Praise for Susan May Warren's Deep Haven novels

ghthearted, punchy story about two wounded souls who
love and a new lease on life . . . [that] nicely balances the
y and realistic."
PUBLISHERS WEEKLY

"Warren's charming inspirational romance has it all: the boy
next door and the princess isolated in her tower, past histories
and new beginnings, poignancy nicely blended with hopefulness,
and troubled, everyday people doing their best to live according
to their faith. Highly recommended."
BOOKLIST

"Delightful . . . a story reminiscent of both *Steel Magnolias* and
the Mitford novels, but with a personality and charm all its own."
CROSSWALK.COM

"A truly delightful tale straight from the heart."
ROMANTIC TIMES

"This delightful tale centered on family, friends, football, and
trust in God's wisdom . . . is a very entertaining and inspiring
romance."
FRESHFICTION.COM

The Shadow of Your Smile

"Warren handles well the many facets of lives intertwined by
love, hope, and tragedy. This is a book of second chances for the
Hueston family, for those who care about them, and for readers
looking for clarity in their own lives."
PUBLISHERS WEEKLY

"Quiet, yet powerful . . . Warren's latest inspirational novel is a story of hidden pain. . . . At the end, hope is in full bloom."
BOOKLIST

"A warm and charming tale that features well-developed characters and a solid story line."
LIBRARY JOURNAL

"This heartwarming story serves as a gentle reminder of God's faithfulness and that He is always near."
CHRISTIAN RETAILING

"Warren handles [the story line] with such grace that the reader is drawn into the tale. . . . This is a beautifully written book."
ROMANTIC TIMES

"An eminently readable story, perfect for book clubs . . . or to read on your own."
CROSSWALK.COM

"*The Shadow of Your Smile* confronts the pain of tragedy, reminding those suffering that loss may define us, but God will not leave us."
CHRISTIAN RETAILERS + RESOURCES

"[Warren] explores serious themes that impact marriages and relationships with authenticity and honesty, while maintaining the charm and whimsy that have marked her Deep Haven stories. . . . *The Shadow of Your Smile* . . . will undoubtedly garner her readers for life."
TITLETRAKK.COM

you don't
know me

You Don't Know Me

Susan May WARREN

a deep haven novel

TYNDALE HOUSE PUBLISHERS, INC., CAROL STREAM, ILLINOIS

Visit Tyndale online at www.tyndale.com.

Visit Susan May Warren's website at www.susanmaywarren.com.

TYNDALE and Tyndale's quill logo are registered trademarks of Tyndale House Publishers, Inc.

You Don't Know Me

Designed by Erik M. Peterson

Edited by Sarah Mason

Scripture quotations are taken from the *Holy Bible,* New Living Translation, copyright © 1996, 2004, 2007 by Tyndale House Foundation. Used by permission of Tyndale House Publishers, Inc., Carol Stream, Illinois 60188. All rights reserved.

You Don't Know Me is a work of fiction. Where real people, events, establishments, organizations, or locales appear, they are used fictitiously. All other elements of the novel are drawn from the author's imagination.

Library of Congress Cataloging-in-Publication Data

Warren, Susan May, date.
  You don't know me / Susan May Warren.
    p. cm.
  ISBN 978-1-4143-3484-4 (sc)
  1. Politicians' spouses—Fiction. 2. Family secrets—Fiction. 3. Witnesses—Protection—Fiction. 4. Minnesota—Fiction. 5. Domestic fiction. I. Title.
  PS3623.A865Y68 2012
  813'.6—dc23   2012018897

Printed in the United States of America

18   17   16   15   14   13   12
 7   6   5   4   3   2   1

For Your glory, Lord

Acknowledgments

I couldn't write a book without the following people in my life watching over me:

Rachel Hauck: Thank you for answering the phone every time I call (even if it's the twenty-seventh time that day) and having an answer for "What happens next?" You are a gift to me.

Steve Laube: Thank you for your pastoral heart and your voice of wisdom. I am so blessed to have you as my agent.

Karen Watson: To have an editor believe in you, know how to guide you, and work with you to help you create a great book is a tremendous gift. Thank you.

Sarah Mason: You are a delight to work with! Thank you for knowing just how to make me feel brilliant, even when you are smoothing out my mistakes.

Andrew Warren: My hero. You are my Nathan, and you are my happy ending. I love you.

David, Sarah, Peter, and Noah: You remind me that the greatest identity I could ever have is being your mother.

Prologue

THERE SIMPLY WASN'T ENOUGH GRACE to survive saying good-bye.

Claire O'Reilly knotted her hands on her lap as the plane lifted off, leaving her heart, her stomach, even her resolve, behind her on the St. Louis tarmac.

She couldn't do this. She wasn't finished being Deidre's mother.

Claire leaned her head on the seat rest, drew in a long breath. Three-plus hours to reconsider the decision she'd already made. Three hours to let the regrets gnaw at her. Three hours until she had to live with her decision for the rest of her life.

How did they expect her to let go, to never know the woman her daughter would become?

"Why are you going to Portland?"

The woman next to her, a blonde dressed in a business suit, had pulled out a notepad from the seat pocket and was lowering the tray to work. She looked about thirty, old enough to have children, but not yet so old that she'd have to watch them make the decisions that would scar the rest of their lives.

"I'm going to Portland . . ." *To say good-bye.* She'd already made the decision. Why could she not push the words out? "To see my daughter."

"How old is she?"

"She's eighteen."

Eighteen and just finding herself, just breaking free of the chaos years. Just becoming the woman Claire knew she could be. No, she couldn't talk about this. "Do you have children?"

The woman flipped the pages of her notepad. "Yes, four. All in grade school."

Claire smiled. "I remember those days. When you wonder if anything you say to them will take."

"Oh, I hear you. I keep thinking that if I do the hard work now, I'll reap the rewards when they become adults."

Claire kept her smile, but the words found tender soil. She'd never see those rewards, would she?

She would never hold her daughter's precious babies, never smell their skin, never delight at their lopsided smiles. She'd never see them grow to become teenagers, maybe a replica of her daughter, smart and beautiful and strong.

This wasn't the ending she had planned.

Claire looked out the tiny window, watching the earth slip away, turn into precise boxed squares of farmland. If only people could have this vision, the order of it all, before they decided to fall in love, to run away from home, to throw away their futures.

Why was it that Deidre thought only until her next pocket of fun instead of looking ahead to the ending God would give her? What had Claire done wrong to make her child so reckless?

"How many children do you have?" the woman asked.

"Three," Claire said. But she'd have to get used to a different answer, wouldn't she? *Two. A boy and a girl.*

She'd have to forget her oldest child, the one who had broken her heart, the one she hardly recognized last time she saw her.

"Your daughter is very brave," a man named Frank Harrison had told her while she paced outside Deidre's hospital room.

Brave. Bravery was three broken ribs, a collapsed lung, her daughter's beautiful face turned purple and grotesque. Claire probably wouldn't have recognized Deidre anyway, with the short, midnight-black hair, her wan face, bones protruding from the form under the sheets. Once upon a time, Deidre plowed through college brochures, fielded calls from volleyball coaches.

Then she met Blake Hayes.

Claire swallowed the acid pooling in her throat as they announced the beverage service over the speaker system. Her seatmate began to write on her notepad.

Claire closed her eyes. *Oh, God, I can't do this. I don't know how I'm going to do this.*

No, not nearly enough grace to say good-bye.

1

Days like today, Annalise Decker's happily ever after almost seemed unbreakable. With the perfect blue sky suggesting the golden days of autumn, the hill overlooking the town of Deep Haven a cascade of jewels—gold oaks, crimson maples, lush green pine—the hint of woodsmoke filling the air, she could stop, breathe in, and believe she belonged here.

Believe that she deserved this life.

"Mom! Watch this!" Henry's voice caught her attention back to the soccer practice—twenty youngsters outfitted in wool hats, fleece jackets under their club T-shirts, and sweatpants under their shin guards. Henry needed a haircut, his own hat discarded on the sideline bench, the wind parting his hair as he chased the ball. She wanted to yell at him to put the hat on, but that might only encourage his sudden propensity to shy away from her good-bye kisses.

She would do anything to keep her eleven-year-old in her embrace, before he was yanked into the world of cell phones, dating, and drama. Perhaps she held him with a tighter grip than her older children, but motherhood turned out to be rife with too many small sorrows for her liking.

Once he was gone, she wasn't sure what she'd have left.

Annalise winced as his kick flew past the goal and into the tangle of forest beyond the field.

His shoulders slumped.

"It's okay, buddy!" she yelled because she couldn't help herself.

"C'mon, Annalise, give me your cookie recipe." Beth Iverson, dressed for soccer in her jeans, boots, a red parka, and a hat over her short brown hair, handed Annalise the Tupperware container, now half-empty. "And I'll promise Nathan my vote."

"You'll promise him your vote anyway," Annalise said as she pinched the cover back on. "He's the only one running."

"You are not putting those away." Lorelei reached for the container to pick out a chocolate chunk cookie, then passed it again to Karin, in the front row, cheering for her daughter as she chased the ball down the field. Their club team still played co-ed. "Jerry never served us cookies."

"Or put up signs or ran ads or hosted a luncheon," Karin said. "Nathan *does* know that no one is running against him, right?"

"He just wants to . . ." Win. For some reason, Nathan breathed and dreamed of this mayoral position. As if his entire life hinged on landing the electoral approval of the town of Deep Haven. Like he didn't already have it? "He wants to do a good job."

Apparently Annalise's role as his wife was to secure votes across

Deep Haven, from the PTA to the thrift store to the soccer field. She had Election Day circled in red on her calendar in the wild hope that then the Nathan she knew might return to her instead of this man who crept into their room long after the lights dimmed, after meeting with locals and knocking on the well-worn doors of their neighbors and friends.

As if anyone in Deep Haven didn't know Nathan Decker. Or his family.

Then again, that precise fact might be what drove him. What made him stretch the hours down at the realty office and over at his mother's house, or volunteering at the care center or running the church finances, and generally serving on too many town committees.

He probably didn't even need her campaign cookies with all his activities, but that's what wives did.

They campaigned. They kept everyone's lives running.

They made sure the secrets stayed in the dark.

"Please, Annalise. Tell us your secret," Karin said, catching cookie crumbs on her hand.

For a second, the question jolted Annalise, found the last patch of guarded soil in her heart. She looked at Karin, her brain blank, and couldn't breathe. Shoot, she wasn't made of glass—no one could see inside her.

"Not until after the election," she said, and her voice sounded just fine.

"Which is Minnesotan for no." Beth shook her head. "You Deckers know how to keep us in suspense."

"Uh-oh, here comes Henry." Karin handed her the container.

Annalise watched as her son trudged to the bench, kicked it, and sat down. She reached for her bag. "I think that's our cue."

"You're leaving?" Beth asked.

"I gotta run. The auditions for *Romeo and Juliet* are today, and I have to take Jason some food before Colleen's game."

Please, please let him get the lead. Because it was the only chance for redemption he had after turning down a job offer at Licks and Stuff Ice Cream. Nathan was always so tied up over finances and their children's education that he'd practically demanded Jason drop out of theater and get an after-school job to help pay for college. But the kid could get a scholarship with his acting abilities. Let him land a role, and then they'd tell Nathan together.

She didn't really want to keep things from Nathan, but she didn't want to cause tension either. Besides, every marriage had secrets, right?

Like Colleen and her new boyfriend. Annalise and her sixteen-year-old daughter had a showdown ahead over that lowlife Tucker Newman. If Colleen came to her senses, Annalise wouldn't have to tell Nathan about finding them in the front seat of Tucker's Jeep parked down by the lighthouse during lunch hour on Tuesday. Really, it wouldn't do Nathan's campaign any good to appear on Tucker's doorstep, ready to tear him limb from limb.

Yes, secrets protected them. The small secrets . . . and the large ones. Like the fact that "Nathan Decker for Mayor" just might get her—maybe even all of them—killed. The remote possibility hovered over her with every step Nathan took farther into the spotlight.

Okay, the *very* remote possibility. So remote that Annalise shrugged off the brush of fear that had traveled up her spine when Nathan announced today at breakfast that the media would be interviewing him—and her—at tomorrow's luncheon.

After all, they lived in a town of less than two thousand, in the northern tip of Minnesota. And after twenty years, she could stop looking over her shoulder.

Probably.

"Of course you're taking Jason dinner. Probably some home-made energy bars or a plate of casserole you have cooking in the Crock-Pot," Beth said.

Actually, yes, but she must have frowned because Beth laughed. "You're such a curve wrecker. Can't you leave some of the all-star mothering for the rest of us?"

Annalise stared at her.

"You're at all the practices—too often with cookies. You make bread from scratch. You attend every PTA meeting, every field trip, every school party. You make the rest of us feel like we're bums when we serve a frozen pizza."

"There's nothing wrong with frozen pizza—"

Karin had turned, listening to the conversation. "When is the last time you cooked a frozen pizza?"

"I happen to like homemade—"

"And let's not talk about the Christmas decorations." This from Lorelei, who tossed her long black ponytail over her shoulder as she gathered her stadium blanket and rose from the bench. "I feel like I'm the Grinch with my wreath and twinkle lights. I think Deep Haven needs its own electrical grid just for the Decker Christmas display."

They laughed, and Annalise forced a smile. "I'm not that bad. . . ."

Beth shook her head. "Oh, Annalise, we're just giving you a hard time. Listen, you're not *bad*. You're wonderful. And Nathan is a shoo-in for mayor, so please don't tempt us with cookies next week." She leaned forward and caught Annalise in a one-armed hug.

"Uh-oh. Kelli Hanson just made a beeline for Chip," Beth said, releasing her.

Annalise glanced at the field as Kelli sidled up to Beth's husband, the assistant coach, catching him in conversation. A tie-dyed bandanna caught her long cherry-red hair, the rest of it blowing in the afternoon breeze. She wore green Army pants and an oversize wool sweater, a pair of purple Converse, and looked like she might still be in high school and not married to a local landscaper. She waved to her sixth-grade daughter, Marin, playing midfield. Her son, Casey, played football for the Huskies—Annalise remembered seeing him make the front page a few times.

"I better get over there. She doesn't mean to, but she's a natural flirt, and my husband is befuddled by her."

"Kelli is a flirt?"

"I know you've only lived here for twenty years, Annalise, so you'll have to trust me—Kelli is a little bit of trouble. You know she had Casey when she was seventeen." Beth raised a perfect eyebrow. "And she has a tattoo." She leaned over to Annalise. "A tramp stamp—right here." She placed her hand at the small of her back. "That should tell you something." Beth's mouth tightened into a knot of disapproval. "I know I shouldn't be judgmental, but . . . a gal can't be too careful. You might want to keep an eye on her around Nathan."

Annalise had no words for that. She'd always considered Kelli . . . well, original, if not pretty. She watched Beth climb down the bleachers and jog onto the field.

Not that Nathan would notice Kelli, anyway. He barely noticed Annalise these days.

"Are you kidding? Nathan's only ever loved Annalise. I've known him since grade school, and he was a changed person when

Annalise came to town. I've never seen him so happy as the day they got married." Lorelei winked at her. "They were love at first sight. A storybook romance."

Well, not really. But they had managed to build a life together. "See you all next week," Annalise said.

Sunbaked, crispy leaves tumbled along the edges of the field as she tucked the empty container into the bag, then pulled out her keys, heavy with pictures of her kids and emblems of her life—a plastic volleyball, a Decker Real Estate fob, her Java Cup discount tag.

Henry trudged by her, and she jumped off the bleachers to catch up to him.

"It's okay, Henry," Annalise said as he reached the Suburban. He opened the hatch, then slid onto the bumper and began to pull off his cleats. "You don't make every shot."

"I quit." He wiped the back of his hand across his face, leaving a trail of grime. "I hate soccer. Why did you have to sign me up?" He turned and climbed through the car, disappearing behind the backseat.

"You hate soccer? Since when?" Ten minutes ago he'd been waving for her attention on the field.

"Sheesh, Mom. Since *always*."

Annalise checked her watch. They had about an hour before Colleen's game. As she closed the tailgate, she glanced around the parking lot for Nathan's Ford, but clearly he hadn't been able to make it to practice. Not that she expected him, but . . .

"Can you drop me off at the skateboard park?" Henry shoved his uniform into a ball in the backseat and climbed into the front.

"What about supper? You need to eat something before Colleen's game."

"I'm not hungry. Besides, Grandma always brings snacks."

"Popcorn isn't dinner." At least it shouldn't be. But even she looked forward to Helen's contraband volleyball snacks. What were grandmothers for but to spoil their grandchildren?

She often wondered how her own mother might have spoiled her kids. Would she have made them her homemade hot chocolate? Maybe the snickerdoodles that Annalise just couldn't seem to perfect?

"Fine. Buckle up."

"It's two blocks."

"I don't care. It's the law."

Henry rolled his eyes, and she quelled the urge to push his hair from his face. He looked so much like Nathan's boyhood pictures—round face, dark hair, vivid green eyes that took in the world. So much energy—just not for sports. The kid could probably win an Xbox gaming competition.

Henry also reminded her too much of her little brother, Ben.

Someday she'd love to see him again, know the man he turned out to be.

Annalise pulled into the parking lot of the skateboard park. "I'm going to get some coffee. Walk over to the school for Colleen's game. I'll meet you there. Do not go anywhere else."

"Thanks, Mom," he said as he slid out of the car. And he gave her a real smile as he tucked his skateboard under his arm.

Almost as good as a kiss.

She passed Marybeth Rose in her RAV4, dropping her daughter off at the curb for tonight's volleyball game, and lifted her hand to wave. Colleen had stayed after school to practice her serve. At least, Annalise hoped that was the truth. Just in case, she searched the parking lot for Tucker's Jeep and hated herself a little for it.

But she saw herself—too much—in Colleen, and it raised the tiny hairs on the back of her neck.

She drove down the hill toward the coffee shop, her hand closing around her phone. Maybe she should text Nathan, remind him about Colleen's game. Poor man spent most of last night going over his responses to the preposted questions for tomorrow morning's radio call-in show.

She passed houses decorated for Halloween—orange lawn bags packed with leaves, hay bales stacked in yards with stuffed scarecrows or hoboes leaning against them, a display of pumpkins. They still had weeks to go before Halloween—a holiday she'd forever been trying to get Nathan to celebrate. But their church had a moratorium against Halloween in any form and, well . . . she didn't like to make trouble.

One of these days, however, she might like to dress up. Maybe as Alice in Wonderland. Days like today, she could relate to Alice.

A local had propped up a homemade sign with *Go Husky Volleyball* written in blue paint against the white background. A win at tonight's final regular season game would take them to the conference sectionals.

How Annalise loved volleyball nights. They helped her remember who she'd been—the good parts—and added a little flavor to their weeknights, something different from the usual dinner and homework. On every other night, for high fun, she might read a book while Nathan went over his campaign finances.

Then, if she were extra lucky, he'd come to bed the same time she did. Maybe give her a good-night kiss.

Okay, a lot of people longed for their kind of ho-hum. A life without drama. She should be thankful for a man who came home every night, lived a life of faithfulness. And just because they'd never had the type of romance with sparks, candlelight, and swooning, that didn't mean they didn't love each other. Not every marriage had to come from a romance novel.

Besides, she probably didn't have the right to long for anything more.

Yes, volleyball nights made her realize how grateful she was for all of it—her safe, ordered, happy life.

The Java Cup hosted a giant painted moose on its window—a nod toward the Moose Madness celebration this weekend. A tourist town, Deep Haven depended on visitors from the south craving fall color and perhaps a glimpse of wildlife—eagles, bears, foxes, deer, and especially moose. So the tourism board created an entire community event around the hunt for moose, including this weekend's Mad Moose community dance. This season, Indian summer eluded them, so they'd had to move their booths and outside activities to the local community center.

"What's in a Wild Moose Mocha?" Annalise said, reading the menu.

Kathy, the blonde owner, wore a fuzzy brown headband with giant moose ears. "It's a dark chocolate mocha with whip and a caramel drizzle."

"I don't know . . ."

"C'mon, Annalise, you only live once."

Actually . . . "Okay, yes. That. Please."

Nathan didn't need to know she was annihilating her diet. Again. Another secret kept for the sake of their happy life.

For a late afternoon, the Java Cup buzzed with conversation. She nodded to Jerry, the incumbent mayor—talking with Norm, who ran the fish place, in the corner easy chairs. At a long table sat the football coaches, Seb Brewster and Caleb Knight.

On the bulletin board, someone—possibly Nathan—had hung a Decker for Mayor pin. She'd handed them out at Nathan's booth at the Fisherman's Picnic this summer. Seeing all those faces, shaking all those hands—it made her realize just how embedded she'd become in Deep Haven.

"One Wild Moose Mocha," Kathy said and handed her the cup. "Careful, it's hot."

Annalise paid Kathy with the card on her key ring.

"See you at the game? I just love watching Colleen play. She's got a good future in Husky volleyball." Kathy handed the card back.

"She's thrilled to be a starter," Annalise said. She took her cup to the coffee counter to grab a stir stick and work in the whipped cream. Indeed, at any other school, sophomore Colleen would sit the bench until her junior year. Being in a small town gave all of them opportunities unheard of in a big city.

Like hiding out where her sins couldn't find her. And starting over. And becoming someone who desperately wanted to deserve the life God had given her.

Outside the giant picture windows that overlooked Deep Haven's harbor, Lake Superior had kicked up, the waves platinum as they rippled against the brilliant late-afternoon sun. Sunlight poured through the windows, marinating the smells of leather and coffee. Outside, ruby and amber leaves tumbled down the sidewalk, gems bullied by the wind. She'd have to cover her mums tonight.

Soon snow would turn the world white, hiding the rocky shoreline and capturing them in ice.

But today—today her world was unbreakable.

She replaced the lid, took a sip, then turned.

And everything stopped. Sure, conversation in the coffee shop continued to hum, and outside, the wind tickled the hanging wind chimes, but as Annalise stared at the man seated by the door, the one who looked up at her with sad eyes, apology in them, she couldn't breathe. Couldn't move. Couldn't think beyond . . . *No.*

Perhaps she shook her head, because he rose to his feet. "Annalise."

He didn't look so different from the last time she'd seen him—a moment so vividly etched in her brain that she had no trouble pulling it out, comparing him to the man he'd been. Faded, even unremarkable leather jacket. Short, now-graying hair. Jeans and boots—attire designed to blend in. Hands in his pockets. He could be her uncle visiting from Hoboken for all the presence he had.

He hadn't changed a bit.

He'd always be the man who had saved her life. The man who had given her a new identity. Who had helped her build this amazing, normal, perfect lie.

The man who could steal it all away.

"Hello, Frank," she said softly to her Witness Security agent.

&

Nathan Decker stood on top of the world.

He stood at the apex of the foundation of the unfinished house, where the Palladian windows would be, and held his camera to his eye, panning for exactly the right shot. So many choices—with the twilight drizzling crimson across the crisp waves of Lake Superior, foaming along the rocky shore; the sky stirred with the palette of magenta, chartreuse, and turquoise; the sun a simmering ball of hot pumpkin. Any one of these shots might catch the eye of a curious Internet surfer.

The right buyer could turn this house into a castle.

Hopefully one with a healthy credit rating and a desire to live on the most beautiful tip of Minnesota, tucked away in a half-finished shell of a house twenty miles from the nearest grocery store. He'd list it as needing TLC, call the location charming and nestled in the woods, and use words like *privacy* and *retreat* and *hideaway*.

He still couldn't believe he'd finally talked Nelda McIntyre into parting with the place. That's what years of Sundays singing ancient hymns at the senior center could do for a man's career. And reputation.

Most of those old folks grew up with his grandfather, his uncles, his cousins, and remembered when the Decker name meant success, even honor.

He intended to bring that back.

For a moment more, Nathan watched the waves crash on the rocks below the cliff that dropped straight down some twenty feet. The violence of waves against the rocky shoreline had the power to trap him with their rhythm—the sound of the surf hitting the cliff like a punch, deep inside the gut of the rocky wall. The giant gulp as the water rushed away only to hurl itself again against the rocks. Over and over, never ending, until he could feel it pulsing within him, a heartbeat of doom, reminding him of who he was, imprisoning him inside the Decker legacy.

It had taken him thirty years, but with this mayoral race, he'd break free from the current of shame and failure.

Nathan took a few more pictures of the tall cement beams that comprised the shell of the massive great room, then moved to capture the building's layout, how it curved along the shore like it belonged there. A cement shell, really, a dream unfinished by Nelda's husband, a man taken before his time.

The right owner simply needed the vision to see beyond its legacy to the potential.

Nathan crunched across the gravel driveway and climbed into his used Ford Focus. He'd purchased it for the gas mileage, no frills, something Jason and Colleen could drive. Someday, he intended to get something fast and shiny. Maybe after he got Jason, Colleen, and Henry through college. And after he replaced Annalise's beater SUV. And his mother could use a new deck after forty years of living in the same tiny bungalow.

But someday.

He glanced at the dashboard clock as he turned around for the trek up the long dirt drive to the highway. Annalise had mentioned something about Henry's soccer practice—he'd wanted to stop by. But he needed to log in these pictures, get them up on the Net before Colleen's volleyball game. Still, a sudden longing to see his wife, maybe spend five minutes holding her hand while watching their son, churned inside him, rearranging his plans.

He'd stop by, say hi, then pop into the office to post the listing.

His campaign depended on his selling this property and digging his bank account out of the red. Thankfully, Annalise had no idea how far he'd plunged them into debt or she'd start talking about working at the nursing home again. Not that he'd mind the extra paycheck or her having her own career, but she loved her volunteer work at the school, around town at the Goodwill, the blood drive, and on the theater board, and she liked being able to attend the kids' events, go to lunch with the soccer moms, hit the gym.

And he loved giving her the freedom to do it. Sometimes, when he saw her wave to him from the stands at the volleyball games, in front of the entire town, looking pretty with her long blonde hair and incredible blue eyes, that old feeling swept through him.

Disbelief that he'd married so well. That God had given him the most beautiful woman in Deep Haven. It was all he could do to keep up with the grace, to be the husband he'd pledged to be. Honestly, she probably deserved better, but he wouldn't tell her that.

All he wanted was to do right by her. To grow old with her.

Most of all, to never end up like his old man.

Nathan pulled out onto the highway and turned on the radio, catching the local broadcast. Vern and Neil, the sports jockeys, were on, giving a pregame analysis of tonight's volleyball game. They mentioned Colleen and her spike, the stats of the team.

He punched the gas, glancing again at the time.

The soccer players were just winding up the post-practice pep talk when he pulled in to Rec Park. He spotted Kelli Hanson, coach Chip Iverson, and his wife, Beth, handing out cupcakes to the line of boys.

No Annalise. He let his car idle for a moment, debated asking, then figured she'd bundled Henry up to run him home before Colleen's game.

Which meant he had time to upload these pictures and at least get them posted in the listing he'd created today. He'd add the tags, features, amenities, and put out a few nibbles to past clients tomorrow.

With luck—a lot of luck—this property would move within a week. Sure, they were in a recession, but the right property, with the right salesman and a motivated seller . . . He just had to work his contacts. He knew a few investors who might be interested.

He pulled out of Rec Park, waving to a couple of the parents, and onto Main Street. His office overlooked the lake at the far end of town—which, in a town the size of Deep Haven, wasn't saying much. Still, sitting in his chair watching the sun over the harbor, turning the masts of the moored sailboats to gold, he could convince himself that he'd made the right decision staying in Deep Haven.

Nathan was motoring past the Java Cup when he spotted Annalise's truck. Hard to miss—the Husky Volleyball sticker on the side, the dent in the fender where he'd backed into his snowmobile trailer. Maybe he'd stop in and surprise his wife.

She'd pay him with a smile, one that reminded him why he got out of bed every morning and headed in to work.

He parked and climbed out, noticing he'd gotten dust on his dress shoes tromping around the old McIntyre place. He bent for a moment, wiped them off with his leather glove, then smacked his hands and headed for the coffee shop.

The bell above the door jangled as he walked inside. A few heads popped up. Mayor Jerry Mulligan, in one of the chairs in the corner, talking with Norm, the bait shop owner. Nathan lifted a hand and smiled.

Then he looked around for Annalise.

He found her sitting at a table in the corner of the adjacent room, deep in a conversation huddle with someone he didn't recognize. Graying hair, leather jacket. Dark, almost-pensive eyes. The man was talking with Nathan's wife as if he knew her, his hand on the table about to reach out and touch her arm.

They didn't hear Nathan approach. In fact, Annalise was leaning forward, wearing a strange expression. He might even call it fear, although he'd seen fear on her before—that time Henry drove off the cliff on his bicycle and broke his shoulder. Or the time Colleen wandered off for over an hour at the Minnesota State Fair. Or that day Jason crashed the snowmobile and had to hike back in the darkness, two hours late.

No, this didn't look like that motherly fear.

This fear he didn't recognize, and eerie fingers curled around him.

"Lise?"

She looked up and for a moment just blinked at him. As if she didn't know him.

The expression flushed words out of him. If he didn't know better, he would have thought he'd walked into something clandestine.

But this was his wife. The woman he'd known for twenty years. She couldn't keep a secret from him if she wanted to.

Then her smile appeared, and the tightness in his chest broke free.

"Nathan. Hi." She reached out, took his hand. "I'm sorry; were you looking for me?"

His gaze darted to the man and back. "No . . . I was driving by. I stopped by soccer practice. Where's Henry?" He turned, expecting to see their son at the book corner, working his iPod, pretending not to know any of them.

"He's up . . . he's . . . I dropped him off at the park. He'll meet us at the game."

Annalise glanced at her companion, and for a second, the eerie feeling returned. But Nathan shook it away and held out his hand.

"I'm Nathan Decker, Annalise's husband. I don't think we've met. Are you new in town?"

The man looked Nathan over as if assessing him. Then he stood, smiled, and took his hand. Nathan had apparently passed. "I'm Frank Harrison." He glanced at Annalise. "Annalise's uncle."

Uncle.

Nathan opened his mouth, waiting for words. "I . . . I didn't know that Lise had an uncle." He looked at her. "You didn't tell me you had an uncle."

Funny, she appeared almost as shocked by this man's pronouncement. She gave him an odd smile. "My . . . uncle Frank. From . . . Pittsburgh."

Nathan turned back to Frank. "This is wonderful. I thought her family was all killed in the accident."

Frank blinked as if he had forgotten the demise of her family. Then he nodded. "Yes. They were. Except I was out of the country. On business. I haven't been back for . . . a while."

Frank let him go, and Nathan reached for a chair. "What kind of business are you in?"

"Military." Frank sat and leaned back, crossing one leg over the other, folding his arms. "What do you do?"

"I'm in real estate. And I'm running for mayor."

Frank drew in a breath. "Really. Hmm."

"It's a small town," Lise said, almost too quickly, as if Nathan's bid for mayor were inconsequential. "Very small."

"Not so small that we can't make a difference," Nathan said, casting a glance at her. She turned away, took a sip of her coffee. Huh. "We actually swell to about twenty thousand in the summertime with all the tourist traffic up here. The right laws on the books and we can encourage more tourism, more growth, really help the families who live here year-round survive. In fact, we're having a luncheon tomorrow with a few media folks from Duluth to talk about fresh ideas I hope to bring to the mayor's office."

Frank flicked a gaze over to Annalise, now staring at her coffee. She drew in a breath as she looked up. "Nathan will make a wonderful mayor. But I'm really very behind the scenes."

What was she talking about? "Hardly. This woman is on every

committee in town—from the PTA to the blood drive. She's the backbone of my campaign." Nathan reached for her hand, but she had tucked it into her pocket. And her smile—yes, that was fake, like the time he'd given her touch-on lamps for Christmas.

"We need to get going to the game." She stood. "It's great to see you, um, Uncle Frank."

What? "Lise, what are you doing? You suddenly have family and you're sending him away?" Nathan turned to Frank. "Where are you staying?"

He seemed to catch Frank off guard, as if the man hadn't thought about it. His eyes flickered to Annalise's.

"At the Super 8," she said.

"No, you're staying with us. You're family—the first of Lise's we've ever met." Nathan stood and slipped his arm around her waist. "She's always so quiet about her family. As if they never existed."

"She suffered a terrible loss," Frank said quietly.

"I know. Which is even more reason for you to stay with us. We're delighted you're here. And if you haven't eaten dinner, I'd love to buy you a hot dog at the volleyball game. Our Lady Huskies are undefeated in the conference and my daughter—your great-niece—is a starter on varsity. She's got a spike that will turn you cold. Probably my wife's genes because I was never any good at sports, although she claims she never played volleyball."

He waited a beat for Frank to contradict him and, when he didn't, added a shrug. "Anyway, our two boys and my mother will be at the game. They'll be thrilled to meet you too; won't they, honey?"

Annalise was staring at him wide-eyed. What did she want him to do? This was her only living relative. Finally a connection to his wife's past. Maybe he'd get more information about the accident that had claimed her parents and two siblings. And left her with that scar on her leg. The accident that still woke her, weeping, at night.

Nathan held out his hand again. "Welcome to Deep Haven, Uncle Frank."

2

FRANK SORT OF WISHED that the name *Uncle* actually belonged to him.

Deidre—er, Annalise had built a life for herself after all, and he *felt* like her uncle.

Frank had even wanted to give her a hug. But that might be too much for her. It wasn't every day a woman he'd placed in WitSec saw her past appear in the coffee shop like a ghost.

But it also wasn't every day he had to check in on one of his charges with the bad news that she might be in danger.

He'd followed her into the coffee shop, not wanting to pounce on her at the soccer practice. She looked good. She'd let her hair grow out into its natural straw-blonde color, now past her shoulders. It softened her, made her elegant as opposed to the harsh teenager she'd been with her midnight-black hair spiked around her head, her bloodshot eyes crayoned so dark he could barely see the blue in them. She'd filled out, too, no longer drug-thin and bony, and she sported the remains of a summer tan instead of the pasty, scaly skin of living on the streets.

Annalise looked like a woman who had grown up in a healthy home, married well, and lived a life she might be proud of.

He was certainly proud of who she'd become.

Unfortunately he might have to take it all away. He'd directed her to a private table in the back and jumped right in with the bad news. "Garcia is out of prison, and he's jumped parole."

Annalise had slid onto the chair and blinked at him for a full second as if cataloging the name. But he knew better.

How would she ever forget any detail of what Luis Garcia had done to her? Or the threats he'd leveled against her?

Her voice emerged, low, feeble, as she set down her coffee. "How did Garcia get paroled? I thought you said that no one would let him out."

"Luis Garcia got out because the federal prison system is overcrowded and he apparently behaved himself for the last twenty years."

"Or he bribed someone in the system."

He heard her cynicism and couldn't deny the truth in her statement as she shook her head and sat back, staring out the window at her world.

"I'm sorry, Annalise. What you did saved lives. You got a murderer and drug dealer off the street—"

"And now he's back on the streets." She turned to him with the same dark, piercing eyes she had twenty-plus years ago. "You know he's going to keep his promise to find me and kill me."

He met the look with his own, the most solemn assurance he could give her. "I've hidden you well. No one knows you're here—in fact, only two other people on the planet know you're still alive."

She drew in a breath, and he saw her chin quiver. "How are they?"

"Older. But in good health. Your father retired two years ago. They gave him a gold watch. He was in the paper."

"I know. I googled him."

"You shouldn't—"

She held up her hand, and in her expression he saw a hint of the former Annalise, the one known as Deidre, who had once told him just what he could do with his idea that she should turn informant on her drug-dealing boyfriend, a lackey of Garcia's. "I miss them. And I'm careful."

"I hope so." Frank leaned toward her. "Please tell me—does anyone else know?"

She drew in a breath, looking at her coffee, which she had yet to sip. "No one."

"Not even your husband?"

She pursed her lips, shook her head. "When I met him, I was starting over. I . . . I didn't want to tell him who I'd been, so . . . I made up a past. I told him my family had been killed in an accident and that I had come here to forget."

"Good lies are based on truth."

She lifted a shoulder. "After twenty years, it's easy to believe. I've never had any relatives show up. My family believes I'm alone."

"So you should be safe. We'll find Garcia."

She closed her eyes. So long that a chill brushed through him, made him ask, "What aren't you telling me?"

"I could be in trouble."

It was the way her voice pitched low, the word *trouble*, that dredged up the memories, the failures. "I can't keep you safe unless I know."

She leaned close. "Right after . . . after I moved here, I . . . Well, I was still in love with Blake."

Blake Hayes, the no-good boyfriend who had convinced her to run away from her perfectly decent family, made her live on the streets, and talked her into using various drugs until she forgot her own name. Thankfully, a rookie cop found her in an alley and hooked her up with Frank and an escape into WitSec in exchange for her testimony against one of St. Louis's most wanted drug lords. It had only cost her best friend's life. And, well, her own.

"I told you to stay away from him."

"Frank—I was stupid back then. Blake was all I had. I was lonely here, and . . ."

"You wrote to him."

She actually looked like she might cry. He resisted reaching out to her and instead let his hand rest on the table.

"Please tell me you didn't use your new name."

"I can't remember. But I did tell him where to find me if he wanted me. Then I met Nathan and from then on lived in mortal fear that Blake would actually show up."

"We moved him to Fairbanks, Alaska, after he got out. I didn't want him near you, regardless of what you said." Because, well, she'd sorta felt like his own daughter.

She met his eyes. "Thank you. You probably saved my life again."

"All I did was offer you choices. You saved your own life. Listen, my partner is headed up to Fairbanks right now to deliver the same news to Blake. We'll feed him a story about you being killed and end it right there."

"Another obituary."

He didn't comment—couldn't, actually, because that's when her life caught up to them.

"Lise?"

Frank felt like a father meeting the boyfriend for the first time as he shook Nathan's hand. Nathan Decker was exactly the kind of man Frank hoped might marry Annalise. Love her. Protect her. The lie didn't feel too far from the truth when he introduced himself as an uncle.

Frank never expected, however, to end up in the bleachers of their small-town school, cheering for Annalise's daughter. A cute blonde who was Annalise's spit image. If only her parents could see their granddaughter. Even Frank could feel a tinge of grief over Annalise's loss.

No wonder she googled her family.

"C'mon, Colleen, dig it out!" Annalise shouted.

The girls on the court were up by one game, the gym packed with fans dressed in blue and white, their roar nearly drowning out the screech of shoes on the court. The smell of popcorn and grilled hot dogs seasoned the air, along with the scent of body odor.

A crew of young men had painted their faces blue and now led the crowd in a cheer as a tall brunette took the ball back to serve. The other team, dressed in red, crouched to receive.

"Colleen's strength is the spike. She knows how to find the hole and slam it right in the center," Nathan said.

Nathan had taken to Frank like he might truly be family. On the other side of Nathan, their son Henry ate popcorn. Frank pegged him about ten, but he already had the wide shoulders and charming grin of Annalise's younger brother, Ben. Probably she knew that.

Her oldest son, Jason, had joined them after the game started. Tall, also wide-shouldered, he looked like he could play middle linebacker. He sat down beside Frank, curling a small booklet in his hands. Frank had snuck a glimpse—*Romeo and Juliet.*

Annalise had finally stopped looking at him as if he might bolt. Now she cheered—and coached—as her daughter positioned herself for a spike. The other side dove, dug it out, and returned it. The brunette bumped it to the front, another set; then Colleen went up again for the spike.

It landed out of bounds.

The crowd groaned.

"C'mon, Huskies! Get the serve back!" This from the woman beside Annalise—Nathan's mother, Helen.

She'd handed Frank a bag of popcorn about 10.4 seconds after Nathan introduced him. "About time we met a relative," she said, but her smile suggested that she was delighted. He'd stolen a couple glances at her. Slender, even regal, with graying hair and beautiful green eyes.

Colleen went up to block. The ball bounced off her arms and slammed onto the Cardinals' court.

"Attagirl, Colleen! Now play the net!"

Colleen glanced at her mother, grinned.

It was the grin from Annalise's daughter—easy, whole, without fear—that convinced Frank.

He was sticking around until he knew that he'd done his job and that Annalise could indeed live happily ever after.

❧

Annalise simply had to act normal, and they'd all live through this.

"Take it slow, Henry. Each word—sound it out."

She sat on Henry's bed, her arm around him, holding one side of his book, the lamp spotlighting the page. She cherished these quiet moments, helping him untangle the letters that still plagued him. Like *B*. And *D*.

He ran his finger along the line like she'd taught him to and lurched out the sentence.

He'd get this. She'd never been the best student either, but by eighth grade, she could read with the rest of her class. It just took someone never letting him give up.

He went on to the next sentence. She tried not to glance around, to the shirt hanging over his chair, the puddle of jeans and socks in the corner, the debris—he called it his treasures—piled on his dresser. Clay ashtrays and Bionicles and a couple pinewood derby cars. Ribbons and soccer participation trophies. Even a picture of him and his brother wrestling.

She probably wouldn't change his room until he moved out.

Henry finished the paragraph and turned the page with a sigh.

"That's enough for now, buddy. You're doing great." She kissed the top of his head as she stood, let him settle into the covers.

"I hate reading," he said.

"Not forever. You're getting better," she said, returning to the edge of the bed. She prayed for him, then kissed his cheek, pausing for just a moment to inhale what remained of his little-boy scent. Their surprise child after two miscarriages. Named after her father.

The cherry on top of her already-blessed life.

"I like Uncle Frank," Henry said as she got up. "He's funny. And he knows magic. He can make things disappear."

Exactly. But the last thing she needed was for Frank to actually become an *uncle*. More lies for her to keep track of.

"Yes, he's real nice—"

"How come he's never visited us before?"

At the door, she took a long breath, her hand hovering over the light switch. "He was out of the country a lot."

"Why did he come to see you?"

"He was in the area and wanted to say hi. Good night, Henry."

"I hope he stays forever," Henry said as she turned off the light.

Oh, please, no.

She stopped by Colleen's room, knocking on the door before opening it.

Colleen slid her cell phone beneath the covers.

Wonderful. Texting, probably with that troublemaker, Tucker. His name nearly rose to her lips, and the confrontation hovered there for a second.

She'd seen him tonight after the game, lingering by the drinking fountain. With black hair that hid his eyes, he carried the aura of a snowboarder, an irresponsible, bad-boy magnetism that clearly had her daughter mesmerized. He wore a snap-button black-checkered shirt over a black T-shirt, a pair of painter pants. And ear gauges.

Just the kind of boy she hoped her sweet, beautiful, smart daughter might date.

Stay away from him. He'll destroy your life. The words filled her throat, but she couldn't bear to dismantle their triumphant night.

Another day.

"You were amazing tonight, honey."

Colleen grinned.

Sometimes, in moments like this, the past echoed back to her, and Annalise was again sixteen, bundled in her bed with the pink knit afghan pulled up to her chin, bidding her mother good night.

It had all gone wrong so quickly after that.

Annalise could admit that she lived in perpetual fear that Colleen might one day fall in love with Tucker or some other greasy-haired boy who charmed her with the wrong words and stole her away from Annalise's arms.

Yes, twenty years later, Annalise knew exactly what she'd put her mother through.

"Thanks, Mom. We should have won three in a row."

"You're not a one-person team out there. Remember to listen to your teammates. They can see the blockers and tell you where to attack. I definitely heard Ashley shout, 'Hard line' on that last volley in the second game."

"I know. I have a hard time listening—I get into the game and I can't hear anything but my adrenaline." Colleen smoothed out the purple fleece blanket, catching the fur between her fingers, a common behavior when she was reliving a game. "And I need to work on my vertical. Coach says I'm not extending, so I'm not hitting at full power."

"It helps if you jump with both arms up—you have more power that way. Don't drop the other arm while you're bringing your hitting hand back, or you'll lose momentum."

At least that's what Annalise's coach had told her, and it had launched her to varsity as a sophomore, just like Colleen with her power attack. If she'd only believed in herself a little more . . .

"I'll try that." Colleen frowned. "Been surfing volleyball coaching sites again?"

Annalise laughed, but her heart stuck in her throat. What was wrong with her family knowing she'd played volleyball? That piece of truth shouldn't matter. But she'd rewritten so much of her life, determined to delete every piece of herself in her bid to start over, that she'd lost tidbits that might have turned into treasures.

Like being a volunteer volleyball coach for her daughter's team.

"Get some rest. You only have two days before sectionals." Annalise gave her a wink before she switched off the light and closed the door.

She wandered past the gallery of her children's pictures. At the end of the hall, she stuck her head into her room, where Nathan lay in bed in his gray-striped pajamas, the news humming from the television. He wore his reading glasses, but she could see where they'd been propped on his head, mussing his short brown hair, and a hint of five o'clock shadow suggested he hadn't shaved twice today. He'd been doing that since the start of his campaign, ever the well-groomed candidate. He balanced his computer on his lap, typing.

Always working, her Nathan. Always striving. Always trying to be better.

"I'm not sure we should have given Colleen a cell phone or her own set of keys for her birthday."

Nathan flicked his eyes up at her. "Colleen's a smart girl. She'll be responsible."

Except her mother had probably said that about her, too, at the age of sixteen. "She's just growing up so fast . . ."

Nathan had returned to his typing.

Annalise sighed. "I'll be right in. I'm going to make sure Uncle Frank is settled."

He nodded, and she shut the door, making her way to the kitchen.

Jason sat at the table, the overhead light shining on his calculus. She slid a hand onto his shoulder, squeezed. Such an honorable young man. And handsome, too, with that slightly curly brown hair, the physique of an athlete, even if his passion leaned toward theater.

"I noticed that you didn't mention your audition to your father tonight."

He glanced up at her. He had her father's amber eyes, and sometimes that simply took Annalise's breath away. And he'd inherited her acting ability, one she didn't realize she had until she moved to Deep Haven.

"They'll have the cast lists up tomorrow. I'll tell him if I land a part."

His expression bore a hint of pleading. Oh, what was she supposed to do?

She gave his shoulder another squeeze.

Outside on the deck, wind piled leaves against the railing as the trees shivered off what sounded like rain. Or sleet. She turned on the outside light and let it shine across their covered grill, the now-empty planters.

She preferred to sleep with the outside lit up like a ballpark. A remnant of those early days in Deep Haven when the night seemed to swallow her, when she sat up on the sofa, wrapped in a blanket, afraid to sleep.

No wonder she married Nathan the second he asked—she needed to hang on to someone to keep the memories away.

But that wasn't entirely why. Nathan was an amazing man who offered her the life she needed. And her damaged heart had loved him the best it could. Still did.

She nuked a mug of water, added hot cocoa, and wandered down to the basement, where they'd tucked Frank away in the den. She knocked on his door, hoping he wasn't yet asleep.

He answered fully clothed, his spectacles down over his nose.

"I brought you some hot cocoa, Uncle Frank."

"Oh, Deidre, you're so kind."

"Shh. Annalise, please. Jason is upstairs."

"Of course. Sorry. Sometimes I forget."

"Sometimes I forget I was ever Deidre."

He gave her a smile, then took the cocoa and blew on it before taking a sip. "Delicious."

"My mother used to make it this way—with cinnamon and nutmeg. I don't have her recipe, but I kept experimenting until I found something that tasted similar." She folded her arms over her chest. "Do you have everything you need?" She looked past him into the den, where Nathan had pulled out the sofa bed before turning in. She didn't spend much time down here—it smelled like gym socks. But Nathan had nearly worn out the treadmill in the corner of the main room, and he and the boys sometimes watched TV down here. She had big plans to paint the dark paneling cream, maybe install track lighting, replace the tweed furniture. For now she'd slipcovered. But change took time. It didn't happen overnight.

Unless someone was in WitSec, of course.

"If you get cold, there's a linen closet next to the bathroom. It has a couple blankets." She pointed it out, not sure what else to say to Frank.

Or rather, wanting to say so much and not knowing where to start.

She turned toward the stairs.

"You made the right decision, Annalise."

Maybe that was it, what she needed to hear, because it stopped her and, for a crazy second, burned moisture into her eyes. "Really?"

"Yes. I know what it's cost you, but . . ."

She turned back at his pause. Searched his eyes. They were always kind, even when she hadn't been . . . well, cooperative. In fact, she remembered once frisbeeing a plate at his head. His quick reflexes had rescued him from a beheading.

"They're okay. It was hard at first. Your mother would call me every once in a while, and of course I couldn't tell her anything. They finally accepted it and the calls stopped."

She drew in a breath at that, sinking into Nathan's old recliner in the main room. "I think about my parents, especially on nights like this, when everyone has grandparents at the game. My mother would love to see Colleen play. My father would want to take Henry and Jason fishing."

Frank carefully moved from the den doorway to sit on the sofa, cradling his cocoa.

"Funny, having you there tonight was the closest thing to having a relative."

"I know what you've accomplished."

"I haven't accomplished anything. It's Nathan. He found me; he built this life."

"No, Deidre, you built this life with him. You created Annalise. You became a mother, a wife. You took your second chance and did something amazing with it."

"I sometimes wonder what would have happened if I . . . well, if I had turned you down."

He met her gaze.

Yeah, she knew the answer to that.

She ran her hands together. They were cold—always cold during the winter. "I hate keeping secrets from Nathan."

Frank nodded.

"It's like . . . there's this part of myself that I've walled off. I sometimes feel like I'm staring at my life from a different vantage point, like it doesn't really belong to me. And Nathan doesn't understand why I have to keep the outside lights on or why I can't watch shows like *Law & Order*. Or even why sometimes I climb into bed with Colleen and hold on."

Frank just kept nodding.

"Did you know that every year my mother would buy me a Christmas ornament for my collection? I wonder if she still does that." She drew up her knees onto the chair, pulled her sweater around her. "My sister's baby is named Deidre. But you probably knew that."

He nodded once more, setting his cocoa on the side table.

"Sometimes I want to call them so badly, I find myself walking around the house with the phone."

"Don't do it. You'd come back from the grave, and . . . there would be too many questions. And who knows but Garcia still has connections in St. Louis."

She looked away, wiping her hand across her cheek. "I thought I was over this. Sorry."

"It's my fault. I shouldn't have just appeared. But I didn't want some other agent popping into your life . . . and I wanted to see how you were doing."

The affection in his voice reminded her just how much she'd depended on him in those early days. "How's Margaret?"

Frank leaned forward and pressed his hands together. "She passed about eight years ago. Cancer."

"Oh, Frank, I'm so sorry."

"It was fast. She didn't tell me until the end, and by that time, well . . . we only had a little time together."

"You have a daughter, right?"

"She and her husband live in California, and I have a grandson. He's twenty. Sometimes I see pictures on Facebook."

Strange, he sounded even less connected to his family than she was. "Aren't you getting close to retirement? Why don't you move to California?"

He made a face. "You know, she's busy, and she doesn't need me loitering in her life."

"Frank—"

He held up a hand. "I'm okay, Annalise. People don't know what they have until they don't have it anymore. Someday she might figure it out."

"I know what *I* have, Frank. And I'm not going to lose this. But . . . I can't look at Nathan without feeling the lie. I want to tell him the truth. I think he deserves it. But then what? I can see his face, and . . . maybe not knowing is better."

Frank had this annoying way of not answering her. It made her words echo back to herself, made them pinch and burn.

"I should have told him in the beginning."

Frank picked up his cocoa, took a sip.

"You drive me crazy, you know that?"

"I think I'm going to hang around here for a couple days. Make sure Garcia doesn't show up."

She stood. "Do me a favor: try not to blow my cover, will you, Uncle Frank?"

He grinned. "Listen, missy, don't get snippy with me, or I'll put you over my knee."

She threw a pillow at him.

He ducked. "Still quicker than you."

She left him downstairs, hiding a smile. Wasn't that the way with relatives? You wanted to throttle them. But you couldn't live without them.

She was still chuckling when she opened the bedroom door.

Nathan looked up again from his computer. "What's so funny?"

And right then, for a golden moment, the door to her past opened and her opportunity appeared on the threshold. Maybe she *could* tell him the truth. How Uncle Frank wasn't really a relative but her protector, the man who had saved her. How he'd brought her to Deep Haven because he loved this little town. How she'd taken one look at Nathan, standing in the vestibule of the community church, his hand extended, and seen a future she wanted.

How she'd been afraid that Nathan would run away at the first glimpse of her past, so she'd hid it from him. And ever so slowly, her secrets wove into a web of lies so well constructed that it became the fabric of her world.

But maybe if she told him now, it would cut through this veil that hung between them. He'd see all of her and . . . and . . .

Then what? Nathan hated betrayal. His father had betrayed his mother, and it destroyed all of them. He'd never forgive her. Worse, he'd despise her.

She couldn't bear to see the reflection of Deidre in his eyes. The Deidre who had once bartered herself for drugs. Who'd awoken in an alley with no recollection of who she was, where she'd been. Who'd gotten her roommate and best friend murdered.

Even Annalise despised that Deidre.

And her children, what of them?

She couldn't lose them.

"Nothing's funny," she said finally. "I'll be to bed in a moment."

He flicked off the television as she closed herself in the bathroom, reaching for her nightclothes hanging on the hook. Long flannel pajamas, wool socks, an extra sweatshirt. Sometimes she even slept with gloves.

Sexy.

She considered the layers. No, she couldn't tell him the truth—not yet—but perhaps she could put a little spice back into their marriage. Help them find that spark, that intimacy she'd always longed for. Maybe then he'd understand.

She stripped off her clothes, examined for a moment the scar on her knee, then grabbed a towel and wrapped it around herself. She sprayed on some of the perfume he'd given her last Christmas, pinched her nose to keep from sneezing, brushed her teeth, and finally exited the bathroom, her pulse pounding in her throat.

The light on her side of the bed bathed Nathan's face, his eyes softly closed, eyelashes curled against his cheeks. His computer lay on the floor next to the bed, in sleep mode.

She padded across the room. He didn't move.

Sitting on her side of the bed, she laid her hand on his chest. "Nathan?"

Nothing.

She leaned close, smelling his neck. She loved his aftershave, the way it sank into his skin, turning his smell masculine and strong. Despite the lack of spark, their romance had healed her, their love life always making her feel safe and cocooned.

He emitted a snore.

She ran her hand along his chin, feeling the whiskers there. Then pressed her palm again to his chest, gauging his breath as it rose and fell.

Yes, this was enough. To share this life, these children. To know they had a future. She didn't need spark.

She returned to the bathroom to don her layers before slipping into bed.

Once upon a time, Tucker Newman had a family waiting for him when he came home. A mother who set a tuna casserole in the middle of their scratched pine table at six o'clock. A father who sat in the frayed green recliner, channel surfing. A brother who might drag him into their room to check out the newest boards in *Snowboarder* magazine.

Once upon a time, Tuck didn't open the front door to a cold, dark house, with creepy shadows that lurked in the corners and the smell of old milk in the air, evidence that someone—aka him—had forgotten to take out the trash. When he flicked on the light, it spilled into the kitchen, over the pile of mail strewn in the center of the table, across sticky, egg-encrusted dishes in the sink.

"Mom!" he called but didn't really expect a reply. His mother had pulled a couple double shifts down at the Deep Haven Tavern—working as a waitress, then her regular position as bartender. She'd probably be out past two again tonight. But they needed the money.

Maybe this year they wouldn't be eligible for the community church's Thanksgiving basket. He hated answering the door, accepting the basket from Pastor Dan and his wife. Like they were poor or something.

They weren't poor. Just . . . just . . .

Hungry. Tuck found a box of generic macaroni and cheese in the cupboard. He pulled out a pan, filled it with water, and set it on the stove to boil.

Then he toed off his shoes and lifted Rusty off the table, setting the old tabby on his lap, running his hand over the cat's back as he sifted through the mail. The folks at Midwest Ski Supply still hadn't figured out that his brother died three years ago. Nevertheless, Tuck opened the catalog, checking out the new equipment for the season. Rusty settled into a rumble of pleasure on his lap.

What he wouldn't give for a Burton Nug. His board was heavy and longer, and by the looks of the Nug, he could get by with a 142, cut down from his 150. And with the V-Rocker reverse camber, jumper cable suspension, and frostbite edges, it could still perform in every condition—through the woods, in spins, jumps, boxes. He could probably land in the Sugar Ridge Free Boarding finals with it.

And it cost a mere $400.

He closed the catalog. Picked up Rusty around the shoulders. The cat stretched out his body, yawning. "Who am I kidding? I'll probably spend my whole life here, busing tables, shoveling, and taking out the trash at the Sugar Ridge Resort for $7.25 an hour."

It wasn't like his grades were going to land him any scholarships. Reading gave him the most trouble—he just couldn't figure out the words. The letters lifted off the page and rearranged themselves. He'd rather skip class than read aloud.

They'd probably keep him in high school until he hit thirty.

No, he'd drop out long before then.

He set the cat on the floor, and Rusty curled around his legs. Tuck tried not to accidentally kick him as he returned to the stove and poured in the macaroni. The water bubbled up, then flowed over the side onto the white cooktop.

He turned down the heat a little, stirred, and dropped a lid onto the pot.

Then he pulled the dishes out of the sink, stacking them on the side so he could fill it with hot water, and let Colleen tiptoe into his head.

He'd caught her today practicing her serve in the gym, her blonde hair pulled into a long, beautiful tail, her blue eyes like the sky on a crisp winter day. They could hold him captive, make him forget his name.

Just like that day when he'd seen her watching one of his competitions. It took him a full eight months to ask her out. But who could blame him? She was a Decker.

Colleen had stopped her warm-up this afternoon to run over to him. He'd plucked the volleyball from her arms, twirled it on his finger.

She snatched it away. "Show-off."

He grabbed her around the waist, pulling her to himself as he leaned against the wall. "This is showing off." Then he ducked his head and kissed her.

He'd kissed his share of girls—after all, he was a senior—but none of them like Colleen. She tasted like pure sunshine, and kissing her made his entire body feel golden. She wound her arms around his neck and leaned into him.

The memory of Mrs. Decker catching them at the park on Tuesday had vanished.

Colleen broke away, and he nuzzled her neck, drew in her smell—something floral lingering on her skin—then landed a kiss by her ear. "You're going to annihilate them tonight."

Biting her lip, she glanced at the door to the locker room. "Technically we don't have to be in warm-ups for another twenty minutes. Wanna drive me downtown for coffee?"

He considered her. "Are you sure?"

She nodded. Smiled.

"Let's go."

He'd parked out back by the gym doors, and since she didn't

bother to grab her jacket, he turned the heat on as soon as he fired up his ancient soft-top Jeep.

"I heard that it's already snowing in Montana," Tuck said as he pulled out of the lot. "What I wouldn't give to be on the slopes."

They drove to the Java Cup and were pulling in when she put a hand on his arm. "Wait. There's my mom's SUV."

He scanned the coffee shop but couldn't see Mrs. Decker through any of the front windows.

"I don't need coffee," Colleen said, stiffening.

He frowned. "Just because your mother is here? Listen, Colleen, I know she freaked you out when she caught us kissing—"

"My mother is paranoid I'm going to get pregnant or something. Wreck my life."

"With me." He hadn't wanted it to leak out quite like that. It sounded a little too vulnerable.

"So what they don't like you. I don't care," she said, shrugging.

And then he made it worse. "You know, it wouldn't be terrible if they liked me."

He knew she didn't mean for her laugh to be so harsh, but it cut a swath through him. "Oh, Tuck. *Really?*"

He tightened his jaw a bit. "Right. What was I thinking?" He put the car into gear. "Let's go to the harbor. I'll give you a pep talk."

Then he winked because he needed her smile.

Colleen played an outstanding game that night, and he cheered her on, despite her words burning inside him. Especially as he watched the entire row of Deckers eating popcorn, laughing. Like they belonged together. Like they were happy. Mrs. Decker had surely seen him as she entered the gym, but she didn't invite him to sit with them.

He wasn't that unlikable, was he?

Tuck set the egg-crusted plates in the hot, sudsy water to soak. Added water to the egg pan and set it on the counter.

Once upon a time, their dishwasher worked. But that was when his dad lived with them, when he could fix nearly anything.

Except his marriage.

Tuck had stopped trying to figure out which weekend he might spend with his father. Truthfully, it seemed his old man couldn't care less. Sure, he gave Tuck a free pass to Sugar Ridge, where he worked maintenance. And Tuck had seen him on the sideline at a few of last year's competitions. But only because he worked the lifts or the snowmaking equipment or ran the graders.

Tucker's memories of the life they'd once had were fading.

Behind him, the lid on the pot rattled. By the time he turned around, more milky foam covered the stove. The air reeked of burned pasta.

He turned off the heat and moved the pot away to let it sit. Then he dove back into the dishes. The water scalded his hands as he scrubbed at the egg residue.

So what they don't like you. I don't care.

He couldn't erase the words, that expression on Colleen's face, from his brain. As if she might be dating him to spite her parents.

Yeah, that felt good.

What he really wanted was to knock on their door, hold out his hand, and apologize for what Mrs. Decker saw going on in his Jeep in the lighthouse parking lot at lunchtime on Tuesday. Not like he hadn't gone farther with a few other girls. But they weren't Colleen Decker, daughter of the almost mayor, part of one of the most respected families in town. Everyone knew Nathan and Annalise Decker. And the fact that their daughter liked him almost made him feel . . . like he wasn't such a loser.

He rinsed the plate, set it in the drying rack.

It wasn't like he expected them to invite him over for Thanksgiving dinner, but . . . okay, that might be nice. A real family dinner like the kind he used to have.

Sheesh, he was turning into a Hallmark commercial. He rinsed the next plate.

So what they don't like you. I don't care.

Someday he was going to show them that he wasn't what they saw—an irresponsible board bum trying to steal their daughter.

He rinsed the last plate and grabbed a towel, wiping the dishes dry before he added them to the cupboard. He drained the water from the sink, then grabbed a colander for the pasta. It fell out into the colander in one rubber lump.

When he rinsed it, the pasta loosened. He added it back to the pot, then opened the fridge. Sure enough, the milk smelled like it had gone bad a week ago. He found a container of old margarine, cleaned it out, added some water, and managed a weak replica of macaroni and cheese. Scooping it onto a plate, he took it to his bedroom.

He'd kept his brother Jazz's Tom Sims posters plastering the room as a way of keeping him alive. Tucker straightened the blue denim comforter before he sat on it. Probably he should clean his room—at least try to separate the clean laundry from the dirty, now a jumbled mess on his floor.

He hit the Play button on his old television/VCR unit, and up popped an old snowboarding video, the kind that his brother ordered every month, with tricks and spins and excellent snow. Sitting cross-legged on the bed, Tuck lost himself in the freedom of the board as he shoveled dinner down.

When he finished, Tuck returned the plate to the kitchen, ran some water over it, added it to the drainer. Then he washed the stove of the residue. He drained the milk from the carton, smashed it, and tossed it in with the recycling.

He turned off the lights in the kitchen, leaving the outside light burning for his mother, a glow over their weathered porch and the now-yellow hosta overgrowing the stone walk.

This time of night, with the house so quiet, his room echoed with memory—his brother, on the other side of the room, telling him stories of snowboarding or the girls he'd met in Colorado when he'd hitchhiked out to work one summer.

Tuck lay back with his head on his hands. Stared at the poster of the glistening white snow, the spray of a boarder as he did a McTwist.

How he missed his brother.

Hopefully he had gone fast when the avalanche took him. Hopefully he hadn't lain there entombed for days until he finally suffocated. He hated to imagine what that might feel like, suffocating.

Or maybe he already knew.

He closed his eyes, listening to the silence.

Yeah, Colleen was hot, but he wanted more than just her in his arms.

He wanted her perfect life.

3

Any day now Helen Decker might wake to a frost, and all the apples on her Honeycrisp tree would be ruined. But picking them early meant she'd never get that perfect crunch.

Helen stood in the yard, the sun just cresting over the lake, testing the scent of the air, smelling the loamy briskness of autumn. She pulled an apple from the overladen tree, checking it for brown spots, wormholes, disease.

The Honeycrisp sported a perfectly speckled red skin, with shades of yellow and lime green, hinting at the delicious sweet-sour crunch that sucked the moisture from her mouth and left it tingling with a refined tartness. Perfect for apple pies and apple crumble and caramel apples, and the pride of her corner lot on Third Avenue and Sixth Street for the past forty years.

Yes, today she could harvest.

She would take the first barrel to Nathan's house. Thankfully he lived just across the street, kitty-corner—his idea of keeping an eye on her. Maybe Colleen and the boys would want to take one to school. Later, she'd make a pie—or three. Bring one to her sister Miriam's, another to Nathan's. She'd keep one for herself, although she'd end up freezing most of it. A pie might last her two months if she cut it up and froze the pieces individually.

Still, she always netted enough apples to make twenty quarts of applesauce, enough apple crisp to outfit church potlucks for the winter season, holiday pies for her sister and her family, and sometimes even apple cider for the annual Mad Moose community dance.

She could probably manage hauling out the apple press by herself. It wasn't heavy, just bulky, and Nathan had enough on his plate today.

She'd have to make sure she listened to the radio show this morning. Maybe call in with a question that Nathan could brilliantly answer. She'd also call Miriam, remind her to tell the ladies in her apartment building.

Nathan would be the best thing that ever happened to this town. He'd certainly been the best thing that ever happened to her.

Helen worked on her gloves, then began pulling the apples from the tree, checking for only the ripest. She'd harvest them slowly over the next few days, even week, praying away the frost, although she guessed they'd have real snow on the ground before Halloween.

Those with bruises or worms or bird dings she dropped into a paper bag. The good apples she placed in the red wicker bucket, working her way around the tree, filling it until the apples brimmed the top.

The first harvest of the season.

She couldn't wait to show Annalise and the grandkids.

And maybe Annalise's uncle Frank, if he was still in town.

Not that she noticed him really, but to have one of Annalise's relatives turn up after so many years . . . Helen could admit to her curiosity.

And he wasn't a chore to look at, with that short salt-and-pepper hair, blue eyes that seemed to take her in with one gulp. He'd met her gaze without guile and shaken her hand.

She liked that kind of frankness in a man. Made her want to trust him.

If she ever had a mind to trust a man again.

Lugging the apple basket to the porch, she set it on the steps, avoiding the broken boards, then pulled off her gloves and went inside.

The coffee had finished, so she poured herself a cup and added some almond milk and sweetener. She used to take it black but over the years began to soften the bitter edge with milk. Sometimes she even went down to the Java Cup and had one of those lattes. She'd noticed a new flavor this season—pumpkin.

Maybe she'd give that a taste.

She jumped into the shower. The phone was ringing when she finished. Dripping wet, she grabbed it, wrapping her bathrobe around her.

"I left a message. Where have you been?"

Miriam had gotten more demanding after her husband, William, passed three years ago. Helen hated to think that she might have done the same thing after Dylan died . . . but no, he'd been gone months before that.

Helen had since spent her life making sure she demanded nothing from anyone, thank you.

"It's apple day. The Honeycrisps are ready. I was out in the yard. Where did you think I was?"

"I didn't know. I saw you at the game last night, talking to some man."

"And what? Did you think I took off dancing with him or something?" Helen put her on speakerphone and wiped cream on her face.

"What's got into you, Helen? Of course I didn't think that. You're used to being alone." Her tone changed, turned quiet. "It's not like being widowed. There's always that empty place on the other side of the bed."

Helen stared at herself in the mirror, at the lines etched around her eyes. Right. She knew *nothing* about the emptiness on the other side of the bed. She shook her head. "It's Annalise's uncle Frank. He's visiting her for a few days."

"He's Annalise's uncle? I thought she didn't have any family."

Helen sawed her makeup drawer free. So it had been a few years since she'd dug through it. She found some blue eye shadow—or how about pink?—and layered it on.

No, that didn't look right. She took a tissue and wiped it off. "He's just back from some overseas trip. Or maybe he lived there. I didn't get all the details."

When she found the mascara, she pulled out the brush. It clumped like paste on the end. She dropped it back into the drawer, shut it. "He's not in town for long, I don't think. Listen, I meant to tell you—Nathan has a radio show today at nine o'clock. He's answering questions on some community issues. I know he'd be grateful for an audience."

"I can't believe he's running for mayor. Jerry was doing a fine job. I don't know why he's quitting."

"Miriam, Jerry wants to retire. And Nathan's your nephew. Vote for him."

As Helen towel-dried her hair, she considered herself again in the mirror. She'd aged, yes, but her eyes were still young. At least today.

Maybe she should color her hair. Imagine, showing up again as a blonde, especially after all these years. Her battle with cancer had stripped the color from her hair way too early. Painfully early. She'd aged a decade or two practically overnight. In fact, she'd looked about sixty for twenty years.

"Of course I'll vote for him," Miriam said. "Say, I might stop by and pick a few apples off Mama's tree. You don't mind, do you? I want to make a pie for Janice and the boys."

"That's fine." Never mind that her mother had planted the tree when Nathan was born. That she'd sold her house to Helen after her divorce. That Helen had owned the bungalow free and clear for twenty years. Miriam still thought the house belonged to her, too.

"I'll see you later." Helen hung up before her sister could drive her to her final nerve.

Miriam never could forgive her for throwing Dylan to the street. Well, she hadn't been there that night he'd come home, tanked up and angry.

Or rather, Helen had been angry. And kept being angry. She closed her eyes against the memories swelling in her mind. So long ago. And yet she was still paying the price.

She had no doubt Nathan's bid for mayor would drag up a few dormant accusations. But she'd become calloused to them.

And frankly, Miriam was right. She wasn't going to find anyone to marry this late in the game. Besides, the divorce label still hung over her head, despite Dylan's passing so long ago. Divorced . . . not widowed.

She combed her hair, then changed into jeans and a clean denim shirt with a pumpkin stitched on the lapel. She looked for earrings and found a couple matching pumpkins Colleen had given her a few years ago.

She caught her image again in the mirror.

She looked frumpy.

But maybe that's what she was. Old and frumpy.

A grandmother.

Well, that wasn't such a terrible thing. She should count her blessings.

She could too easily be dead.

Pulling on a jacket, Helen turned up the collar, added a pink scarf—Annalise had purchased it at one of their local street fairs this summer—and grabbed fresh gloves.

The sun had cleared the horizon, brilliant and burning off the lightest haze of white from the tips of the grass as she descended her steps.

She heard the crack on the third step and swung her hand out to catch her fall. Her foot went through the board anyway, and she stumbled, pitching forward off the step.

"Oh!"

Helen landed on her hands, rolling out into the yard and coming to rest faceup under the apple tree.

Nice. So very nice.

"Are you okay?"

She heard the voice from across the street, coming toward her, and closed her eyes.

Perfect. Yet she couldn't help a laugh. Oh, how graceful. If she had any lingering thoughts about impressing Uncle Frank . . .

She sat up, icy dew saturating her jeans. "I'm fine!"

But of course, the man, wearing a baseball hat, a pair of worn jeans, and that leather jacket, came trumpeting into her yard as if he were playing fullback for the Vikings.

She scrambled to her feet in case he had a case of overblown chivalry and decided to scoop her up.

"I saw you fall—"

"I just tripped. My front steps are in need of repair." She turned and checked the damage. The board had broken all the way through, and worse, her bushel of apples had spilled down the steps, into the grass.

She hated bruised apples.

"You could have gotten hurt."

"What, I look that old?"

That comment worked some color into his face.

She smiled. "I'm kidding. You're sweet to run over here, really. But I'm fine. What are you doing up this early?" She rescued the bushel basket and began picking up apples, checking them for bruises.

"I'm an early riser, and I saw you out here picking apples this morning." He bent beside her to retrieve the apples. "What kind are they?"

"Honeycrisp. They're a delicacy." She handed him one and he cleaned it on his jacket, then took a bite.

She grinned at the way his eyes blinked, the twist of his face.

"Sour," he said between chews.

He had nice eyes. Grayish-blue, with a touch of humor.

"They make for great pies. And caramel apples." She finished picking up the apples and hoisted the bucket.

He took another bite before tucking the apple in his pocket, reaching for the basket.

She held on. "I can carry this."

"I'm sure you can, but indulge me." He smiled, one half of his mouth tweaking up.

"I was bringing them over to Nathan's—"

"Perfect. I'm going that way." He winked.

She didn't know what to do with that.

And then, she wasn't sure why, but the words just sort of erupted from her, like she'd been holding them back for years. Like they'd been waiting to ripen and were suddenly ready to harvest. Before the frost came and destroyed them.

"Would you like to come in and I'll make you an apple pie?"

&

He just meant to explore Annalise's world and meet the people in her life. Frank didn't really mean to stay for pie.

But what was a guy to do? Helen had a laugh about her—the way she rolled out from under that tree, bouncing up as if she were twenty-three.

Cute little pumpkin-shaped earrings dangling from her ears.

And the smell of cinnamon and nutmeg drifting from her kitchen as she sang Sinatra while he fixed her front porch step . . . Yes, he liked her.

It felt good to work with his hands, pry up the broken board, cut a new one, replace it, and while he was at it, patch two more. Helen wouldn't be falling through her porch anymore, at least not while he was around.

And when she invited him into her kitchen for a slice of crisp, tangy, warm apple pie à la mode, for a moment his life stopped spinning and settled into a sweet, perfect place.

He'd been unmoored since Margaret died. But sitting in Helen's kitchen, letting her tell him about how Nathan and Annalise met and fell in love, and about the early years of their marriage, felt like coming home after a long stint at sea.

"It seemed to be love at first sight. The minute she walked in the door, I knew she was right for Nathan. She looked at him like he was her hero. And she's treated me like a second mother."

Helen set coffee in front of him alongside a carton of milk, then slid back onto her chair. "So sad she had to lose her own family. I'm glad Annalise has you."

Frank nodded, ignoring the twinge inside.

"Nathan says you were in the military? Where?"

He poured the milk in, stirred it. "All over, really. Mostly stuff I can't talk about."

"Oh, some sort of secret agent?"

He liked the way she teased him, even if it felt wrong to lead her astray. "Something like that. I was away too many years, unfortunately. My poor wife went for weeks without hearing from me."

Her smile dimmed at the mention of his wife, and he saw her glance to his ring finger, so he just said it. "She passed away about eight years ago from cancer." He ran his thumb over the handle of the coffee mug. "We have one daughter who lives in California."

"I'm so sorry, Frank."

He lifted a shoulder.

She seemed as anxious to change the subject. "Annalise has a cousin? Another relative she hasn't mentioned."

Nice, Frank. That was the problem with lies—they were like trying to seal leaks in a submarine. "They haven't seen each other in years, I'm afraid." He'd have to alert Annalise to that tidbit.

"Shame. Nathan has cousins all over the county. The Decker family has been in the area for nearly five generations. My former husband's grandfather came here in the early nineteen hundreds as a trapper, settled down in Deep Haven, married a local Ojibwa girl, and, well, now if you throw a rock, you hit a Decker relation."

"A lot of people throwing rocks at the Deckers?"

He meant it as a joke, but something he'd peg as sadness edged her eyes. She picked at her pie. "Unfortunately, yes. Nathan and I are the black sheep of the family."

"I hardly see you as a black sheep, Helen."

She looked up and smiled at him, and for a second his world moved—just a little—a feeling he'd nearly forgotten. "You're sweet. The truth is, I was married thirty years ago, to Dylan Decker. A local boy who wooed me into marrying him and then broke my heart." She pushed her pie away. "We divorced after thirteen years of marriage—Nathan was twelve. I still remember him standing in the family room, holding a football, watching his daddy drive away. He spent the summer sitting on the steps, waiting for him to come back. Me, I was relieved."

She paused, drew in a breath, and he knew a secret when he saw one.

"Dylan showed up a few times after that, often three sheets to the wind, demanding to see his son, but I wouldn't let him—not in that condition. One night he got behind the wheel drunk and hit a local man head-on. Dylan died when his car went over the edge of the highway into the river, off the Cutaway Creek Bridge. The other man—Moe Jorgenson—died on impact. His son Shawn played football with Nathan, and my son quit immediately. He never played again. And . . . and this town never forgot the Decker name."

"I'm so sorry."

"Nathan and Annalise and their kids are enough for me. I don't care what the town says about us. As long as I have my family, my life is whole."

He gave in to the urge to reach out and touch her hand. She had strong, soft hands, a little chilly under his. She didn't move away but didn't turn her hand to hold his, either.

The moment passed and he heard only the tick of the clock.

Helen gave a small shake of her head. "I'm sorry. I'm being . . ." She pulled her hand out, patted his. "You're a nice man, Frank. Thank you for listening—"

"What is going on here?"

Frank jerked his hand away. Out of reflex he found his feet, tipping over his chair in the process.

A woman who could be a more padded, shorter version of Helen let the screen door slam behind her as she stalked into the kitchen. She wore a brown fleece jacket open over a sweatshirt with a purple flower embroidered on the front, her hair pulled back with a knit headband. She stared at Helen as if she'd caught her necking in the backseat of his old Mustang.

And where had that thought come from?

"Please come in, Miriam." Helen stood, glanced at Frank. "This is Annalise's uncle, Frank Harrison."

Miriam had a round face, tight, thin lips, and cold eyes that grew inexplicably colder as she turned to him. "Hello. I'm Miriam, Helen's sister."

He picked up his chair. "Nice to meet you."

"So odd that after all these years, a relative of Annalise's shows up."

He wanted to cheer when, right then, his phone rumbled in his pocket. He pulled it out, checked the number, and kept his voice even. "I need to take this. Please excuse me."

Helen gestured to another room, and he accepted the escape, opening the phone.

He kept his voice low. "Did you talk to him?"

"Hello to you, too, Frank."

"For crying out loud, Boyd, I know it's you. Did you talk to Blake? What does he know?" Six years of working with Parker Boyd and Frank still couldn't get the word *rookie* out of his head.

"Actually, boss, there's a problem."

This had probably been Nathan's room—the walls brown, the single bed covered with a quilt, a framed photo of Annalise and him on their wedding day on the old bureau.

"What kind of problem?"

"Blake Hayes is dead."

Frank sat down on the bed and cradled the phone against his head. "Say again?"

"He's been murdered. He's been dead maybe a day at most. The coroner is just getting here. Looks like he's been tortured—he's tied to a chair, and . . . well, he's missing parts."

Garcia. Frank didn't speak it out loud, but he knew the man's MO.

"And the place has been tossed like the perp was looking for something."

A letter, perhaps? One dated twenty years ago? He ran his thumb and forefinger against his eyes. Probably a remote chance, but Blake might have hung on to Deidre's address for insurance against Garcia's sudden reappearance.

Oh, how he hoped she hadn't told her old boyfriend her new name.

"Could be a random murder," Frank said, more hope than truth in his words.

"Could be," Boyd said softly. "Boss, I think we have to move Annalise—"

"Stop talking. Just . . . let me think."

How would Garcia have found Blake? He couldn't have known . . . unless Blake refused to stay hidden. Unless Blake had contacted his cohorts from so long ago.

"Look into Blake; see if he's made contact with any of Garcia's old gang."

"If this was Garcia, then he's on the move, and he could be heading her way."

"Alert the airlines—"

"I did that when we discovered he had jumped parole."

"Which means he's traveling by car. How long does it take to get from Fairbanks to Minnesota?"

"I don't know, maybe a few days? Hang on; I'll MapQuest it."

Outside the door, he could hear Miriam's voice. "What's going on, Helen? Was he holding your hand?"

Helen answered with a sibilant *shh*. But Frank moved toward the door anyway.

"I just invited him over for pie!"

"You should be ashamed of yourself."

"I'm not dead—I'm divorced."

"Exactly. Something you should think about before you jump into another relationship—"

He stepped away from the door, stared at the pictures on the wall above the bed, one of Helen and her grandchildren. She was crouching between them on the steps he'd just repaired, arms over their shoulders, grinning into the camera.

"It's sixty-seven hours, give or take a few."

"So maybe three days?"

"He's gotta avoid the main roads, and if he's traveling alone, he'll need sleep. There's a storm moving in from the north that will slow him down . . . Still, I think you've got five days max, boss."

Five days.

Five days to tell Annalise to pack up her life. To give her a new identity, find her a new place to live, create a new life for her. With or without her family. He stared at himself in the mirror, hearing the voices of the past.

He had to move her if he wanted to keep her alive.

And he very much wanted to keep Annalise alive.

"Find him, Boyd," he said and clicked off.

He looked again at the picture, hating this job and people like Garcia. Hating that in five days he'd take everything away from Annalise.

From Helen.

Unless . . .

Unless he could convince Helen to trust him. To put her life in his hands. To let him build her a new identity along with Annalise and her family.

"What, are you going to invite him to the dance tonight?"

He paused, listening, suddenly wondering about the answer.

"I—"

And then, not caring because he'd found a way to fix this, he opened the door and pasted on a smile. "Actually, I'm inviting *her* to the dance." He met Helen's eyes. "Will you go with me?"

It almost felt like a real date when she smiled at him, eyes shining, and said yes.

4

How Nathan had landed in the doghouse, he didn't know. But he'd done something to make his wife betray him.

Okay, *betray* didn't seem fair. But he hadn't the faintest idea how to respond when she'd turned to him this morning and said, "Are you sure you need me at today's luncheon? You're running for mayor, not me."

What was that supposed to mean? They were a team, and frankly, there wasn't a person in Deep Haven who didn't like Annalise Decker. He knew she'd been campaigning for him at every PTA meeting, every soccer match. Through every volunteer hour at the Goodwill, at the hospitality committee meetings at church, on the theater board, and at the blood drive.

Her words had burrowed into him all morning, especially

during the hour on the breakfast show today with Isadora Presley, local talk show host turned political interviewer.

Annalise was his secret weapon, and he needed her more than ever if he hoped to beat Seb Brewster.

Until today at 9 a.m., Nathan Decker had believed he'd be the next mayor of Deep Haven. Then Jerry—tricky Jerry Mulligan—just had to show up, right there on the radio show, and endorse Seb Brewster's late-entry run for mayor.

Nathan should have guessed. The man had been threatening a run since he returned to Deep Haven over a year ago.

Which meant that Nathan needed every vote he could get. He glanced at the calla lilies on the seat beside him. They filled the Ford with a freshness, a grace, that his marriage suddenly needed.

Truth was, Annalise had been acting remote, even jumpy, since her uncle arrived yesterday. He'd nearly startled her out of her robe when he found her at the window this morning, watching Frank pick up apples in his mother's yard, a strange look on her face, and when Nathan came up beside her, she gave a small yelp.

Very reminiscent of those first years of their marriage, when he'd walk into a room and she'd spook like he might be a bandit. Or worse.

"Sorry," he'd said, and she gave him a tepid smile as though still returning from wherever her thoughts had taken her.

Maybe across the street, where her uncle was hitting on his mother.

Yes. He saw the way his mother laughed. The way Frank took the basket from her hands, Mr. Chivalrous. It tightened something inside him.

He'd have to keep his eye on the guy. Maybe Frank *had* put Annalise on edge.

Still, it was Nathan's job to fix it.

He pulled up to their ranch house and didn't bother to park the car in the garage. Her SUV took up the other side of the driveway. He hoped to catch her in the shower, getting ready for the luncheon. Maybe even rekindle some of the old, impromptu moments. He missed their closeness, but that's what happened when you lived a busy life.

He stepped past the pumpkins lining the steps, the pot of red chrysanthemums on the bent twig bench on the porch. She'd hung a wreath made of fall leaves and grapevine on the door.

Nathan recognized the pungent smell of fresh paint the moment he opened the door. Oh no.

Toeing off his shoes, he walked across the Berber carpet into the kitchen, then down the stairs to the basement. "Lise!"

He'd blame Uncle Frank for this sudden urge toward home renovation. Not that Annalise needed much of an excuse. His wife thrived on remodeling. She'd single-handedly refaced the old cupboards in the kitchen, turning it into a French Renaissance style, and retiled the backsplash not only in the kitchen, but in both main floor bathrooms. She'd repainted their bedroom twice and each of the children's rooms three times as they grew out of Thomas the Tank Engine, Bob the Builder, Dora the Explorer, and then through the Marvel Comic stages until finally letting them choose their own themes. With supervision, of course.

In the family room, she'd painted the walls red and a burnt-yellow faux stucco and replaced the carpet with Berber. He couldn't count how many times they'd resurfaced the driveway, and he never thought he'd survive digging up and re-laying the brick walk or the patio pavers in the backyard.

Sure, the house dated from the early fifties, and the foundation had a few cracks, but she was always slapping paint over it, as if she'd never quite get it right.

Not that he minded. But it all cost money.

More, it wasn't like they'd ever sell the place. Or leave Deep Haven. Their life was here, in this small town, in this old ranch-style house. They had to make the best of it.

But for Annalise, it had to be better. Perfect.

Down in the basement, she had draped plastic across the carpet and had nearly finished covering the brown paneling with what looked like eggshell-white paint. She wore one of his old sweat-shirts, her hair tied up in a high ponytail, protected with a blue bandanna. The nip of the October breeze snuck into the room through the open windows, tempering the odor of paint.

"Lise, now? You're painting now?"

She stepped off the footstool, holding a roller. "Have you ever noticed how dark it is down here? And those old sofas—they stink, you know."

"Yes, like Mountain Dew, Cheetos, and sweaty boys playing Xbox. Trust me, we're not replacing them until after our children are out of the house."

She set the roller in the pan. "I know. I just . . . I can't bear to look at this dark paneling one more second."

He pulled the flowers out from behind his back. "I'm sorry for being testy this morning."

She gave him a soft smile, and suddenly his world slowed. Righted. Sometimes, when their life seemed to overflow with school events and church board meetings and mayoral races, he forgot the easy, simple days when just looking into her eyes made him feel as if he already had everything he needed.

As if he was already someone.

She picked up a rag, wiped her hands on it, then came over to him and took the flowers. "They're beautiful, Nathan. Thank you."

Her words curled around him, empowered him. He wrapped his arm around her waist and pulled her close. "Are you okay? You just seem so distant, even angry." He tried to wipe away a smudge of paint with his thumb, but it wouldn't clean off. "I'm not sure what I have to do to get your vote, Mrs. Decker, but I'm willing to try."

"Really. How hard?"

Oh, he could meet that challenge. He tipped up her chin, held her eyes for a moment, and kissed her.

She had a way of making him believe that he could save her with his touch, that when he took her in his arms, he became a hero. Maybe it was her surrender, how she usually molded herself to him, her fingers looping in his hair. He could get lost in the little sounds she made, soft sighs, like he could put all things right.

Not today.

Today she gave him what he called her duty kiss, the one where he knew she was thinking about the laundry or signing permission slips or what new pillows she'd buy for the old slipcovered sofas.

Like kissing him was on her to-do list, the one she kept to make her life ordered and perfect.

He let her go. "Okay, what did I do?"

"What are you talking about?"

"You. I could be kissing a walleye for all the love here."

"Nice. Thanks." She shoved the lilies back at him. "I have to finish painting before the kids get home."

"Lise." He dropped the flowers onto a table. "C'mon, that isn't fair. You've been acting strange. What did you mean when you said you're not running for mayor? You might as well be—this town looks up to you."

"They shouldn't—"

"Yes, they should. And I need you at the luncheon. You know how much this means to me."

She picked up the roller, drove it into the paint, then turned to the wall, her movements brisk. "That's what I can't figure out. Why do you have to be mayor? You're already so busy. You already miss soccer games, and . . ."

"Once. I missed one game."

"And you missed a volleyball game."

"I had a church board meeting."

"Exactly. And now you'll be mayor."

"That's right. I'll be mayor. *Mayor* of Deep Haven, Lise." He wanted to grab her, make her listen to him. But she kept painting.

And sighing.

How he hated the sighing. "What?"

She rolled until the paint ran out on her roller, then turned to plunge it back into the paint tray. "You know, you don't have to prove anything to anyone. You're not your father, and everyone knows that. You're Jason and Colleen and Henry's dad. And my husband."

"It's not enough." He said it without thinking, just let the words slide out, and hated himself the moment they emerged.

She drew in her breath. "Thank you for the honesty."

"Lise, I didn't mean it like that." He reached for her, but she moved away. "I just want more for us." Oh, he was making it worse. "Not that I'm not happy—"

"I need to finish this."

"Could you just shower and get dressed for the luncheon? We can talk about this later."

She stood there, paint dripping onto the plastic, her shoulders stiff.

"I need you there. The voters expect to see you, to see us. And with Seb Brewster running . . . please, Lise."

"Seb Brewster is running?"

Had she not even listened to the radio show? He tried not to let her question spear him through the chest, but it must have shown on his face because she shook her head and made a sound of defeat.

"Fine. I'll be there." She dropped the paint roller into the tray, grabbed the rag. "But I don't really care if you win or lose, Nathan, because I *am* happy with our life. And your being mayor just might destroy all that."

Her words jolted him. What—?

A door upstairs slammed, and he heard footsteps on the landing before a voice called, "Annalise?"

Frank.

"Down here!" she called, nothing of welcome in her voice.

Nathan would agree that her relative had lousy timing. He heard Frank's footsteps thump down the stairs.

"Annalise, I have to—"

Nathan turned at Frank's clipped sentence.

"Nathan. Uh, what are you doing home?"

Nathan couldn't help his tone. "I live here."

Frank had seemed friendly when he showed up, sort of an unassuming man, the kind who might take his kids fishing. Now the old man pulled himself up and for a second looked like, indeed, he had military training. His eyes went cold, his mouth tight.

Then it passed and he nodded. "Right. Sorry. I need to talk to Annalise. Family stuff."

"I'm her family."

Funny, though, the way Frank looked at him, Nathan didn't feel that way. The eerie feeling climbed back into his belly, latched on. For a moment, it seemed that he stood outside a secret, that he knew nothing of a sacred, even terrible truth.

It reminded him of the way people looked at him that day so many years ago when he went to school, unaware of the wretched news of his father's death.

Then Annalise saved him like she always did. "Oh, for pete's sake." She dropped the rag and brushed past him, leaving the calla lilies behind. "I have to get to the luncheon. Whatever it is, I'll talk to you tonight, Uncle Frank."

Strange, the way she said *Uncle*. Like it might be a threat.

But as Nathan watched Frank's eyes on him, perhaps it was.

&

Annalise had stood, hands folded in front of her, Nathan's hands hugging her hips, and tried to find a real smile. Something that didn't betray panic.

"One more shot," Erland said, looking over his camera.

She'd tried to manufacture an expression that would make her unrecognizable to anyone who might have once known her. Like Luis Garcia.

Or her mother.

She hadn't realized how much of her life had gone public. Viral, even, if Lorelei's words as Annalise escaped to the punch bowl held any truth. "I love Nathan's new Facebook page. Such a cute picture of you and the family. When did you have the photo taken?"

Annalise scrolled back to the last time they'd all been in one place, with clean shirts, combed hair, and smiles.

Maybe this summer, when Jason had his senior photos taken.

She'd asked the photographer to snap a few shots of their family. The one with them sitting on the rocks with the lake in the background and Nathan holding her hand had turned out well.

The perfect family.

Not for long if Garcia ever saw her picture. But would he know her? Twenty years ago she'd had short black hair, angry eyes. He hadn't a prayer of finding her. And Blake—Blake wouldn't mention it. He'd probably forgotten her.

She should just relax. "Thanks, Lorelei."

In the corner, next to the expansive picture windows that overlooked the lake, Nathan talked with Lorelei's husband, Barry, who owned the convenience store in town. Nathan was gesturing as he spoke—dangerous with the cup of coffee in his hand. She walked over to retrieve it from him before he spilled it down his pressed shirt or across a prospective voter. Their fingers brushed as she took the cup, and their fight burned inside her. She set the cup on a table beside him. He caught her eye, smiled.

She shouldn't have been so hard on him today—the flowers were sweet, his apology for nothing he'd done even more so.

She was just on edge. Having Frank around made her lies, her secrets, seem so large. Fresh. Inescapable.

Still, she couldn't erase Nathan's words. *It's not enough.*

Which meant she wasn't enough. Their lives weren't enough. Everything she'd done, sacrificed . . . wasn't enough.

"Annalise?"

The voice startled her, and she moved out of the way of the punch jostling from her hand. Oh, shoot, and on her black pants, too. Thankfully they wouldn't show the punch stain.

She set the cup down on a table, grabbed a cloth napkin.

"I'm so sorry." Lee Nelson handed her another napkin. "I'm

doing a piece for the Deep Haven paper and was hoping you'd answer a few questions for me."

She knew Lee—the widow of Clay, the deputy who had died in that terrible shooting a few years back. Lee looked good—slender, her auburn hair freshly cut—clearly healing from that terrible day.

Then again, did anyone heal from the traumas that changed their entire lives? Even if they started over?

Lee reminded her—everyone—of how quickly everything could be taken away.

Annalise longed to grow old in Deep Haven beside Nathan. The thought wheedled through her even as she fixed on a smile. "Lee, I'd love to help you, but Nathan's the one running."

"Please. You're just as much mayor material as your husband. You're the one on the community boards—theater, PTA, and aren't you running the blood drive again this year?"

It was the least she could do since she couldn't actually give blood. Not since she'd once had hep A running through her bloodstream. It kept her out of the spotlight, always working behind the scenes to drum up volunteers. But when asked, she'd used a blood transfusion after the car accident as an excuse.

After so many years, she even believed it.

"I am. Want to join my team?" Annalise winked.

"I'm giving for Lucy Brewster's team."

Lucy Brewster. Seb's wife.

Lee shrugged. "It's a small town. I haven't figured out who I'm voting for yet."

"Well, let me tell you why Nathan is perfect for the job." Annalise pulled out a chair for Lee and sat down opposite her, outlining Nathan's position on the new tax levy for the county, the tourism tax increase, the school referendum, the proposed bike path expansion.

Lee took a few notes. "Will you still be running the Give Drugs the Slip campaign this year?"

"Of course. And the abstinence program."

"You're so involved at the school, Annalise. The perfect mayor's wife."

Right. Oh, she had these people fooled.

What would this town do if they discovered she'd lied to them for over twenty years? Probably feel the same way Nathan would. Betrayed.

It wasn't like she had a choice, however. She'd made an agreement to become a new person, to let the past die. To erase it, like she had her sparrow tattoo.

"I'm not the perfect mayor's wife. But I am sure Lucy Brewster would be."

"You're not supposed to root for the competition."

"Lucy and her shop are fixtures in this town. Of course she would be an excellent mayor's wife."

Lee grinned as she scribbled down Annalise's words. "I'm going to be posting my article and your picture on the newspaper's website. I'll send it to you so you can put it up on your Facebook and tweet it out."

Oh, boy. "Thanks." She wrapped her hand around her neck to rub the muscle there.

Lee frowned. "Are you okay?"

"I'm just a little tense."

"You should see my chiropractor. He's great. Maybe you just need an adjustment."

She needed an adjustment all right. Back to reality. Only, what was that, anyway?

"The first time I went, he found old injuries that I didn't even remember. It took a bit of work, but finally I started to feel better than I had in years. Amazing how we get used to living with aches and pains."

"Maybe I could use a massage."

"That too." Lee dug into her purse and pulled out an appointment card. "His number is on the bottom. And he has a massage therapist who works for him."

Annalise's entire neck screamed—had been tight for days. Long before Frank showed up, if she were honest.

Isadora Presley hovered over them, finally pulling up a chair. "Can I get a sound bite from you, Annalise?"

A year ago, Issy Presley had been a name on the radio—Miss Foolish Heart. No one in town knew she ran the late-night lovelorn talk show, although Annalise would confess to tuning in more often than she should. She hadn't been lovelorn. Lonely, maybe, but that was to be expected for such a busy family, wasn't it? Now Issy ran special programs like Nathan's interview today.

Which she'd forgotten to listen to, so intent on buying the right color paint. And he'd caught her.

She felt a little sick then.

"Nathan Decker is an honorable man who will bring his integrity and passion for family and community to the office of mayor." She spoke into Issy's handheld recorder, reciting the line she'd memorized at their kitchen table. But she believed it. No lying there.

"Thanks," Issy said. The silver diamond engagement ring sparkled on her finger. "I'll use it as filler between station breaks and for a promo when you come on the show."

When she—"What?"

"Nathan said you'd be happy to be interviewed for our *Deep*

Haven Digest hour next week. You'll come on, talk about yourself, your family, the things you believe in, some of the boards and charities you serve on. You know, what makes Annalise Decker our next mayor's wife."

So an hour of deceit, then. Perfect. She swallowed, glanced at Nathan. He was smiling at her like she hung the moon.

When in fact she might cost him everything he'd worked so hard for.

"Okay," she said. Not one quaver in her voice.

But, oh, maybe he hadn't anything to worry about. Because she was good—so very good—at lying.

5

HELEN STARED AT THE ARRAY of clothing in her closet, pretty sure she hadn't purchased anything new since 1983. And even then, maybe it hadn't been in fashion.

That stupid man—why did he have to invite her to the dance tonight? Like she needed a date.

Or romance. Or love.

She wasn't that silly girl anymore. The kind of girl who swooned when a good-looking man asked her out. She definitely wasn't the kind of girl to fall in love on the first date or rush into marriage.

Well, maybe she had rushed a little with Dylan, but at eighteen she'd fallen so hard, so fast, that it felt like forever before they'd married.

Maybe if she'd waited longer, she would have seen his lies, the fact that he had hidden his scoundrel, cheating ways, and saved herself from heartache.

Not that she would trade Nathan for anything.

But she might not have lived with the legacy of betrayal, the scourge of divorce.

Men were trouble.

Especially Frank, the way he sauntered into her life, those deep-blue eyes watching her as she'd rolled out pie dough. And those wide shoulders under his flannel shirt as he'd fixed the porch.

It frightened Helen how easily she could see Frank Harrison in her life. How she could get used to watching him drink coffee, listening to him talk.

Not that she'd enjoyed hearing about his wife and her death. Poor man. Eight years gone, however, felt long enough to enjoy his laughter without shame.

Of course, according to Miriam, these very thoughts were sacrilege.

She closed the closet door. Stared at herself in her white full-length slip in the long mirror on the door.

Maybe she should stay home. One date might lead to more.

And then what? Marriage? Hardly. She had a nice life, one she liked just the way it was. She didn't need a man messing it up.

She sat on the bed. Ran a hand over her arm. Flinched.

She'd managed a bruise already from her fall today. Holding up her arm, she found the purple-black smudge.

She prodded it, wincing. She had another one just like it on her shin, probably also from the fall. And a third on her hip where she'd wrestled with the apple press today. She'd given in to Frank's request to help her without too much fight.

It did make the juicing go faster. And was it so terrible to have company?

She pressed the bruise again, pain bleeding through her. Yes, perhaps asking for help, letting someone into her life, could save her from the bruises.

Or would it cause more?

"Helen?"

She grabbed up her bathrobe, shrugging it on as Annalise came to the door.

"Oh! Excuse me!" Annalise ducked away.

"For cryin' in the sink, c'mon in, Annalise. It's not like I'm standing here in my birthday suit."

But Helen had to go out into the hall to retrieve her daughter-in-law. The woman had picked up the family picture they'd taken this summer by the lake, staring at it as if she'd never seen it before.

"Such a beautiful family," Annalise said softly.

Was that a tear she whisked away?

"Are you okay, honey?"

"I'm fine."

But she looked tired. Of course, Annalise could still turn heads in town, with her long blonde hair, her figure, those blue eyes. Helen wasn't blind to the attention she received from the few bachelors—and nonbachelors—in town. But she wasn't Dylan, wasn't a liar, wasn't a cheat, would never betray her family. That's why she'd been the perfect choice for Nathan.

As if God had looked down upon them, forgiven Helen for her bad choices, and dropped into their lives the woman who could remind them exactly what fidelity felt like. Helen loved her daughter-in-law as much as she might love her own daughter. Annalise had healed all of them when she married Helen's son.

"How did the luncheon go today?"

"Nathan is still there, meeting with people. I had to come home to get something for the kids to eat before the dance tonight. Although what I'd really like to do is read a book." Annalise rubbed her hands down her arms. She wore a pretty red shirt, black dress pants, her hair in a loose bun. "Nathan says we have to go, though. Community spirit."

"Is that white paint on your chin?"

Annalise scrubbed at it with her hand, giving Helen a wry smile. "Oh, shoot, I thought I got it all."

"You can hardly see it," Helen said, moving into the kitchen to hand her a wet rag from the sink.

"I was painting the basement. Someday I'm going to gut it, start over."

"That sounds pretty drastic. Maybe it doesn't need to be gutted—"

"It smells. And I think there might be mice down there. No, a complete gutting. Not even the white paint is going to save it." Again the tight smile.

"Annalise, are you okay? You seem tense—would you like some pie?"

"I'm fine. It's just . . . all the media attention. Nathan had his picture taken today and there's a television interview next week . . ."

"Elections are in three weeks and it'll be all over. Life will go back to normal."

"I hope so." Annalise didn't smile. "I came over to ask if you'd check in on the kids tonight. Jason is going out with friends, but Colleen and Henry will be at home. And Tucker said he's going to stop by, so . . ." She made a face.

Tucker. Yes, that's right—Colleen had mentioned a boy she liked at school.

See, she didn't need to go to the dance.

"Sure, I'll be glad to check in on them."

Except, right then, of course, the doorbell rang. And before Helen could stop her, Annalise turned to look out the front window.

Frank Harrison stood on the stoop.

With flowers.

And looking dapper in black pants, a tie under his leather jacket.

"What is going on, Helen?" Annalise said softly. "What is F— Uncle Frank doing here?"

Oh, shoot. "We were supposed to go to the dance." She tucked her bathrobe tight to her neck and crossed the room. Opened the door. "Frank, listen—"

"I have to admit, I thought you might be in something different."

"Funny."

"What are you doing here?"

Even Helen started at Annalise's tone. She felt the frown on her face as Annalise charged up behind her.

"Are you taking Helen to the dance?" Annalise pushed past Helen, toeing up to her uncle. "Have you lost your mind?"

Okay, that hurt a little. "Excuse me?"

Frank narrowed his eyes. "Trust me, Annalise." He said her name slowly, as if it were rarely used.

"I'm not sure I should."

Oh, boy. "Listen, sweetie, your uncle Frank asked me to the dance and apparently dinner . . ."

She glanced at Frank. When he met her eyes, he gave her a smile. It ignited something inside her, something long dormant.

No. She wasn't a silly girl. "But I can't, Frank. Annalise needs me to check in on the kids—"

"You're going to the dance." He let himself in the house now, brushing past Annalise, then turning to her. "If you're going to the dance, so are we."

Meaning flashed in his eyes.

Annalise put her hands on her hips. Cocked her head. "What if I stay home?"

Helen had never quite seen this side of Annalise before. Nor heard that tone.

"You're going. Helen and I have dinner plans. Then we're going dancing. So go home, change, and we'll see you there."

A muscle ticked in Annalise's jaw, and for a second, something dangerous and even angry flashed in her eyes. "You watch yourself, Uncle Frank. She's my mother-in-law. My *family*."

Frank glanced at Helen, then back to Annalise. He leaned close and whispered into Annalise's ear.

Whatever he said jerked her upright. Made her glance at Helen. "See you at the dance," she said quietly.

See you at the dance?

Annalise closed the door behind her—not quite a slam, but something near it.

Frank turned to Helen and extended the flowers—roses. Yellow roses. "I'm okay with the bathrobe, but if you want something a bit easier to dance in, I'll wait."

Helen didn't care how long she had to look; she intended to wear something fabulous tonight.

❧

Why couldn't Colleen just give him a chance to meet her parents? Tuck hated sneaking around.

He nearly drove away, waiting for her like a gangster in his Jeep, parked in the shadows of the Laundromat, two blocks from her house. The moon was a giant eye overhead, watching as she emerged from the Johnsons' yard, around the end of the Magnussons' hedge, and onto the pavement of the shadowed lot.

She slid into his car, breathing hard. "Sorry I'm so late. My parents wouldn't leave until Jason promised to stay in. And then he gave me the third degree about why I wanted to watch a movie in my room. Like he didn't spend hours in his room on Facebook with Harper Jacobsen."

She leaned over, snaked her hand around Tuck's neck.

She looked amazing tonight in a short black skirt, leggings, and a low-cut sweater. His irritation dissolved at the look in her beautiful blue eyes.

"I missed you," she said right before she kissed him, a recklessness in her touch that set off alarms inside him. He put her away from him before they ended up not going to the dance.

"I missed you too. I would have picked you up at your house, you know. I don't like sneaking around."

"Right," she said, turning to slide onto his lap. "Like my father would greet you with open arms. Trust me—you don't want the third degree."

Ouch. He shook her words away and ran his finger down her face. "You look pretty."

Catching his hand, she wove her fingers through his. "Pretty enough to take me home?"

He swallowed, not sure what to say. "Colleen, I, uh—"

"Later." She gave him another kiss, this time longer.

He pulled away. "What's with you tonight?"

"What's with you?" She slid off his lap. "Drive me down to the lighthouse. We're meeting Brianna and Ronnie there."

"Why?"

She rested her hand on his leg. "Why do you think? To score some entertainment."

He grabbed her hand, put it back on her lap. Okay, really, she was starting to freak him out. "I thought we were going to the dance."

"What? The dance? My parents are there. As is half the town. They're playing old-people music from the eighties. Or the sixties."

"I thought it would be fun."

She stared at him like she didn't recognize him.

"Seriously? Ever since the coffee shop yesterday—no, wait—since my mother caught us kissing, you've been acting weird. Like you . . . what? Do you feel guilty?"

He swallowed. "I . . . I just keep remembering the way she ordered you out of the car, the look she gave me, like she wanted to skewer me alive."

"She did." Colleen laughed, nuzzled close to his ear. "And that's part of the fun."

"What fun?"

His tone must have startled her away.

"You think I like having your parents look at me like I'm a criminal?"

Eyes wide, she shook her head.

Okay, so maybe he wasn't preppy and slicked up like her brother, but just because he didn't own an Abercrombie & Fitch wardrobe didn't make him dirt.

There it was again, the sense that maybe she was dating him *because* he looked like a criminal.

"Let's just go. They're waiting." She scooted a little away from him.

He breathed finally. But he didn't put the car into drive.

"What now?"

"Have you ever even smoked weed before?"

"Sure I have."

"No, you haven't."

"Sheesh, Tuck. I thought you'd like this."

"I don't smoke pot anymore." Not since he'd started seriously training for snowboarding. Even when his buddies did. He couldn't end up like his brother or, worse, wrap himself around a tree. "Can't we just go to the dance?"

"No. I don't want to go to the dance. I want to meet Ronnie and Brianna and have some fun."

"I just don't want to be the guy getting you in trouble. Listen, let's go grab a pizza. We can go back to my place, I guess."

"Forget it." She reached for the door handle.

His hand on her arm stopped her. "Wait."

"Why?"

He put his hands on the steering wheel. His knuckles turned white. He wanted this girl to like him more than was good for him. Maybe she'd get it out of her system. He'd keep her safe, make sure she didn't do anything stupid. "Just this once, okay?"

She frowned at him. "Yeah. Sure."

He drew in a breath as he put the car in drive. Hating himself a little.

Silence filled the car as they drove to the harbor, to the shadows behind the Coast Guard building, where Ronnie waited by his

Mustang. He had his back to them, both arms braced on the roof of his car, Brianna wrapped around him, probably already wasted by the way she was inhaling him.

Colleen glanced at Tuck and smiled.

His stomach clenched.

It wasn't supposed to be this way with her. She made him feel clean and bright and not at all like he might belong in a trailer park, eating lumpy macaroni and cheese for dinner. He wanted to do this right, not dodge her parents when he saw them in school.

She slid out of the Jeep and walked over to Ronnie.

No way was he letting her do this alone. Tuck turned the engine off and got out. He stood behind her as she handed over a rolled wad of cash. Ronnie didn't look at Tuck as he fished a bag out of his pocket and they made the exchange without a word.

Brianna stared at them, her long black hair tied back, whipping in the wind. Her eyes were far away, her smile uneven.

Colleen shoved the bag in her pocket.

"Climb in," Ronnie said. "Let's try it out." He pulled away from Brianna and opened the passenger door.

Tuck caught Colleen before she could acquiesce. "I don't think so."

Ronnie frowned at him. "Dude. Let the lady do what she wants."

Ronnie wasn't a big guy, though he had a couple inches on Tuck. But Tuck had just made his personal best in squats, and the way he felt right now, if Ronnie wanted to go, he wouldn't turn him down.

"Back off," Tuck said quietly.

Brianna saved them both. "C'mon, Ronnie." She kissed his neck. "Let's get out of here."

As the Mustang drove away, Colleen turned to Tuck, her eyes shiny. "You could have taken him."

"Let's just get in the car before we get caught."

She made a face but climbed in. "And now what?" She sniffed the bag, then reached into her pocket and pulled out a tiny pipe.

"Where'd you get that?"

"Alexis. She borrowed it from her boyfriend."

He shook his head.

"When did you turn into such a prude?" But her hands shook, and she spilled a little as she pushed the dried pot into the bowl.

"Don't get that in my car."

"Stop yelling at me! Just take me home."

"So you can get high at home?"

"Maybe. Yeah, what if I did?" She spilled some more.

"You're getting it everywhere." He reached for the bag, the pipe. "You gotta pack it in or it won't burn right."

She released it into his hands, smiled as he loaded the pipe.

The way she looked at him made him feel like the bad boy she wanted him to be.

Lights flashed across the lot and he looked up. A patrol car had pulled in.

Tuck swore. "It's Deputy Hueston."

"What do we do?"

But he'd already shoved the bag, the pipe, into his pocket. He curled his arm around Colleen and pulled her to himself. He didn't mean it, but his kiss was rough and almost angry as he kissed her for show until the light shone into the window.

"Hey, you two."

Tuck released Colleen, feigning surprise. He rolled down the window. "Hey, Officer."

"Tuck. What are you doing here?" Deputy Hueston flashed the light around the Jeep's interior. Tuck's heart banged in his throat as Colleen put her hand over the scattered remains dusting the seat.

Tuck smiled, trying to keep his voice smooth. "Just . . . hanging out."

Deputy Hueston shone the light into Tuck's face. Tuck blinked it away.

"Okay, get out of here. Go to the dance. Stay out of trouble." He glanced at Colleen. "Hi, Colleen. I'm going to vote for your dad."

"Thanks, Kyle." She gave him one of her shiny smiles and it squeezed a fist inside Tuck.

The guy had it so easy. Everybody loved the former Deep Haven basketball star. Hueston and guys like him had no idea what it felt like to watch your family fall apart.

Tuck watched the deputy return to his cruiser, barely able to push breath out of the web of his chest.

"That was wild," Colleen said.

"That was stupid!" He put the car into gear. She slid toward him as if expecting him to take her hand.

The entire night made him a little ill.

Tuck drove up to the convenience store and pulled in.

"Why are we here?"

"Stay here. I'll be right back." Tuck got out, striding into the building.

Thankfully, all the bathroom stalls were empty. He poured out the contents of the bag and flushed. Watched it spiral down, disappear.

When he returned to the car, he slid inside without looking at Colleen.

"Are you okay?"

He nodded and put the car into drive.

"Where are we going?"

"You're going home."

"What—why? I thought we were going back to your house. Getting loose."

He drew in a breath. "I flushed it, Colleen."

She stilled. "You what?"

"I flushed it. The pot. Here's the pipe, by the way." He handed it back to her, empty. "I don't need to end up in juvie, and neither do you."

"It's my life—"

"And it's a decent one. Not sure why you're determined to blow it."

"I thought we were going to have some fun. I thought that's what you wanted."

Her words made him feel dirty, like he'd brought her to this. "No, it's not," he said softly.

She pocketed the pipe. Shook her head. Added venom to her voice. "You owe me fifty bucks."

He nodded, then drove through town in silence.

When he pulled up to the house, he put the car in park, letting it idle. "Last chance to go to the dance."

She told him where to go and let the word ring into the night.

He watched her stalk to the porch. She slammed the front door. Flicked off the light.

Tuck sat there like a fool way too long before he finally drove away.

⁂

Annalise didn't know what kind of games "Uncle" Frank had decided to play, but she wanted him out of town. He scared her with the secrets he knew.

The way he could destroy her life with a word. Or a name. Like Garcia. Or even Deidre. And he'd whispered it in her ear, reminding her that he was here to protect her, which meant going to the dance. And he needed a good reason.

Like a date.

And now the man danced with her mother-in-law, ballroom style, like some sort of Fred Astaire. Wooing her in front of the entire town as the local band JayJ Bump played slow standards.

Even Nathan noticed. "What is your uncle doing?"

Then, "How long is he staying?"

Finally, "When did Mom learn to dance?"

She had no answers to any of his inquiries. Just stood at the edge of the crowd, watching Helen smile at Frank and trying to figure out how she might convince him to leave.

Now.

Forever.

"C'mon, baby, let's dance." Nathan didn't wait for her response, just took her hand and pulled her onto the Moose Lodge dance floor. A giant moose head hovered over the room, dripping its beard onto the dance floor, the horns like wings from its head.

She'd seen a moose once, stepping out onto the dirt road on the way to visit Nathan at one of his showings. The animal stared her down, and for a moment, safe in her car, she dared to stare back, right into its cold, dark eyes. Its breath puffed hot into the night, crystallizing on her windshield, heavy jowls that took a bite out of her heart.

She shrank back, held her breath, then landed on her horn. The moose had darted off the road, crashing through the bush, the pine trees, the poplar, into the clasp of forest.

She hadn't forgotten the animal, however—it found her sometimes in the dark of the night, made her wake with a shiver.

She refused to look at the moose head now as Nathan took her in his arms and moved her around the floor to the music.

Out of the corner of her eye, she saw Helen curl her hand around Frank's neck.

She had to put a stop to this before Helen got hurt.

"Ow, Lise—" Nathan said.

"Sorry."

Okay, so maybe this confrontation could wait until tomorrow, if Nathan went for his Saturday morning run. She'd march downstairs, rouse Frank, and tell him to pack. So sorry, but Uncle Frank had urgent business to attend to. In Chattanooga.

Clearly, Garcia wasn't headed this way. It had been twenty-four hours since Frank showed up, and he had chosen well when he picked Deep Haven for her to hide in.

Annalise tucked her chin on Nathan's shoulder, smiled at Eli Hueston and his wife, Noelle. Poor Noelle had fallen last winter, wiping out her memory, but Annalise had heard that in the past months, bits and pieces had returned. Maybe that was a good thing—she didn't know.

Nathan turned her on the dance floor.

"Seb Brewster is here," she said quietly, seeing the former star quarterback and current mayoral opponent dancing with his petite wife, Lucy.

"I'm pretending he's not," Nathan whispered in her ear. Then he moved his lips to her neck, where he brushed them against her skin. "You look beautiful tonight. I love this dress. You should wear it more often."

Okay, so maybe she should just relax. How much damage could Frank do? He was a good man—she believed that. And Helen deserved a dance or two. Frank would leave in a couple days at most, and would it do any harm to show Deep Haven that Helen could still attract a handsome, eligible bachelor?

Her mother-in-law didn't deserve the slander, the rocks thrown in her direction over the years. Annalise didn't know the particulars, but she did know there was no truth to the stories that Helen had thrown her husband out into the street, turned him into an alcoholic, rejected him when he pleaded for forgiveness, and deleted him from his son's life.

She knew Helen. The woman didn't have a mean bone in her body. She would forgive. Especially if the person was sorry. Repentant. If they had no choice about their decisions.

"That's the second time you've stepped on my foot," Nathan said. "Are you okay? Usually I'm the one walking on you."

"Sorry." She untangled herself from his arms, catching his hand and pulling him from the floor. "How about some punch?"

The community had set up a table of potluck treats—brownies, chocolate chip cookies, Bundt cake. Annalise spotted the remains of a Helen Decker Honeycrisp apple pie and decided to save it for the less fortunate.

Nathan handed her a glass of punch as Ellie Matthews came up behind them. "Congratulations, you two."

Annalise lifted an eyebrow.

"Jason's role as Romeo—don't tell me you didn't know. I saw Chloe Jacobsen at our women's Bible study and she said that Harper came home thrilled to play Juliet opposite him."

Nathan wore his mayoral candidate smile. "Yes, of course, we're excited."

Annalise managed a nod, kept her smile as Ellie moved away. She listened to the music, feeling Nathan's eyes on her, and took a sip of punch.

"You knew about this." His voice, calm and dark, cut through the words of the next song. She couldn't look at him.

"Jason loves the theater."

"How about loving a job to pay for college? Theater isn't a profession. It's a hobby."

She didn't want to fight, not here. "Let's talk about this at home."

He shook his head. "Lise, you can't keep these secrets from me. What's next?"

Oh, boy.

He set his punch down. "Let's go home. I'm tired. I'll get our coats."

He left her there, winding his way through the crowd.

Three people stopped him and shook his hand while she listened to his question. *What's next?*

Maybe she conjured him up, because Frank almost materialized beside her. "I need to talk to you."

"Not now, Frank. I'm tired. Nathan went to get our jackets."

"Yes, now. This is the only chance we'll get." He put his hand on her elbow and directed her through the crowd, out into the chilly parking lot.

The moon had risen, haunting the night, and the smells of woodsmoke and the loamy decay of the crisp leaves hung in the air.

She shivered, running her hands over her bare arms. "What?"

Frank turned to her. "We found Blake."

She hadn't realized how tightly wound she'd been over the past twenty-four hours. She put her hand on his shoulder. "Good. How did he take the news of my death?"

Not that she wanted Blake to grieve her—probably he wouldn't pay her a second thought. But years ago they'd had a wild, passionate—albeit dangerous—romance. The kind that Romeo had with Juliet. The kind that had cost Annalise her life.

"Annalise . . ."

It was the way Frank said her name that made her withdraw her hand. Clutch herself around the waist. "No."

"We think he's been dead for a day at most."

"No." She was shaking her head, moving away from him.

Frank caught her hand. "Shh. Breathe. It's going to be okay. We'll just find you another location—"

"What?" She pushed his hand away. "No. *No.*"

"You need to leave."

She blinked at him, his words rattling through her.

"Did you hear me?"

"I . . . have to *what?*"

"Listen, Annalise, Blake wasn't just murdered. He was tortured. Garcia wants to hurt you. Which means he'll hurt your family. Your children. Your mother-in-law."

"My . . . You're trying to get Helen to leave with me. That's why you asked her to the dance."

He nodded.

"I'm not leaving, Frank. I have a life here. A *great* life."

"You can have a great life somewhere else."

"Really? And what about my children?" She heard her volume and cut it to low. "Colleen starts on the volleyball team. Jason just landed the role of Romeo. Henry is eleven and has the perfect special ed teacher at school. The last thing he needs right now is to move. And I don't suppose you've noticed, but my husband is *running for mayor*. I can't take them away from here."

Frank glanced toward the door, back to her. "You could always leave them behind."

His words landed like a slap. "Leave . . . leave my *family*?" She swallowed. "Again?"

"Blake didn't know you were married—which means that Garcia doesn't know it either. You could leave, and he'd never know where to find your family."

She could feel herself coming apart, the words shaking through her, deep inside. "Can you guarantee that?"

His mouth turned into a grim line.

"I hate you. I hate what you made me do. I have a life here—a good life. A happy life! You can't just come in and yank it away, destroy everything I've built."

His hands came down on her shoulders—hot, warm, solid. "Shh."

She shook them away. "Don't *shh* me. Do you have any idea what you're asking of me?"

To her surprise, he nodded. "I do. Which is why I'm giving you a couple days to figure out what you're going to do."

"I don't need a couple days. I'm staying."

"Then you'll do it without any protection. You'll be on your own."

"Frank—"

"That's the deal. I'll give you up to five days to figure out what you want to do with this life you've been given. Take it with you, leave it behind, or risk it to Garcia's vengeance."

"That's not fair." She pressed her hand over her mouth. "It's not fair!"

"I know."

She turned away as the door opened behind them.

"There you are, Annalise." Nathan came out, holding her jacket over his arm. Behind him, Helen also stepped out into the cold.

Nathan looked from Frank to Annalise and back. "Everything okay?"

No. Never. Annalise ground her teeth, managed a nod.

Nathan draped her jacket over her shoulders. "I take it you'll deliver my mother home?" he asked Frank.

Frank glanced at Annalise one final time, words in his eyes. *Trust me, Deidre.*

Then he turned back to Nathan. "I promise to take good care of her," Frank the liar said.

6

BLAKE SO EASILY TIPTOED back into Annalise's dreams, as if he were always lingering on the outskirts, waiting to sidle up to her, wrap his arms around her waist, lean in close, and stir a terrible impulse inside her. "Hey, baby, miss me?"

She didn't. Or maybe she did. She knew, even as she turned in his embrace and slipped her arms around his neck, that she was dreaming, and something niggled at her, telling her to run away, that it didn't feel right. But she never could refuse the lure of those dark eyes, of the lazy, almost-daring smile, given only for her. He hooked his fingers through her jean belt loops, like she belonged to him, and drew her against the hard planes of his chest.

Then he was kissing her, and she lost herself in the feelings that sparked inside her, danger and recklessness. And victory. Only she could tame Blake Hayes.

He ran one of his hands through her short black hair, his rings tangling in it. "Where've you been? I've been looking all over for you."

She saw herself now, recognized the place in downtown St. Louis. The bluesy joint rocking out mood music behind her. A group of guys looking for trouble beneath the overpass. The smell of cheap beer sifting into the street. Yeah, she knew this place. Had even slept here a few times.

The wind caught her jacket, and she shivered as a car drove by. Blake had his lips against her neck. Where *had* she been? The question rattled around her brain.

And then, as Blake backed up, as she looked into his nearly black eyes again, it came to her.

She'd been safe. At the Seventh Street homeless shelter, serving meals in exchange for a room because her sins wouldn't allow her to go home. But she'd escaped Blake and his boss, Luis Garcia.

She'd been healing. Gaining weight. Getting clean.

"I gotta go, Blake," she said as she untangled herself from his arms.

"No, baby, stay with me. I miss you."

I miss you too. The words hung in her throat, stayed there, glued. But if Blake found out—

"D'Nell is waiting for me."

He caught her arm. "Who's D'Nell?"

Who's D'Nell?

She saw herself now, out of body, over the city, having shaken free of Blake, the question driving her through the streets. Who was D'Nell?

The Seventh Street shelter looked just as she remembered, a three-story brick building in the center of a fenced lot, with a wide porch and dark windows like eyes mourning the city. From a block away, police lights banked against the building, turning it bloodred. A crowd lingered around the entrance, around the cruisers, the ambulance.

She slowed her step, tasted her heartbeat.

The EMTs carried the stretcher from the house, parting the crowd.

Deidre pressed her hands to her mouth, caught her scream.

She barely recognized the girl on the stretcher as her best friend. D'Nell's face was swollen, her body torn—too much blood to know exactly what had happened.

"They found her in the alley," someone said beside her. "Beaten and stabbed."

She might have known the voice, but she couldn't tear herself from the scene as the EMTs stopped, began to do CPR.

They loaded D'Nell into the rig, still pumping.

And that's when Deidre ran. Her legs grew heavier with each step, and instead of carrying her, they simply churned as the road moved beneath her. She hadn't made it a block from the shelter, still caught in its shadow and the bloody lights, but she ran with her breath hard.

And then a hand hammered her shoulder.

It jerked her back, slammed her to the pavement, and she sprawled there, gasping.

A form silhouetted above her.

"Blake?"

"You can't run from me, Deidre." The voice reverberated as the man dragged her to her feet, grabbing her jacket, pulling her to his face.

Luis Garcia.

She screamed.

It emerged in a whimper but Annalise woke herself anyway, shooting up in bed, shaking, a chill slicking down her spine. She blinked away the darkness, clutching the warm blankets and inhaling the silences, the safety, of her home.

Not St. Louis. Deep Haven. Safe Deep Haven, tucked away so far from the overpasses and the memories that no one could find her.

The furnace kicked on with a low hum. The outside lights shone into her windows, the sound of Nathan's even breathing calming as he lay with his back to her.

She pressed her hand on his arm. Safe. They were safe.

For now.

But what if Garcia *had* found Blake? Had tracked him down in Fairbanks?

What had she done?

She covered her face with her hands. She never should have lied to Nathan, but now . . . now they all might have to leave.

You could always leave them behind.

No. She shook Frank's words away. Never. Growing up without a father had etched deep scars into her husband. She wouldn't make her children grow up without a parent. Besides, how could she live without them? They were her breath. Her life.

God, please don't take them from me.

The prayer leaked out, a moan more than a thought. But there it was, and it felt raw, too real.

God had given her this life that she didn't deserve. And it seemed that now, finally, He was going to make her pay for it.

Apparently He hadn't forgiven her. And why would He? She hadn't exactly run from her sins. She built a life on them and embraced them every day.

Annalise threw off her covers, the cold bracing against her skin, and reached for her robe, sliding her feet into slippers. She just needed some tea, to think, to figure out what to do.

She heard the sounds of hiccuping breaths as she shuffled out to the family room. Who—?

Colleen sat in her father's recliner, her knees drawn up to her chest, wrapped in the purple afghan Helen had knit her. Shadows fell upon her face, but Annalise saw the glisten of tears on her cheeks.

"Honey?"

Colleen jumped, startled. "Mom."

"What are you doing up?"

Colleen lifted a shoulder and turned back to stare out onto their lit porch, where the wind's fingers scraped leaves across the planking. She looked so broken that Annalise wanted to pull her into her lap, smooth her hair, kiss her forehead.

Instead she sank onto the leather sofa. "What's the matter?"

Colleen sighed. Lifted a hand to wipe her cheek. "I'm so stupid."

Annalise held her breath, trying to keep her voice even despite the lurch of her heart. "Why?"

"I don't know. I just . . . I just want him to like me." Colleen covered her face with her hands.

Shoot, just as she feared, they were talking about Tucker.

Annalise let the clock tick through the silence, tasting dread. *Please . . .*

"He's really not a bad guy, Mom."

Colleen glanced up at Annalise as if looking for approval. Annalise gave her a smile, not wanting to start a fight. Miraculously, she kept her voice soft. "What happened?"

"Not what you think."

"I'm not accusing you of anything. You are the one calling yourself stupid."

Colleen blinked, looked away again, and Annalise wanted to wince. First rule of parenting teenagers—don't panic. But she would do nearly anything to keep Colleen from repeating her mistakes.

From ruining her life with a Blake Hayes.

"I just want to fall in love. Get married, be happy, like you and Dad."

Yes. Of course. Because Annalise pretended just that well. Or maybe it wasn't all pretend. She hoped not. "You will, honey. God has a good plan for your life."

"You really believe that?"

Outside, the wind played the chimes, rattled the windows. "Yes, of course." Her voice didn't at all betray the hole inside or the laughter now mocking deep in her heart. She found her confident smile. After all, she'd been using it for years. "I promise, the right guy will walk into your life. You just have to wait for him."

"I don't know. What if God doesn't want for me the same things that I want? What if He doesn't give me the happy ending I want?"

That was the big question, wasn't it? Annalise's eyes burned. Had she ever really trusted God? Or had she simply jumped into this new life and looked behind her, hoping God would catch up, would bless it?

Yeah, look how that turned out.

Colleen seemed not to see her mother bite her lip, swallow hard. "I just keep thinking, what if I make some giant mistake?"

With Tucker? Yeah, that was Annalise's fear too. Finally they were on the same page.

"What if I lose the only guy who will ever love me?"

Or not.

Do not fall in love with Tucker Newman! But Annalise schooled her voice. "I know that God gives us second chances. And that He can fix anything, even use our mistakes for good."

At least, she used to believe that. Until Thursday at 5:42 p.m. Her words tasted like ash in her mouth.

"Mom, did you ever do something stupid for a boy to get him to like you?"

Annalise's throat closed. How had Blake materialized right in the middle of their conversation, seated on the arm of Colleen's chair, smiling at Annalise with that intoxicating grin, his eyes holding so much dare? In that instant, the old feelings churned to the surface and held her in their grip.

She met her daughter's gaze, longing to tell her the truth. But how could she peel back her past to find the nuggets of wisdom without laying everything bare?

Her lies stole her right to parent her child.

"I've made lots of mistakes, Colleen. And . . . and God has blessed me anyway."

Her words found soft soil. God had blessed her anyway. At least this life had seemed like His blessing.

But why would He bless someone living a life of deceit?

"Would you like some tea?" She stood.

Colleen nodded, her bottom lip trembling.

Annalise did know this much. "I love you, honey. And God loves you, very much. I know you are going to fall in love and live a happy life."

As long as her mother didn't destroy it.

❧

Nathan couldn't pinpoint exactly how the fight had started. Or why it escalated so fast, so loud, especially while standing in line at the Java Cup. Maybe it had been lurking for days and he simply hadn't seen the signs.

Most of all, he didn't know why he'd let it end the way it did.

He knew only two things.

He'd need more than calla lilies to fix this one.

And by tomorrow, the entire town would know that Nathan Decker had screwed up, again. There he went, keeping that family legacy alive.

He walked ten paces behind his wife, who seemed determined not to let him catch up as they marched toward home. Her blonde hair twisted in the wind under a knit cap with a cute flower embroidered on the side—his mother's handiwork. She had her hands shoved into the pockets of her lime-green jacket. This morning, before they left the house, he'd grabbed ahold of her matching knit scarf, brought her close, and kissed her.

"Thanks for going out campaigning with me today."

She'd smiled, but he couldn't tell if it was real or not. Darkness hung under her eyes as if she hadn't slept well. Had he heard her get up? He didn't remember, but he'd tossed the night away himself, catching only snippets of REM sleep.

Nathan couldn't deny the wound inside him from her lie about Jason's theater role. He'd tried to let it go as he watched her grab brochures about his campaign and head out into the bright Saturday morning, but as she pushed through the door into the brisk fall air, it irked him that she'd decided not to trust him. She'd simply made a ruling to keep their son's activities to herself, decided not to honor his input, and given Jason permission to disobey.

And what was Nathan supposed to do now? Make the kid quit the lead?

Yeah, the wound burned a little, and not just because of her lie. If Nathan hadn't plunged them so far into debt, Jason wouldn't have to find a job. He could count on the college fund his father had promised him.

Maybe this was his fault after all. And that truth only dug the ache deeper as they began to canvass their neighborhood.

Nathan had left the closest homes for last, knowing that he'd need to do some extra canvassing as Election Day closed in. But now that Seb had decided to run, Nathan wished he'd stopped by before. Maybe he wouldn't sound so desperate.

No, not desperate. He wasn't desperate. Just determined.

He found a smile as he knocked on the door of the Buchanans' tiny bungalow. They too had a grapevine wreath, and it listed as Shelly answered, still in her bathrobe, surprise on her face. She pushed open the storm door. Although Shelly had graduated two years after him, Nathan knew her well, along with her husband, Brian, an auto mechanic down at Buchanan Auto and Tire. Everyone in Deep Haven knew each other well.

"Well, if it isn't the Deckers. Out early today, huh?"

"Good morning, Shelly." Nathan extended his hand. She shook it, her other hand wrapped around the neck of her robe. "I know it's nippy out here, so I won't keep you. I just wanted to ask if you and Brian would consider voting for me for mayor, leave you this information, and see if you had any questions or concerns for me."

He'd rehearsed his speech in the bathroom mirror so long that it flowed out without a hitch. He smiled.

Shelly took Annalise's proffered brochure, flipped it open. "I think I know what you stand for, Nathan," she said.

For a second, her words shook him. Like what?

"Your family is a delight. We love them all. Mikey plays football, so he and the boys always cheer on the girls' volleyball games. Colleen is a real star. Probably just like her mom." Shelly grinned at Annalise.

Annalise smiled back, but she seemed a little wan at the compliment. Could be the cold. "Thanks, Shelly. We'd really appreciate your vote."

Shelly's smile dimmed. "Seb is Mike's coach," she said softly. "Thanks, Nathan. Good luck."

He managed a smile and a good-bye, but his chest tightened as he walked down the driveway. Annalise walked beside him, quiet. Finally she said, "So what if Seb is running. You've been here longer than him. And people love you."

"People don't love me."

"They do too, Nathan. You have a successful business and a good family."

"Seb married into the donut legacy of Deep Haven. And he's the star quarterback from our only championship season. And now the assistant football coach, as well as the head basketball coach." He shook his head as he strode up the walk of the next house. "This town is crazy about their sports."

She put a hand on his arm, turned him. Met his eyes with a pretty smile, the kind that could yank him out of his crazy spirals of despair. "If they see in you what I do, I promise you'll win."

Yes, he wanted to believe her. More than that, he wanted to pull her into his arms, right here on the Michaels' doorstep. For a second, everything seemed healed. Whole. Perfect.

Joe answered the door and spent five minutes talking with Nathan about the issue of the new pool at the community center and the funding for the school gym. Nathan must have caught the guy writing one of his bestsellers because Joe nursed a cup of coffee, wearing a Deep Haven Huskies sweatshirt and a pair of lounge pants, his glasses up on his head.

"See, Joe will vote for you, and he works with Seb in the volunteer fire department," Annalise said as they walked away.

When Nathan took her hand, it reminded him of those early days when they'd walk hand in hand around town after dinner, trailing behind Jason on his bike and Colleen on her tricycle. He had so many dreams back then, hopes of what he'd give them.

Twenty years later, they lived in the same run-down house, trying to get ahead.

Still, he wanted to believe what Annalise said, what she saw in him.

Maybe everything was about to change for him—for them. Then this distance he felt from Annalise would vanish. Frank would leave and everything could go back to normal. No—better. Happier.

Nathan walked up to the old Svenson place. He'd heard they moved, but he hadn't yet met the new owner. Obviously he had the same taste as the Svensons because he hadn't removed the deer skull tacked to the tree in the front yard.

Nathan knocked, smiled at Annalise. "Let's stop by Java Cup after this," he said.

"You have to try their Wild Moose Mocha—it's fabulous."

And that's when the door opened.

Nathan stood there a full thirty seconds before his heart started beating again. Thankfully, by that time, Annalise had glanced at him, seen him go white, and rescued him. As usual.

"Hello, I'm Annalise Decker, and this is Nathan, my husband. He's running for mayor, and we just wanted to stop by to see if we could get your vote and do anything for you today."

She didn't know. She didn't recognize the man.

Shawn Jorgenson, son of the man his father killed, stared at Nathan with folded arms over his extended belly, his eyes cold. "Get off my property."

Nathan hooked Annalise's arm. "Let's go."

But she frowned at Shawn. "I'm sorry; did we offend you?"

"Get off!"

Nathan was already stalking down the driveway. The back of his neck burned.

In an instant, he'd turned twelve and a coward.

"Nathan, what's the matter?"

He didn't say anything, just kept walking, all the way to the street. Toward the corner. "Let's get that coffee."

She was scrambling to keep up. "Why was he so angry with us?"

When had Shawn Jorgenson moved to Deep Haven? Nathan knew he'd left town after high school and had heard he returned to work for a lumber mill nearby, but he thought Shawn lived at his father's place, back in the woods.

"What is going on?"

He slowed, turned. Winced as he saw Annalise nearly jogging to catch him. She was a little out of breath. "Sorry."

She curled the brochures in her gloved hands. "Who was that?"

How he didn't want to relive this again. "That was Shawn Jorgenson. His dad was Moe."

Nothing registered. But maybe he shouldn't expect it to. He hadn't really told her anything about that part of his life—just the facts, and he let his mother fill in the rest. "His dad was the one my dad killed."

Oh. Her lips formed the word, but no sound came with it. Then, softly, she said, "But why is he angry at you? You didn't kill his father."

He tried not to, but he couldn't hold it back—he emitted a laugh that had nothing to do with humor. "Because it's a small town, Annalise, and people hold grudges. You don't know what it's like. You had the luxury of coming here and starting over. But I didn't." He shook his head. "Sometimes I wish I could start over too. But I'm trapped here in Deep Haven. I'll never escape."

He hadn't exactly meant it that way. More like he had too many responsibilities, too many threads holding him here. But she winced like he'd slapped her.

That, added to his brilliant remarks yesterday, and . . . well, no wonder she didn't look at him.

"C'mon, let's get some coffee." He tried a smile, longing to fix it.

Annalise walked with him to the coffee shop, too quiet, and he tried to assure himself that she'd forgiven him. But when he saw her holding back tears while standing in line at the Java Cup . . . "Annalise, I'm sorry. I didn't mean *trapped.*"

She bit her lip.

He should have left it there. Especially since this Saturday morning, coffee groups were huddled in chatter, probably about him, and despite the noise, everyone listened to every nuance of their conversation.

But the wounds of the past day wouldn't stay down. "I just meant you don't know what it's like to have your past always lurking. Not being able to escape it."

She wiped her cheek. Yeah, like everyone didn't see *that.* Super.

"Let's talk about it at home." She turned to leave the line, but he caught her.

"We have more campaigning to do."

Something sparked in her eyes and for a second, he didn't recognize her. "What if I don't want to be a mayor's wife? What if I just want to be *your* wife? The mom of our kids? That's not enough for you, is it? You have to be mayor and destroy everything."

What?

"Well, guess what, Nathan. I like our lives. I'm *not* trapped. And there's nothing I want to do more than stay *right here*. I just wish you liked our lives as much as I do. But maybe we want different things—maybe we've *always* wanted different things. Maybe we were never right for each other."

Huh? And of course, the entire coffee shop had silenced until he could hear only his heartbeat and the jangle of the door as Annalise yanked it open and left him there in his puddle of shame.

Nathan ducked his head and charged after her.

But he never caught up to her the entire way home.

JOHN CHRISTIANSEN probably knew Nathan better than anyone
in Deep Haven. He'd been the only one who still talked to him
after his father killed Shawn Jorgenson's. Twelve-year-old John had
deliberately set his lunch tray at Nathan's table after that terrible
day on the football field. He'd kept Nathan from quitting school—
quitting life, really. He'd invited him out to his house on Evergreen
Lake and made him believe he wasn't alone.

John Christiansen just might be Nathan's only real friend even
after all these years.

Which was why Nathan showed up on his doorstep at three
o'clock on a Saturday afternoon, wearing his running gear.

John was a big man, the kind who preferred time in the weight
room to long hours of solitude pounding his feet on the dirt road

that led back to his family's lodge and rental cabins. He'd long ago lost his hair—or at least most of it, opting to shave what remained. Today he wore his signature black ball cap, the one with the family logo across the top, but it did nothing to shield his eyes, dark blue and too knowing as he opened the door to Nathan.

John took one look at Nathan and hollered to his wife, Ingrid, that he was going running.

No, he didn't know how long he'd be.

Yes, he'd be back for the play-off volleyball game tonight.

Which, Nathan had to admit, was more than he'd promised when he left the house this afternoon. Annalise's voice, with just a little hiccup on the end, had followed him down the hall— "Please don't miss Colleen's game. We're a family; we have to stick together."

Then maybe she shouldn't embarrass him in the middle of town.

She didn't have to listen to the accusations—and they were there, all right. Not just in Shawn's eyes. Nathan saw them in Jenny Jorgenson, Moe's widow and the city clerk, every time he had to search a lien on a house. And any time he drove past Cutaway Creek, he heard the voices that told him he'd never escape this town, this legacy of shame.

His wife had to pour gasoline on it by dismantling their marriage in front of the entire town.

So maybe he hadn't helped, barging into their room after she locked him out—locked him *out*! He'd had to find the wire master key that opened all the locks in the house. And then he found her standing by the window, staring out, not looking at him, like he might be invading her privacy or something.

She'd never locked him out of their room, not once in twenty years.

But everything seemed different in the past couple days . . . and the more he thought about it, he pointed to Frank's appearance as the ignition.

For the first time he considered that Frank hadn't appeared in Deep Haven on happenstance, a nice family visit.

His brain tracked back to that huddle he'd walked into at the Java Cup. Perhaps he should have paid more attention to the expression of fear on his wife's face. That feeling in his gut.

She and Frank had something between them, something unresolved. But as long as Annalise locked Nathan out of their room, he hadn't a clue how to solve it.

"How far are we going?" John said as he came onto his porch after changing into a pair of black track pants and a black short-sleeved shirt with the Huskies emblem on the front. He sat on the steps made of rough-hewn logs, probably felled by one of his Christiansen ancestors and dragged by hand through the piney woods to the homestead. John lived in a house bequeathed to him by his father, four generations of family running the Evergreen Lodge Outfitter and Cabin Rentals.

John, of course, had updated the place, just like his father before him, and he now had a home that rivaled anything out of *Log Cabin* magazine.

Sometimes Nathan stood in John's massive gourmet kitchen, peering out the picture window that overlooked the expansive lawn, the indigo lake, and just wanted to sink into one of those handmade oak chairs and quit.

He would never build a family legacy like the Christiansens'.

"I don't know. Five miles? Seven?" Nathan said.

"You bet. However long it takes." John finished tying his shoes, descended to the lawn, and stretched out a bit.

Nothing Nathan did would ease the tension inside him, but he stretched his calves, his hamstrings, noting the burn in his legs.

He hadn't run in . . . well, maybe weeks. Not since he'd thrown his hat into the mayoral ring. But Annalise had suggested it yesterday, and after their fight, he needed something to help air out his thoughts.

Maybe he'd convince himself that he shouldn't quit the mayoral race. Although, at this point, he still held on to that as an option.

How was he supposed to beat local hero Seb Brewster?

"Along the lake, then?" John said as he jogged up to him.

Nathan nodded and fell in beside him.

John had played football for the University of Minnesota and had never shed his bulk. He ran with effort, like a bull clearing a highway. Nathan, however, had turned to running that spring of his seventh-grade year, joining the track team. It kept him far away from Shawn Jorgenson, who played every other sport, and it had slimmed him down, made him lean, empowered him.

Yes, Nathan could do anything when he ran.

"Colleen was in the newspaper this week. They're saying she'll make all-conference. She's got over two hundred kills this season and almost as many digs," John said between labored breaths.

Nathan could probably be labeled a poor father when his best friend knew his daughter's volleyball stats better than he did.

It must have been clear in his silence because John added, "It was right next to the football stats."

Nathan nodded. They hit the dirt road that wound through the woods back to the Evergreen cabins. The breeze swept the scent of pine into the air, crisp and clean. He inhaled, then—"I'm thinking of quitting the race."

John didn't look at him.

That helped a little.

"Did you know that Seb Brewster threw his hat in yesterday?"

"You're going to let Seb intimidate you?"

John never pulled his punches, not even thirty years ago.

"I decided to canvass the town today, do some door-to-door campaigning."

John was still running well, but he slowed slightly. Maybe he knew Nathan would rather run than talk. "And?"

"Did you know that Shawn Jorgenson moved into town?"

"No."

"He lives on Third Avenue in that A-frame with the triangular porch, the one with the deer skull in the yard, tacked to the tree."

"The old Svenson place."

"Right. I didn't know that. He answered the door and just stood there this morning, staring at me. It was awful. I saw that day again, every second of it. Walking out onto the field all suited up, ready for practice. Shawn standing next to the coach, the man's hand on his pads. For the life of me, I can't figure out why they let him come to practice."

"Coach Presley was more than a coach to most of us. Shawn probably needed someone to tell him it was going to be okay."

"Yeah. Me too. I don't know why no one told me what my father had done—or what had happened to him—before I got there. I saw Shawn, then the rest of the team, turn and stare at me. I saw it in their eyes—they hated me."

"They were kids, afraid and angry. And Shawn was a year older, had even played a little junior varsity. They saw you as a red dog, someone expendable."

But John hadn't. He had the crooked nose to prove it. That hadn't been a practice anyone wanted to recall.

"Shawn still feels that way."

"And do you expect anything different from him? He grew up without a father because of your old man."

"Thanks for that." Nathan slowed to a walk. "I thought I'd finally put that behind me."

John caught up to him. "But see, that's the thing. It's not yours to put anywhere. You didn't have anything to do with Moe Jorgenson's death."

"It doesn't matter. No matter what I do in this town, I'll always be Dylan Decker's son. The son of a drunk. A cheater. A murderer. And my kids will bear it too. That's why I was running for mayor, John. Not for me, but for my kids. For my wife. They deserve a better name."

"Decker is a fine name."

Nathan started running again.

"Don't quit the race, Nate."

They rounded a bend and cut through the woods, down a trail toward the lake, their feet soft on the bed of pine needles.

The trail opened at the end to a view of the lake. The wind chapped Nathan's skin as it skidded off the water. He stopped, bent at the waist. "Annalise and I got into a fight."

John had come up behind him. He heard the man breathing hard.

Nathan closed his eyes. *I'm trapped here in Deep Haven.* "I know I started it, but . . . she lied to me, John. Or at least she kept the fact that Jason had tried out for the play a secret." He watched geese fly overhead, a V headed south. "He got the part of Romeo."

"That's great, man."

"No, it's not. I deliberately told him to get a job. He needs it to pay for school." Nathan watched John haul in breaths, hands on his knees. Now or never . . . "I've charged nearly ten thousand dollars on our credit card for this race. I'll have to use Jason's school savings to pay it."

John raised his head, met Nathan's eyes.

Yep.

"But you didn't have an opponent. Why—?"

"I don't know—I just wanted to do it right. To convince everyone they were making the right decision, believing in me. But . . ." He blew out a breath. "Annalise doesn't know."

"So she's not the only one lying."

Nathan looked away. And that made it all the worse. Because his being trapped probably had more to do with his own web of secrets than what Deep Haven dished out. "C'mon. Please don't tell me that you and Ingrid don't have secrets."

John leaned against a tree to stretch. "Secrets sabotage a marriage. Doesn't matter how big they are."

"Secrets are normal. They save a marriage. I mean, there are all sorts of things that I don't know about Annalise. But that doesn't mean I don't love her, that we don't have a great marriage."

Until today. But it was just a fight. It wouldn't dismantle their lives.

"Isn't that the point of intimacy? To share yourselves with each other? To close the gap between you?"

"I know my wife, John. And she knows me. We're intimate, I promise."

Although John's words stung. Sometimes Nathan did feel as if a canyon existed between him and Annalise. As if they stood on opposite sides, not hearing each other.

Her words in the coffee shop suddenly made sense. *Maybe we've always wanted different things. Maybe we were never right for each other.*

No. He refused to believe that.

"I'm not talking about physical intimacy, Nate. I'm talking about truly knowing each other. No secrets. Full acceptance. That's what God gives us, and that's what marriage is supposed to be."

Nathan stared out at the lake, the way the wind ran across it in tiny ripples all the way to the shoreline.

Wasn't that what they had? He thought so, but . . .

No. He wasn't his father. He loved his wife, and they would work this out. Besides, he had a plan.

"I landed the McIntyre house. I'm hoping that commission will pay the debt off."

"You need to tell Annalise, Nathan. You can't fix this by hoping you'll sell the house. You have to fix it by telling the truth."

He stared at John. The man had it so easy. He owned his own home, had a rock-solid legacy of character in his lineage. And his children—"I heard that Owen finally decided to sign with the Minnesota Wild. That's awesome."

"He'll probably sit the bench for a while, but we hope he gets to play. He loves the game, and playing for Minnesota is perfect. We'll get to see some of his games." John folded his arms over his barrel chest. "But we never intended for him to play pro hockey. He just loved the sport so much, we kept encouraging him to play. One game at a time until one day he's on the Wild roster." He shook his head. "That's how you build a life. One day at a time. Until you realize you've built something solid."

Something solid. "I used to think that. The day I met Annalise. She didn't see me as Dylan Decker's loser kid, but . . . like she needed me. She believed in me. And she made me believe in myself." He ran a hand behind his neck, squeezed the tight muscles there. "Only, she's been so distant recently. Ever since her uncle arrived. And there's something about him—I can't put my finger on it, but I don't trust him. He watches me. Watches our town. And he took my mother to the dance last night."

"Your mom had a date?"

"Let's not call it that, okay? It's . . . Fine. Maybe it *was* a date. They danced all night together."

John smiled, something like humor in his eyes. "You should be happy for her. She gave you everything, put her heart into raising you. She deserves a date. Maybe even to fall in love—"

"She's not falling in love with him."

John laughed. "Right. Because she's your mom?"

"Let's just run."

Nathan took off, back up the spongy path to the road, hearing his heartbeat in his ears.

Wouldn't that be fun—his mother falling for Frank.

He shook the thought away. But he'd keep an eye on the guy, just in case.

Maybe whatever was bothering Annalise would shake loose along the way.

"So are you going to quit the race? Let Seb Brewster beat you?" John ran up beside him.

Nathan broke free of the forest, emerging onto the road, and set a quick pace, John huffing behind him.

If there was anything running taught him, it was endurance. No, he wasn't going down yet.

⅍

Frank could play uncle with very little effort. The kind of uncle who showed up with fabulous Christmas gifts, like fishing poles and bowie knives and a pet Labrador retriever.

This house could use a Lab. A black one, named Winifred.

He'd always liked the name Winifred. It meant "blessed reconciliation" or "peace." And he wanted to bring peace to the war between Annalise and him.

Even from the early days, Frank had been a guy who liked names. And since he was in the business of helping people reinvent themselves, he took the name game seriously.

Like he had with *Annalise*. It meant "the grace of God." Receiving something undeserved. Not that Annalise didn't deserve starting over in Deep Haven. She had testified, lost a friend, had to surrender her entire family for justice. But perhaps the very fact that a person could start over, reinvent herself, had grace attached to it.

If Frank were to start over, it might be here in Deep Haven. Maybe in this very house, surrounded by Annalise's family. They seemed to like him.

All except Annalise, who looked like she might be ready to take an ax to his head in the middle of the night. Not that he blamed her.

Her expression last night at the dance, when he'd delivered his ultimatum, had dredged up all the old nightmares. How he'd wanted to take back his words, to tell her that she didn't have to uproot her entire life and remake it somewhere else.

But he had no choice. He'd been there before. Seen the grisly end of the terrible decision to stay and fight.

People didn't fight Luis Garcia. They ran from him. And Frank had roughly four more days to keep Annalise safe while she figured that out.

"Your move, Uncle Frank. Be ready to pay up."

Oh, her son Henry had her sass. He'd already wiped Frank out of Marvin Gardens and Ventnor and Atlantic Avenues, and now owned everything from St. Charles Place to Pennsylvania Avenue, not to mention being a railroad magnate. Frank's low-rent properties between Go and Jail would fall next. His only hope was to hang on to Boardwalk and Park Place.

Or maybe . . . Frank glanced at the clock. Yes, maybe they'd have to call the game on account of concession duty at the volleyball tournament.

The rest of the afternoon had moved too quickly, despite being trapped in Annalise's home. Despite the fact that she spent the last hour, after she'd emerged from her room, glaring at him.

He rolled the dice. Moved his Scottie dog to the community chest. Picked up a card. "Are you sure we can't play Clue? I'm much better at Clue."

"Read the card, Uncle Frank."

He cupped his hand over the card. "It says you have to give me all your income from this year. And all your properties."

"It does not!" Henry reached to swipe the card, but Frank yanked it out of his reach, holding it above his head. "Let me see it!"

Frank got up, danced away from the table, stiff-arming the kid and laughing. "Yes, it says all your money and all your properties, and—oh, wait, I get two hotels, too."

Henry was jumping now, and Frank turned his back, tucking the card into his pocket.

"That's cheating!"

Frank turned, grinning at him. The kid resembled Taylor, his grandson, that year before Margaret died. The year his daughter, Caroline, had come home with the twelve-year-old for Thanksgiving. Frank had played Risk and enough games of Scrabble to make his eyes bleed. Taylor had been the perfect age to not demand anything but a competitor, and Frank could do that. He could thrive on outwitting his opponent, on making sure he won.

As long as he didn't have to have some sort of deep, soul-baring conversation. And as long as the kid stayed out of trouble.

But Taylor hadn't. Not with Caroline spending months at a time nursing her mother, commuting from California to Portland. It took a few more years, but Taylor found the wrong crowd, got busted for possession, and of course Caroline looked right at Frank.

He couldn't bear it, so he stopped coming around. Just like he'd stayed away after Margaret's diagnosis. He couldn't watch his wife suffer. It just felt easier to treat his family like he did the witnesses in his job. Don't get attached, because that way, a guy could get hurt.

Really hurt.

Yes, Frank could play this game and be Henry's fake uncle until the end of time. As long as he didn't really care.

But he had to admit, it felt good—fake as it was—to be a part of something, a family. To listen to Helen humming in the kitchen, to smell the cinnamon and nutmeg from whatever delicious apple dessert she concocted.

How convenient that she lived across the street. And that she'd been outside this morning, cleaning up her apple tree—a ready excuse for him to go out and keep an eye on Annalise and Nathan as they tromped through the neighborhood stumping for votes.

He was ready to jump in his rental car when he saw them disappear down the street, headed for town. He'd followed them, but they'd disappeared. By the time he returned to the house, he spotted them on their way home, Annalise with her hands balled in her pockets, looking a little like she had that day he busted her out of lockup with the offer to help her get off the streets.

Yes, her husband had made her mad—Frank deduced that much from the way she folded her arms across her chest and wouldn't look at him as they marched home.

Nathan had stormed out of the house an hour later in his running gear. Frank tried not to hear the pleading in Annalise's voice as she asked him to attend the game. *We're a family; we have to stick together.*

He hoped Nathan took her words to heart.

"Fine. Okay. The card actually says . . ." He pulled it out. "State tax of 10 percent. I think you're going to wipe me out, kid."

Henry grinned, sat down, and held out his hand. "Hand it over to the bank."

Frank rolled the dice, then peeled off the right amount of hundreds while Helen chuckled from the kitchen.

"He'll grow up to be a Wall Street tycoon," Frank said to her.

"No, I'm staying in Deep Haven forever," Henry said, piling the money in the bank. "I'm going to be mayor like my dad."

Hmm.

"Then running the concession stand will give you good practice," Annalise said, breezing down the hallway. She wore a blue sweatshirt emblazoned with *Husky Volleyball Conference Champs*, and volleyball earrings dangled from her ears. She didn't look at Frank as she kissed Helen. "See you at the game."

"Mom, I want to finish Monopoly."

"He'll find a way to win, Henry. Better to quit now while you're ahead."

Hey, now. Frank frowned, then caught her arm as she walked by. "You can't go up there by yourself. I'll be right behind you."

Annalise jerked away and rubbed her wrist. "I'm selling hot dogs and Snickers bars, Frank. I'm in no danger."

He shot a glance toward the kitchen. Helen had disappeared behind the counter, rummaging through pots and pans.

"Still—"

"Can you leave me alone for one hour?" Annalise hissed.

Uh, no. But she was probably right. And she would be surrounded by people.

Although—

"Frank, can you get that popcorn popper down for me?" Helen was pointing to a stovetop popper on the top shelf of the cupboard. She glanced at Annalise. "You moved it."

"You're the only one who uses it, Helen. No one makes popcorn like you."

"Make us peanut butter popcorn!" Henry said as he pulled on his skater shoes by the door. He stood and grabbed his jacket.

"Only for you, Henry." Helen winked at him. "But Frank will have to help me. I can't stir and pour at the same time."

Annalise raised an eyebrow. "Behave yourself."

He had no words for that. "One hour. Don't go anywhere else."

She rolled her eyes. "Where do I have to go? C'mon, Henry." She grabbed her keys from the hook by the door and stepped into the garage, closing the door behind her.

Frank barely restrained himself from running after her, his best judgment screaming at him. But she was right.

Hopefully.

Either he could follow her out and raise questions or . . . Or stay here with Helen. Maybe convince her that he could be trusted. So when he suggested that she leave with Annalise . . .

He pulled down the popper. "How do you make peanut butter popcorn?"

"It's popcorn with a peanut butter—honey sauce poured over it. But the sauce cools quickly, so you need two people—one to pour, one to stir. It's a little like caramel popcorn but sweeter." She set the popper on the stove. It had a handle like an old-fashioned ice cream churner.

Helen lit the stove, then took oil from the cupboard and poured some into the pot. "I started making popcorn for Nathan when he was little. He and I would sit and watch movies together on Friday night. Our town doesn't have a theater, so it was the best we could do. We did it all the way through . . . Well, it was what held me together during my cancer treatments."

Frank stilled at her words. Tried not to be jerky as she handed him oven mitts and said, "You get to turn the handle."

She dropped a couple kernels of popcorn into the oil and closed the lid, seemingly oblivious to the way he had stopped breathing as she measured out a half cup of unpopped kernels into a glass. "It was such terrible timing for Nathan. He had a partial cross-country running scholarship from Winona State and wanted to become a lawyer. Instead, he turned it down to stay here and take care of me. He saved my life by donating his blood marrow. Then he drove me back and forth to Duluth for my treatments, made sure I ate, took care of paying the bills. That's when he got his real estate license and discovered he had a knack for it."

The kernels popped and she opened the lid, pouring in more kernels. "Stir."

Frank obeyed, turning the handle.

"He met Annalise about a year after I went into remission. She'd only just moved into town, was living at the old Sjoderberg place on Fifth Avenue . . ."

Frank remembered it well. A yellow bungalow with black shutters, a rose garden in front. The agency had purchased it under an assumed name, knowing that someday they'd need it.

"She was looking for a church and came in the front doors one Sunday. Nathan was greeting."

Frank had told her to do that. To go to church. He'd meant it as a way to change her life, to establish her new identity.

Apparently it worked.

"Nathan seemed happy enough. He's never mentioned wanting to leave." The popcorn began to burst in the pan. "I wonder sometimes, though, how his life might have been different if I hadn't gotten sick." She retrieved a jar of peanut butter from the pantry. "Or if I hadn't told him."

The popcorn burst like gunfire in the pot. Frank stirred with fury. "Is there somewhere to pour this?"

Helen slapped a giant plastic bowl on the counter.

He took the popcorn off the heat and dumped it in. It sizzled and glistened.

"Now the sauce."

But instead he put the popper back on the stove and grabbed Helen's wrist through his pot-holder hands. "You did the right thing."

She glanced at him.

"Would it have been better if he'd just come home one weekend and discovered that you were dying? That he'd missed his chance to fix anything, make things right, say the words he needed to say? Maybe by then you would have been too far gone for him to make amends or become the man he needed to be."

She swallowed, frowned at him.

He looked away. "My wife didn't tell me she had cancer until she was in stage IV. Didn't want me to worry about her."

Sometimes, the old anger could tighten his chest.

He nearly jumped when Helen put her hand on his, over the oven mitt. Her voice softened so much it hurt. "I'm sorry about your wife, Frank. But if she decided not to tell you, you can't blame yourself."

Oh, but he could. He'd been afraid of her pain—or maybe his pain. He'd spent all his time fighting emotions; it had terrified him how much losing Margaret tore at him. "I don't know, Helen. I shut her out, so afraid of losing her. I lost her before the cancer ever took her."

But if he'd allowed himself into the pain, he might not have lost her with so much regret that he couldn't look at Caroline. Couldn't call her. Couldn't write to Taylor in jail.

"I do blame myself."

He hadn't realized he'd said that out loud until he felt Helen's hand on his cheek. Until she met his eyes with so much compassion that it burned inside him. Until she rose up and kissed him softly on the cheek.

"You're a good man, Frank Harrison. Your wife was lucky to have you. And Annalise is lucky to have you." She patted his cheek again. "Now, if you'll hand me the honey, we'll make some treats for the grandkids."

༄

The nausea had nothing to do with the greasy hot dog Annalise had eaten between the second and third games. Or the nachos she'd split with Henry. Or her mother-in-law's gooey peanut butter popcorn.

No, Annalise would attribute it to watching Helen glance now and again at Frank, almost as if—no, she couldn't actually like him, could she? It was one thing for her mother-in-law to get out, have some fun. Completely another for her to fall in love with Frank, a man who would only break her heart. Even if he was trying to keep the family intact, Helen was headed for heartbreak.

Oh, who was she kidding? Frank had a sort of scoundrel charm to him. And he could be terribly kind when he tried. Like when he'd taken her out of police custody and to his home in Portland—breaking protocol—to feed her. She well remembered Margaret, his wife, the way the woman helped Annalise dye her hair close to her real color and restyle it more softly around her face. How Margaret let her sleep for days, it seemed, and twice Annalise found Margaret holding her hand, asleep in the chair beside her, as if she'd come in the middle of the night to quell a nightmare.

Not unlike Nathan in those early years. He'd endured enough of the scars of her mysterious past to earn him a bye for the way he'd acted today.

Sometimes I wish I could start over too.

Probably she could blame her nausea on the fact that with one word, she could make Nathan's wish come true. She wasn't sure how Frank might do it—a nasty car crash, perhaps a fire in the house. But they'd disappear in the night like bandits, taking nothing with them.

Not a picture. Not a journal. Not a book. Not a memento. Maybe not even their wedding rings.

She turned hers around her finger.

Frank would find them new names. Like Kirsten or Gretchen,

Neil or Thomas. Names designed to blend in, although not too much. No John Smiths or that too would raise suspicion.

"C'mon, Colleen!" Jason sat beside her, digging into his bag of popcorn. He'd been away most of the day reading through his script with members of the cast. Like Harper Jacobsen. She sat one aisle over and three rows down with her friends, and Annalise didn't miss his occasional glances that direction.

Jason would have to start his acting career over, playing bit parts again until he worked up to the lead.

And Henry—she glanced toward the opposite bleachers, where he sat with the other skater hoodlums. Maybe it would do her younger son some good. He could find new friends. Maybe jump into a different sport, one he liked, just in time for adolescence.

"Point for the Huskies!"

She heard the announcer and focused again on the game. Huskies in the lead, 20–13, in the third game. Five more points and they'd advance to the semifinals. Colleen had landed eight decisive kills tonight and at least four digs. She'd even aced a serve.

Colleen would find a new team. Maybe if Frank moved them to a bigger town, she could play in the bigger conferences, with better competition. She was that good, wasn't she?

Or maybe this was the better competition. Maybe all this playing time on the tiny Husky team meant that she would excel in the big schools.

But a move would mean Annalise could get her daughter away from Tucker Newman, troublemaker. The kid had even raised his hand to her tonight from his spot in the bleachers, waving as she walked in. Weird. He should be skulking away in shame.

Annalise pressed a hand against her stomach. She shouldn't have had that cotton candy.

At least Nathan had decided to come to the game. He sat with John Christiansen on the far end of the bleachers. He'd made a point, however, of finding her as he walked in and smiling.

Offering forgiveness.

She had too many of her own sins to stay legitimately angry at Nathan. Instead his words had dragged a lethal trail through her heart.

Not enough. Trapped.

She couldn't believe she'd embarrassed him like that in front of the entire town. But maybe they *weren't* supposed to be together. Maybe they'd never had that spark because she'd been broken and afraid and he'd been safe and reliable. And handsome, yes. And kind.

And Nathan Decker, the most trustworthy man she knew.

But did that constitute love?

What if she'd never *really* loved her husband?

Maybe she'd had no business getting married, ever.

Yes, she just might be ill. She got up, moved past Jason.

"Are you okay, Mom?"

"I have to use the ladies' room—"

"There's only three points left!"

But she ignored him, heading down the bleachers, along the edge of the court, past Nathan, who grabbed her hand. "Lise?"

She didn't slow, feeling green.

She marched past the ticket table and into the hallway, past the concession stand—the odors of greasy hot dogs didn't help—and nearly broke into a run to the bathroom.

Annalise dove into the first stall just in time.

Nice. Oh, so nice.

She tore off toilet paper and wiped her mouth. Leaning back against the wall of the stall, she closed her eyes.

And saw the Nathan of her youth. A summer tan still embedded in his skin, tousled brown hair, those green eyes—he stood in the vestibule of his church in a pair of khakis and a white oxford shirt. He had never dazzled her like Blake had, but she would still call him handsome. Especially when he smiled—her entire body turned warm, like a summer day, when he smiled at her.

Are you new in town? His first words to her before he handed her a bulletin and showed her where to sit.

After the service, he took her out for coffee and spent the afternoon showing her around Deep Haven before teaching her how to skip rocks into the lake. She could still remember how he'd hunted for the perfect rock, then stepped behind her to help angle her wrist. She let him because he had strong arms, and she needed to be in someone's embrace. A month in Deep Haven by herself had hollowed her out. She hadn't slept a night all the way through.

She had no idea how Frank expected her to build a life here.

Annalise got three skips on the first try. Five on the second. She could have stayed on that beach all day listening to Nathan cheer for her.

Later they'd watched the sunset dip into the horizon, and for the first time in longer than she could remember, listening to him tell her about his life, this town, she inhaled peace.

No wonder she said yes when he asked her out, standing on the doorstep to the yellow house on Fifth Avenue.

No wonder she lied to him—the lie Frank had constructed, but the first time she used it—when he took her to dinner and over candlelight asked about her family.

No wonder she let him take her into his arms after he walked her to the door.

His kiss had been gentle and ministered to her soul in its

tenderness. He wasn't Blake. And frankly that's what made her say yes when, four dates later, he asked her to marry him.

Annalise scrubbed her hands over her face.

She loved Nathan; of course she did. She'd given him three children. She supported him. Just because he never ignited the dangerous, reckless pulse inside her didn't mean they didn't belong together.

They had a family. A life. And she couldn't take any of them away from it.

"Annalise?"

Oh no, Helen had found her. The woman had the tenacity of a bull. "I'm okay."

"Really? Because you didn't look okay."

"Too much concession food."

Annalise heard the towel dispenser rolling out, then water running.

"I've always said that no one should eat dinner at the concession stand. It's why I bring popcorn. It keeps temptation away." Wet towels appeared under the door.

"Thank you."

"There's more where that came from."

Through the crack in the stall, she saw her mother-in-law hunker down against the wall.

"You don't have to stay. I feel much better."

"Oh, darling. Maybe I need to catch my breath too."

Annalise unlocked the door. And stared at her mother-in-law.

Helen looked . . . younger somehow. She wore a cute white scarf at her neck, like a pinup girl from the fifties. And—"Are you wearing makeup?"

Helen pressed her hands to her cheeks. Nodded. "I . . . I don't know what came over me."

Annalise washed her hands in the sink, debated a moment, then slid down beside her.

"He's an awfully nice man, your uncle is."

Oh, Helen. "He is nice." When he wasn't destroying lives. Okay, he'd saved them too.

"I am just a silly woman." Helen clasped her hands between her knees. "I realize he's leaving."

She did? Had Frank told her—?

"He *is* leaving, right?"

"I . . . Yes. When he's finished with his visit . . ."

Helen drew in a breath. "See, I keep thinking about Dylan. Nathan's father."

Yes, Annalise knew who he was. Hard to forget a man who haunted Nathan's every decision.

"I fell so hard for him, so quickly. Although I went to high school with him, I hardly knew him." She shook her head. "I don't want to make that same mistake. But a woman my age . . . Well, this sort of thing doesn't come around often."

Oh no. She'd been hoping she was wrong about the way Helen looked at Frank.

"And I . . . He's just such a nice man."

Annalise tried not to wince. "Helen, Frank is . . . complicated."

Helen looked at her, a bit of mother in her eyes. "I know about his wife—your aunt, Annalise. You don't have to shield me. He told me how she died of cancer and how he wished he'd been around more. How his job consumed him. But he's nearing retirement age, and it would be nice to have someone—"

"No, Helen, uh—" Shoot. Annalise hadn't quite meant to cut her off like that, but—"Frank isn't exactly who he seems."

Helen frowned. "What?"

Oh! Her lies were like soup around her, filling her pores, dragging her under.

"He's just . . . he's got a bit of a checkered past."

"You mean his military experience? He told me how he was involved in . . . something *off the books*."

She said it like he might be James Bond or something, not enough fear in her voice. *Way to go, Uncle Frank.*

"I just don't want you getting hurt."

Helen smiled. "You're so sweet, Annalise. The perfect daughter-in-law. I'm so thankful you came into our lives." She leaned over, popped her a kiss on the cheek, then wiped off the lipstick. "I promise to be careful."

She made to get up, but Annalise caught her hand. "Helen, can I ask you a question?"

Helen sat back down on the hard tile. "Of course, honey."

"Would you ever want to leave Deep Haven?"

Helen frowned, then gave a quick laugh. "Why? This is my home."

"But—well, Nathan said he sometimes wishes that he could start over, and . . . it got me wondering."

"Oh, sweetie, I'm too old to start over. No. We belong in Deep Haven. I can't imagine living anywhere else. Sure, we've had our troubles here, but you don't quit on your life, don't leave it all behind. Hard times make you stronger. More compassionate." She covered Annalise's hand with hers. "Nathan struggled with that, I know. He bore so much of the scandal on his shoulders. But he belongs here too. And when he becomes mayor, he might finally believe it."

Annalise leaned her head back against the cold tile. "What if your mistakes are so big they could destroy you?"

She didn't really mean for that to slip out. But sitting here with a woman who had been everything of a mother to her, she had to ask.

To her surprise, Helen didn't startle, didn't even flinch. She just squeezed Annalise's hand. "Then you press on and pray that those mistakes don't come back to find you."

Annalise drew in a breath, held it.

The door opened. "Mom!" Colleen danced into the bathroom. "What are you and Grandma doing in here? We won!" She hovered above both of them, holding out her hands, palms up.

Annalise slapped one. Helen high-fived the other.

"We're going to the sectional semifinals on Tuesday!" Behind Colleen, two more players pushed into the bathroom, cheering, high-fiving, hugging.

No. By Tuesday they might have vanished from Deep Haven completely.

8

THEY WERE RIGHT FOR EACH OTHER, and they did want the same things. Nathan just had to fix this, tell Annalise the truth, and everything would go back to normal.

His marriage wasn't in trouble.

He had to face the fact that he'd made a mess of things. John's words just wouldn't let him go: *Secrets sabotage a marriage. Doesn't matter how big they are.*

Indeed, how many times had he heard Pastor Dan say it— a marriage filled with lies was a leaky ship.

He tugged his bathrobe tight around him and stepped into the leather slippers Annalise had given him for Christmas last year.

Stopping by Jason's room as he walked down the hall to the kitchen, he knocked, then stuck his head in.

Jason sat on his bed, his computer on his lap, typing.

"What are you doing?"

Jason turned the computer screen. Facebook. "Chatting with the cast of the show. We're talking about costumes. We're thinking of doing *Romeo and Juliet* as steampunk."

Whatever that was. But, "Hey, Son, congratulations on getting that role." Nathan wrapped his hand around the doorframe. "You know, you could talk to me about it next time. I don't like you hiding things from me."

Jason closed the computer lid. "I know. I'm sorry, Dad. I just thought . . . I thought you'd be angry."

"That's fair. How about I try not to be angry and you give it to me straight, like a man?"

Jason smiled.

Maybe he should take his own advice. He closed his son's door.

Annalise sat at the kitchen table, only the glow of the computer lighting her face. The outside light illuminated their front porch, the street, all the way over to his mother's stoop. The light glowed through the curtains at her window.

He'd become accustomed to Annalise's addiction to having their house lit up like it was high noon outside.

Annalise still wore her Husky fan attire. The woman knew how to deck out for a volleyball game. She had taken her earrings off, however, and the two volleyballs lay on the table, where she played with them as she stared at her computer.

He slid onto a chair beside her. "Hey."

She glanced up, and if he didn't know better, he'd think she was looking at something, well, illicit. Wide eyes, drawn breath.

He couldn't help leaning over and checking her screen. "You're reading a blog?" He read the top. "Kylie's Korner. Cute."

Nathan scooted his chair over to study the picture. The woman looked familiar, but he couldn't place her. She held a pretty baby—big blue eyes, dark hair. "Who is she?"

He glanced at Annalise. *Did she just wipe her cheek?*

"No one. I just follow certain blogs. This woman posts pictures of her daughter. Lives in St. Louis."

"Cute kid." He touched the screen. "Reminds me of Colleen. The same chubby cheeks."

Annalise closed the notebook. Palmed the top of it. Gave him a smile in the semidarkness. It didn't meet her eyes.

"Are you okay?"

She nodded. "Great game tonight, huh?"

He didn't want to talk about the game. "Lise, I have to talk to you about something."

Another fake smile. So maybe he should start with an apology. Again. Better than the one he'd given her in the coffee shop.

"Honey, I'm so sorry for . . . for hurting you." He took a breath, finding solace in how her eyes softened. "I'm not cut out to be mayor."

"Oh, Nathan." Her hand closed over his. "If anyone should be mayor, it's you. You know this town and what it needs more than anyone. And you're not just aware of the issues, but you care about the people in this town. You're practically on staff down at the senior center. They love you. I know you'll be the best mayor this town has ever had."

Her words could slake his thirst, keep him sane. He touched his forehead to her soft hand.

They *were* meant to be together. She confirmed it in her quiet words. "I'm sorry I embarrassed you at the coffee shop."

He waited for her to take back what she'd said about their marriage too, but she didn't speak.

Okay. Fine. "It's okay."

Looking up, Nathan found her gaze on him, her eyes watery. He ran his thumb across her cheek, catching a tear. "We're supposed to be together, Lise."

She gave him a smile. Nodded.

The tension eased out of his chest. John was wrong: Nathan knew his wife, knew she hadn't meant it. They had a great marriage. It wasn't going down in the storm.

Still, he had to do the hard part.

"I need to tell you something. . . . I charged over ten thousand dollars to our credit card."

This did get an eyebrow raise. A swallow. "Oh."

"I know; I'm so sorry. I was buying these lawn signs and the banner and the radio spots, and then I had to put down a deposit on the luncheon space, and the food cost more than what the donors gave, and . . . I'm sorry. I should have told you."

She just watched him, waiting. See, this was why he loved her. Because no matter what he did, what he said, what mistakes he made, nothing seemed to rattle her. She was solid. Unflappable. A rock to his crazy shifting sand.

She made him believe that, yes, everything would work out fine.

"But listen, I just acquired the old McIntyre place, and . . . well, the commission on that might be tidy. We'll get the card paid off, no problem."

She reached up to touch his cheek. "I'm not worried. You're the most responsible man I know, Nathan. And the most honorable." Her eyes glistened. "I don't deserve you."

He frowned at that. "Of course you do."

"No." She shook her head. "No, I don't. There are things . . ."

Her hand slid away from his face, back to the laptop. "Things you don't know about me. Things I didn't tell you."

Oh, Annalise. He took her hands. "Honey, I know there are things you haven't told me. Sometimes I think there's a line in your past, and I just can't cross it, no matter how hard I try. And with Uncle Frank here, you've been acting . . . Well, it's made me realize that perhaps I should pay more attention to you. But I've decided that if you don't want to tell me, I don't need to know. You're an amazing woman, an amazing wife. Your past is behind you—it's not a part of our lives. And I promise, there is nothing you could tell me that would change the way I feel about you."

She looked stripped. Not quite the expression he'd thought to evoke from her.

"Really?"

The way she said it, almost a whisper, caused that eerie feeling to creep up his spine, settle in his chest. But he nodded.

"Nathan, I—I'm not who—"

"What is your uncle doing at my mother's house?" Nathan stood up so fast that his chair dumped over, clattering on the floor.

Frank was on his mother's front porch, one hand braced on the frame, leaning in like . . . like . . .

"Stop!" He'd reached the door before he could stop himself. Flung it open. Barely heard Annalise.

"Nathan, stop—"

But he was already outside and charging across the lawn. "Don't you dare kiss her!"

It occurred to him that he might have simply stood on the porch. Or stayed in his driveway. But he'd lost a good part of his head seeing the way his mother—his mother!—smiled at the man. As if she *wanted* him to kiss her.

Halfway across the road Nathan began to slip. Frost already slicked the street, and his leather slippers skidded like skis, first one foot, then the other. With a shout, he felt himself pitch forward. He overcorrected and spilled back. Then his arms flailed as he flew into the air and landed with a spark of heat and stars on the pavement.

He lay there, just breathing, dressed in his drawers, his robe, and nothing else. His slippers had abandoned him, and perhaps even the stars laughed, winking as they were.

"Nathan!"

And now he felt about five years old as his mother jogged toward him. He sat up in time to see Frank's hand extended to him.

He wanted to slap it away. But Nathan was going to be mayor, after all, and his training kicked in.

You never knew who was watching.

Frank helped him up. "You okay? That was a pretty spectacular spill."

Nathan glanced at his mother, still coming toward him, then stepped close to Frank, cutting his voice low while he still had the chance. It took everything inside him not to grab him by the neck. "You watch yourself, Uncle Frank. That's my mother you were . . . leaning toward."

Frank's eyes searched Nathan's, something of sadness in them. "I know," he said softly. Then he turned to Helen.

She stood in the street, her mouth open.

Apparently Nathan hadn't been as quiet as he'd hoped.

"I'll see you in the morning?" Frank said to her.

Helen directed her words to Nathan. "Yes. Church starts at ten." Then she tightened her mouth into a tiny bud of fury and strode into her house, not looking back.

So he'd end the day as a twelve-year-old also. Nice.

Nathan followed Frank inside and stood like a gladiator at the top of the stairs, making sure the man descended into the basement. Then he sat in the kitchen, watching his mother's light until it finally flickered off.

When he returned to his room, Annalise lay on her side of the bed, bundled for Siberia, asleep.

&

Tucker just wanted to apologize. Colleen's words as she'd slammed her way out of his car had eaten at him all day. Sure, he'd had girls yell at him—one even slapped him—but . . . what had gotten into her head?

Maybe she'd been feeling angry or lonely. He'd done crazy, stupid things that first year after his parents split. Ditched school, some vandalism—though, c'mon, everyone wanted to spray-paint the giant bear statue in the park. And yes, he'd even ended up in foster care for a while.

But then he'd started snowboarding, and that funneled his energy into something useful and good.

He'd started lifting to feel stronger. Healthier. As if he might belong in the weight room with the other jocks, even if he could lift only a fraction of the weight the arrogant football players could.

He probably shouldn't tell Colleen that he also hung around with the gymnastics team sometimes, using their trampoline to work on his slope style and half-pipe techniques.

And he'd started running. Saturday mornings, usually, before he went to work. It helped his endurance and his ability to recover his energy between events.

Maybe he should have explained some of that to Colleen when

she wanted to smoke dope. Didn't she want to play college volley-ball? She'd worked so hard to do something with her life. Her behavior last night made no sense. He just wanted to make things right between them, start over. Fix it.

Which could explain why the smart part of his brain clicked off. Why he found himself parked at the Laundromat after the volleyball game, then heading to her house. Inside, the windows were dark, even if the outside glowed like a giant Christmas light. He felt like a burglar as he snuck up to her window in the back of the house, just outside the glow.

He climbed onto an overturned tin bucket, probably covering one of the rosebushes Mrs. Decker tended. Then he rapped on the window. Waited. Knocked again.

They'd done this once before, a few weeks back when Colleen called him at 1 a.m. He'd been home alone and yes, sure, he'd come over. He didn't expect her to want to sneak out, but she had—trundled right out of her window and into his arms.

They'd made out under the stars. It scared him a little how far she'd let him go, and he'd been the one to stop.

He'd gotten her back to her room by 3 a.m., skulking away like a bandit.

Now he just wanted her to look in his eyes and tell him that she still wanted him in her life.

He tried not to admit the entire thing felt desperate. He knocked again.

The curtain moved away, and there she stood, wearing blue pajamas, her long blonde hair loose. She stared at him with a frown as he held his breath.

Then she slid open the window. "What are you doing here?" But she didn't sound angry—only curious. And oh, she was so pretty, even with her makeup off—especially with her makeup off. Fresh and pure and sweet. Like the first time he saw her, smiling at him after he'd come off the half-pipe.

He liked her just like this.

"I came to say I was sorry about last night."

There was that smile that could turn him to lava. Colleen crouched down, put her arms on the windowsill. "I'm the one who should apologize. Deputy Hueston freaked you out, didn't he?"

Tuck lifted a shoulder.

She rested her hand along his face. "I'm sorry, Tuck. I . . . I shouldn't have done that. I thought you'd like it. I guess . . ." She caught her lip in her teeth. "I guess I just wanted you to like me."

His heart nearly exploded from his chest. "I like you, Colleen. I promise."

"You do?" She smiled, starlight in it.

When she was close to him like this, her smell around him, her skin so milky soft, his brain turned to noodles. He ran his hand up into her hair, letting it fall between his fingers. "Yeah."

Tuck kissed her. And when she put her arms around his neck, pulling him closer, he lost himself.

She drew away, nuzzled his neck. "Want to come in?"

Oh . . . uh . . . Tuck couldn't answer. He felt himself agreeing as he climbed over the sash and into her room.

The place smelled like her, her double bed a tumble of comforter and white sheets, her walls plastered with inspirational posters—an athlete's room.

Colleen caught her lip again, folding her hands over her pajamas. "Like my room?"

He might have nodded, but she suddenly pressed herself into his arms, her body soft and flannel.

What was he supposed to do? He nudged up her chin and kissed her again, until he forgot his name, where he was, and . . .

Tuck pulled away, breathing hard. "Colleen, I don't think—"

She laid a finger over his lips. Smiled, a little tremulous around the edges. He saw a hint of fear in her eyes.

He had to keep his head here. "I should go."

"Yeah." She nodded. "But . . . not yet. We'll be quiet."

Oh, this wasn't a good . . .

No. He'd only come to apologize. Tuck blew out a breath, held her away from him. "I shouldn't be here—"

"I don't want you to go." She slipped her arms around his waist.

"I know." He pushed her hair back from her face. "And I don't want to go. But . . . Colleen, you're not making this easy. I didn't come here to make out with you." Not really.

She frowned, stepping away from him. "What?"

"I thought maybe I could go to church with you and your family tomorrow."

"You did?" Then she slapped her hand over her mouth. "Sorry."

"I . . ." Now he felt like an idiot. "I thought maybe I could talk to your dad, you know, introduce myself. Maybe he wouldn't think I was such a bad guy—"

"I know you're not a bad guy, Tuck. But . . . well, really? Why?"

Good thing night filled the room, hid his face, because it felt like it was on fire. "I want your parents to like me. I don't want to sneak around. I want to sit with your family at the games and eat popcorn with them. Maybe come over on Sunday and watch football."

Colleen was staring at him as if lobsters were growing from his ears. "I guess that would be all right. I could ask . . ."

"Really?"

She nodded. He caught her wrists, leaned down, kissed her softly.

A board creaked in the hallway outside the door. Colleen looked up, her eyes wide. "Hide."

He doubted he'd fit under her bed but dove there anyway, feeling like a criminal. Colleen yanked the curtain across the open window and leaped into bed. He prayed that she'd pulled the comforter over her and feigned a deep sleep by the time the door eased open.

If he could have stopped breathing, turned off the telltale thunder of his heartbeat, he would have.

Whoever opened the door paused, watching.

If he could just get away, he wouldn't sneak into her room ever again. *Please, please . . .*

Colleen must be an Academy Award–worthy actress because, finally, he heard the click of the door closing.

Tuck rolled out from under the bed, crept to his feet.

Mrs. Decker stood in the room, her eyes on him, her arms folded over her bathrobe.

He swallowed. "It's not what you think."

"Get. Out."

Colleen sat up, throwing off the comforter. "Mom—"

Mrs. Decker held up a finger, and even Tuck went cold with her look. "Stop talking right now." She raised an eyebrow at Tuck. "Go."

Yes, ma'am. He felt the words even if he couldn't say them.

Tuck nearly dove out the window, tumbling onto the grass, and lit out for the Laundromat in a full run.

He wiped his eyes twice before he reached the Jeep.

⁂

Frank lay on the lumpy sofa, his phone to his ear, listening to it ring in Canada. Or at least, that's where he thought his partner was. Last time he'd received a text, Boyd said he was headed southeast.

He cradled his head on his arm, still feeling Helen's hand upon his cheek, imprinted there. He liked it. Too much.

He shouldn't have walked her home from Annalise's after the game, but, well, the road was slippery, and she'd already fallen once.

Then Helen had invited him inside for pie. Which he should have turned down also, but he enjoyed her stories about Colleen and Henry and Jason, about Nathan and especially Annalise. He liked seeing her world through her eyes and knowing that for a brief time, he could share it.

He nearly kissed her too. A colossal mistake that Nathan saved him from as the man had barreled out into the street.

That's my mother.

Yeah, okay, Frank knew that. Yet the words hit him like a roundhouse. Nathan's *mother.*

But oh, the unfairness hit him too. The fact that the first woman who made him feel whole happened to belong to a family whose lives he was going to destroy.

You're a good man, Frank Harrison.

Not so much.

He was stuck there, reliving the many reasons why, when— miracle of miracles—Parker Boyd picked up. "Frank. I suppose you're looking for a sit-rep."

"Please tell me you've located Garcia or at least his trail."

"Good news. We had a sighting of his car at a motel in Whitehorse in Yukon Territory. I've alerted the locals, we have surveillance on him, and we're going to close in tonight. Hopefully we'll have him in custody by morning."

Frank ran his thumb and forefinger into his eyes, seeing splotches of gray. "I need to know first thing, please."

"You sound tired, Frank."

He blew out a breath. "I just don't want to have to uproot this woman's life. She's been through a lot."

"I know she testified against Garcia—"

"And three of his gang members. Her file reads like a bad novel. She hooked up with Blake in high school, dropped out her senior year, and ran away with him. She lived on the street about a year while Blake was a runner for Garcia. Did some drops, started to climb up the ladder. They ran out of money now and again, and I think things got a little rough for her. I don't know the details—I don't want to. We stepped in when she was picked up for vagrancy and drug use. She cut a deal with the St. Louis narcotics division to testify against Garcia. But Garcia found her in a homeless shelter she had escaped to before we were able to pull her off the street. Beat her up, left her for dead. Blake went on the run. Annalise was hurt pretty badly—Garcia broke her jaw, a bone in her neck, three ribs. Margaret had a soft spot for her, so before we moved her, she moved in with us."

"Seriously? Isn't that against protocol?"

"She reminded Margaret of our daughter, Caroline. And frankly, me too. She was a good girl, just got mixed up with the wrong kid. Garcia threatened to kill her even from prison. And he could do it with his connections, so we decided on an extreme placement."

"You faked her death."

"Yes. Only her mother and father know she's still alive. She's dead to her siblings. She removed her tattoo, her piercings, colored her hair, and I moved her to Deep Haven, where I'd gone fishing a few times. Quiet, safe community. The kind of place where she could find a nice guy, get married, start over."

"Which she did."

"Until I walked in with the news that Garcia is out and looking for her."

"Maybe she won't have to leave. If we find him, this is all over. You can leave her be, and she can grow old there."

"I hope so."

"I'll let you know what we turn up," Boyd said. "If he's there, I promise to get him, boss."

Okay, he could like the rookie. A little.

Frank hung up. Annalise was right—the den in the basement smelled funny, and with the paneling on the walls, it sort of felt like a prison. Not to mention the toxic fumes of the fresh paint she'd tried unsuccessfully to fan out with the open windows. He wasn't sure what might be worse: freezing to death under the flimsy blanket—she only had one extra in the closet—or asphyxiating from the paint. As long as he was alive to protect her if Garcia showed up.

He listened to the sounds of the house. The dishwasher humming. The heat kicking on. The creaks of the floorboards overhead.

He sat up. Heard more steps. Silence.

Then, suddenly, the thump of feet, someone running.

Frank had his gun in his hand, pulled out from his ankle holster, before he could form a thought. He launched himself off the bed, taking the stairs two at a time.

No movement in the hallway. Outside, he thought he heard footsteps. He went to the window. The place was lit up like a high-security prison, but he saw nothing beyond the rim of light.

Down the hall, a door opened and closed. Then more footsteps.

He hid the gun behind his back as Annalise came into the family room, her eyes wide, her jaw tight, like she might want to hurt someone.

Maybe him.

"Are you okay?" he said in a harsh whisper.

"What are you doing up?" she snapped.

"I should ask you the same question."

She ground her jaw, stared out the window. "I can't sleep."

"And you think I can?"

She narrowed her eyes at him as if she hadn't thought of that.

Yeah, Deidre, I don't find it easy to rip your life apart, okay?
"I thought I heard something up here."

She shook her head and turned away, studying the wall of pictures, from baby shots to the large portrait of their family in sharp white shirts, seated on rocks, the lake behind them. A beautiful family shot.

Her breath shuddered out of her.

Frank tucked his gun in his belt in the back, pulling his shirt over it. His voice softened. "Really, Annalise, are you all right?"

"No," she said softly. "I'm not all right. I'm not sure I'll *ever* be all right." She looked at him then, her mouth a grim line. "I've made my decision. We're leaving Deep Haven."

Then she turned and walked away, closing her bedroom door behind her.

HOW HAD IT COME TO THIS? Standing in the Decker family pew, third row to the left of the altar, gripping the smooth wood, singing, "'As the deer panteth for the water, so my soul longeth after Thee,'" with so much anger in her heart that Annalise could barely stand.

Barely muster a smile.

Barely keep the charade intact.

What she wanted to do was grab her daughter, drag her into one of the Sunday school rooms, and tell her how close she treaded to destroying her entire life.

To ending up just like her mother.

She couldn't sear away the image of Tucker standing there in the moonlight, deer-eyed. Nor the way she'd wanted to lunge at him and rip him limb from limb.

Leave her alone, Blake!

The impulse, the anger, shook her through. Tucker should count himself blessed to have escaped with his life.

Yes, she needed to get her daughter far, far away.

Either that, or Annalise would let Frank shoot Tucker Newman.

"'You alone are my heart's desire, and I long to worship Thee.'" The words tasted like dirt in her mouth as she sang. She couldn't even feel her soul right now, numb inside her with the circumstances of the past days.

She glanced down the row, past Henry and Jason to Colleen, who didn't look at her, that wan, petrified expression still fixed to her face as she swallowed hard.

Colleen probably hadn't a clue what she sang either.

Beside Colleen stood Helen, bright and shiny and aglow. Like she might be in love or something. Because standing next to her, the culprit of this entire fiasco, was Frank, all shined up for church. His hair combed, wearing a dress shirt and a tie under that leather jacket. A proper gentleman.

He hadn't looked the gentleman last night when Annalise found him wielding a gun in her family room. Yeah, she'd seen it before he slipped it away.

Frank should know there was no use pretending with her.

She glanced up at the screen behind the worship team, realizing she'd lost her place in the song.

But no, she couldn't sing, not with the darkness inside nearly choking her. She gripped the edge of the pew and managed to glue her smile in place, as if she were contemplating, worshiping God Almighty in the swell of music around her. Instead of bracing herself for some divine lightning to part the roof of the church and turn her into ash right here in the middle of the sanctuary. Good thing the rest of the congregation at Deep Haven Community Church couldn't see through her to the lies, like a bacteria, festering inside. They'd cast her out into the parking lot. Maybe throw a few stones.

Not like she'd stop them.

Nathan stood between her and the end of the pew, where she might escape. She hadn't even been needed in the nursery today—although she'd inquired. She was trapped.

Trapped to face God with her black, disobedient, empty soul. And the truth that she would have to destroy the lives of everyone in the pew because of it.

They ended the song and turned to greet each other in Christian love. Annalise shook the hands of the Kings behind them, Julie holding their cute towheaded toddler.

"I can't wait until we have a pew like yours," Julie said. "Such handsome men, and your daughter is your spit image."

Thanks for that, Julie. "Little Matthew has grown up so much." Annalise ran her hand over the one-year-old's hair, feeling a squeeze in her heart. They all grew up so fast.

They sat and Pastor Dan dismissed the worship team.

Twenty minutes and she could escape to a world of football and hot wings. One last happy moment with her family.

The silence from the podium made her look up.

Pastor Dan stared out into his congregation. She'd liked him the moment she met him—a hands-on kind of pastor who volunteered with the fire department and wore jeans and a flannel vest to preach. He sometimes even took text questions from the congregation during his sermon.

They knew to expect unorthodox sermons from him. Sometimes impromptu prayer for healing. Occasionally a skit or a story instead of a sermon.

Now his eyes surveyed the crowd, something of pain on his

face. "I'm discarding my sermon for today because God has given me something else."

Annalise stared at her hands, praying that he wouldn't announce an unscheduled open forum to praise God publicly. Today of all days, she could not stand up, driven by the pressure of the Decker name, and declare something fabulous God had done for her, for her family.

"I'm going to start by reading Psalm 103."

She drew in a breath, stared out the window toward the parking lot. A flock of Canada geese had landed in the pond outside, probably en route to Florida.

"Let all that I am praise the Lord;
with my whole heart, I will praise his holy name."

Annalise opened her bulletin to read through the announcements for the week.

"Let all that I am praise the Lord;
may I never forget the good things he does for me."

Potluck next week. She'd bring a macaroni . . .
Oh, wait. No.

"He forgives all my sins
and heals all my diseases."

Henry had opened his Bible and was running his finger across the lines, following along. She swallowed down the burning in her throat.

*"He redeems me from death
    and crowns me with love and tender mercies."*

Nathan leaned back and put his arm around her, tucking her into his embrace. She blinked, fighting back moisture.

*"He fills my life with good things.
    My youth is renewed like the eagle's!"*

Jason reached over to Colleen, offered her his hand for a thumb war.

*"The Lord gives righteousness
    and justice to all who are treated unfairly."*

The geese outside lifted suddenly in flight.

*"He revealed his character to Moses
    and his deeds to the people of Israel.
The Lord is compassionate and merciful,
    slow to get angry and filled with unfailing love."*

Annalise widened her eyes to dry them, willing herself not to move her hand to her cheek.

*"He will not constantly accuse us,
    nor remain angry forever."*

Oh, why had Nathan trapped her in this row? She took a breath—too big, for it shuddered back out, and Henry glanced at her.

"He does not punish us for all our sins;
    he does not deal harshly with us, as we deserve."

She patted her son on the knee, found another smile, and used the opportunity to run a quick swipe across her face. There. Normal.

"For his unfailing love toward those who fear him
    is as great as the height of the heavens above the earth."

Had she taken out the wings to thaw?

"He has removed our sins as far from us
    as the east is from the west."

She'd make snickerdoodles this afternoon.

"The Lord is like a father to his children,
    tender and compassionate to those who fear him."

She closed her eyes, the walls pressing in around her.

"For he knows how weak we are;
    he remembers we are only dust.
Our days on earth are like grass;
    like wildflowers, we bloom and die.
The wind blows, and we are gone—
    as though we had never been here."

She looked down the row at her amazing family, at Helen seated beside Frank. *Never been here.*

"But the love of the Lord remains forever
with those who fear him."

Annalise looked up at Dan, who was reciting the passage from memory, his eyes closed.

"His salvation extends to the children's children
of those who are faithful to his covenant,
of those who obey his commandments!"

And right there lay the problem. She might have had no choice but to run, and yes, she might have saved lives, but she'd created a life full of deceit. And her children would pay.

"The Lord has made the heavens his throne;
from there he rules over everything.
Praise the Lord, you angels,
you mighty ones who carry out his plans,
listening for each of his commands."

She'd tell them this afternoon, after the game.

"Yes, praise the Lord, you armies of angels
who serve him and do his will!
Praise the Lord, everything he has created,
everything in all his kingdom."

She closed her eyes again, willing herself to listen, to dare to feel anything of life inside her, anything of praise.

"Let all that I am praise the Lord."

Nothing. God had abandoned her in her sin.

Silence filled the church.

Except, of course, for her heartbeat, thundering in accusation.

Annalise opened her eyes and found Pastor Dan standing in front of the altar, on the floor of the sanctuary.

"I have a word from the Lord for you today, church. I don't know who this is directed to, but someone needs to hear it." He smiled, something so kind in it that Annalise had to look away.

"'I love you,' says the Lord. 'I see you, and I know you, and I love you. Period. I know stuff about you that you don't even think I know, and yet I love you. I know the things you're hiding, and yet I love you. I love you so much that even what I know about you didn't stop Me from sending Jesus to the cross to save you. In fact, the very fact that you are suffering is why Jesus went to the cross. To redeem you. My love is not an equation, something you have to earn or barter for. I love you—I bless you even in the midst of your sin. Not to condone it, but to remind you of the glorious reunion that awaits when you come to Me. My blessings are to remind you of My great love and to turn you in to My arms. You cannot repay My love. Or My grace. You can only rejoice in it.'"

Annalise couldn't breathe. Couldn't move. Perhaps her heart had stopped. She prayed that Dan's gaze wouldn't fix on her because she might shatter into weeping in the pew.

"Here's my only sermon today. Do not let your circumstances define God's love for you. He loves you. Period."

Period.

She closed her eyes again, afraid of how the words seeped inside, almost painful.

"I'm going to ask the prayer team to come and stand at the altar. If these words were for you today, please come and let us pray for you. Let's rise and sing our closing hymn."

Prayer team. Annalise froze. Nathan unwound his arm from around her.

Oh. No.

But what was she to do?

As the congregation sang the closing song, she slipped out of the pew and, head bowed, joined Pastor Dan at the front. His wife, Ellie, stood on the other side of him.

Please, please don't let anyone come to me.

They sang through one verse, the next. She saw a pair of hiking boots standing before the elder next to her. A woman in heels chose Ellie.

The last verse. *Yes, please*—

Someone in leather cowboy boots stood before her. She smiled and looked up.

Good thing she'd spent years honing her reactions. Kelli Hanson stood before her, tears streaking her thin face. She had her hair in two long red braids, a green bandanna holding them back, and wore a pair of patchwork jeans with the same oversize wool sweater Annalise had seen her in at Thursday's soccer practice. Her green eyes were red-rimmed, defeated, broken.

"Hi, Kelli," Annalise said softly. "How can I pray for you?"

Kelli drew in a breath and swallowed, then closed her eyes. "Help me believe in grace."

Help her believe in grace.

Yes.

Annalise closed her eyes too and took Kelli's cold hands. And then because she had no choice, or because she longed to hope, or simply out of pure desperation, she prayed for Kelli.

Hoping that God might hear the silent cry from her own heart.

᠊᠊᠊᠊᠊᠊ ❧ ᠊᠊᠊᠊᠊᠊

"Maybe God is giving me a second chance."

Helen studied her sister for her response, watching for any twitch on Miriam's face, any stiffening in her shoulders, any rolling of her eyes.

But Miriam continued to pour the batter for the apple bread into the pan, cleaning out the bowl with a rubber spatula, as if oblivious to Helen's bait. The late-afternoon sun filled the tiny kitchen with the color of orange marmalade, and the smells of cinnamon and nutmeg and cloves could season her home for a month. Across the street, Helen had no doubt Annalise and the boys huddled around the big screen, watching the Minnesota Vikings get annihilated by the Chicago Bears. Poor Nathan. For some reason, Annalise seemed to like the Arizona Cardinals.

Miriam had shown up at Helen's house, bucket in hand, and if her sister wanted to cook here after picking another bushel of apples, Helen wouldn't complain. She was sure Miriam intended to deliver a rebuttal after seeing Helen seated next to Frank in church this morning, but so far, she hadn't mentioned it.

Her sister's silence could drive Helen to her last nerve.

What was she to do? It didn't help that the man had *handsome* written on him from head to toe. And he smelled good, spicy, armed with the cologne he wore to the dance. She'd spent too much time during the service remembering what it felt like to sway in his arms. Probably not appropriate thoughts for church.

But weren't men and women designed to get married? To have

companionship? Frank made her laugh, and he came without pre-loaded opinions about her life, her reputation in Deep Haven. She liked the way he looked at her, as if he enjoyed listening to her. Even last night, when he walked her home after the volleyball game and came inside ever so briefly for coffee and another piece of pie. He'd asked about her life, her job—yes, she'd loved being a nurse, but not retirement so much. No, she hadn't traveled much. Where would she go if she could go anywhere? Maybe Italy, but she liked Deep Haven, had never had much of a wanderlust.

And when he turned to her as he left, his hand braced on the doorframe, the desire to step up to him, to kiss him, to find herself in his arms—just like on the dance floor—nearly took her breath away.

She should thank her crazy, overprotective son for interrupting them and making a fool out of himself before she did.

Or not. She didn't know what she wanted.

Nathan had even tried to sit between her and Frank today in church. But Frank got up and returned a few moments later, scooting in beside her.

Perhaps this was her second chance at happily ever after. Her only chance.

And Helen didn't particularly want to argue with Miriam about it, but her sister had stood by her for so many years, welcoming her into her pew at church and even inviting Helen and Nathan to every family celebration. She just wanted her sister to understand, perhaps.

If not give her blessing.

"I mean, why not? You heard Dan today. 'The Lord gives righteousness and justice to all who are treated unfairly.' Maybe he's saying that I need to ignore the gossip . . ." Helen lifted a warm snickerdoodle from the cooling rack, broke off a piece, let the cinnamon sweetness dissolve in her mouth. Annalise's recipe—perfection.

"It's not gossip that's kept you from being married all these years, Helen. It's yourself."

Helen pressed a hand against her chest to keep from choking. "What? You're the one who's always implying I shouldn't get married again because I'm divorced. Because I've *sinned*."

Miriam put the bowl in the sink, ran water into it. Although two years younger than Helen, she had a wiser and older air about her. Just because she'd been married for thirty-six years, had three children, hadn't sinned a day in her pristine life . . .

"Would you agree that God hates divorce?" Miriam wiped her hands with a dishrag.

Here they went again. "Yes. But I don't think that means we're supposed to live punishing ourselves, never allowing ourselves to find happiness again."

"Really? You could have fooled me." Miriam opened the oven, placed the pan on the center rack.

"What are you talking about?"

"You have spent your entire life shutting out people, almost as if you *are* punishing yourself." Miriam set the timer. "A man couldn't get close to you if he tried."

"That is not true. I don't push everyone away."

Miriam crossed her arms, leaning against the counter. "Please. You've spent thirty years making sure everyone knew you could take care of yourself. I'm not stupid, Helen. I was there when you caught Dylan cheating. I remember our conversation."

"Me too! You told me to forgive that louse and let him back in my front door. All I got was the Christian answer, the legalism, from you."

Miriam rubbed her arms. "Have you considered the fact that when you married Dylan, you said yes for better or for worse?"

"Not that kind of worse. Even the Bible says you can divorce if your spouse is cheating on you."

"Yes, it does. That's true. But . . ." She looked away. Widowhood had aged her, etching tiny lines into her face and adding a few pounds. But Miriam was still pretty with her dark-brown hair, gentle hazel eyes. Helen supposed there might be a second chance out there for Miriam, too. "I'm just wondering what would have happened if you had forgiven him."

"Why would I do that? He betrayed me. And then look what he did. He turned to alcohol . . . and killed someone."

Miriam nodded. "I know. And none of that is your fault, Helen. Dylan made his own choices." She smiled at her sister as the aroma of the bread baking began to scent the kitchen. "But I've long believed that marriage isn't just for our joy, but to make us stronger, better people. To change us into the people God wants us to be. And we do that through better . . . and worse."

"How much worse are we supposed to take?"

Miriam took a hot pad and opened the oven. The bread was just rising. She closed the door. "I guess that depends on the worse. But I do know that during the worse, we draw nearer to God, and that's a good thing. And maybe we even see His redemption of our marriage."

Helen pulled out a plastic container, ripped off paper towels to line it, and started loading in the warm cookies. "That's easy for you to say. You and William never had a quarrel in your life."

"Actually . . . I fell in love with another man about ten years into our marriage." Miriam said it without emotion, without drama. But it stilled Helen nonetheless.

"It was an office romance. Nothing happened except for a few flirtatious moments, but William and I were going through a distant, kid-focused time in our marriage. We'd forgotten the romance of our youth, and I let my heart be tempted."

Of all the hypocritical—

"I stood in church one Sunday, surrounded by my family, and I realized that I was on the verge of destroying everything. It shook me back to myself." Miriam picked up a rag, wiped the counter. "I remember the day when I told William. I tried to convince myself that I didn't have to, but secrets are cancer to a marriage, and . . . and I knew I couldn't live like that. I wanted us to not just survive, but thrive. So I confessed what happened, expecting him to hate me, maybe even throw me out."

Helen kept putting the cookies in the container, trying not to break them.

"He forgave me, Helen. And God redeemed our marriage."

Helen turned and held out the container. "I think I need you to leave, Miriam."

Miriam looked at it, then shook her head. "I'm not surprised. That's what you do when people hurt you. Kick them out of your life."

"Now, please."

Miriam took the container. "I want you to be happy, Helen. I loved seeing you dancing with Frank. But I'm afraid you're going to get hurt again."

"I won't marry a man like Dylan."

Miriam set the cookies on the counter. "You'll marry a *man*. By definition, they will drive you crazy."

Funny. But she wasn't laughing.

Miriam opened the oven again, where the bread was starting

to form a crust. The smell could make Helen's eyes water. "Are you ready to commit to 'for better or worse' with Frank? Or anyone?" Miriam met her eyes. Gave her a smile. "I agree. God *does* give second chances. And He does protect us—even fixes the unfixable. Especially when we stand firm in our commitments. Frank seems like a nice man, but the biggest question is, are you ready for your second chance?"

Her words made Helen's eyes burn, tightened her throat. "What if it's my last chance?"

Miriam took out a cooling rack for the bread. "William loved my apple bread." She took off the oven mitts. "It's got a little while left to bake. I'm leaving it for you. Thanks for the snickerdoodles." She turned to Helen, pulling her into a hug. "God loves you, Sis, and He wants His best and highest for you."

Crazy, Helen actually thought she might cry.

She pulled away.

"Helen, you're bleeding!"

Helen's hand went to her nose, came away stained with red.

Miriam tore a paper towel and Helen pressed it against her nose, tipped her head back. She felt Miriam's hand on her elbow, helping her to a chair at the kitchen table. "It's probably this dry weather," she said.

Miriam went to the sink, grabbed a cloth, dampened it, and returned. Helen checked her nose as she switched the paper towel for the cloth.

"Really? Are you sure?"

Helen recognized the fear in her sister's eyes. "Yes. I'm fine. I had a checkup just three months ago. Still cancer free."

But Miriam's smile seemed forced. "Maybe I should stay."

"I'm fine." Helen pulled the cloth away. "See, it's already stopped bleeding."

"I would feel a lot better if you'd go to the clinic tomorrow."

"Miriam—"

"Please, Helen." Miriam pressed her arm. "I couldn't bear to lose you, too."

Helen washed her hands, her nose, wiped her eyes with a towel. "Thank you for the bread."

The fragrance lingered long after Miriam left, long after the bread finished baking, the harvest sweetness twining through her small house. Helen ran a bath, loading it with sea salts, and lit a candle.

Miriam's words hung around her like a noose: *Marriage isn't just for our joy, but to make us stronger, better people. To change us into the people God wants us to be. And we do that through better . . . and worse.*

Helen undressed and sank into the bubbles up to her chin.

If she closed her eyes, she could still remember that night she had confronted Dylan on his cheating. Nathan crying in his room, twelve years old, looking like he might be six, in the fetal position with his football clutched tight to him.

I'm sorry, Helen—it was a stupid mistake.

Just like mine was, marrying you. Every time she remembered her words, they stung her afresh, and she recoiled from them now. Would she ever erase the hurt on Dylan's face from her memory? The way he shook his head, the slam of the door as it rattled their home to its foundation?

She had climbed into bed with Nathan and listened to Dylan's car fade into the night.

What if she had forgiven him?

Dylan had a way of making her laugh that sloughed off

the problems of her shift at the hospital. How many times had she arrived home late and found a pot of chili on the stove, little Nathan curled in his daddy's arms as they watched college football?

A stupid mistake.

Like turning him away that night, months later, when he'd begged yet again for her forgiveness. No wonder he'd tempered his pain with too many beers. Taken that curve at Cutaway Creek too fast.

Her fault. A mistake she could never repair.

Helen climbed out of the water, blew out the candle, and wrapped a towel around herself.

Maybe, if she had it to do all over, she would have paused for one moment before she threw him out, thought about her life instead of her broken heart, and listened to his apology.

Given him a second chance.

For better or worse.

Yeah, well, at the time, *worse* felt insurmountable.

She drained the tub, then pulled on a pair of flannel pajama pants, a sweatshirt, her wool socks. A glass of tea, popcorn, and a movie would erase the memories.

Perhaps it was the shadows or the heat of the bath in the cool of the house, but her head spun as she walked into the family room. She had to brace her hand on the doorframe to right herself.

Tea, yes, and a slice of bread. Miriam did make excellent apple bread. Helen filled the kettle and lit the stove.

Her hands shook as she took out the bread and grabbed a knife. She put it down, held her hands together.

The sense of the room tilting made her grab the counter.

And then she felt the trickle of moisture down her face into her lips.

She grabbed the washcloth from the sink and held it to her nose as she stumbled onto a kitchen chair, pinching back the blood flow.

The lighthouse clock in the kitchen ticked off the seconds. The minutes.

Maybe it was too late for second chances after all.

⅋

Annalise felt bruised. All the way through to her bones.

Bruised and mocked by Pastor Dan's message. *"The Lord is compassionate and merciful. . . . He does not punish us for all our sins; he does not deal harshly with us, as we deserve."*

Except with her. Because this felt harsh.

Annalise dumped the gnawed chicken wings into the trash, then set the tray in the sink. She squirted dishwashing liquid onto it, turned the hot water on full blast. The barbecue sauce from the wings needed soaking to work free.

Behind her in the next room, opposite the kitchen, her family cheered on the Sunday night game. The Eagles were down against the Patriots by one touchdown late in the third quarter.

Based on the roar of her crowd, the Eagles had just managed a fantastic run. Or catch. Or something. Not that she cared oh-so-much about football, but Nathan loved it, so she did too.

Or pretended to.

Her life had become one big game of pretend.

At least it suddenly seemed like it. Three days ago, it felt real and right and whole. Three days ago she was Annalise Decker. Today she felt like Deidre O'Reilly.

And today she wanted to call her mother. To hear her voice, to tell her how sorry she was, every day, over and over.

She picked up a scrubber and began to attack the pot, not caring how the hot water scalded her.

Or better, she wanted to fly down to St. Louis and walk in the front door of their ranch home. Smell the cinnamon and sunshine embedded in the walls; hear the owl clock ticking away the hours in the kitchen; see the brightness of the yellow Formica counters, the light-blue cupboards, the old oval table with the doily in the middle. She'd catch her mother at the sink or drinking coffee at the kitchen table.

Hi, Mom. It's me. Deidre.

Her mother's breath would catch, and then she'd smile, forgiveness in her eyes. *Oh, please, let there be forgiveness.*

She'd get up from the table and enclose Annalise in her arms.

And they'd simply hold on.

"Annalise?"

The soft voice behind her made her jump. She turned, foamy bubbles dripping onto the tile floor. "Frank! Sheesh—you should know better than to sneak up on me."

"I wasn't sneaking. Sorry." He set a stack of dishes on the counter. "I thought we could talk. About what you said last night. Leaving."

"Shh. They can hear you."

He reached out and took the scrubber from her hand. "Let's step outside."

Frank guided her toward the door off the kitchen, where they'd built a screened-in porch. They had a deck off the family room, too, but she'd made this tiny porch her escape, with a pair of rattan chairs, an ottoman. Sometimes she read her Bible here, even wrapped in a blanket in October, with the autumn breezes ruffling the pages.

Now she sank into one of the chairs and pulled the blanket around her, having left it outside this morning, when she'd sat riffling through too many imaginary conversations with Colleen.

She couldn't remember how early she'd risen or even if she'd slept.

Frank stood away from her, hands in his pockets. "When are you going to tell them? We need to get this in motion."

Regardless of how gently he delivered them, his words were like acid.

She swallowed, looked at her hands, wrinkled from the water. "I know what I said last night. But . . . I don't know, Frank. What if you're wrong? What if Garcia didn't kill Blake? What if I'm perfectly safe here—and I decide to rip apart my family's world?"

Frank took a breath, but she ran over his words before he could utter them. "Jason's shot at a theater scholarship. Colleen's chance at all-conference volleyball. Henry has a great team at the school to help him read. And let's not even start with Nathan and his mother. All Helen has is us. And she's not about to leave."

"I know," he said softly.

He did? "What did you tell her?"

"Nothing." He sat down on the opposite chair, running his hands over his face.

Hmm . . . "By the way, my husband wanted to murder you last night. You should stay away from her if you want him to trust you."

Frank looked away. "I know this isn't easy—"

"Isn't easy? Frank, you're asking me to walk away from everything that makes me who I am. I've built a life here. I'm Annalise Decker and that actually means something."

"I know it does." He kept his voice quiet. "I've seen your life here, and it kills me to take you from it."

"Listen, last night I panicked. I caught Colleen with a boy in her room. I don't think anything happened, but I heard voices and got up in the nick of time."

"I heard the floorboards—"

"I saw your gun." She raised an eyebrow. "You're better than a watchdog."

"I think that's a compliment. You want me to track down this kid, have a talk with him?"

"I think that's Nathan's job. But . . . but that's why I said we'd leave. I don't want to go through what my mother did."

He nodded.

"But then . . . I don't know. I want to believe that . . . Well, you heard the sermon today. I know you once told me to go to church, Frank, and I listened. And God gave me this amazing life and . . . I want to believe that Pastor Dan was talking to me today . . ."

She ignored his grim expression. "Nathan is a righteous man, and we just need to trust that God will protect us . . ."

But Frank was shaking his head. "No, Annalise. You can't stay. You—"

"Why not, Frank?"

"Because you're going to get yourself—and your family—*killed*!"

She recoiled at the panic—even the anger—in his voice.

"You have to trust me," he said.

"I do trust you. I just think you're wrong. I think you don't understand—"

"I understand! Annalise, I've been doing this for nearly forty years. *I understand.*"

Something in his voice, the way it cracked on the end—"What aren't you telling me?"

He released a long breath, then got up, walked to the edge of the porch. "I'd been doing this for about ten years when I placed a young girl, about your age back then. She . . . well, she was a lot like you. Brave and feisty, but broken and afraid. I told her she'd be safe. And I checked on her. A lot."

The wind tumbled leaves against the screen. Annalise drew her blanket tighter around herself.

"About five years into her placement, the man she'd testified against escaped from prison. Of course, I went to her, told her she might be in danger. But like you, she'd gotten married. She was pregnant with her second child. She had created a new life, one filled with healing and love. And like you, she'd never told her husband."

He didn't add any indictment to his words, but she felt it anyway.

"I . . . I was young and let her pleading sway me. She wanted to stay and I promised I'd keep her secret. I didn't make her relocate."

Annalise poked her fingers through the tiny holes in the blanket, dreading his next words.

He turned to meet her eyes. His were glossy. "Her entire family was murdered, including her two-year-old."

A hand pressed the air out of her. "That's not going to happen to me," she said on a wisp of breath.

"You're right. Because I'm not going to let it. I talked to my partner last night, and he thought we had a bead on Garcia, but I just got off the phone with him. Garcia gave them the slip outside Whitehorse. He traded Blake's car for a truck, probably switched the plates a few times. We've lost his trail. And unless we can pick it up again and capture him, you're leaving, Annalise. You can take your family with you. Or . . . or not. But I just can't let you stay."

She drew up her knees, wrapped her arms around them. Inside she heard more yelling. Someone must have scored a touchdown.

"What if . . . what if *I* left—only until you found him?"

He looked like her uncle sometimes, the way compassion hued his face. "And how long do you think it'll take for us to find him, Annalise? Maybe years. And in the meantime, what about your husband, your family? Are you going to tell them the truth? Or are you just going to walk out on him? Make him think you're leaving him?"

"I'm not leaving my husband!"

He held up his hands as if surrendering.

"Frank, it's not fair. I did what I was supposed to; I gave up everything. And . . . and I felt like God rewarded me for it with my children, my husband, this community. But now, what—it's all a joke? It feels like I'm being punished." She wiped her cheek, shook her head. "Of course I'm being punished. I don't know why I didn't realize that sooner. I knew I didn't deserve to be happy. I should have never stopped holding my breath."

She looked away, the wetness stinging her face. "There's no happy ending for people like me."

"Annalise? Are you coming in to watch the game?" Nathan stood at the door, frowning. He stepped onto the porch. "What are you doing out here? It's freezing."

Frank looked at her as if waiting for her to answer.

But she couldn't take her eyes off Nathan. He had a fierceness that she'd never seen before, his jaw tight as he glared at Frank.

Like he'd come out here to protect her or something.

He'd changed out of his suit, put on a pair of faded jeans,

with a black turtleneck that might have shrunk just a bit in the wash because she'd never truly noticed the way it stretched across his chest. Had he dropped some weight? Because his shoulders seemed wider. His hair spiked up, having suffered the abuse of too much frustration over the Vikings game. And he hadn't shaved this morning for church, giving him a layer of stubble that added an oddly rough-hewn edge to his good-boy persona.

She didn't quite recognize this man.

And now he narrowed his eyes at Frank, almost in warning, before turning to her. "Are you all right, Lise?"

Something in his expression made her nod.

Nathan's mouth tightened in a grim line as she wiped her cheeks. But he played along with her charade. "Good. Because the Patriots are behind and we need you."

He held out his hand for her. She took it, let him help her up, and grabbed the blanket that slipped off her shoulder.

Nathan tucked it around her before following her inside.

10

Annalise's words had skewered Frank right through. *There's no happy ending for people like me.*

Certainly there had to be. He couldn't be the guy who destroyed her life—again.

The football game played in the next room, in the final quarter, but he sat at the kitchen table in the darkness, drinking a cup of nuked coffee, too on edge to watch.

Instead, his gaze fixed on Helen's light shining like a beacon.

Nathan had nearly glared him right out of the pew this morning. But what was Frank to do—trust that Garcia wouldn't find them in the house of God?

Although his gun tucked into his ankle holster had felt just a smidge irreverent. And really, did they have to sit near the front? What happened to being a good Baptist and filling up the back row?

But they'd survived church, and frankly, sitting there, singing "Amazing Grace" and "How Great Thou Art," along with a mix of contemporary praise songs, had stirred a dormant thirst inside him. Margaret had been a churchgoer, and when they first married, they'd attended together. But then he began to travel, and his schedule became so busy . . .

Still, that pastor had some good words, and they rang in Frank's head as he stared out the window at the light. *"He redeems me from death and crowns me with love and tender mercies. He fills my life with good things. My youth is renewed like the eagle's!"*

Being here with Annalise and her family, with Helen, he felt redeemed from the death that had become his life. Felt again like a young man every time Helen looked at him.

I knew I didn't deserve to be happy.

Maybe none of them did. But suddenly he wanted to try.

He took another sip of coffee. Then he put it down, grabbed his jacket, and slipped out the front door.

He had a moment of pause right after he knocked when he heard voices inside. Oh, what if—?

"Frank." Helen stood in the door, dressed in flannel pants, an oversize sweatshirt, her hair tied up in a hair clip. A movie played behind her—something in black-and-white. "Come in."

Her house smelled like apple pie, and the dishwasher hummed below the voices on the screen. Only the glow of a lamp lit the family room, where she'd created a nest with a red afghan on the old tweed sofa.

"I interrupted you."

"You interrupted Bing Crosby. After the dance the other night, I was in the mood for a musical." She walked over to the sofa, picked up the remote, and turned off the television.

The room went quiet with the exception of his thundering heart. His palms were sweating, so he shoved them into his pockets.

Good grief, he felt like a teenager on a date.

"Would you like some coffee?"

He shook his head. He wasn't sure what he wanted.

Okay, maybe he knew, just a little. For one moment, he wanted to be someone safe and honest. Not fake Uncle Frank, but Frank, a guy who lived in an empty house in Portland, surrounded by memories he didn't make.

"You look upset. Did Nathan—?"

"No. He and Annalise are watching the game."

Helen nodded, running her hands up her arms. She looked thinner today, maybe even a bit pale.

"Are you okay?"

She gave him a smile. "Yes. Of course."

"Maybe . . . Would you like to take a walk? It's nice outside— no clouds. The stars are out." Fresh air. Yes, that's what he needed.

The second smile looked real. "Yes, actually. I would."

She didn't change out of her flannel pants—he liked that—just pulled on a pair of black fur boots, added a winter jacket and a knit hat. Her hands she left bare.

"Aren't you going to lock your door?" he said as she pulled it closed behind them.

"This is Deep Haven. I don't lock my door. Ever." She stuck her hands in her pockets and descended the front steps. Thankfully he'd repaired them. Maybe she had some other projects around the house he could attend to. Just while he waited for Annalise to come to her senses.

Please, let Annalise come to her senses. As long as Garcia was out there, she wouldn't be safe.

But then, of course, he'd have to leave too. Which meant he'd never see Helen again.

He too pocketed his hands and followed her down the walk.

"Where do you want to go?"

He shrugged.

"Perfect. Follow me." She grinned at him and headed toward the harbor. The moon had risen, tracing a path of brilliant milky white along the dark water. Stars trickled down upon the surface, winking at him.

Scurried up by the wind, leaves tiptoed down the street behind them as they walked.

"Are you cold?"

"I'm from Minnesota. This is bikini weather." Helen turned to him, winked.

They crossed the road, and she led them to the walkway along the lake, her hands still tucked in her pockets. Waves combed the shore as Frank and Helen cut through the park, past where the last of the boats were moored, past the Coast Guard station, and along the rocky path to the breakwater. The lighthouse rose at the far end, unlit.

"Why is the lighthouse not shining?"

"It has a red light that they turn on during storms. It's quite beautiful." Helen sat down on the breakwater, staring out into the darkness.

Frank sat beside her, watching the waves hit the cement pier, rush back out, slam against it again.

"I used to bring Nathan here at night. We'd make wishes on the moon. After his father died, he was deathly afraid of the water. But he'd still sit here with me, listening to the waves. As if he didn't want it to defeat him."

"How did his dad die?"

She sighed and braced her hands behind her on the break-water. "His car spun out over the bridge and landed in the water. He drowned. Or maybe hypothermia killed him first. This water is pretty cold. I never got a coroner report. Dead was dead, and Dylan wasn't coming back."

"I'm sorry."

She shrugged. "I wasn't supposed to be devastated—I'd divorced him, after all—but I was. I grieved for Nathan. And a part of me always waited to hear Dylan coming up the drive. I'd thrown him out, yes, but it didn't mean I didn't miss him."

After a moment, she smiled. "Nathan asked Annalise to marry him on this pier. It's sort of a romantic tradition in Deep Haven. Something about the way the sun shines through the lighthouse. As if guiding them to a happy ending. I know, sappy, but . . . well, it seemed to work for Nathan and Annalise. I spent my entire life trying to give Nathan a good childhood, a good upbringing. The happiest day of my life was when Annalise walked into his life."

Helen shivered. Frank hesitated only a moment before putting his arm around her. She scooted into the pocket of his warmth.

And wouldn't you know it, she fit perfectly.

"I remember the day Margaret agreed to marry me. I was just graduating from West Point. I had the day all figured out—roses and champagne on the beach by the sea. She was a waitress, going to school part-time to be a teacher. My car died, it rained, and we finally had to hike back to the diner for dinner. She said yes anyway."

Helen laughed. "It sounds like she wanted the man, not the magic. Life doesn't have to be perfect to be happy. And sometimes you have to find those happy places in between the pain."

Happy places between the pain. Like now, the rhythm of the water at their feet, the canopy of stars above, the music of the night around them. He could be happy here. Here, he was just a guy sitting on a pier with a beautiful woman. A woman who enjoyed his company.

A woman who considered him a good man. He wasn't the man, but it did feel like magic.

"Thank you for taking me out for this walk. I needed it."

When Helen looked up at him, Frank couldn't help it. He leaned down and kissed her. Softly. More a whisper of longing than a kiss, but she opened her mouth softly to kiss him back.

He hadn't kissed another woman since Margaret, but it contained the essence of a first kiss, the rush of his heart in his chest, the sweet hint of intimacy.

For a delicate, perfect moment, the world became safe, easy. Young.

Then, with a crash, a wave slammed into the pier, water splintering into the air, dousing them. Icy splatter prickled his skin, ran down his jacket. Helen's hat glistened with water and her flannel pants were soaked.

"Oh!" she said, then laughed. "Oops."

He pulled her to her feet. Oh, he wanted to kiss her again, but . . .

But what was he doing? He was leaving in two days, never to return. If they were lucky. He swallowed, hard, then took her hand. "Careful now," he said as they worked their way along the pier. "It's slippery."

&

I'm not leaving my husband!

Nathan couldn't shake the words from his brain. He'd stood at the kitchen sink rinsing his plate and heard Annalise's voice reverberate through the flimsy porch door, loud and clear.

For a long second, he'd wanted to turn away, to ignore what she said, the shock of it stealing his breath.

But then he'd watched her through the door, and something about the way she looked at her uncle Frank ignited an anger inside Nathan that forced him out onto the porch to send the guy packing.

Annalise had appeared shaken. And Nathan couldn't help but think he'd walked into a family secret that he deserved to be a part of.

He blew out a breath, ran a hand around the back of his neck, and closed his laptop, setting it on the bedside table. Not one hit on the McIntyre place. *Please, God, don't let me destroy everything my family has worked for.*

Annalise was with Henry in his room, reading. He could hear his son's hiccup of sentences. His heart went out to him—good thing he had Annalise to help him. Nathan just didn't have the patience to sit by his son's side and watch him struggle. But perhaps that's why God had made them a team.

He should do his part better. The thought dug at him as he got up, went to the kitchen for a glass of water.

Along the way, he caught Jason's voice sneaking out from under his door. Probably practicing for his production at school.

He stopped to listen.

*"Let me not to the marriage of true minds
Admit impediments. Love is not love
Which alters when it alteration finds,
Or bends with the remover to remove:
O no! it is an ever-fixed mark
That looks on tempests and is never shaken."*

Shakespeare. No wonder they were performing *Romeo and Juliet*—it probably matched some Shakespeare unit in English class. Nathan well remembered having to learn a few sonnets during his stint at Deep Haven High School. Things hadn't changed so much in twenty years.

He went to the kitchen, opened the fridge. His stomach growled, or maybe he just imagined it as he searched the contents. In the end, he pulled out the bottled water and poured a glass.

"Love is not love which alters when it alteration finds." He sort of liked Shakespeare. It felt like decoding something.

He moved to the picture window at the front of the house, staring out at the lit walk.

A figure moved into the glow and he watched Frank ease open the door.

Nathan set down his glass. "Please tell me you weren't over at my mother's house." He kept his voice quiet, controlled, because he feared what threatened to escape.

Frank looked up at him.

Nathan had been the father of a teenage boy long enough to recognize guilt. "I can't believe it. What are you *doing*? I told you to stay away from her."

"No, actually you reminded me that she was your mother. Which I know." Frank held his hands up. "Nathan, just calm down—"

"Why do I need to stay calm?" He had advanced around the table. "What's going on?"

"Nothing. We went for a walk."

"At ten o'clock at night?"

A muscle pulled in Frank's jaw.

Never had Nathan wanted to hit someone like he wanted to lay one against Frank. Why had he ever invited him into their lives? He'd send the guy to the Super 8 tonight if he thought Annalise wouldn't be hurt.

"Listen to me. My mother has been through a lot, and she doesn't need to get hurt again."

"Not going to hurt her."

"I need to know right now. How long do you plan on sticking around? Because your three days are up, pal. Like fish, you're starting to smell."

Frank didn't even blink. "Nathan, I promise you that I'll be out of your life as soon as possible."

"Awesome. And until then, I'd like you to stay as far away from my mother as a town the size of Deep Haven allows. Got me?"

Frank nodded. "I'm sorry—"

"While you're apologizing, maybe you could tell me what you said to my wife that has her so upset. What were you two talking about?"

When Frank pursed his lips, Nathan wanted to wrap his hands around the man's throat and squeeze it out of him.

"Ask her," Frank finally said. Then he went downstairs.

Nathan stood in the kitchen a moment, shaking, resisting the urge to go downstairs and throw Frank into the street.

He finished his water.

Set the glass in the sink.

Drew in a breath.

Yes, he'd ask his wife.

But Annalise lay curled under the covers in their bed, the blanket up to her ears. Her eyes were fiercely closed, as if she were already at battle in her dreams.

Shoot. But she'd slept so poorly the night before . . .

Nathan went into the bathroom and stared at himself in the mirror. He looked old. Even angry. He almost didn't recognize himself.

Annalise had left her body cream jar open on the counter, and he reached to close it, taking a whiff first. Lilies. So that's why she always smelled so good.

He replaced the lid, then brushed his teeth, changed into his pajamas, and crawled in beside her, listening to her breathe.

They hadn't made up since their fight. Not really. Not like he wanted to.

I'm not leaving my husband! Her words ricocheted inside his brain. Again. And again.

Please, God, don't let her leave me.

Nathan turned to her, closed his eyes, smelled the skin of her neck. Then, because he didn't want to wake her, he gently tucked his arm around her.

It took him a second, but he realized she wasn't asleep.

"Lise, are you crying?" He rolled her to her back.

She covered her face with her hand.

"Lise, honey. What's the matter?"

She didn't answer him, just shook with her tears. Her grief had claws that dug into him as he lay there, helpless, swallowing his frustration.

She possessed the power to dismantle him when she cried.

He rested his forehead against her shoulder. "Please, Lise. Tell me."

She shook her head, but he gently pulled her hand away and kissed her cheek, salty with tears.

"I . . ." She pressed a trembling hand to her mouth. "I miss my mother."

Oh. Of course.

That's what all this was about. What kind of idiot had he been not to figure it out? Maybe Frank was here to ask her to participate in some memorial or something. Something that bubbled the grief to the surface and trapped her inside the trauma of losing so much.

He'd been a jerk, caught in his own world, this stupid election. "Lise, I'm so sorry. Of course you do."

"And my sister and brother. And my father. I really miss them."

He resolved to be a better man, one without such a thick head, as he leaned back and drew her into his arms. He ran a hand through her soft, beautiful hair. "I know you do. I'm so, so sorry. I would have liked to meet them."

Her breath hiccuped as she curled her hand into his pajama top. "You would like my father. He was a lot like you. Sensible. Kind. He . . . he helped people."

She rarely talked about her family, so he didn't interrupt. Just held her and ran one hand down her arm and felt a little bit like a heel for trying to remember the last time he'd had her in his arms like this.

"He was on the police force."

Her father had been a cop?

"My mother loved to eat ice cream in the winter. She used to take my sister and me over to this Ferris wheel near our house. Once, Kylie got too close to the edge, and my mother went crazy. She was so overprotective."

Kylie. She'd never told him her sister's name, either. Or the story, but it did account for the way she had to ride the Ferris wheel at every amusement park they visited.

See, it was the little things that he longed to know about her. The little things that seemed to pain her too much to share.

"I'm so sorry about your family, honey. I can't imagine losing my mother, and so suddenly. One day they're with you, the next gone." He kissed her hair. "I know it's been hard. And having Frank here—I'll bet he churns up all sorts of memories."

She mumbled something. It sounded like *You have no idea.*

Then she sighed and lifted her head.

Oh, she had beautiful eyes. Like the lake on a hot summer day, inviting and freeing, and in them he could forget who he was and just be. Just enjoy.

"He reminds me of all I have here. All I love. All I would never give up."

Never give up. It almost felt like relief, the way her words settled into his chest and allowed him to breathe again.

"You are so beautiful."

Probably not the right moment to say that, with her face reddened, her hair stringy . . . but she'd never looked more beautiful to him. In fact, she might have grown more beautiful every day.

"I'm sorry we fought, Annalise. I promise I'll be a better man for you."

Her smile dimmed, and for a moment he thought he'd blown it. But then she gave him a look he'd never quite seen before.

And she kissed him.

She tasted like salt and the toothpaste she'd used before bed and the sweetness of the wife of his youth. She sank into him. He rolled over, cradling her in his arms, deepening his kiss.

Oh, how he loved her. The day she had walked into his life, everything turned bright and crisp and colorful. How he'd missed her these last few days—or maybe weeks. Months?

Now, in the dim light, her smile in her eyes as he leaned back and ran his thumb down her face, it felt like eternity.

"I love you, Lise. We belong together, always."

She only nodded and clung to him.

But her words on the porch returned to him.

Nathan had the eerie feeling that she was saying good-bye.

11

"If I have cancer, I'm not telling Nathan, and you can't either, Paula."

Dr. Paula Walgren sat on a rolling stool at the exam room desk, wearing a lab coat over her black sweater, matching pants, and felt clogs. With her short blonde hair and hazel eyes, she could be Helen's younger sister. She'd been a young woman out of medical school, doing her residency at the local hospital, when Helen came in the first time. Paula had walked with her through chemo, her bone marrow transplant, and every year she held her breath with Helen as they waited for test results.

Now she looked up from the chart at Helen, who sat on the exam table, nearly frozen in her flimsy cotton gown. Outside, the air smelled of rain, chilly as a mist drifted off the lake.

"Helen, if your cancer is back, you'll need your family around you."

"Of course. After the holiday season." She gave Paula a smile, hoping it looked real.

She couldn't do this to Nathan again. Not now, when he was going to win the mayoral race. He had his own life to live—he couldn't drop everything to nurse his mother to health again. And Annalise had a full life too, taking care of the children, volunteering in town.

Helen understood exactly why Frank's wife had kept her secret from him. Frank might blame himself, but no one wanted to be treated like an invalid. No one wanted pity.

No, she definitely wouldn't tell Frank. Not after last night.

Not after that kiss.

Her hand nearly went to her lips when she remembered his touch, brief and whisper sweet. She still had a difficult time believing it.

Life doesn't have to be perfect to be happy. And sometimes you have to find those happy places in between the pain. Her own words echoed back to her.

Last night had been a happy place.

She intended to stay there as long as possible. Selfish, perhaps, but she couldn't bear to have her family drop their lives for her, knowing that this time, well . . . . "And no chemotherapy. I'll take a vacation to Italy, enjoy my days."

Her own words made her chuckle. Italy. Right. But Frank's questions had stirred a curiosity inside her. Why didn't she travel, see the world? Now might be her only chance.

Funny how since he'd smiled her direction, second chances seemed at her fingertips.

"Let's not get ahead of ourselves here, Helen. Let's get some blood, run some tests, and we'll go from there." Paula stood, tucked the chart under her arm, and touched Helen on the shoulder. "In the meantime, take it easy and see if you feel better. I promise to call you when we get the results."

She left, but Helen didn't have to wait for the results to know. The bruise on her arm had faded, but she had another on her hip where she'd banged into the counter yesterday and a third on her forearm, although she had no idea how she'd gotten that.

No more nosebleeds, but today she'd lain in her bed like a sack of potatoes, looking at the ceiling, wondering how she'd aged a year overnight. Her bones became rocks, her muscles like noodles.

If she wasn't ill again, she would sign up for Pilates or something after the New Year. Or look for a vacation home in Florida. Something on the beach. She'd use her savings and live large. Go deep-sea fishing, catch a shark.

A knock came at the door and a nurse entered. How well Helen remembered the days when she'd been the one drawing blood, taking temperatures and blood pressures. She'd finally transferred to the hospital, working in maternity, then the ER.

She liked being needed, helping others through traumatic moments. Retirement had left her with long, empty days, and without Annalise and the children, she might have lost herself.

But perhaps even they didn't need her as much anymore.

"Helen Decker?" the nurse asked. She wore pink scrubs and had her long brown hair pulled back into a messy ponytail.

When Helen was her age, they wore white uniforms *and* a cap. "Yes."

The nurse rattled off Helen's birth date and Social Security number, which Helen confirmed. "I'm just going to take some blood," she said as she pulled out the phlebotomy kit.

Helen watched her movements, trying not to be critical.

She found the vein in one stick.

"Good job," Helen said as the nurse removed the tourniquet.

"Thank you." The nurse filled the tube and labeled it. "You're done." She covered the wound with a cotton ball and a Band-Aid. "Have a nice day, Mrs. Decker."

Mrs. Decker. She'd opted to keep her name, believing it easier for Nathan. But perhaps she didn't want to be Helen Decker anymore. What if she went back to her maiden name, Helen Gilbertson? Or even . . .

Helen Harrison.

She might indeed be a little ill . . . in the head. Still, she glanced at herself in the mirror and smiled.

Helen changed out of the gown, back into her clothing, then waved to the staff as she exited. Outside, her dress shoes sloshed through puddles, and the air smelled soggy. The sky betrayed nothing of the sun.

Soon, however, the wind would turn crisp, and maybe even before Halloween, flakes might drift from the sky. She loved the change in seasons, the anticipation of sparkling light on new-fallen snow, the harbor iced over for skaters, Christmas wreaths decking the old-fashioned lamps along Main Street. And then, just when she tired of winter, spring arrived with the buds on the mountain ash, the freshness of the pine trees sporting their new growth.

Yes, she liked change. So what had held her back from embracing it outside Deep Haven?

Helen turned up her collar. Watched her steps. She could imagine the spectacle of falling in the parking lot, adding another bruise to her collection.

She made it to her car, climbed in, and turned on the heat, tucking her hands in her pockets to warm them up.

What if she did have cancer? Would she really keep it to herself?

More importantly, what if she *didn't* have cancer?

She remembered Miriam's words: *A man couldn't get close to you if he tried.*

Not true. Okay, maybe a little true. But she'd let Frank close last night and it wasn't terrible. Far, actually, from terrible.

Maybe she had been punishing herself for thirty years.

Whether she had cancer or not, it was time to live.

She put the car in reverse, pulled out, then drove across town to the grocery store, passing the lake, white-peaked and restless today. She needed milk, eggs, flour, and she had noticed a special on pork roasts in the paper. What if she tried one of those fancy resort recipes in the cookbook Miriam had given her for Christmas a few years ago? Maybe that roast pork with the lingonberry glaze. She could mash golden potatoes, bake homemade orange rolls. She would invite her family—and Frank, of course—for a nice dinner tonight. Pull out her unused china, the fancy cross-stitched tablecloth her aunt Audrey had given her for her wedding.

Yes, she'd start living large. First in Deep Haven and then the world.

After dinner, she could sign on to the Internet—Nathan could show her how—and look for vacation places in Florida. Or even Italy.

Maybe Frank would want to go with her.

Her thoughts stopped right there. She just might be rushing things a little with Frank.

But he *had* kissed her.

She could start living large in love too.

Helen felt a smile through her entire body as she floated through the grocery store, picking up the pork roast, the can of lingonberries, and enough potatoes to feed an army. She lifted the bag off the bottom shelf. Oh, how had she gotten so weak?

Maybe she shouldn't wait until the New Year to join a Pilates class or one of those kettlebell classes she kept reading about in the Deep Haven paper.

She loaded the groceries onto the checkout belt, swiped her card, and watched as the bagger packed them in a couple plastic bags.

"I can carry those," she said and lifted them, one in each hand.

Black spun before her eyes and she wobbled back, banging her hip against the counter.

"Are you sure?" the bag boy said.

Helen blinked away the blackness. "Yes, of course. I don't need any help."

She gritted her jaw as she walked out and piled the bags into the backseat of the car.

Thanks, but she could take care of herself, and she wasn't going to let anything get in the way of her second chance.

❧

If she could talk some sense into her daughter, maybe Annalise could stop panicking, think clearly.

Maybe she could talk herself into doing what was right.

She had to leave. She had to let her family keep their lives while making sure they stayed safe.

As soon as Annalise uttered the words to Frank, they'd clung to her, rooted, taken on life. She could leave, hide, and when—okay, *if*—Frank caught Garcia, she'd return.

Maybe they'd never forgive her. But they'd be alive. And they'd have their lives intact.

That had to be better than running.

Anything had to be better than holding on to lies.

Please, let Colleen see that and confide in her. See that her mother just wanted the best for her. Take with her some nugget of truth to guide her.

Tucker wasn't some sort of Romeo, haunting her window to win her heart. He'd take it, use it, and tear it to pieces. Nothing of romance in that picture at all. The fact that he'd snuck into her room should shout it in stereo to Colleen.

She prayed that Colleen would hear her, believe her, decide to wait.

Wait for someone like Nathan.

Annalise closed her eyes, the memory of his embrace enfolding her. Last night he'd made her feel safe and comforted, and he'd reminded her that he was exactly the man she expected him to be. And because she knew how fragile life had become, she nudged away her doubts and just loved him back.

So he wasn't wild and reckless. So he'd never turned her to fire inside with some romantic passion.

He kissed her tears.

Told her she was beautiful.

I promise I'll be a better man for you.

It broke her heart to think that he believed he wasn't.

If anyone could take care of their family after she left, Nathan could. That part gave her peace.

She'd met him for lunch today—and tried to ignore Frank

sitting outside in the parking lot, watching her like a dog. After she left, she wanted Nathan to believe that it hadn't been his fault. That he'd done everything right. So she'd glad-handed his eager constituents and eaten a dry salad and kissed him good-bye, smiling.

Aching inside.

Then she'd gone home and spent too much time packing a bag with some of her memories. Nothing that would reveal too much of her life, but things like the diamond necklace Nathan had given her on their twentieth anniversary.

And Colleen's old blanket—she wouldn't miss that. It had been balled in the back of her closet for at least a year. But it still smelled like her.

A poem Jason wrote in fourth grade listing his favorite things, *Mommy* written right below *Christmas*.

Henry's favorite book, the one she read over and over—*Corduroy*, the bear without a home.

She'd packed it all up and shoved the bag in the garage for that moment when she would tell Frank she was ready. She'd have to wait until she left for her makeup, her shoes and clothes, if she didn't want Nathan to suspect something. But she could replace all that if she had to. She couldn't replace her memories.

Once the bag was stowed, she'd gone to the school and parked there. Watched the kids stream out. Now the other volleyball players had begun to emerge, their athletic bags swinging over their shoulders.

Annalise pressed against the swill in her stomach. She'd been dreading this all day, remembering too well a similar conversation playing out so many years ago with her own mother.

Annalise had run away that night and given her life over to a nightmare.

Colleen appeared through the double doors. Annalise found a smile for her as she climbed into the SUV. "Hey, sweetie. How was practice? I'll bet you're tired." Oh, too bright, too happy.

Colleen shot her a look, wariness in it. "I'm okay." She swung her backpack into the seat behind her.

"Did you eat your snack before volleyball? I packed an extra apple in your lunch." Now she was just trying too hard.

Colleen leaned back, closed her eyes. "I'm fine, Mom."

Any second now, Colleen would pull out her iPod and tune her mother out. Annalise put the car in drive and pulled away from the curb, searching for the right words. "I thought we could grab a cup of coffee and talk."

Beside her, Colleen tensed, and Annalise could nearly read her daughter's thought: *Coffee in public, where no one can make a scene.*

"Whatever you want to say, say it here. Besides, Coach doesn't want us to have any coffee this week."

Annalise suspected a lie there but didn't go after it. She took a calming breath as she drove toward the library. They'd wait for Henry's reading group to get out. Colleen was right. No need to unravel their family business in front of the town. Again.

She pulled into a parking space and took another long breath. If God was listening at all to her, she could sure use some wisdom. "I want to trust you, Colleen. What am I supposed to think when I find Tucker in your room at 2 a.m.?"

Colleen bolted upright. "See, you're always so judgy! We weren't doing anything. *Nothing.*"

Yep, that had been building for at least a day, hadn't it?

Annalise tried to keep her voice quiet. But she couldn't help it. "Of *course.* I should have noticed the Scrabble board out. And I suppose he was looking for a fallen piece under the bed?"

"Funny, Mom. He came to talk. Just *talk*."

"Talk about what?"

"Well, if you must know . . . he wanted to go to church with us." Colleen raised her eyebrow, a dare.

Oh, please. "So you were just doing a little evangelism there, huh?"

Colleen ground her jaw. "It's the truth whether you want to believe it or not. Tuck is a nice guy and he only wants you guys to like him."

"We'd like him a lot better if he stayed out of your room in the dead of night, Colleen. We could start with that." See, she hadn't raised her voice, not a bit.

Colleen crossed her arms over her chest, looked away, toward the sunset. It shimmered through the trees, casting long shadows across the streets.

Annalise softened her voice. "I just don't seem to know you lately. You have such a bright future ahead of you. A possible volleyball scholarship—schools already courting you. Why would you choose someone like Tucker Newman?"

"Mom, you act like I'm going to run away with him. We're just *dating*."

"That's where it starts, Colleen. You pick the wrong boy and he can derail your entire life."

Colleen stared at her, shaking her head. "You are completely overreacting."

"He was in your *room*!" Whoops, there went her control, all the emotions of the last week boiling over. "And what would have happened if I hadn't walked in, Colleen? Is this how you want your life to end up? Marrying someone like Tucker Newman? Living in squalor with a boy who can't possibly provide for you? I'll be sure to add you to the turkey dinner list at church."

Colleen's mouth opened. "That's amazingly unkind. Wow."

But Annalise only heard the roaring in her ears. "I'm just trying to plan ahead here. How many kids will you fit into the trailer, or do you want to live in the basement? And do you want to get married first, or should we go ahead and use your wedding fund for a trip to Jamaica? Or an Alaskan cruise? Your father's always wanted to see a killer whale."

"Nice, Mom." Colleen's eyes reddened.

Annalise wasn't handling this at all like she'd hoped. But she couldn't seem to stop the overflow of words, flashing back suddenly to her past and her mother's desperation.

Yes, she now forgave her mother for every nuance of that altercation. Another apology she'd give her when—no, *if* she ever saw her again.

"I just want to make sure that I'm keeping up with you, Colleen. Because a year ago, you wanted to be on the Olympic volleyball team. And was it six months ago that you thought you'd study for a term in New Zealand? You're right—Tuck is a *much* better choice. He does have great hair. Maybe you and he could share hair accessories."

"I love him," Colleen snarled.

That stopped Annalise. And made her stare at her daughter, so much dread in her heart that she could barely speak. "No. No, you *don't*. You haven't a *clue* what it means to love someone. To commit to him for better or worse. To stand by him, to believe in him, to care more about him than you do yourself. *That's. Love.*"

Colleen lifted a shoulder in an I-don't-care-what-you-say shrug. "I love him."

Annalise wanted to wrap her hands around her daughter's shoulders and shake her until she came to her senses. She managed not to yell, but disgust layered her voice as she leveled it at Colleen with as much deadly accuracy as she could muster in the hope that her daughter might be stunned into hearing her. "Your kind of love will force you to make the stupidest decisions of your life. Letting a boy in your room in the middle of the night is just the beginning."

"You have him all wrong," Colleen snapped, her blue eyes flashing. "Tuck's awesome. You don't know him. You don't even care about him."

"You're absolutely right: I don't care about him. I care about *you*. I promise you—boys like Tuck only lead to trouble."

"You are so judgmental! What do you know about boys like Tuck? You've taken one look at him and decided he was a loser. That's real Christian, Mom."

Annalise let everything she knew emerge in her calm, almost-distant tone of regret. A tone that she should have used ages ago. "I know plenty about boys like Tuck. And I know they want one thing, Colleen. Lucky him, you nearly gave it to him on Saturday night."

Colleen stared at her, mouth open. "Seriously? That's what you think of me?"

"I think you're my daughter, Colleen. And unfortunately, I know exactly what you were thinking on Saturday night when you allowed Tucker into your room."

Colleen's eyes filled and she shook her head as if angry that she might be crying. "Because you, in your perfectly pure life, know what it's like to want the cutest boy in school to notice you? You have even a clue what it feels like to have pressure from everywhere—grades, the state championship tournament, your own family expecting you to be some kind of princess so your dad can get elected for mayor?"

"Really, Colleen, that's what this is about? Your father's mayoral candidacy?"

Colleen just looked at her.

"You must think I'm an idiot. You haven't thought one second about your father in this or you wouldn't be fooling around with Tucker, knowing your father would lose his mind if he knew what was going on."

"I—"

"And we don't expect you to be a princess, to shoulder it all— but we do expect you to behave like we've taught you."

"A nice little girl."

"A smart young woman. The kind who thinks before she opens her room to a teenage boy who is only looking to sleep with her."

"Mom!"

Annalise raised an eyebrow.

Colleen's face reddened—whether from anger or embarrassment, Annalise didn't know. "I'm so sick of you dictating to me how I should live my life. You're so perfect, so . . . small town. Did you ever think that I don't want to live your life? I want something better, bigger. I want to live life, to taste it, to be a part of it. Most of all, I don't want to be *you*."

Oh. For all her angry defenses, Colleen found soft soil with her accusation.

How had Annalise let it come to this? This was not the conversation she was supposed to have with her daughter. Especially not—oh, please, no—the *last* conversation. She wanted to take every sticky, sarcastic word that hung in the car and shove it back inside. She desperately longed to believe everything her beautiful daughter had said, to believe that indeed, she'd just made a mistake. That she and Tucker *had* been talking about church.

Right. Fear pushed out Annalise's words in a soft, almost-horrified whisper. "Too bad, Colleen. You might not want to be me, but I'm afraid you already are."

Colleen's eyes widened. And then she shook her head, opened the door, got out, and slammed it with everything in her before stalking away into the dusky night.

&

On days like this, Nathan just wanted to hold his breath, never let the feeling go.

Like the sunrise as he'd run this morning, a golden streak of hope and peace on the dark horizon, spilling across the indigo lake, the breeze crisp and startling. He'd worked up a healthy sweat, running with power for all five miles, feeling like he was eighteen again, his entire life ahead of him.

He returned home invigorated and found his wife in the kitchen making breakfast, a smile tipping her lips, no hint of the desperation in the darkness from the night before.

Perhaps he'd made everything better.

Then, as he'd driven to work, the Deep Haven morning show played an analysis of the Friday morning political chat and decided that Nathan had a shot at beating Brewster.

So he could hardly believe it when, speak of the devil, Seb left a message on his business voice mail requesting a viewing of the McIntyre property.

Add that to the three online requests for showings and he just might get the place sold. His bills paid. Might actually land the mayoral position.

And then his name might vanish from Deep Haven lore, or at least he'd shine it up a bit. Give his children a reason to be proud. Give his wife justification for her belief in him.

He'd even called Lise to join him for lunch today, and they'd eaten at the Blue Loon Café—well, he'd intended to eat. But so many people congratulated him on his daughter's championship run, Jason's new role, and even his platform as mayor—lower taxes, an increase in a concentration of tourism—that he'd had to send his soup back for reheating. Even then, the wild rice soup turned out to be mushy and cold by the time he wolfed it down.

And so much for talking to Annalise. But she'd kissed him sweetly, as if she hadn't minded, and offered to make him pork chops for supper.

God had surely given him a good wife.

And now, prosperity and even honor.

Yes, he just wanted to stand on the edge of the McIntyre property, watching the sun trace a Midas finger along the darkness of the water, and soak it in.

"So how long has this thing been empty?" Seb Brewster said as he joined Nathan along the edge.

Nathan turned his back to the scenery and folded his arms against the brisk chill seeping into his wool coat. He probably should have changed out of his dress shoes—after all, Seb appeared ready for a tromp through the woods in a pair of hiking boots and an orange hunting jacket, a Huskies baseball hat.

Then again, Seb always dressed as if he might charge into battle any moment. And why not? The guy sported his football build, even ten years after the state play-offs, and still had the aura of champion about him, even if he looked a little older, more responsible. Nathan well remembered watching him from the stands, cheering for the team, if not for Seb. Back then, he remembered an arrogant young man owning his fame as if he might deserve it as he glad-handed fans around Deep Haven. Apparently no one cared that Seb's father was a drunk and that Nathan had helped scoop him off the street a few times after finding the man curled in the alleyway between his real estate building and the old fire department.

But Nathan wasn't going to let Seb intimidate him with his hometown charm. Seb hadn't worked for twenty years in this community trying to earn their trust.

Except perhaps that was the problem. Seb already had it from the beginning.

"I think she's had the place for about twenty years. Nelda couldn't bring herself to part with it, although she never could figure out how to create something from it. She was stuck."

Seb stared out over the lake. "I understand that. Not sure how to get out of a rut." He adjusted his cap. "That's why I came back to Deep Haven. To break free of the man I was becoming. To find a fresh start." He glanced at Nathan. "I have a lot of catching up to do in this election."

Seb, catch up with Nathan? "Seb, if I remember correctly, you were the grand marshal in this year's Fisherman's Picnic parade. The town is ecstatic to have you back." He resisted the urge to suggest that Seb might beat him handily—no need to be overly magnanimous.

But Nathan wasn't stupid. Seb even looked the north woods mayoral part, a flannel shirt under that jacket, his hair just a little long and woolly under his cap.

"Aw, they liked me when I could throw a touchdown pass. But that was then." Seb smiled. "A man has to prove who he is every day, not rely on his past to build it for him."

Nathan was starting to get the feeling that Seb had dragged him out here for more than a tour of the old, unfinished shell on the hill. Thanks, but he didn't want to talk about the election. Or make Seb feel better in case he stole it from Nathan.

Which he wouldn't.

"I hope you can see the potential of this place." Nathan gestured toward the house, turning Seb from the view. "Put the living room here, with giant windows in an open floor plan. Over here is the kitchen." He walked across the cement patio. "And what about here for a master bedroom? Wake up every morning to the sunrise over the lake?" He smiled, hoping Seb could see it.

But the man was looking at Nathan, his green eyes considering him. "You really are a visionary, aren't you?"

He wasn't sure—

"I admit, Nathan, that I came out here wondering who I was running against. But I suddenly feel like buying a house." Seb walked past him. "Yeah, we could put our bed here, and on the other side of the house, two more bedrooms."

"For kids?"

"Maybe one for my dad. The trailer is getting old. And he could use someone to watch over him. He's in better health since he stopped drinking, but all those years wasted him away."

"I'm sorry to hear that."

Seb walked to the rough-in for the expansive bathroom, the walk-in closet. "He just kept trying to outrun his demons. Until he finally figured out that he'd already been forgiven and there was nothing to run from anymore." He turned in the space. "I think I could fit a sauna in here."

Nothing to run from anymore. Or maybe it was a matter of not running. Standing firm.

"Absolutely. And a hot tub." Nathan walked into the room, mapping it out for Seb. Joked about wives needing two or three times the closet space.

They worked out a plan for the kitchen, then talked about the easements on the property along the shoreline for water and gas lines and electricity.

"It's a lot of work, but it could really be a magnificent place when it's finished," Nathan said.

Seb nodded. "Anything worth doing well takes work. Coach Presley used to tell us that. If we wanted something of value, like a state championship, we had to be willing to fight for it."

Of course everything came back to football. Football players thought they owned the corner on toughness, on courage. But just because Nathan had never really played didn't mean he didn't know how to fight for what he wanted. He'd been doing that his entire life, hadn't he?

Besides, try running a marathon and say it's not about courage.

Nathan resisted the urge to roll his eyes and instead managed a smile. "Let me know when you're ready to make an offer."

Seb shook his hand, held it a little longer than Nathan expected. "Thanks for showing me the house, Nathan. You have an eye for a treasure. I'll have to sit down with Lucy and see if she's willing to go on this ride with me. I'd love to roll up my sleeves and see what we can build together."

Nathan recognized the spark of a newlywed in his expression. Oh, to be young and starting out with Annalise again. "If you need help crunching the numbers, give me a shout. I'll be glad to work through an offer with you," he said as they walked to their cars.

Seb turned to him, holding open his door, and gave a slow

smile, the kind that probably won him his team's trust—and the voters'. "I'd rather not lose to you, but if I do, I know the town will be in good hands."

Nathan had no words for that as he climbed into his car, followed Seb's to the highway.

He could be in big trouble against Seb Brewster and the way he disarmed his opponents.

Nathan called his office on the way back to town, pulling over when he hit the zone for a cell signal. Along this stretch of highway, the service spotted in and out. Today, with a clear sky, it worked.

Only then did he notice he was at the corner of Cutaway Creek. He'd been so engrossed in thought, he'd taken the curve without hearing the voices. Without seeing, in his mind, his father swerving too hard, slamming into Moe Jorgenson's Subaru.

Then vaulting over the guardrail into the river.

He couldn't remember the last time he'd stopped, let the curve lure him to the edge to examine, to imagine the tragedy. He debated a moment, then got out.

A crisp wind rushed into his ears, tugged at his tie, wrapped it around his neck.

The Cutaway Creek gorge ran from some northern lake right down into Lake Superior, a tumble of jagged boulders cutting through the landscape to form more of a frothy river than a creek. In the springtime, the runoff could nearly reach the bridge with its force.

Tourists stood with their cameras, tracing every jagged edge, every turn of the water.

Nathan knew it by heart.

He too had spent hours here, angry that his fear held him captive. Because of Cutaway Creek, he'd become too terrified to swim.

Because of Cutaway Creek, he woke—sometimes even now—with nightmares of drowning, grit in his throat, the icy grip stealing his breath.

Just the thought of water rushing over his head could paralyze him. Turn him into that twelve-year-old kid who refused to get in the pool during gym class. The one who hid in the locker room like a coward until his mother managed to get him excused from class.

Even now, as he ventured to the edge, the roar of the water in his ears wrapped a fist around his heart. He willed away the slick rush of fear and checked his voice mail.

No messages. Turning his back to the river, he called Annalise at home, but the phone went to the machine, and she didn't pick up her cell.

He watched the creek, this time from the north, where it dropped from a waterfall and into the gorge.

Maybe he came here just to confirm that he wasn't his father. That he'd never, ever give up on the people he loved.

He got into his sedan and pulled away. Maybe he'd sneak up to the school and watch Jason's rehearsal.

Or perhaps he should stop by and have a heart-to-heart with his mother before Frank could wheedle his way further into her life. Nathan swallowed back the acid in his throat. He didn't know why the thought of Frank courting his mother set his insides to roil, but he had to get a handle on the fact that his mother did seem to enjoy the man's company.

Didn't she deserve to fall in love? To be happy? She'd sacrificed so much raising him. What if she did fall in love? Would Nathan pick someone different from Frank?

As he entered town and turned toward the school, he waved to Joann Hauck on the sidewalk, walking her little terrier, the dog dressed for winter in a pink sweater. She waved back, thumbs-upping him.

Looked like he could count on her vote.

There was something about Frank he didn't trust, especially after the conversation with Annalise he'd overheard. But maybe he read too much into what was said. Annalise hadn't mentioned it, hadn't acted remote or in the least like she might be really leaving him. Maybe she'd just been reacting to some request for her to travel with Frank, maybe to some family gathering. If Frank moved to town, perhaps it would fill the loneliness, the grief that always lurked inside his wife.

Instead of fighting the man, perhaps Nathan should make efforts to get to know him. To embrace him. To give him a chance to prove himself like Seb had suggested.

Nathan glanced through the school parking lot as he got out, searching for Annalise's SUV. Not here, which meant that she was probably picking up Henry, maybe even at home, cooking. Jason often caught a lift home from rehearsal when he was involved in a show—he would probably appreciate the ride.

Nathan opened the door to the theater. He heard voices coming from down the hallway, along the back entrance.

Lines from *Romeo and Juliet*. Even he recognized them.

> "O Romeo, Romeo! wherefore art thou Romeo?
> Deny thy father and refuse thy name;
> Or, if thou wilt not, be but sworn my love,
> And I'll no longer be a Capulet."

He remembered reading the play in English class so many years ago in this very school. And this voice was sweet and light, as if she meant it. Give up her name, her identity, for the man she loved. It's what women did all the time.

He heard the shifting of pages, then:

"Call me but love, and I'll be new baptized;
Henceforth I never will be Romeo—"

"No, Jason, you skipped my favorite part—'What's in a name? That which we call a rose by any other name would smell as sweet . . .'"

Nathan slowed his step, listening as his son's voice dropped. He had heard Jason rehearse before but never with such depth. Perhaps he was made for this part.

"'By a name I know not how to tell thee who I am: My name, dear saint, is hateful to myself, because it is an enemy to thee.'"

"Jason—"

"Say the line."

"Fine—'Art thou not Romeo and a Montague?'"

"'Neither, fair saint, if either thee dislike.'"

The girl giggled just as Nathan turned down the hall.

"You're not supposed to kiss me yet!"

"I'm improvising."

Indeed. Nathan stopped at the sight of his son, one hand braced against the wall, the other holding his open script, leaning down to kiss Harper Jacobsen. He didn't know what to do. Clear his throat? Turn away? Stand there frozen in the hallway?

But wow, he remembered exactly the moment he'd first kissed Annalise. A quick, stolen moment as he'd dropped her off at her house. She was so jumpy—he walked her to the door and she dropped her keys on the porch. He'd bent to get them and found her crouched beside him.

He wasn't sure why he'd done it—he'd just looked up at her and it felt right to lean forward, to kiss her, to taste the vanilla ice cream on her still-cold lips. She'd stiffened at first and then smiled into his eyes. And the truth was he couldn't be sure, but he thought she'd wiped away a tear.

Then she'd stood and kissed him on the cheek. "Thank you," she said. As if he'd done her a favor.

But really, she'd been the one to bless him. For twenty years they'd lived a calm, safe life. No drama, no Romeo and Juliet tragedy, no theatrics.

Just blessed.

Nathan cleared his throat.

Jason jumped away from Harper as if she were hot to the touch.

Nathan smiled. "Sorry to interrupt. Is rehearsal over yet?"

His son stared at him like he wanted to choke him. Either that or run in horror.

Harper had turned red.

"I'll wait in the car. Unless you'd like to go ahead and drink poison first and put yourself out of your misery?"

"I'll be right there, Dad," Jason said, his jaw tight.

Nathan swung his keys around his finger as he slid into the car, laughing. Yes, he should be grateful he'd escaped the teenage angst of falling in love. When he'd fallen, it had been for real, with the woman of his dreams. His soul mate.

Jason climbed into the car a few minutes later. Didn't look at his father.

Nathan hid a smirk. "So do you like her?" he asked as he backed out of the parking lot.

His son lifted a shoulder.

"Jason, if you kiss a girl, you should mean it."

"I mean it."

Maybe Nathan should have a talk with him later about what it meant to love someone. How it meant respect and belief and loyalty.

Nathan pulled into the garage, hoping to smell pork chops as he walked into the house.

Instead a pall of darkness hung over the lonely kitchen. No frying pan on the stove, no wife chopping salad. No Henry at the kitchen table, wrestling with homework.

"Annalise?"

Nathan set his briefcase on the floor and heard the television downstairs. He went halfway down. Henry sat curled on the sofa, remote in hand.

"Where's your mother?"

"I don't know. She told me to watch television."

Annalise told their son to watch television? Was she running a high fever? He climbed back upstairs, stood in the family room, then wandered down the hall to their room.

The light was off, the shades drawn. He wouldn't have noticed her but for the sobs erupting from the space between the dresser and the closet.

"Annalise?" When he flicked on the light, it washed over her—disheveled, red-faced, her legs caught to her chest. "What's going on?"

She shook her head, then covered it with her arms as if she wanted to curl into a ball.

He crouched before her, put his hand on her arm. What in the world? "I don't understand. Did something happen? Is it . . . Uncle Frank? Mom?" His chest tightened on the question.

"No." Her voice emerged small and shattered. "It's . . . Everything's wrecked, Nathan. Everything." The look she gave him unraveled him from the inside out.

"I can't pretend anymore. It's over." Annalise swallowed hard and, with it, took out his heart. "It's all over."

12

LIKE A MAN WITH AN ADDICTION, Frank found himself on Helen's doorstep, drawn to the light glowing inside as if it were calling him home.

Home. He had the strangest sense of it as she opened the door and smiled at him, her expression so welcoming he might belong here in her kitchen. He sat propped on a stool, eating the last piece of pie, while she drained the potatoes to mash them. The entire house smelled tangy, of something sweet and yet hearty baking, and fresh bread on the counter could make his eyes roll back into his head.

If his partner saw him now, he'd turn Frank in for counseling. Rehab.

Except, well, he'd already overstayed his welcome in WitSec, and they'd been nudging him toward retirement for years now.

He could retire here. In Deep Haven or—

Frank nearly choked on his milk.

"Are you okay?" Helen wore blue oven mitts and a matching apron over jeans and a pretty lime-green blouse that did dangerous things to her eyes. Especially since they lit up, a sort of twinkle in them, when he smiled at her.

He couldn't remember the last time he'd been the reason for a woman's smile.

"Uh-huh," he managed, sounding brilliant. "This pie is so good I nearly inhaled it."

She set the pot back on the stove before dumping the potatoes from the colander into it. "So, what did you do today?" she asked as she added milk and butter to the potatoes. It felt like old times in the kitchen with Margaret. Comfortable. Right.

"Not much." In fact, in addition to following Annalise around all day, he'd spent a good portion of time on the phone working on a new placement for her in eastern Tennessee. He'd found a town there once that felt much like this one, quaint and slower. Kind.

Annalise could become Carrie Ann Fuller, and if the rest of the family decided to follow, then they'd be Justin, Rosie, and Harlan. Nathan could be Nick or perhaps Thad. He liked that name; it meant "praise." Something Frank would do if he could keep this family safe.

And Helen. Oh, Helen. He couldn't think of a better name than Helen. "I have a feeling you spent most of the day cooking."

She glanced over her shoulder. "Make a grab for one of those rolls and you'll pull back a nub." She winked at him, returned to the potatoes, began to mash.

"Let me do that for you." He slid off the stool and came around behind her to take the masher from her hand.

"Thank you." When she stepped back, he wanted to kick himself for letting her get away so quickly.

He wanted to kiss her again. Couldn't stop thinking about it, in fact—the way she'd felt in his arms, made him feel invincible. Young. Full of hope.

Maybe he could live in Tennessee. Helen Harrison . . . that wasn't a terrible alibi.

Or maybe Boyd would catch Garcia and no one would have to leave.

"I think we need more milk," Frank said as he put some muscle into the mashing. "And pepper."

She stepped close and dropped in another pat of butter, shook in salt and pepper. He could smell her perfume, light and intoxicating, rising up around him.

He'd given a good amount of thought to Annalise's suggestion that she simply disappear by herself. Maybe take the entire family on an extended vacation, under protection, until they caught Garcia. How long could that really take?

Years. Garcia was smooth, had contacts and an underground network. He could give them the slip for longer than they could afford to disappear.

No, either Frank moved all of them permanently or he faked Annalise's death. Again.

"That looks about pulverized now, Frank."

He looked down and indeed, the potatoes were milky; not a chunk remained. "Sorry."

"I love them this way." Helen put the top on the pot. "Would you mind pulling the roast out of the oven for me? It gets heavy with all that juice." She handed him her oven mitts.

He had no doubt she had the strength to fetch the roast, but he liked puttering around her kitchen. Puttering around her life, really.

Setting the roasting pan on the counter, he lifted the lid. Inside simmered a trussed-up pork roast, a red glaze over the top.

"Those are lingonberries," Helen said, pushing a thermometer into the roast. "Perfect. Put the cover back on and I'll set the table before everyone gets here."

"The family is coming for dinner?" It took him a while to catch on, but as she pulled out china from the hutch against the wall, he went to help.

"It's been so long since we've eaten together—at least anything but popcorn at Colleen's games. I thought it might be nice to have a real dinner. I left a message on Annalise's cell phone today. I hope she didn't cook anything." She stood at the far end of the table. "Would you help me put the leaf in?"

He joined her, grabbing the other end of the table and giving it a tug. A little too hard. Helen lost her balance and nearly fell onto the chair behind her.

"Are you okay?"

She laughed, but it came out shaky as if the jolt had rattled her. "I'm fine. You're just stronger than most of my other guests."

Frank had the weird urge to become sixteen again and flex or something. Instead he lifted the dressy plates from the hutch and onto the table. He set them around while she went behind him, laying silverware and cloth napkins.

It felt very married couple. Very partnership. Very much like they could spend the rest of their lives setting the table, mashing potatoes, and laughing together.

He'd never met a woman who made him feel more like the man he wanted to be than Helen. At least since Margaret, and after a while, even she had stopped believing in him and simply given up.

Except . . . what if he did that to Helen? What if someday, after

216

being with him, the light went out of her smile, and nothing but a disappointed tweak of her mouth greeted him when he walked in the door?

Hello—he needed an intervention because that would happen the moment she discovered he wasn't Annalise's uncle Frank and was instead . . .

A liar. Pretender.

Playing games with her.

"Frank, are you okay?"

He looked up as she passed him a couple long taper candles and found a smile for her. "I'm fine. Where do these go?"

She handed him a pair of acorn-shaped holders. The phone rang as he wiggled the candles into place. He heard her answer.

"Oh . . . yes, uh . . . thank you for calling."

The hitch in her voice made him look up. She met his eyes, and for a second he thought he read panic there. As if to confirm it, she turned her back to him.

"Mmm-hmm." Helen's hand shook as she picked up a wooden spoon and stirred a pot of simmering lingonberry sauce on the stove. "Right. Okay then. . . . Yes. I'll be in tomorrow, first thing. Thank you."

She hung up and set the phone on the counter. Didn't turn around.

"Helen?" Frank didn't like the clench of his gut, the feeling in the room. "Is everything okay?"

She nodded but still didn't turn. He walked over to her as she picked up a towel from the counter and ran it across her eyes.

He didn't know her that well, but he could recognize a lie when she said, "I'm fine. I'm just going to run across the street and get the kids. I'll be right back."

Then, just like all women could, she left him undone when she rose to her tiptoes and kissed him. Quick and sweet, a brush of hope—or perhaps desperation—against his lips.

He wanted to hold her there, to capture the moment, fading too fast. But she slipped away from him, grabbed her jacket and boots, and was out the door.

Frank watched her disappear across the lawn, then picked up her phone and scrolled through the incoming calls.

The number came with a name. He stared at it, the fist in his chest tightening.

Deep Haven Medical Clinic.

So he wasn't the only one with something to hide.

❧

Annalise stared at Nathan, unable to speak. She wanted to reach out and run her hands through his hair, pull herself into his arms, and just hold on, breathing in his smell.

How she'd miss his smell—the cologne he wore, mixed with the outdoorsy scent from so much time tromping around north shore properties. And the feel of his arms around her. How would she live without that?

She simply couldn't bring herself to dismantle her world with her own hands, her own words.

She thought she'd erased all hint of Deidre, and yet, like a ghost from the past, her daughter had become the girl Annalise had left behind. Rebellious. Angry. Colleen acted like her clone at age sixteen, and Annalise didn't have a clue how to stop it.

She had to leave, but not before she told them the truth. She cupped her hands over her face.

She hadn't meant to let Nathan come home to find her like this—she'd wanted to hold it together at least one more night.

One more night to relish the second chance she'd been given.

"Honey, what's the matter?" Nathan sat on the floor before her and took her hands, running his thumbs over them. "You're scaring me a little."

Nathan had such strong hands. The kind that could toss their children in the air and catch them on the way back down. The kind that could fix the leaky pipes under the sink and change the oil and rub her shoulders after a long day.

His hands made her feel safe.

She couldn't bear to hold them. "I have to tell you something." Annalise paused, listening to her own words to Colleen hammer in her head. *You haven't a clue what it means to love someone. To commit to him for better or worse. To stand by him, to believe in him, to care more about him than you do yourself.* That's. Love.

Nathan didn't deserve this. But . . . but, oh, please, let him love her as he vowed. Please let him understand. She swallowed, pressed her hands together. "I've kept something from you."

"What are you talking about? Are you doing something you shouldn't? Did you overbuy at QVC or something?"

Oh yeah. She wished. Enough fuzzy slippers with the massage soles to last a lifetime. She almost burst out in hysterical laughter except for how horribly wrong he was.

And for the frown on his face. As if he was serious. The poor man had no idea of the magnitude of her deception. And that suddenly made her want to curl into a ball and weep.

She looked away, drew a breath. Closed her eyes.

Dug down for the facts and let them emerge without emotion.

"My name is Deidre O'Reilly. I'm not from Chicago but St. Louis. I moved here because I was—*am*—in the witness protection program."

More silence.

She opened her eyes and found Nathan staring at her like he didn't know her. What else did she expect?

Oh, she couldn't do this.

"I testified against a drug dealer, Luis Garcia, who killed my best friend and who tried to murder me. My boyfriend worked for him, and when his boss found out I was working with the police, he came after me. At the trial Garcia vowed to kill me, even from jail. Frank had no choice but to fake my death and move me." She paused for a breath. "Only my parents know I'm still alive." Only that knowledge, and the hope that her mother still prayed for her, still thought about her, kept her grief safely in pocket. Sometimes she imagined she could even feel the prayers.

Nathan was still staring at her, his beautiful eyes cloudy with confusion.

Yes, Nathan, it's the truth.

Then he swallowed. Cupped his hand to his forehead. In the dim light of the lamp, it seemed he actually paled. "I . . . I don't know what to say." He ran trembling hands down his face.

She had to give him points for staying calm because she wanted to scream.

"Let me get this straight. You are in the witness protection program?"

She nodded.

"And Frank. He is *not* your uncle?"

She shook her head. "He's my relocation agent. I haven't talked to him for years. When I walked into the Java Cup a few days ago and saw him, I couldn't believe it."

"I don't know why that gives me some kind of weird relief. But I guess my next question is, why is he here? And—it doesn't have something to do with why you're hiding, does it?" Nathan winced a little.

She longed to reach out, smooth the frown from between his eyes. Instead, she flicked moisture from her cheeks. "Yeah, well, that's part of the problem. See, the guy I put in jail got out—"

"How? Is he after you?"

"Frank thinks so. Garcia jumped parole and somehow found Blake—"

"Who's Blake?"

"He was . . . he was my boyfriend. The one who was working for Garcia. He was placed somewhere else. Apparently he's been murdered."

Nathan was shaking his head, his eyes wary upon her for the first time. "Can this guy find you, Annalise?"

"Yes. I . . . I wrote to Blake when I first moved here and . . ." She looked at him. "Nathan, I hadn't met you. I was lonely and . . . I thought I loved him."

"You told him where you lived."

She tightened her jaw. Nodded.

Nathan let out a word she'd never heard him use. Turned away from her. "How could you do this?"

"Nathan, I had no choice—I was told to start over. To assume a new identity. I was dead to the world . . ."

He faced her again, wearing an expression she had never seen.

No, wait—she'd seen it yesterday on the porch, when he'd looked like he wanted to dismantle Frank.

It turned her cold and she wanted to shrink away.

Nathan's voice shook. "No, Annalise. How could you not have told *me* sooner? Frank's been here for five days. We're all in danger! We should be gone already."

His words knocked the wind from her, and her voice emerged as a whisper. "I . . . I didn't want to make our children start over. I thought their lives would be destroyed if we left. Jason has the play, and Colleen has her scholarship, and Henry is just starting middle school. It's a terrible time to leave—"

"So we start over! There is someone after you who could *kill* you. Annalise, I can't believe you risked our family like this!" He got to his feet, began to pace, his hands on his hips.

"He doesn't know about you." She said it softly, holding on tight to her arms. "He doesn't know I'm married. That I have children. I . . . I could just leave."

Nathan looked as if she'd slapped him. "You'd just leave me. Us."

Annalise looked away, her eyes filming.

She heard him pull in a long breath. Then, "Yes, I guess you could."

His words sliced through her like a blade.

He was silent for so long that she glanced up at him. He had sunk onto the bed, was frowning at her. "That's why you keep the lights on. And jump when people walk into the room. And don't watch cop shows. It's because of the memories, isn't it?"

She nodded.

He let out a wretched laugh, nothing of humor in it. "Suddenly everything makes sense. Your family didn't die—*you* did. Which is why you don't have any pictures of them and why you never talk about them. You erased them because you erased yourself."

Her throat burned.

"Those people you Facebook stalk? Your family, isn't it?"

She nodded again.

"Your children have grandparents. Aunts and uncles. Cousins."

"I'm sorry, Nathan."

He stilled then, his eyes narrowing, as if assimilating information. "That's why, after only a few dates, you agreed to marry me. Why you acted as if I was saving you or something. Why you became the perfect wife." His voice lowered. "I was your cover. Your hiding place. Part of the pretend world you made for yourself."

"Nathan, I married you because I loved you. *Love* you. And this is my real world—not pretend. There's nothing fake about it." She got to her feet and moved toward him.

He stood, held up his hands, backing away. "Except *everything*. I don't know you at all."

"You know me. You know everything about me." She didn't care that her tone grew desperate.

"Except your name. Your past. Everything that makes you who you are."

"*You* are what makes me who I am. You and Jason and Colleen and Henry."

"I'm so glad we fit into your cover life."

"Nathan, please—"

"Mom!"

She froze as Henry's voice sounded, followed by knocking on the door.

"Grandma's here. She wants us to come over for dinner."

Oh. Yes. The voice mail.

Annalise didn't know what else to do, so she found something of normalcy. "You go over, Henry. We'll be right behind you."

She looked at Nathan. "Right?"

She didn't know him. Not the man who stared back at her—coldness, betrayal, even disgust in his eyes. "Not one word to my mother," he snapped as he wrenched off his tie and headed toward the door.

❧

Sometimes Tuck dreamed of snow. Dreamed of sprawling on the icy blanket, staring at the sky, flakes drifting onto him, covering his face, his body. Encasing him, soft and light, like feathers, until . . .

Until he couldn't breathe. Until his entire body lay entombed, the oxygen waning, the pressure of the snow breaking his ribs, crushing him. Sometimes he even heard voices, shouting like they were searching for him, but when he opened his mouth to yell, nothing emerged but screams.

He woke himself with his own shuddering breaths even as the door banged again. "Tuck!"

Oh, he'd fallen asleep on the sofa, a gold knit afghan over him, the Weather Channel woman still calling for snow tomorrow, flurries of hope upon the ski hill they called a mountain.

"Tuck!"

"I'm coming!" He switched on the light. He hadn't meant to fall asleep—but he hadn't slept well since Saturday night, the image of Mrs. Decker's anger haunting him, and today he'd just wanted to lay out of school. But he'd gone anyway and then worked out after classes, feeling puny as he watched the football players deadlift into the four hundreds. He could barely squat over one hundred.

Still, he worked out because snowboarding was his escape, and this year he planned on winning the Sugar Ridge Free Boarding competition.

He flicked on the outside light as he opened the door. Colleen stood on the step, stamping her feet, her eyes red and puffy.

"Babe, what are you doing here?" He'd tried to track her down today at school, but she wasn't waiting for him in their usual place by the drinking fountain and, well . . . he thought maybe her parents had forbidden her from seeing him or something.

"I hate my mother!" She pushed past him.

He looked out into the street for a car. "Did you walk here?"

He didn't live that far from town, just a couple blocks, but almost a half mile from school and even farther from her house.

She threw her bag onto his dad's old recliner. "Yes. Because I ditched my mom. Because she was . . . she was judging you. She didn't believe you wanted to go to church with me."

"Yeah, well, she's probably pretty steamed after seeing me in your room."

"But we weren't doing anything."

He gave her a look that made her turn a little red. Yeah, they'd been doing enough to scare him. "Have you been crying?" He closed the door, came over to run his thumb across her cheek. "I thought you were going to break up with me."

Colleen smiled through her tears. "No."

He tangled his fingers into her silky hair. She didn't want to break up with him. He couldn't ignore the relief that whisked through his chest even as he tried to hide it. "I was thinking . . . maybe I should go apologize. You know, tell them that I'm not such a bad guy."

"I don't know if that will do any good. My mom seems to think you're just going to get me into trouble."

She was probably right there. Especially the way he was feeling today, his house so lonely, and Colleen looking like she might leap into his arms.

He stepped away from her. "Want a pop?"

He opened the fridge, leaning down so she couldn't see his face. Of course her parents would never like him. He'd never sit with them and eat popcorn in the stands. He grabbed a Dr Pepper and handed it to her.

She considered it. "Got anything stronger?"

He wanted to swipe the can from her. "No. Sheesh, no wonder your parents hate me. What's going on, Colleen? When I met you, you didn't even drink. Now you're buying weed and coming over here . . . I don't get you."

Her eyes went cold. "Forget it."

"I'm not going to forget it. You know what? I would do anything to have my mom here when I got home, fixing dinner. Or my father hassling me about homework. Or my brother—" His voice hitched on the word. "My brother wrestling me for the remote control. But that's not happening, and for a while, yeah, I was mad. So mad that I started hanging around people I thought could make me feel better. They only got me into trouble, and I did stupid things. But I'm not that guy anymore."

"I'm sorry." She started to cry again. "I guess I should go home."

"Good, because that's where you should be." He slammed his hand on the door before she could open it. "But I'm driving you."

"No, you're not." She shoved him and lunged at the door.

He caught her, stepped in front of the door. Folded his arms. "Colleen, what do you want from me? I like you. I think you're pretty, and when I asked you out, I thought it was because you liked me too. I thought I was so lucky having a girl like you in my life. But now I don't get it. I'm trying with everything inside me to help you here and to be a good guy, and you won't let me."

Her eyes had turned glossy. "You're never going to fit in my family, you know. They think you're a loser. My mom wants to kill you—and just wait until my father hears about you in my bedroom!"

The way she said it made him cringe.

"Then why are you here, Colleen? Why do you want me in your life?"

She clenched her jaw. Then she pressed a hand to her mouth, shook her head.

He had no idea how to interpret that. "I'll get my keys. Stay here."

"No—" Colleen caught his arm. "I'm sorry, Tuck. . . . I'm such a mess." She closed her eyes, her shoulders shaking.

He didn't know what to do. So he put his hands on her shoulders and pulled her to himself.

She wrapped her arms around his waist and held on. "I'm sorry. I just . . . I'm scared."

He lifted her chin. Searched her eyes. She had such pretty blue eyes, even when covered with black makeup. "What are you scared of?"

"I don't know. One minute I'm fine, and the next, I'm in a panic about my life. I'm going to blow it; I know I am."

"What are you talking about?"

"My whole life my mother has believed that I was amazing, that I could be just like her. But I can't. I'm not like her. I'm going to let her down."

"You're not going to let her down."

"You don't understand. Sometimes it feels so overwhelming.

I picture all these terrible things happening—dropping a serve, getting a bad grade. What if my life doesn't turn out at all?" She brushed the tears off her cheeks, smearing black across her face. "What if I can't do it?"

He softened his voice. "Do what?"

"I don't know—win sectionals, get a scholarship, go to college, fall in love. Do it right. I want my life to go faster, to be done and happy. I want to know it'll all work out. I just . . . I just want to stop being so afraid all the time."

Tucker whisked another tear from her cheek. Probably he should go to the bathroom, get some toilet paper for that makeup mess.

"And sometimes I get so angry. My parents are perfect. They have no idea what it feels like to be me. They live a charmed life even now, and when they get on my case . . . they don't understand me at all."

She looked up at him. "I really like you, Tuck. I thought you wanted someone more . . . well, a party girl. And I wasn't one, so . . ."

"Colleen. Stop trying so hard." He cupped her face in his hands, lifted her chin. "I already like you."

Tucker kissed her. Softly, like he had the first time because he'd been so amazed that she was with him, he thought she might slap him. But she hadn't. And now, like then, she responded sweetly, with nothing of the ardor of the other night.

It reminded him of the girl he'd fallen for, the one who glanced at him from the volleyball bench, blushing a little because he was in the stands, or followed him around at his snowboarding competitions.

She moved away.

He smiled. "See, that's the Colleen I had a crush on all last year."

"You did?"

He nodded. "I like the real Colleen, not the party Colleen. Maybe you don't have it all figured out, but you don't have to. Maybe you just have to figure it out one day at a time." He kissed her again. "Let me take you home and I can even apologize to your parents, try to get them to like me." He swallowed, forcing out the words. "Make them think I'm not a loser."

Colleen leaned away from him, making a face. "I'm sorry I said that."

Yeah, well, she couldn't help if it was true.

A light layer of snow slicked the road as he drove to her house. He pulled into her driveway, the glow of the outside lights turning the snow orange.

Colleen held his hand across the seat. "I'm scared to go in."

He stared at her house, the darkness. "Are you sure they're home?"

But at that moment, the front light flickered on and Colleen's grandmother walked out of the house. She wore her rubber snow boots and a jacket wrapped around herself, snow dotting her graying hair. She walked right up to the Jeep and knocked on the window.

Tuck braced himself as Colleen rolled down the window.

"Hello, sweetie. I was just reminding your mother about dinner." She glanced at Tuck with kind eyes, and he gave her the best smile he could muster. "Is this your boyfriend?"

He drew in a breath. Colleen's hand tightened in his as she said, "Yes, Grandma. His name is Tucker."

"Glad to meet you, Tucker. Would you like to join us for dinner? I made a pork roast."

Tuck opened his mouth, but nothing emerged.

Colleen glanced at him, smiled, a warmth in her eyes that made his heart flip over. "Yes."

The entire thing felt surreal. One moment he had been debating between microwaved lasagna or Cheerios, and the next he was crossing the threshold into the world of the Deckers.

Colleen's grandma had a clean, tidy home, with a bright-yellow-and-red kitchen, apples stenciled along the ceiling. It smelled tangy and rich, of garlic and sweet jam.

A man stood in the kitchen—not her grandfather because Tucker knew he'd died a long time ago, but still, this man seemed to belong here. He had a presence about him. The way he shook Tuck's hand sent a sliver of cold through him. "Frank Harrison," he said.

"Tucker. I'm a friend of Colleen's."

"He's her boyfriend," Colleen's grandma said and winked at Frank, real friendly.

Weird. Did old people date? Tuck didn't want to think about it.

He heard noise at the door as Henry and Jason, Colleen's brothers, came in.

Jason glanced at him with a frown. "Hey, Tuck."

He knew Jason from a few classes, not to mention his reputation. If they should be on anyone's case . . . "Hey."

Henry, Colleen's kid brother, shucked off his jacket and hung it up, then went to the counter and swiped a roll.

Frank grabbed him in a playful headlock. "Release the contraband, kid."

Henry laughed as Colleen brought a water pitcher to the table, set with fine china and real cloth napkins, white candles flickering with beckoning flames.

"Pork roast coming through," Helen said, holding a plate with a piece of juicy meat centered on it. Red sauce dripped down the sides.

No one seemed to notice Colleen's still-reddened, chapped face, but thankfully it had begun to fade.

When Tuck heard footsteps on the porch, he braced himself as the door opened.

Oh, he'd hoped that Mrs. Decker hadn't yet mentioned to her husband what she'd seen the other night, but Tuck turned, ready to take the punishment. Ready to apologize. Ready, even, to grovel.

He really wanted to stay for dinner.

But Mr. Decker barely looked at him other than a passing greeting before pulling out a chair at the table. He sat there, a strange smile on his face, asking Henry about his day.

Mrs. Decker came in next, and if Tuck wasn't completely made of stone, he could tell she'd been crying too. Her eyes stopped on Tuck and something of surprise flashed in them. Then she glanced at her daughter and offered a smile.

Colleen gave her one back.

Maybe she'd forgiven him. See, that's what families did for each other. Forgave. Showed up for dinner. Sat around the table together. Held hands as they prayed.

Weird to pray like that, and especially to hold Grandma Decker's hand, Colleen on the other side. But he liked the little squeeze she gave him as they began, as though she liked having him there.

And the words of the prayer Grandma Decker offered lingered too. *Grant us Your joy this day as we gather together, and help us to abide in love for one another.*

Someday he would have a family exactly like this. Loving. Loyal. The kind that showed up for dinner and held hands and figured out how to make it through the dark times. He made that promise to himself as the Decker family all responded with "Amen."

13

NATHAN MIGHT FREEZE TO DEATH on his mother's tiny porch before he got answers.

Answers to questions like, how much danger were they in?

And what happened if this Garcia fella landed on his doorstep? Did Frank intend on having a shoot-out right in their front yard?

Even more essential, why were they still having dinner around the family table if someone intended to kill them? Well, at least Annalise . . . or Deidre—was that what she said her name had been?

Deidre.

He rolled the name over his tongue. It simply didn't taste, didn't feel, right.

Tonight at dinner, the entire thing had felt as if he were viewing his life from the outside, watching his wife pass the gravy, chat with his mother, who kept smiling at Frank, his wife's uncle. Only, not her uncle. Her Witness Security agent. Never mind that Frank acted like a *real* uncle as he told the boys a story about catching fish in nearby Evergreen Lake, all the while eyeing Colleen's friend, Tucker, like he might be a hardened criminal.

Tucker seemed like a nice kid—quiet, polite. Needed a haircut, but what kid didn't these days? He avoided eye contact with Nathan, which told Nathan that he must like Colleen more than she knew; although she'd introduced them as friends, she hadn't made any gestures that suggested they might be more.

Even Jason was acting weird, not looking at his father as he speared his pork roast. So Nathan had caught him kissing Harper— the kid was nearly eighteen. He should be dating a pretty girl.

Yes, Nathan's world felt surreal and plastic. Pretty on the outside, empty on the inside. He knew one thing, however—he'd never been an action hero, but he would do anything to save his family.

Starting with getting answers from Frank Harrison, regardless of how long it took him to help Nathan's mother with the dishes.

What was with the man? Clearing the table, taking out the leaf, washing the good china, and now he was wiping the counters?

Nathan wrapped his arms around himself, sitting on one of his mother's deck chairs, glancing between her kitchen and his own house, where the lights glowed like a lantern against the darkness. The cold breeze filtered into his jacket, down his back, raising gooseflesh. They'd get a frost, if not a few more flakes, tonight.

Annalise had left with the kids, returning home to tuck them in bed, and he couldn't get his eyes off his house, waiting for a black sedan to roll up, maybe crank down the windows, and start firing.

No, that didn't happen in Deep Haven.

None of this happened in Deep Haven. They didn't harbor criminals and relocated witness protection victims.

Nathan scrolled through Annalise's confession and tried to get his mind around her words: *I testified against a drug dealer, Luis Garcia, who killed my best friend and who tried to murder me.*

Soft and quiet, they blew his world open, allowing him to get a good peek inside the woman he thought he knew.

No wonder she'd been so quiet, almost shell-shocked, when he first met her. He'd attributed it to the so-called car accident she'd lived through while losing her entire family.

Except she still had family. One of whom was *not* Uncle Frank.

A thousand tiny memories, like pieces of a broken mirror, infiltrated his brain. Some so crisp and bright—like the time he'd walked in on her at 2 a.m., holding baby Jason, her eyes glistening. *I wish my mother could visit. She would love to see him.*

He'd chalked her words up to exhaustion at the time. Now they made sense.

And how many times did he find her leaning over their children after they'd gone to sleep or kneeling beside their beds in prayer?

She still did that—looked in on them every night. Ruffling Henry's hair, picking up his dirty jeans after she'd read to him. Rehearsing a few lines with Jason. Curling up in bed, even for a few moments, with Colleen. Annalise had a routine with each one of them, designed to protect, to nurture.

He never dreamed that it might be because she actually feared for their lives.

Nathan glanced at the kitchen, saw Frank wiping his hands on a towel. So help him, if Frank made a move to kiss his mother . . .

The man had courted her for nearly a week, lying every moment. Only his poor mother's broken heart had kept Nathan from barreling into the kitchen and dragging Frank into the yard during dinner. He noticed the repairs on the porch steps, not to mention the twinkle in his mother's eyes when she looked at Frank.

Oh, the mess the man would leave behind.

Thankfully, Nathan was spared the horror of watching his mother kiss this liar.

The door opened and Frank stepped out onto the porch. He startled when he saw Nathan. "What are you doing out here?"

Nathan got up. "Not here." He stepped off the porch, shoved his hands into his pockets, tight fists, numb with the cold. "We have to talk."

For once, Frank said nothing, though Nathan heard him sigh as they crossed the road. He led them around to the deck of his own house, lit up like high noon, and debated brushing the snow off one of the metal chairs to sit, but decided to stand.

Just in case he had to beat the tar out of Frank.

"Annalise told me everything."

If Nathan doubted that she'd told him the truth, if he'd believed that she might be making up this entire story, Frank's reaction would have set him straight.

Frank blew out a long breath, shook his head. Met Nathan's eyes. "Sorry."

Sorry? "*Sorry? My* wife has lied to me for twenty years because you told her to, and the best you can do is *sorry?*"

"She didn't have a choice, Nathan. What would you have her do—tell you the truth and endanger your life too?"

"Let's start with the fact that I'm her husband. We don't have secrets. Or I thought we didn't have secrets. Apparently we have gigantic, supernova secrets. And as for endangering our lives . . .

well, what am I supposed to do with the words 'Garcia is out of jail and coming to kill me'?"

"Calm down, Nathan." Frank held up his hands.

"I promise you, this is as calm as I intend to get until I know my family is safe."

"That's what I'm trying to do—keep your family safe."

"Funny, I thought that was my job."

Frank drew in a breath. "Not in this case. Luis Garcia is a cruel man. He wouldn't hesitate to torture your entire family while you watched."

Nathan couldn't help a flinch and hated himself for it. He had to be tougher than this. "No one is going to hurt my family."

"Which is why I told Annalise five days ago that she had to move. But she didn't want to take you or your children away from your lives."

She'd known about the danger for five—*five!*—days. There she went again, trying to keep them safe, insulated.

Not trusting—not believing in him—at all. How had he been so incredibly blind?

She'd put up quite a show for him all these years, playing the perfect wife, perfect mother. He didn't even know where to start with the depths of her betrayal. He almost wished she'd done something easier to wrap his feelings around—like cheat or charge them into mountains of debt.

No wonder she'd forgiven him so easily.

He'd deal with it later. For now . . . "You should have come to me, Frank. I'm her husband and the head of this family. I deserved to know."

Frank's eyes narrowed. "Let's just play out that scenario for a moment. I come to you and tell you that your wife used to be a drug-dealing, homeless runaway who mainlined drugs and slept in flophouses while she helped her boyfriend run product for one of the nastiest drug lords in the country, and what? You're going to take that well? You're not going to throw a punch at me and toss me off the deck? Because looking at you right now, I'd make a steep bet that's what is going through your head."

Oh. Yes, well—"She did drugs?"

"Had to get her clean and healthy before we moved her. Blake had her so messed up, she didn't even know her own name when the St. Louis police picked her up the first time. They found her in an alley, half-dressed, hypothermic, and nearly dead when they called me. I offered her a deal—testify against Garcia and she could start over. I'd help her get off the streets, clean, and home. She was terrified. But she agreed and we worked together for three months before she got enough on him to put him away. Garcia found out and beat her within an inch of her life."

Nathan steeled himself, fighting the urge to hit something, to howl.

No wonder she jumped sometimes when he came up too fast behind her.

"I hid her while my wife helped nurse her back to health. At the trial, Garcia promised to find her and kill her—and if he didn't, his men would. We decided to fake her death and move her to Deep Haven. Changed her name, her appearance, got her tattoo removed." His voice gentled. "For what it's worth, Annalise is nothing like Deidre. She's a new person. Or maybe she's finally the woman she was supposed to be."

"She never told me she had a tattoo."

"It was here." Frank put his hand at a space just above his knee.

"She has a scar there. She said it was from the accident."

"She has a lot of scars, Nathan, and I'm sure my arrival tore them all open. The longer we wait, however, the more danger you and your family are in. We need to move you. Tomorrow, if we can."

Tomorrow. The word shook Nathan to his bones.

Tomorrow he'd sever his life in Deep Haven. Leave it all behind. He couldn't help but glance at his mother's house, the porch light still glowing, scattering through the branches of the ancient family apple tree.

"She can come with you," Frank said softly.

"Really?" Nathan didn't mean the sharpness in his voice—okay, maybe he did. It seemed the only place to put everything that roiled inside him. "*Really?* And how fair is that to her? I'm going to uproot my mother, drag her to a new town where she has to make new friends and start her life over? She's lived her entire life in Deep Haven. What did you think—that you'd simply get her to trust you and then drop the bomb on her?"

Frank appeared nonplussed. "Yes, actually."

"You *jerk*. You made her like you, made her believe in you so you could destroy her world."

"So I could keep Annalise's intact. She's already lost so much."

"Which was her fault to begin with! Who does that—leaves her family, runs away with a jerk of a boyfriend, starts taking drugs?"

He could hear his words but couldn't stop them from spilling out.

"Too many," Frank said quietly. "But few get a chance to reset their lives. And few have the bravery that Annalise showed. So yes, I lied to you and to your mother. But I thought maybe you'd be the kind of people I hoped you were."

And what was Nathan supposed to say to that? He ground his

jaw so tight he thought his teeth might crack. "My mother will be devastated."

Frank looked away. "She's not the only one."

Nathan frowned. He didn't even want to begin to unravel that. Frank didn't have actual feelings for his mother, did he?

Even if he did, Nathan didn't want the man in their lives, having to sort out fact from fiction.

Which meant he'd have to leave town without telling his mother.

Nathan sank into a chair. Cradled his head in his hands. He thought he might retch. "We'll leave tomorrow after school."

Frank made a move toward him like he might make some sort of fatherly gesture, maybe dare to put his hand on Nathan's shoulder.

Nathan looked up and tried to turn him to ash, just in case. "You'd better make sure that when we leave, my mother is safe."

Frank nodded. "Don't do anything rash before tomorrow. We'll find you a good place to hide, Nathan."

Nathan held up his hand as Frank gave him a compassionate expression. "Please. Don't."

Frank sighed; then Nathan heard him move off the porch, open the sliding-glass door, slip inside.

Don't do anything rash. His entire life felt like one rash reaction after another. Like quitting football, walking right off the field after realizing what his father had done. And giving up his scholarship to stick around to take care of his mother when she had cancer. And deciding to run for mayor. And now, slinking away from Deep Haven, practically in the dead of night.

Rash reactions to decisions others made for him.

Nathan got up, went inside the house, closed the sliding-glass door, then the drapes to hide them. Dragging a chair to the closet, he climbed up and dug around in the back of the shelf.

There lay his father's .22 shotgun. When he was seventeen, Nathan had used it for target practice at the gravel lot outside Deep Haven with a few of his buddies. Now he took it down. The safety was still on. He checked the chamber and found it empty.

He retrieved the shells from the shelf as well and brought them to the family room, taking a seat in the recliner.

He loaded a shell into the chamber, put his thumb on the safety. Set the gun across his lap.

Don't do anything rash.

Tell that to the woman sleeping down the hall.

❧

He wanted her to leave.

Nathan wanted her to *leave*. Annalise sat in the middle of her bed, dressed in her layers, praying Nathan might finally come in, kindness in his eyes, ready to finish their conversation.

Ready to refute her statement that she could leave. Alone.

Yes, I guess you could.

The words churned inside her, chewing up her life. Her dreams for her children—college, marriage, children of their own. Her memories—the downy smell of her newborns, the laughter of her children on Christmas morning, the warmth of them as they climbed into her lap for a story. How would she live without rehearsing with Jason or cheering on Henry in soccer?

What if she left with the taste of her fight with Colleen still in her mouth?

Please, Nathan, come to bed.

But the light in the family room continued to trickle down the hall. Thin and weak, not enough to chase away the shadows, but enough to reveal the grim edge to Nathan's face as she tiptoed into the family room in her wool socks, her bathrobe snagged tight.

She froze at the glint off the steel barrel of the shotgun. Nathan sat in the recliner, feet on the ground, staring at the front door as if Garcia would knock or something. He still wore his suit pants, although he'd yanked out his dress shirt, rolled up the sleeves, unbuttoned it at the neck. He'd been running his hands through his dark hair, and with the five o'clock shadow, he appeared . . . well, dangerous.

Her voice eked out on just a breath of panic. "What are you doing with that?"

He glanced at her, his expression tight, blame in his eyes. "Go to bed, Annalise."

"I think you should put that thing away before someone gets hurt."

He stared at her, his green eyes icy. "I think we're past that. I just want to make sure we're safe tonight. Tomorrow, we're leaving Deep Haven."

"We're leaving? *All* of us?"

"What did you expect, Annalise? That I'd stay here while Frank stole my wife and hid her from me? No, we are in this together."

Except it didn't sound like they were in it together. It sounded like the last thing he wanted was to be in this with her.

She clasped her arms around herself. "What about your mother?"

He looked away, back at the door, and shook his head. "Please, just go to bed."

She had to press her hand to the wall, had to find balance as she turned toward their room.

How could she leave Helen?

Her eyes burned as she stopped at Jason's room. She watched him sleep, rolled like a burrito in his comforter, the moon's arms over him.

And Henry. She went to his bed, picking her way past the backpack, the clothing debris, the skateboard, to run his hair back from his face and kiss him. She loved the softness of his cheeks, still a baby in so many ways.

Colleen had closed her door, and Annalise listened a moment before she turned the handle and eased it open. Colleen lay on her side, curled into her covers. Annalise couldn't stop herself. She tiptoed into the room and climbed onto the bed, molding herself to her daughter's frame, tucked under the covers.

Her daughter breathed the rhythmic melody of slumber. Annalise draped her arm over her body, settling it lightly. Colleen didn't stir. Then Annalise closed her eyes and breathed in the sweet smell of her skin as she listened to the words of their fight.

I don't want to be you.

The words hollowed her out. It could be her voice, her own words hurled once upon a time at her own mother. *I love him! And Blake loves me! You are so judgmental!*

Annalise tucked her forehead against Colleen's back. She just wanted to stay right here, to hold on.

Oh, to have the chance to erase it all, to rewrite everything.

Annalise couldn't bear to have her daughter disappear forever. There would never be enough grace to say good-bye.

God, I'm sorry. I'm so sorry.

How many times had she returned to that moment, in the

nondescript safe house apartment where they had brought her mother for one final good-bye? Her mother, thinner than she remembered, a forced smile on her face. She'd hugged her daughter and told her she loved her. *I'll never stop praying for you, Deidre.*

At the time, it felt like a religious platitude.

Now Annalise clung to it with everything inside her.

The verses from Dan's sermon yesterday slid through her. *"For he knows how weak we are; he remembers we are only dust. . . . The wind blows, and we are gone—as though we had never been here. But the love of the Lord remains forever with those who fear him."*

She wanted to believe that, but she couldn't get the words to soak into her heart.

Annalise kissed her daughter's shoulder, over her flannel pajamas, got up, and left the room.

She heard only the tick of time in her chest, her ears, as she stood in the hallway.

I'll never stop praying for you, Deidre. I'll always love you.

Annalise closed the bedroom door behind her and climbed into the center of her bed, pulled the covers to her chest.

Then she picked up her phone.

She'd never forgotten the number. As she dialed, time bled away and she was again eighteen, afraid and hungry, wounded and cold and desperate as she huddled in the phone booth. She held the phone to her ear, listening to it ring.

Then, "Hello?"

Her breath caught. Just like then, words abandoned her now.

"Hello?" The voice was just as she remembered, soft yet firm and expectant. Except now with the tenor of age around the fringes. Annalise's hand moved to the Mute button before she betrayed herself.

"Deidre?"

Annalise pressed a hand over her mouth, despite the mute, not wanting her gasp to leak out. *Mom.*

She closed her eyes, just listening to her mother's breathing, wanting to drink it in.

And then her mother began to hum. Softly. It sounded like a moan at first, then became a song, something so familiar that Annalise didn't have to hear the words to know them.

Amazing Grace, how sweet the sound
That saved a wretch like me!

Her mother's humming became louder, and she broke into a whispered version.

"Through many dangers, toils and snares
We have already come.
'Twas Grace that brought us safe thus far,
And Grace will lead us home."

The longing for home could drown her. The smell of her mother's chocolate chip cookies. The step of her father's wing tips on the kitchen linoleum, coming in from patrol. Kylie curling up in her basket chair, tucking her feet under her as Deidre talked about her day. The way her sister's blue eyes admired her. Ben playing hoops on the paved driveway.

Easy, almost-inconsequential memories that she hungered for.

It was too agonizing to conjure a real memory, like Thanksgiving or Christmas. A birthday.

Her mother lapsed into humming again. Annalise tucked the

phone against her ear, curling into a ball, drinking in the sound. *I love you, Mom.*

She finally clicked off, pulling the phone against her chest, willing the melody, the truth, inside her. *"I once was lost but now am found, was blind but now I see."*

But she didn't see. Couldn't see.

And she'd never felt more lost.

In the last several days, God had abandoned her. Worse, He'd laughed at her happy ending. Reminded her that no matter how hard she tried to build a new life, she could never erase her regrets. There was no grace for her.

And now, her entire family would have to pay. Again.

Annalise continued to hold the phone against her chest and wept.

She didn't know how, but she finally fell asleep. She *must* have fallen asleep because otherwise she would have seen the night fade into morning and heard the boards in the hallway creak.

She would have risen, gone to the door, opened it a crack, and seen Henry wander down the hall in search of breakfast.

She might have called out to him, followed him, even stopped him.

Because she could have never forgotten that his father sat in the family room, waiting for danger to leap at them.

Waiting, because she'd all but summoned it to their door.

All but set them up for disaster.

All but caused Nathan, asleep in the chair, to jerk, for his hand to release the safety.

For the movement to cause the .22 to fire.

Annalise sat up, her heart in her throat, every nerve on fire. A shot. She'd heard a shot.

A scream propelled her out of bed and down the hall.

And then the scream became her own as she saw Henry standing in a puddle of glass and plaster, Nathan holding his discharged gun, pale, looking exactly like he'd, indeed, nearly killed their youngest son.

14

FUNNY HOW, once she made the decision to keep everyone in the dark, Helen's world got brighter. As if, by keeping it secret, the cancer couldn't really touch her. Sure, it still lurked inside her—she felt certain that Dr. Walgren would confirm it today at her appointment—but as long as she kept smiling, kept passing the roast and potatoes last night, kept meeting Frank's eyes with a smile, it simply couldn't be true.

Not yet.

She had too much life yet to live.

Helen shrugged on her jacket, bent to pull on her boots. She'd be in and out of the doctor's office before anyone even noticed she was gone. She loved the fact that the clinic opened at 7 a.m.—maybe she'd come home and make another pie, take it over for lunch.

Just to see the look on Frank's face.

Oh, he had her thinking about all the things she still wanted to do. Go on a cruise. Repaint her house. Maybe write a recipe book on pies—apple pies.

Maybe even make a few more family meals like last night. She'd wanted to weep with the joy of her family around the table. And Colleen's boyfriend seemed so nice, the way he walked Colleen back to her house, kissed her on the cheek.

Even Frank had seen that, watching over Colleen like a grandfather might.

Yes, she would add falling in love to her list. Maybe even getting remarried.

In fact, maybe the cancer had lit a fuse on her life. Time to live it to the fullest before it was snuffed out. She'd travel and dance and cook exotic foods and make the most of her final days.

Grabbing her purse, she stepped out into the bright sunshine. The air held the crisp tang of autumn, the sun a glorious rose-gold against the mottled clouds. Yes, this was a good day, come what may.

A shot ripped the air, fracturing the morning stillness. She jerked, and the scream that followed the shot lurched inside her.

It came from Nathan's home.

Then she heard yelling, but she was already scrambling down the drive, across the road, turning the handle on the front door and finding it locked.

She fumbled for her keys, still hearing the yelling—

"You could have killed someone!"

"And this is my fault?"

Someone crying, now another.

Helen banged on the door. "Nathan! It's your mother! Let me in!"

Footsteps. The door jerked open just about the time Helen found her key.

Colleen stood in the doorway in her flannel pajamas, eyes wide.

"What's going on?" Helen took Colleen's hand. "Are you okay?"

"Daddy shot the wall."

Helen blinked at her. Nathan had done—*what?*

But as she came into the family room, she saw that the family picture—the huge three-by-five-foot framed portrait they'd taken last year on the shore—lay splintered on the floor, glass glinting on the sofa, sprayed across the carpet. The plaster behind it bore a hole.

Nathan stood barefoot in the middle of the room, holding a broom, dressed in his rumpled suit pants, his dress shirt untucked and wrinkled as if he'd slept in it. A shaking and crying Annalise clutched Henry to herself so hard that for a moment Helen thought he'd been hurt. Henry had his eyes shut as if trying not to cry.

"What happened in here?" she said.

Annalise looked at her, her eyes red-rimmed. Jason, bare-chested in his pajama bottoms, stood behind her, just staring at the mess.

"He's going to get someone killed." The voice came from Frank, who materialized behind her. He looked wrung out, his hair tousled, a shadow of whiskers on his face, as if he'd been rousted out of bed and had thrown on his jeans and a white T-shirt on the way up the stairs.

It was then Helen saw the shotgun lying on the floor. "Is that your father's?" She looked at Nathan.

"Mom, everything's fine—"

"Everything is *not* fine. Good night, what is that doing out?" She went to pick it up.

"Just leave it," Nathan said. "Go home, Mom, please."

Helen froze. She'd never really heard that tone from him before. "Not until someone tells me what is going on here!"

"How could you do this?"

Colleen's outburst behind her made Helen turn. Her granddaughter wore such a look of fury, of betrayal, her arms wrapped around her skinny body as her gaze pinned on Annalise. "You told him, didn't you? That's why Dad had the shotgun. You told him about Tucker!"

Her words echoed in the silence of the room for one long, unbearable moment as Nathan's face drained. He had bent to sweep glass from the wood floor of the hallway but now slowly stood up. He stared at his daughter in a way that made even Helen want to run. "What about Tucker?"

"I . . . I found Tucker in Colleen's room Saturday night," Annalise said softly.

But the entire room heard her because for a full twenty seconds, no one said anything.

See if Helen ever asked Tucker over for pork roast again. But she reached out and drew Colleen to herself.

Nathan shook his head, venom in his tone. "More secrets, Annalise? Haven't we had enough?"

Annalise pressed her forehead into Henry's hair.

Nathan turned back to Colleen, his eyes hot. "You're not to see him. Ever again."

Helen felt Colleen gasp under her embrace. "That's not fair, Daddy—"

Nathan held up a finger, his mouth so grim even Helen would have stopped talking. "Go to your room and get ready for school."

Colleen untangled herself from her grandmother. Helen pressed a kiss to her head as she let her go.

Nathan turned to Jason. "You too. Henry—"

"I'm sorry. I'm sorry!" Henry looked up at him, his eyes big. "I didn't mean to wake you up."

Nathan closed his eyes as pain streaked across his face. He held open his arms, and Annalise let go as Henry flung himself at his dad. "This is not your fault."

"Then why were you sitting there with the gun?"

"Helen, c'mon. It's time to go," Frank said.

She froze. "For the love of pete, my son just shot a hole in his wall! I'm not going anywhere."

"Everything is going to be fine here. And don't you have an appointment you need to keep?" he said, his voice small. "Please."

Again, the room quieted.

Helen's throat began to swell; she could hardly push words out. "How did you know about that?" She met Frank's eyes, fury building inside her. "What did you do, *spy* on me?"

"What appointment, Mom?" Nathan said behind her, his voice recognizable again.

Frank's mouth tightened around the edges, his eyes sad. "Tell them, Helen."

"Tell them what? I don't know anything yet! I just had some tests."

"Helen? Are you okay?" This from Annalise.

Oh, see if she ever made Frank pie or ever, *ever* invited him into her house—her life—again. She tried to level him with a glare, but he just met her gaze evenly.

Fine. She turned to her son, to Annalise. "The doctor thinks the cancer might be back."

Only a muscle moved in Nathan's jaw.

Annalise slipped a hand over her mouth. "Helen."

See, this was why she didn't want them to know. Now they'd make a big fuss, and she'd . . . she'd feel like an invalid.

"It's nothing. I'm headed over to the clinic, but I think I need to help clean up this mess—"

"I'll drive her to the clinic," Frank said.

Helen rounded on him. "I'm not going anywhere with you. I don't know how you knew, but you invaded my privacy. You betrayed me. Just stay out of my life."

He didn't even flinch at her words. "Let me drive you—"

She held up her hand. "I'm staying right here."

"Mom, please. Go to the clinic. We have to get this cleaned up and the kids to school," Nathan said. "I promise, everything's under control here."

"Hardly! Are you . . . in some kind of *danger*, Nathan? What would possess you to bring out your father's shotgun?"

"Helen—"

She wanted to turn, lay one against Frank's cheek, and considered herself a fine Christian woman when she simply snapped, "Stay out of this, Frank. You're not a part of my life, so stay out of it." Although her voice shook on the end.

She wouldn't cry in front of her family. They needed her to be strong.

"Mom, everything's fine." Nathan came over, gripped her shoulders, and gave her a smile, one that she'd seen him use during his campaign . . . and she'd never felt more betrayed.

Her son was lying to her. Flat-out lying.

He'd finally turned into his father.

The pain in her chest threatened to make her cry out. Instead, she shook her head. "Fine. If that's the way you want it, Nathan, I'll leave." She swallowed. "But I'll be back after my appointment. And then I want to know what made you take a shotgun to the family picture."

She pushed past Frank, outside into the bright autumn day, wondering how it had all become so dark.

&

They'd never escape their fears.

Annalise had known it as she watched Nathan clean up the glass, like frozen teardrops against the wood floor of the hall. He would always live with fear hovering over him, always trying to keep them safe. And in his attempt to be a hero of some sort, he'd get them all killed.

She had to leave, alone, before her choices cost them everything.

"Mom, I need lunch money." Henry leaned forward from the backseat. "Don't forget."

He seemed totally recovered from this morning's near trauma. As though a bowl of Cheerios and some peanut butter toast could set the world right.

"I'll write out a check when we get to school."

She'd tried not to notice as Nathan swept up the mess. He was still working on it when she bundled the kids into the car.

How she wanted to say good-bye. To wrap her arms around his waist and hold on, one last time. To breathe in everything strong and familiar and right about the man she'd married. But then it would be obvious.

And most likely, he'd just push her away. The betrayal on his face after the revelation about Colleen had told her everything.

Beside her, Jason sat without words as if trying to sort out what had happened in his home; Colleen kept glaring at Annalise as if the entire thing might indeed be her fault.

Well, it was.

But this was not how she wanted to leave them. She didn't want this morning to be their last memory of her. If she could have, she would have kept them home from school, but according to Frank, school, with its embedded security, might be the safest place for them.

She turned in to the school parking lot. *Just stay calm. Keep a smile on your face.*

She pulled up to the curb, and Jason reached for the door handle. She put a hand on his arm. "I love you, Jason."

He turned, smiled at her. "I love you too, Mom. Have a great day."

And then, by some miracle, he leaned in and kissed her on the cheek.

She wanted to cry. Managed a smile instead.

Colleen had already climbed out.

Annalise put the car into park, got out. "Colleen, honey!" she called over the hood of the car.

Colleen glanced over her shoulder. "What?"

"It's going to be okay! It'll all work out, I promise. Just . . . remember that."

Colleen frowned at her. "Whatever, Mom. See you tonight at the game."

See you.

Annalise's throat tightened.

"Mom, what about my lunch money?"

Oh, precious, precious Henry. He stood by her door, his backpack over one shoulder. So grown-up. She nodded, her eyes welling, and reached for her purse. Pulling out her checkbook, she wrote the amount, then tore it off, handed it to him.

He took it, and she caught his jacket before he could move away. "Keep reading, Henry. Every day. Keep reading and it will get easier. I promise."

He shrugged. "Okay, Mom."

And then, well, she couldn't help it. She grabbed him in a hug.

For once, he didn't squirm away. Just hugged her back, his arms around her waist. She wanted to weep. "Bye, honey."

He slipped out of her arms and ran toward the building, his backpack bouncing. "Bye!"

She watched him, uncaring that he blurred as he disappeared through the school door.

Then, before she could change her mind, she got in and drove away. Down the hill, along Main Street, and out of town.

Along the lake, the sunny droplets of light on the blue water were too bright, scalding her eyes. The sky appeared clear and unsullied, the balsam and pine trees a lush green, the last of the bedazzled oaks and maples dropping their jeweled leaves across the highway.

A picturesque ending that belied the devastation of her life.

She pressed a hand against her stomach, willing herself to stay upright, not to hunch over the steering wheel, not to end up in the ditch.

Or worse, in the water, to drown or freeze to death like Nathan's father. That would be rich—a final way she could decimate her husband's life.

And now she couldn't see. She tapped the brake, pulled over onto the shoulder, and used the bottom of her shirt to wipe her eyes. She wasn't wearing makeup, but she still felt sodden and messy.

This was the only way. Garcia would come to town, not find her, not know that she married or find her family, and he'd move on.

If he ever did track her down, he could hurt only her.

Yes. This was better.

And if she had any doubt that she should leave, seeing Helen this morning shrug off the fact that she had cancer sealed her decision.

She couldn't drag Nathan away from his mother, never to see her again. Annalise knew *exactly* how that felt.

Helen deserved better.

Maybe if Frank apprehended Garcia, it wouldn't be too late to walk back into her children's lives. Maybe someday they'd even forgive her.

I'm sorry.

She kept repeating the words as she pulled back out onto the highway. *I'm sorry.*

She didn't know how she'd ever stop, really.

Annalise had no plan, no destination, nothing clearly formed beyond the muddle of panic propelling her out of Deep Haven and the packed bag she'd slipped into the back end. Maybe she would drive the SUV to Duluth, trade it in, and buy something else, something used. Then, maybe, she'd call Frank. After her decision had time to take root in her bones.

But she needed to think of a plan beyond that.

Now, thirty miles out of town, an impulse pulled her off the highway, down a side road onto the private acreage of one of Nathan's clients.

For tonight, it made sense. In winter, the Millers rented the place to skiers and other lodgers who wanted a hideaway from the city. They'd offered it to Nathan and Annalise on more than a few occasions free of charge for managing the housekeeping and maintenance, and they always called before they arrived so she could stock the fridge. She kept the key on a ring in the glove compartment.

Here she'd also be out of cell phone range, one of the few pockets left in America that didn't have regular cell signal. Good thing, because if Nathan decided to call her, his voice alone could lure her back, shake her out of her resolve.

She keyed in the security code at the gate and drove down the long path toward the lake. The Millers owned a long stretch of Lake Superior shoreline, their home outfitted with immense picture windows overlooking the rocky lake, an embracive back porch, and a giant stone fireplace made from stones plucked off the rocky beach. But no one could see the vacation home from the highway. More importantly, no one would guess her hideaway.

She'd stop, conjure up a plan. Then tomorrow she'd gas up and leave Deep Haven for good.

But tonight was Colleen's semifinal game. She had to stay at least to listen to it on the radio and imagine herself in the stands.

Imagine her family intact.

Imagine her life with a happy ending.

Annalise pressed her fingers to her eyes again to wipe the wetness from them. She could do this. For her family, for their safety, she could do this.

Down by the lake, the leaves lay upon the dirt driveway, soggy and brown. When she glanced into her rearview mirror, she saw the imprint of her tires. Perhaps it would snow tonight, cover up her escape.

She pulled up to the three-car detached garage, got out, and unlocked the garage door before she pressed the door opener. She parked her car by the Millers' sleek boat, closed the door, and took the path to the house.

Sophie Miller had landscaped the grounds herself with black rock from the lake, chrysanthemums tufted between them, the red and orange blooms stiff with cold. The stone pathway glistened under the thawing frost of the night, the grass brown and scarred with a patchwork of snow.

Annalise fumbled with the keys, stamping her feet on the woven mat. A plaque by the door caught her eye: *Wherever you are going, God has already been there and paved the way for you.*

She doubted very much that God had ever been here. A secret identity, the horror of knowing your actions hurt others. The desperation of loneliness looming in every step ahead. Abandoned. Defeated.

No, she was in this alone.

Those verses in Psalm 103, Dan's words from the pulpit, simply didn't apply to her, regardless of how much she hoped they might. God didn't love her.

She opened the door and listened to the silence as she stepped into the foyer. The door echoed into the massive great room, two stories high, as she closed it. She toed off her shoes. Let her bag drop on the bench by the door.

Annalise walked into the house in her stocking feet, running her hand over the black soapstone island in the kitchen.

She had longed for a house like this. A house that she didn't have to repaint every year. A house that smelled of wealth and safety and success. A house with fitted Italian tile behind an inset stove and hood, a long bar, where her children could belly up and help her cook Thanksgiving dinner. A great room with a massive leather couch, enough to fit all of them as they watched football, and a bearskin rug on the floor to lay by the fire in Nathan's arms. Outside, through the massive windows, the lake could ice over or throw itself against the rocks, and they'd watch it from the warmth of the fire or seated at the immense rough-hewn walnut table with the leather chairs. Or from upstairs, where the master bedroom overlooked the view.

Yes, she'd wanted a house like this, a place where she might raise her children in safety. In happiness.

She walked to the bearskin rug, sat in the middle of it, cross-legged, running her fingers through the fur.

You could have killed someone!

The echo of her shrill voice, the panic embedded in it, made her wince. But she'd seen Henry's wide eyes, and fear simply won.

She curled her arms around her legs, pulling them to herself.

And this is my fault?

No, Nathan. This isn't your fault.

She wished she'd said that, but it all happened so fast, and then Helen arrived and held them hostage in their secrets.

Maybe they'd already spoken everything worth saying anyway.

She leaned over, let herself curl into a ball on the floor. Listened to the silence of the grand home, the rumble of the waves outside, washing the shore.

Heard the lingering song in her mother's voice.

Through many dangers, toils and snares
We have already come.
'Twas Grace that brought us safe thus far,
And Grace will lead us home.

She breathed in the words, over and over. Willing herself to believe.

But there wasn't any grace for her. Not anymore. God had made that much clear.

Which meant she'd never go home.

15

FRANK DIDN'T KNOW where to begin to catalog how this op had ended up so far south. He should have seen the crazy written in Nathan's eyes last night, should have known he'd do something foolish.

The man could have killed his son. Or someone else.

And then there was Annalise. Yeah, she had crazy in her eyes too. He'd recognized it the second he came up the stairs and spotted the glass spilled across the family room floor. Enough crazy to do something rash. Something stupid. Like leave town without telling anyone—including her handler. Disappearing off the planet where Frank couldn't keep her safe.

Of course, no one could be labeled sane after the shot shattered the quiet morning. He'd nearly had a cardiac arrest, practically levitating from the bed and falling onto the floor. He'd scrambled into his pants and was up the stairs with his gun out by the time he took his next breath.

The sight of Henry standing in a puddle of glass, the family picture in shreds, turned him cold.

How close, how very close, they'd come to tragedy.

And if there wasn't enough crazy going on, Helen had to walk in, demand to stay, and he'd let her secret out of the bag.

Her eyes, the look that said he'd destroyed everything good and sweet and magical in their budding relationship, had him calling himself a jerk. He hadn't meant to betray her.

As if things couldn't be any worse, Jason had caught sight of Frank's gun as he slipped it into the back of his pants. Frank would have to level with the kid, and soon. The entire operation was spiraling way out of control.

Regardless of where he started listing his mistakes, he landed on one very real conclusion. He should have been the one sitting up with his gun cocked in the family room.

Protecting Annalise and her family.

Instead, Frank had been in the basement, like a relative, forgetting that he had a job to do. Forgetting, apparently, that Annalise wasn't his niece but rather one of his charges, one whose life seemed to be dismantling.

In fact, he'd been thinking about Helen and that phone call from the medical clinic and what he'd do if her cancer was back and how that thought made him ache to his bones.

This time, he would be there until the end. Be braver. Be stronger.

Be willing to get messy, even hurt.

Which was probably why the truth had just spilled out of him.

If only Helen had waited for him as she banged out of the house. Because that's exactly what he'd wanted to say to her—that he wasn't leaving. That if she needed him, he'd be there.

Maybe he should be grateful his phone had vibrated in his pants pocket. Because if it hadn't, he just might have taken her hand and told her she wasn't alone.

Which meant . . . ?

See, everyone had gone crazy today.

"Take the kids to school; it'll be safer," he'd said, interrupting Annalise and Nathan's low-toned argument. Annalise had looked at him with so much relief in her eyes, he'd wanted to hug her.

Instead, he'd opened his phone and stepped out on the stoop, wanting to hit something. "What?" he snapped into the phone.

"Good news, boss," Parker Boyd said.

"Tell me." He watched Helen get into her car, drive away. Inside, he heard Annalise rounding up the kids for school. Good girl.

"We got him."

Frank kneaded a stiff muscle in his neck as he sank down onto the wooden bench by the door. "That is good news. Where? When?"

"Duluth. Tracked him down in the car he stole—the locals got on it. He gave them a good chase, ended up rolling his car. He was thrown and died on impact."

The knot in Frank's chest loosened as relief set in.

Annalise didn't have to leave her family, her home.

Maybe she and Nathan could finally live in peace. In truth.

But Duluth. That was only two hours from Deep Haven. So close. A chill shook him through. "Are you sure it's him?"

"The coroner said she'll compare DNA. He was pretty mangled, but yes, it looks like Garcia. They're taking him to the morgue, and

I'm on my way. I'll send you a picture when I get it, but it looked like him—same general build, same tattoos on his neck."

"The cobra?"

"It's some sort of snake. Could be a cobra."

"Garcia has gang ink for his dominion. It's specific to his people."

"I have a picture of the tats. Hang on; I'll send it to you."

When Frank heard a beep, he pulled the phone away from his ear to open the text message. He studied the grainy picture. "I don't know if that's him or not. Probably, but . . . listen, I'll come to you. I don't want any chances that you got the wrong guy."

He'd wait until Annalise dropped the kids off at school, then take her with him. Seeing Garcia would give her closure.

"I'll be here." Boyd clicked off.

Frank sat there, breathing in the morning air, wishing he felt better. Hoping the nightmare might be over.

Hoping, because, well, Pastor Dan's words Sunday hadn't left his head. He'd kind of hoped God had been speaking to him: *I see you, and I know you, and I love you. Period. I know stuff about you that you don't even think I know, and yet I love you.*

Maybe not, but it had fertilized all his hopes.

He heard the garage door open, and Annalise pulled out in the SUV. She didn't look at him.

Please, God, heal this family from my mistakes.

Frank returned inside to see Nathan still tracking down the glass chips. The family room looked like a war zone, tiny glass bombs embedded in the carpet, the furniture.

"Where's the vacuum? I'll help."

"I think you've done enough," Nathan snapped as he strode past him.

"Are you kidding me? I'm not the one who pulled out an old shotgun. You're lucky Henry's not dead."

When Nathan rounded on him, Frank took a step back. Nathan looked exhausted, lines embedding his face, his eyes bloodshot. "You should have let her tell me from the beginning—the very beginning. I don't know who to blame, but I do know that when Annalise moved here, she was scared and alone, and she trusted you. You should have let her trust me, too. Maybe it wouldn't have come to this."

"I did manage to keep her safe for over twenty years," Frank said, but his words felt hollow, even to himself.

Nathan shook his head, his voice low, angry. "Now my mother has cancer, and I gotta choose between taking care of my family and taking care of her. Perfect."

"I'm sorry."

A muscle pulled in Nathan's jaw. "You don't know what sorry is."

That wasn't exactly true. "I know you're upset, Nathan. Just stay calm and this will be over," Frank said quietly, glancing at his phone. He didn't want to give them the hope that they might be safe, not quite yet, but still, see what the panic wrought? "That was my partner. He thinks we got Garcia."

Nathan stared at him, nonplussed.

"I'm headed to Duluth to confirm, but I am going to wait for Annalise. I wanted to take her with me, take one last look at Garcia—"

"Are you crazy? She still wakes up with nightmares—I thought they were of the accident, but since there *wasn't any accident*, it can only be from Garcia and what his men did to her. I can't even think of it without wanting to howl, and I've only lived with it for a day. Imagine having that memory in your head for years, having it creep back up on you without being able to tell anyone why." He put his hand up as if to push back the suggestion. "No way is she going to look at his face and relive what he did to her again."

"It might help—"

"Nothing is going to help. In the last few days you've managed to dismantle everything Annalise is. Everything we built together. Just leave, Frank. Please, just leave, and don't ever come back."

"I can't do that, Nathan. She's still my charge. I have to make sure she's safe."

"She's *my* charge. She became that when I said, 'I do.' We're in this together, and I can promise you nothing is going to happen to her on my watch."

"Like her getting shot?"

Nathan took a swing at him.

Frank sidestepped it, grabbed him by the arm, muscled him into a choke hold. "Seriously, Nathan! Who do you think you are? You're a small-town real estate agent. You haven't dealt with this kind of person. I know what I'm doing here, and you have to let me do it."

"Get off me!"

When Nathan elbowed him, Frank took it in the ribs, released him. "I don't want to do it this way, Nathan. But the fact is, you're not responsible for her—I am. And you getting involved is only going to get somebody—" and he was deliberate about the way he glanced at the picture on the floor—"hurt."

Nathan swore at him. Something soft and angry and deserved.

Frank tightened his jaw. "I'm sorry, but I'm finding your wife and I'm taking her with me."

"Over my dead body."

"Hopefully not."

Nathan said nothing. But Frank recognized the frustration in his eyes. The same frustration Frank had probably worn as he'd watched his wife slowly slip away. Even before the cancer.

Frank's voice gentled. "Listen. How about a compromise? You wait for Annalise, and when she gets here, lock yourselves inside this house. I'll go to Duluth and call you. If there's trouble, I'm calling the sheriff's office to see if they can send over someone to take you into protective custody. But please, don't do anything crazy."

Frank glanced at his phone, his throat thick. "Would you tell your mother I'm sorry?"

"What do you want me to say? That you were just playing her?"

Frank felt his words like a blow to the sternum. "Tell her whatever you want." He didn't look at Nathan as he stalked out of the building toward his rental car.

Maybe Nathan was right—he could never be sorry enough. Especially if Luis Garcia wasn't dead.

$\approx$

Nathan just wanted to hurt someone. Something.

To put a physical response on the roiling pain inside.

He could have killed his son.

Killed.

The moment grabbed him, sucked out his breath, held him hostage as he replayed it in slow motion.

He'd fallen asleep, his hand on the trigger.

A noise, and deep in his subconscious, panic lit a fire. He'd woken, already in fight mode, swung the gun toward the noise.

And he'd pulled the trigger before his aim centered on his son. *God, thank You.*

His skin flushed hot and sweat trickled down his spine as he shook himself out of the moment, as he pressed a hand to his chest, feeling his thundering heart.

Henry was okay. They were all okay.

Nathan checked his watch as he finished vacuuming. Annalise should be home by now.

Maybe school would be the safest place for the kids today. He'd give Frank that much.

He ran the vacuum over the sofa, took off the cushions, found glass even in the pillows. He vacuumed his recliner, then went over the carpet once more, listening to the crunch of glass under the beater bar.

He should have worn something more than his flip-flops, but they'd been by the door and he'd grabbed them out of habit. A shard shot out from the force of the vacuum and embedded in his foot. He shook off the flip-flop, pulled out the glass.

Blood trickled off the end of his foot. He turned off the vacuum, limped to the kitchen sink. Grabbing a towel, he pressed it to the wound.

He'd left bloody footprints across the white carpet, the wooden floor.

Holding the towel to his foot, he hopped down the hallway to his room.

The disarray wasn't unusual for a morning, but something felt . . .

Wait.

Annalise's dresser drawers lay open, the contents scattered on the floor, on the bed. Shoes littered the floor like bomb debris. In the bathroom, her makeup box sat on the counter, empty, as if she'd dumped everything into a bag.

She hadn't taken much, evident from the remains.

She had, however, taken the Bible by her bed. And the wallet-size baby shots in the three-hole frame. She'd left the bigger photo of their wedding and the five-by-seven of their family, a replica of the destroyed shot in the family room, but he couldn't shake the feeling that once again climbed into his belly.

Annalise had left him.

Nathan sat on the bed.

Sure, she'd probably fled out of a desire to protect them, but . . .

But she hadn't believed in him enough to trust that he'd protect her, stick by her. Which meant she'd been lying to him about that, too, for years.

For better or worse—yeah, right.

He sat there, listening to his heart thump. Glanced at the clock.

Then he picked up the phone, his hands shaking just a little. His call to her cell went to voice mail.

Maybe she had it turned off.

He set the phone back on the mount. Stood. Took a breath.

So this was what it came to. He stared at their mussed bed, usually so perfectly made up every morning by his wife. Today the sheets lay in a tangle, evidence of a restless sleep—if she'd slept at all—and their turbulent morning.

He wanted to rip them off the bed. To throw them in a ball across the room.

Instead, he found himself hopping back to the bathroom. He opened the medicine cabinet and grabbed a box of Band-Aids.

He sat on the toilet to affix one over the wound.

Then, getting up, he limped back into the bedroom, his thoughts strangely quiet.

She'd left him.

With this mess she'd created of their lives.

He took the covers, pulling them up, then smoothed the comforter over the top. Tossed the pillows—maybe a little too hard—at the head.

Nathan turned and left the room, pausing at the edge of the family room. Droplets of blood embedded the Berber carpet, so recently laid. They'd saved every penny for a year for this carpet, and Annalise had waited until the yearly sale, picking out exactly the stain-resistant variety she needed.

Going to the kitchen sink, he grabbed an old ice cream bucket from under it and filled it with hot water and some Pine-Sol.

He didn't care that it scalded his hands as he plunged a rag into the water, then began to attack the stains. He scrubbed each one, practically wearing away the carpet in his effort.

He'd shot at his son and his wife had left him.

The water turned metallic, roughened his hands.

This was Annalise's fault. If she'd just trusted him—and not only today, but at the beginning, the very beginning . . .

And she said she believed in him. "'You can do anything, Nathan. You're my hero,'" he mimicked. He knocked the bucket, and the bloody water sloshed out onto the other side, the clean carpet, soaking it through.

Perfect.

Worse, he could still see his bloody steps.

So much for stain-resistant.

He hefted the bucket back to the sink and poured out the bloody water, rinsing the bucket and adding fresh, scalding water.

He'd get the stains out. The carpet would be good as new.

And if she wanted to do this on her own, if she wanted to abandon him . . . She'd gotten them into this mess; she could just take it with her out of town. Out of their lives.

He yanked the bucket from the sink with so much force that the water sloshed down his legs. He cursed, for the second time today—see, she was turning him into a person he didn't even know—and carried it to the family room. His legs burned with the heat of the water, and he couldn't even feel his hands as he squeezed out the rag and then decided to just pour the water onto the stains. It saturated them, flooded out beyond the borders into clean carpet.

He kept scrubbing, moving again to each one. "I didn't marry Deidre O'Reilly, thank you very much."

"Nathan?"

He startled, jerked back, hitting the bucket. It turned over but Nathan ignored it, instead staring up at John Christiansen. The man wore his EMS jacket, concern on his face. "Who are you talking to?"

Nathan ground back a word and turned to rescue the bucket. "No one. Myself. The idiot cleaning up his wife's mess."

John turned and went to the kitchen without speaking. He returned a moment later with a wad of towels. He threw them on the carpet, over the water, and began to step on them.

Nathan climbed to his feet. He was soaked through—his pants, his shirt. They were starting to chafe.

"I was on my way to the school for CPR class, thought I'd stop by and see if you wanted to grab some coffee first. Uh . . . what's going on?" John raised an eyebrow, his gaze scanning over Nathan, landing on the bandaged foot, then the broken picture frame. Finally on the hole Nathan's shot left in the wall. "Everything okay here?"

Nathan scooped up the bucket, biting back a "Does it *look* okay?" Instead he said, "I'm fine."

"Of course you are. Clearly."

"John—" He wanted to round on the man, to put his anger somewhere.

John held up his hand. "I'm on your team here. What happened?"

Nathan stared at the towels soaking up the blood and water. "Annalise has left me; that's what happened."

"I doubt that."

"Really, she's left me."

"She wouldn't do that, Nathan. She loves you; she loves her kids. There hasn't been a time I've known you that she wasn't bragging on them or glowing about her husband. She didn't *leave* you."

"You don't know Annalise."

John frowned. "I've known Annalise nearly as long as you have."

"No, you don't get it. Neither one of us knows Annalise. She's not who she says she is." Nathan heard a warning in the back of his head, but frankly, he couldn't bear another moment carrying these secrets. How had Annalise done it for twenty years? "Her name is really Deidre O'Reilly, and she's been in the Witness Security Program since she came to Deep Haven."

Nathan gave himself points for reacting better than John, who stared at him as if he'd spoken Portuguese.

"Yes. She's lied to us all these years. Lied to me. Evidently she's been hiding from some drug lord who is now on the loose and hunting her down."

"Nathan—"

"Oh, it gets better. Uncle Frank? *Not* her uncle. Feel free to sit down because Uncle Frank is really her WitSec agent and is here to *move her and our entire family*."

John did sit down.

"Meanwhile, he's been dating my mother, who I think has fallen for him. Need a paper bag yet? Because I'm just getting started. My mother . . . has . . . cancer."

He delivered that as best he could, hoping the words wouldn't touch him; he'd been dodging them since the moment she—or rather, Frank—confessed it.

"I'm sorry."

"Oh yeah, life is super fun in the Decker house right now. Especially for Colleen because apparently her boyfriend was here the other night in her room."

"What?"

Good man—John found his feet, looked like he might be willing to go tear the boy limb from limb for Nathan.

"Yeah. I had dinner with him last night. Thought he was a nice kid. Shook his hand. I should have ripped it from his body."

"It can't be that bad."

"I wouldn't know because Annalise didn't breathe a word about it. Just another secret she's kept from me. And you didn't get the best part . . . Who put this hole in the wall and nearly killed my eleven-year-old? Me. I nearly shot my son, John." He shook his head, walked to the window. "I sat up all night like an idiot with my dad's old .22 in my lap, and this morning when Henry walked in, I woke up, jerked, and the gun went off." He felt his voice begin to crack, his chest tighten. "By the grace of God, Henry isn't dead right now."

He felt nauseous, had to bend over, grab his knees. Breathe. He could barely hear his own voice over the thunder of his heart. "So when I say that Annalise left me, believe me, I'm not kidding. She ran from me, from this mess, and I pray she takes it with her and lets us all live in peace."

He closed his eyes, trying to lay hold of his words, to bring them into a place where he could mean them.

At the moment, he hated no one more than himself. "How did I let this happen? How did this get so bad?"

"Sit down, Nathan. You look like you're going to keel over."

Nathan felt a hand on his shoulder, shrugged it off, but managed to sink into his recliner. No, not there. He moved over to the sofa. Hid his face in his hands.

"I feel like I'm walking onto the football field thirty years ago, into the mess my father made. Seeing the destruction of his decisions, his mistakes, and now I gotta live in the debris." Nathan ran his hands behind his neck. "A huge part of me wants to just say . . . good riddance. Let her go. Forget about Annalise—or Deidre— and salvage what we have left."

He closed his eyes. Salvage what they had left. Like his mother had done. He'd done fine without a father—his children could learn to live without their mother.

What choice did they have?

"So you're going to give up. Walk away. Do what your father did."

Nathan looked up at John, who had his hands in his pockets. Made for an easy tackle if he wanted. "I'm not my father. Besides, I'm not the one doing the leaving."

"Yeah, you are, Nathan. You're turning in your equipment, just like football. And maybe you didn't betray your wife, but you're doing it again—letting what someone else did sideline you instead of fighting for what you want."

"This isn't football. This is our lives, John. This is twenty years of deceit. Please, no more football metaphors."

"Okay, fine. Here's the truth. When you married Annalise, you married her past—her good and bad past—as well as her future. You agreed to the whole package when you said, 'I do.'"

"I don't even know the person I married. If she's not who she said she was when I married her, are my vows even valid?"

He hadn't thought of that before, and suddenly it scared him how easily that excuse fell into place. He'd never married Annalise . . . because she didn't exist. God couldn't hold a divorce against him when he'd *never married her*, right?

"You're hearing a lie, Nate. Annalise *is* the person you married. It doesn't matter what her name was. You married her heart, her soul, her mind, her body, and have been loving her for twenty years. So she didn't tell you all her secrets—did you tell her about the time you got wasted at homecoming and were arrested for indecent exposure?"

Nathan glared at him. "That was a childish prank in ninth grade. Not even a comparison here."

John lifted a shoulder. "Full disclosure, pal. Skinny-dipping in Lake Superior might be a no deal for her."

"Stop."

"See, that's my point. That's not you. You wouldn't do that now—and she's not the person she was in her past. Annalise is who she's been every day for twenty years. She loves you, Nathan. And God loves you both. He's blessed you, and by His grace, you can fix this."

Nathan didn't move. "Don't talk to me about God's grace. I did this right, John. I kept my promises to my wife. I've been faithful; I've provided. I've tried to be a good husband. And what do I get? Lies. Where is God's grace, God's blessings, now? Where are my promises?"

"Your promises are found in staying the course. In obedience.

In the *yes* and *amen* we say to God's work in our lives, whatever it might be. That's when God's promises show up."

Nathan shook his head.

"Don't judge God's love for you on your circumstances, Nathan. Judge it on what you know to be true. God loves you, and He'll give you the strength to do what's right. Just stay the course. That's what God wants for you—everyday faith. Not . . ." John pointed at the wall.

Nathan followed his gaze to the jagged hole in the plaster. Cracks ran through the walls in a spiderweb away from the gash. But like so many other cracks in their house, he could repair this, plaster over it, repaint, make it look good as new. Even better. Stronger. And while their home might never be fancy, it would be . . . home.

And Nathan Decker knew the worth of a home.

He might not be a tough guy, might not know how to handle a gun, but as long as he had breath, he wasn't going to let Annalise leave without a fight.

16

THE CLOCK IN TUCK'S ENGLISH CLASS had ceased to function, the minute hand permanently stuck at 11:33.

Two minutes. Two grinding, jaw-breaking, stomach-churning minutes before Tuck could escape Mrs. Hallberg's prattle about the relationship between Macbeth and Darth Vader—not a bad comparison if he were at all interested in learning about tragic heroes. But he needed to see Colleen. To pull her close, maybe give her a kiss.

And to confirm that, indeed, he'd had dinner with her family last night and no one brought him to trial, no one tried to execute him. No one even made him feel like he was the homeless guy eating Thanksgiving dinner at the table.

He had felt like one of them—a Decker. A member of her family. Like they might invite him back.

Oh, he was a fool, wasn't he? To actually think that Mr. Decker had meant it when he shook his hand? To think that Mrs. Decker had forgiven him?

One minute.

He'd seen Colleen as she walked into school today, looking a little angry—as if she'd had another fight with her mother.

Please let it not be over him.

He'd tried to catch up with her, but the bell rang and she ducked into her English class.

She hadn't answered his text either.

He'd have to meet her in the lunchroom. Thankfully, she hated Taco Tuesday, so he'd suggest they go down to the coffee shop or maybe over to the sandwich shop for lunch. Of course, that's what busted them last week—their Taco Tuesday run and the brief tryst in the lighthouse parking lot. But things had turned around since last Tuesday.

This Tuesday, Mrs. Decker liked him. This Tuesday, he would ask Colleen out on a date for Friday night, and by Sunday, maybe he'd be watching football with the family.

Thirty seconds.

Mrs. Hallberg was writing the assignment on the board. He usually had to read it a few times before he could unscramble the letters. Now he stared at it, trying to decipher the page numbers correctly when finally—yes!—the bell rang.

Tuck grabbed his books—he'd figure out the assignment later—and flowed into the hall with the other students.

He dumped his books in his locker, then headed to the lunchroom. The jocks had linebackered to the front of the line, their girlfriends glued to their bodies.

A few of Colleen's volleyball friends already filled their booth.

She used to sit with them, but when she started dating Tuck, she'd joined him and a couple of her friends with boyfriends. He knew them—one played basketball; another was on the ski team. Not his friends, but he hadn't that many anyway.

Tuck leaned against the door, pulled out his phone, scrolled down for a message from her. Nothing. He watched as the line filled. The smell of spicy ground beef and grease seasoned the lunchroom, along with the hum of conversation, punctuated by occasional shouts. Probably everyone was staring at him, so he scanned the room, then headed toward the volleyball table.

"Hey, Tucker," Amelia Christiansen said as he approached. Her family owned a resort on Evergreen Lake. She was pretty enough with her dark hair, those green eyes.

"Hey. Have you seen Colleen?"

Ginny Iverson sat beside her, her blonde hair pulled into a high ponytail. "Yeah. I think she's in the gym, working on her serve. She seemed pretty upset today in English, so Coach told her she could work out during fifth period."

Upset. Maybe she *had* gotten into a fight with her mother. That sort of punched some of the breath from his lungs.

He pulled out his phone again. R U OK?

C'mon, Colleen, answer.

But she didn't text him back and he pushed his way out of the lunchroom, heading toward the gym.

He was just rounding the corner when Jason appeared out of the boys' bathroom.

"Hey, Jason." Tuck brushed past him but jerked back.

Jason's hand had clamped him on the shoulder. "If you're looking for my sister, stay away." Jason spun him around, his eyes dark.

A hand crawled through Tuck's gut, squeezed. "Why?"

"You two are done. Over."

He shrugged off Jason's hand. "Back off, dude."

Jason stood there for a moment, his face tight. He wasn't a big kid—spent most of his time spouting Shakespeare on the stage—but he had a presence about him as he stood in the hall, kids now walking past them, eyeing them.

No way did he need a fight here in the middle of the hallway. Tuck put up his hands. "Dude, I don't know what this is about—"

"How about your midnight visit to my sister?"

"What—? Wait a second—"

Jason took a swing at him. Not close enough to connect, but the fist still grazed him enough for Tuck to jump back. "Dude!"

But Jason didn't stop, came right up in his grill, gave him a push. Tuck went down, hit the floor, but bounced back up and circled him.

A few of the kids had stopped to watch.

Tuck kept his voice low. "Jason, it's not what you think. Nothing happened."

"You're a dirtbag, Newman. You stay away from my sister." Jason lunged at him again.

Tuck stepped aside, tripped him. Jason skidded into a bank of lockers.

More crowd appeared. He felt the words pulsing in the air. *Fight. Fight.*

Tucker held up his hands. "You gotta calm down, dude."

Jason hit his feet and charged. Tuck caught him around the waist as Jason slammed him into the other bank of lockers. He shoved Jason away, landing his hand into his breastbone, punching out his breath. Jason fell back, gasping.

Tuck scooted away. "What is your deal?"

"The deal is you keep your hands off my sister." Jason had his hand on Tuck's chest, his breath heaving.

Oh no. "You got it all wrong, man. I'm not sleeping with Colleen. In fact, I keep trying *not* to sleep with her. Try that on for size, jerk."

Tucker heard a gasp, glanced behind him, and spied Colleen.

She stood in the hallway dressed in her workout gear, her face white. She hadn't said a word in his defense. Hadn't come out to rescue him. Another man stood behind her. A big man—Tuck thought it might be Amelia's dad. He wore an official-looking jacket like he was an on-campus cop.

Well, they weren't going to drag him away to detention without someone hearing the truth. He turned to Jason, letting the venom fill his voice. "Please. Everyone knows you're getting it on with Harper Jacobsen. But it doesn't matter, does it? You're a Decker and you're perfect. You can do no wrong. But when you're a guy like me, no matter what you do, you can't get a break. Guess what—I really liked your sister, and I was just trying to find her to make sure she was okay. Try to keep her out of trouble, will ya? You might need a leash."

When he glanced at Colleen, he saw her jaw tighten as she looked away.

He sorta regretted those last words. Or maybe he regretted the entire thing—thinking that a girl like her might hang with him, thinking that he might belong in her family, that he could rewrite his rep.

He pushed past Colleen.

Amelia's dad stood in his path. Tuck shot him the finger. "Move."

He regretted that too, but that's what they expected of him, and he liked to live up to expectations.

To his shock, the man stepped aside, staring at him with something of sadness in his expression. "Do what you know is right, Tucker," he said loud enough for Tuck and the entire school to hear.

Yeah, well, he'd tried that route.

He nearly broke into a run as he stalked out of school, heading them off on the detention, the suspension. Maybe he'd never come back.

He pushed through the doors, not stopping until he reached the parking lot.

An old beater Honda, grimy from the road, sat at the curb, idling. He kept his head down but shot a glance at the guy inside. His eyes raked over Tuck, his mouth pursed, a layer of whiskers on his chin. And he had a tattoo that wound up around his neck all the way to his chin. Tucker snuck another peek at it as he stormed by. He thought it was a snake.

The man looked like some kind of criminal.

Probably how Tuck looked to the Decker family. He'd been a fool to think he'd ever fit into their world.

&

After hours of tests and more waiting, at least Helen didn't have to take the news while wearing a cotton sheet, her backside open to the wind. Paula granted her the dignity of putting her in a private waiting area, letting her watch the sunshine as it poured down from the skies.

It couldn't reach her spirit.

How could Frank have betrayed her? Spied on her and then spilled her secret to her family?

She should have listened to her instincts and kept him out

of her life. She didn't need Frank Harrison. So he had made her feel young and alive and helped her believe she could live beyond Deep Haven. She didn't need him in order to be happy, to change her life. For pity's sake, she'd only known him a week or less, and she'd decided to build her life around him? Maybe she had a brain tumor too.

For a few days there, she hadn't recognized herself. Had actually wooed herself into believing that she might have a second chance at love.

Foolish old woman.

She should be concentrating on what had happened at Nathan's house to make him sleep with a shotgun.

Helen pressed her hand to her chest. Good night, she barely knew him this morning when he asked her to leave. Worse, he'd looked at Annalise with such venom . . .

It had reminded her too much of how Dylan had looked at her that last day, when she told him he'd never see his son again if she had anything to say about it.

She swallowed past the tightness in her throat. *Please, God, don't let Nathan make my mistakes.*

A knock came at the door and Helen looked up as Paula entered. She looked so crisp and young this morning, dressed in a white jacket, a stethoscope around her neck.

"Helen, thank you for coming in."

Oh, she couldn't go through this again. Helen took a breath. "Before you start, I've already made up my mind. I don't want chemotherapy. I can't put my family—"

"Helen." Paula shook her head. "You don't have cancer."

Helen stared at her, her pulse in her ears. She didn't have— "Then what's wrong with me?" Oh no, what if it was something worse? Like Lou Gehrig's disease or Huntington's? Her hand wrapped around the arm of her chair.

"You may have lupus. The fatigue, the weight loss, even your headaches and upset stomach. All symptoms. I need to do a few more tests—an ANA test, and we'll need a urinalysis to see if it has affected your kidneys. Your hemoglobin is low, and you're a bit anemic, but you had a full body scan three months ago." Paula leaned forward, pressed a hand to her knee. "You don't have cancer."

"And the bruises?"

"They're called purpura—looks a lot like a bruise, and some of these are actual bruises, of course, which is also a symptom of lupus."

"What is lupus?"

"It's a chronic autoimmune disease that presents when your body's immune system attacks your own tissues and organs, including your skin, blood cells, brain, heart and lungs, kidneys, and especially the joints. It can often be accompanied by fibro-myalgia and lead into more serious complications like a stroke or heart attack."

"So I'm not going to die a slow death. I could drop right here."

"Helen."

"Calm down, Paula. I'm just giving you a hard time."

Paula offered a tight smile. "There's no cure, but we treat the symptoms, and there are a number of homeopathic options as well. We'll do more tests, but at this point, I don't think you should be announcing to your family that you have cancer. They might panic."

Oh, boy. She had no idea. "Thank you, Paula."

The doctor left Helen in the waiting area.

No cancer.

So she didn't face a slow death. She didn't have the dire push to change her life, to see the world, to live dangerously, as if for the last time. She stared at the clock, watched the long hand tick toward noon. It matched her heartbeat, the pace of her life.

But perhaps she didn't need a reason to jump into a second chance.

Maybe she'd just been looking for a reason like cancer to risk loving again. Risk being the woman who still stirred inside her. The woman who had, once upon a time, climbed onto the back of Dylan's motorcycle.

The woman she'd been before he betrayed her.

The woman she'd seen returning . . . until Frank betrayed her.

Except maybe she'd been the one doing the betraying. People who loved each other didn't keep secrets.

Maybe Frank had deserved to know the truth. Be given the choice to stay . . . or leave.

She pulled on her coat, fighting the burn in her throat.

Yes, she should have been honest with Frank. Now the poor man was probably trying to figure out how to walk out of her life without hurting her. She stood in the hallway, staring through the window at the parking lot, where the glistening maple leaves splotched the ground like blood.

Why did she have to live her life by impulses, scraping up the results of her actions?

She'd just call him. Maybe . . . maybe ask him out to lunch. Or coffee. Most of all, she'd start with telling him the truth. No more secrets.

Helen fished out her cell phone. Dead. Or maybe just off. . . . Right. She'd shut it off in church a few weeks—maybe months?— ago when the pastor suggested it.

She pressed the Power button and it came to life.

Wait . . . did she have Frank's number? Maybe Annalise had it . . .

Her phone beeped as it found a signal. Four missed calls.

How did she get her voice mail again? Helen dialed and waited for the beep, then entered her Social Security number. It was the only thing she could remember.

Behold, it worked.

The first two were calls from the prayer chain, old news that she deleted. She'd have to update the records at church. Or perhaps just keep her cell phone on.

The next was an automated call from the library. She'd returned that book a week ago.

The last came from an unfamiliar number. But the voice she knew.

"Helen. I don't know if you'll get this or not. Or when. But . . . I had to tell you I'm sorry."

Yes, well . . . her too. Helen sank down on a bench, pressing the phone tighter to her ear. Frank sounded like he was outside, the wind against the phone.

"I have to leave. I know you're angry with me for telling everyone your secret, but . . . I have to talk to you. I know what Nathan told you, but I can't let you believe that what we had was a game or lies."

A game? Lies? What was he talking about?

"Or that I didn't care. By now you probably know about Annalise and why we did what we did. It was for her safety, and I promise I didn't want to deceive you."

Her chest tightened.

"I was just hoping that you'd learn to trust me, and that if we had to relocate you, you'd see that I was trying to help."

Relocate her? What was he talking about?

"You changed me, Helen. You awoke something inside me and . . . I'm so sorry I won't be with you. I want you to know that if you do ever need anything, you can call me. I . . . I'm so sorry."

The line went dead.

Helen stared at the phone.

She had no idea what to make of his words. Relocate her? What about Annalise?

I promise I didn't want to deceive you.

Which meant that he did lie to her . . . at least about something. She closed her eyes, willing herself not to do something rash like throw her phone across the room. Or call him back, tell him to stay out of her life or . . .

Her phone vibrated in her hand. She stared at the number.

No.

She didn't want to know. Didn't want to care. Didn't want to relive the past.

She answered, "What?"

"Helen, please don't hang up—I have to talk to you."

"No. You don't. We're done talking. Please, don't ever call me again."

She hung up and pressed the Power button. See, she'd never liked these things.

No more silliness. Second chances just cost too much.

&

Tucker!

His name was glued in Colleen's chest.

Don't go.

Colleen stood at the door, watching Tucker drive away, so much anger in the spin of his tires, the way he barreled out of the school parking lot.

She didn't blame him. She should have said something, stopped the fight, but she'd just stood there with the rest of the crowd, watching him fight her brother in the hallway.

She'd caused this, and now she wanted to run. Maybe after him. Maybe just away.

Ever since the shot that woke her this morning, seeing her brother standing in the hallway surrounded by glass, and then . . . Why hadn't Mom told Dad about Tucker? The horror on her father's face made her want to weep.

Maybe her mom had just been trying to protect her. The thought thickened Colleen's throat, and the memory of their fight replaying in her head didn't help.

And now Tucker had left her too.

Try to keep her out of trouble, will ya? You might need a leash. Tucker didn't mean that the way it sounded, so full of hurt.

She stalked back up the hallway, saw Jason standing there, surrounded by his congratulatory friends. She hooked his arm, yanked him toward some privacy. "Is it true—what he said about Harper?" she asked quietly.

Jason glanced over his shoulder. "Shut up."

What—?

"Just stay away from that jerk." He disappeared down the hall.

She stared after him, feeling punched. So Jason had secrets too. The only difference was he never got caught.

She watched him walk away and tried not to throw something at him.

And yesterday, sitting at dinner, she'd thought everything

would be okay. That her mother had forgiven her for their fight. In fact, she'd almost climbed into bed with her mother last night, as if she were ten years old. She'd thought about lying there with her, their hands wound together. She loved her mother's hands, the strength of them.

She should have been nicer when she got out of the car today.

The bell rang for the end of fifth period.

Colleen debated, then went to her locker, pulling out her phone and her jacket. She shrugged it on and headed out the front doors. She could walk home—it wasn't that far. The wind caught her hair, tumbled leaves before her as she crossed the parking lot. Regret burned inside, distracted her.

She didn't hear the car until it had stopped, until the driver got out, moved toward her.

She turned, startled. A man about the size of her father, with dark hair, a dark beard with strands of gray. He smelled like he hadn't bathed in weeks, wearing a dirty canvas jacket, a blue stocking cap.

She glanced around, looking for others in the lot, but this time of day, it was empty. Even the gulls had abandoned her.

She thought about screaming but had no breath for it when the man grabbed her wrist, yanked her close, and pressed a blade to her neck.

"Get into the car, little Deidre."

17

ANNALISE STEPPED INTO THE SHOWER, lifting her face to the spray, allowing the water to wash away the horror of the day. It might also put heat back into her frigid bones, warm her core, make her feel new.

After all, she couldn't be Annalise Decker anymore. She'd have to find a new name. A new identity.

But how could she erase the memory of her eleven-year-old holding on to her as he said good-bye today? Of reading to him at night, Henry tucked in the safety of her embrace?

Or Colleen's delicious smell, her amazing smile, the way she could crawl inside Annalise's heart, even when she wanted to ground her daughter to her room for a year?

Or Jason? Listening to him recite his lines, watching him strut around the family room like a real Romeo. He'd been the first of her babies to take her breath away.

How would she forget Nathan? The taste of his lips against hers, the feel of his strong hand around her waist?

She shivered under the heat of the shower and turned it off. Grabbed a towel. No, she could never be anyone but Annalise Decker. Her name might change, but her identity wouldn't.

She'd spent the past four hours or more staring at the cold fireplace, then the glow of the afternoon light on the lake, imagining what her family might be doing. Did they even know she'd left? Helen would be furious with her. And Nathan . . .

Nathan was long past forgiving her.

When Colleen found out about her mother's lies . . . oh, Annalise prayed her daughter wouldn't use it as a one-size-fits-all excuse to run off with Tucker.

Maybe she should have taken Colleen with her. But then what? Tear their family further apart?

Annalise wrapped a towel around her, combed out her hair, then sat on the side of the soaking tub in the massive master bathroom. She could hold a Super Bowl party in here, practically heard her heartbeat echo off the Italian tile.

How could she leave them?

But how could she stay? As long as Garcia knew where she was, they weren't safe.

She'd gotten them into this danger. She'd do anything to keep them safe.

Annalise reached for the lotion on the side of the tub, squirted it into her hands, began to smooth it over her legs. Her hand ran over the scar by her knee. Misshapen, about the size of an eraser.

"What was it?"

She dropped the lotion bottle. Nathan stood in the doorway, his green surplus Army jacket open over a flannel shirt, a pair of faded jeans, his hiking boots now dripping onto the clean carpet. He hadn't shaved and looked a little raw-edged and even . . . scary.

He didn't smile, and she couldn't place his expression. Angry? Worried?

"You didn't think I'd let you just leave, right? That I wouldn't come after you? That I'd let you face this alone?"

She braced herself. "How did you find me?"

"I've been looking for hours. . . . I was halfway to Duluth, and then I realized . . . you'd stay in town for Colleen's game. At least to listen to it on the radio. So I thought, where would you go to feel safe?" He looked past her to the lake. "You love this house. I should have figured it out right away."

Her throat closed. "You shouldn't have come. You should have let me go."

"No." He came into the bathroom, knelt on the soggy bath rug before her. Oh, he had beautiful eyes, the kind that riveted on her now. However, something about them seemed . . . different. Stronger. "Annalise, you're my wife. And I meant that—for better or worse."

"This is definitely worse."

He shook his head. "This is most definitely *not* worse. *Worse* is you walking out of our lives. *Worse* is not knowing where you are and going crazy with worry. *Worse* is the thought of waking up every day without you, knowing how broken our children are without their mother." He swallowed and looked away, closing his eyes as if gathering himself before he met her gaze again. "*Worse* is thinking every day that you might be dead."

She ran her fingers under her eyes.

His jaw tightened then, as if pain gathered in his throat. "*Worse* is knowing that you thought I didn't love you enough to stay with you. To fight for you. To be your husband. *Worse* is you giving up on us."

"I didn't give up on us. . . . I just . . ."

"You stopped believing in us." He caught her hands.

"And why not? Nathan—Henry could have been killed today because of me."

"What are you talking about? Henry nearly got hurt because *I* did something stupid and rash, like you did by running away. I thought I could solve this on my own. But we're not in this alone, babe. I recall adding a 'so help me God' to our vows. I'm taking that to mean God's in this with us."

"God can't fix this. He's laughing at me. I'm finally getting what I deserve." She pulled her hands away.

"Seriously? That's what you think?"

"Yes. Everything was perfect and then—"

"Everything *wasn't* perfect, Annalise!" Nathan stood. "Jason has a girlfriend we know nothing about, and who knows what is going on there. Colleen had a boy in her room the other night—"

Annalise looked away.

"Yes, you should have told me, although I have to admit, murder wouldn't look good for my campaign."

She glanced up at him, unsure if he was kidding or not.

Maybe not.

"I'm so sorry, Nathan. And your poor mother. I can't believe she has cancer again."

He drew in a breath. "Yeah, well, life is messy and painful and unpredictable. And this guy Garcia is just one of the horrible things that could happen to us. But we can't run away and change our name every time something threatens our happy lives."

"It wasn't like that—"

"I know, babe. I know." He crouched in front of her again. "And maybe leaving Deep Haven will be the wisest thing we can do." His voice gentled. "But we make that decision together. You and me. For better or worse. Richer or poorer. Deckers or Smiths." He caught her eyes. "You told me that we didn't belong together. But we do. We belonged together the day we said, 'I do.'"

How she wanted to believe him. "You don't understand. Garcia is an evil man. . . ."

"Lise, I know. Frank told me." He cupped his hand on her cheek. "He also told me that they might have caught him."

She stilled, caught her breath. "Really?"

"But even if they didn't, I'm not going to let him hurt you. Or our family. If he's still out there, we'll leave."

"And your mom?"

He swallowed, his mouth a grim slash. "We'll figure it out. She can come with us."

"I don't know what to do. I'm . . ." Her vision blurred. "I'm scared, Nathan. I am scared that it's all going to end badly." She pulled her hands away to wrap them around herself. "I don't deserve you. I knew that the moment I met you. I knew that someday you'd find out who I was, and that it would all crumble. This life we built—our happily ever after. I feared it would come crashing in and I'd lose everything again."

His expression twisted and he shook his head, cradling her face. "No, Lise, I don't deserve *you*. You walked into my life and suddenly I wasn't who I thought I was. I looked into your eyes and saw the man I wanted to be. You believed in me and I wanted to be the man you saw."

"You are that man, Nathan."

"I'm trying to be. Every day. And that's the key. Maybe we don't deserve each other—but that's what grace is. Getting what you don't deserve. God loving us, even with His knowing everything, including our mistakes, our failures." He ran his thumb down her cheek with a tenderness that sent heat to her bones, filling her entire body.

"I love you, Annalise. I would die for you. You are the sweet reward between all the chaotic, painful, dangerous moments of life. You and Jason and Colleen and Henry. Happily ever after isn't a place; it's a perspective. We just gotta hold on to that because that's how we're going to get through this. Trusting in God's love, His grace, one moment at a time. That's how we live happily ever after, every day."

"Grace will lead us home." The words stirred in her heart. "But I wrecked everything. Nothing will ever be the same. You'll never look at me the same. I'll always see Deidre in your eyes."

She looked away, but he brought her gaze back to his face.

"Lise . . . I married *you*. I don't care what your name was or is. The circumstances don't change my love for you. It is. And will be. I love you, period."

I love you, period.

She stared at him, the way he held her with his eyes. The smell of him so close, drawing her in. The edge of whiskers darkening his skin. He hadn't even combed his hair today—instead he'd spent it looking for her.

Like he needed her.

Like, yes, he couldn't live without her.

He lowered his voice, his eyes soft, a smile tipping his mouth. "But you're right. Nothing will be the same. It'll be better. Because finally, *finally* . . . I know you."

Nathan leaned forward and kissed her. Softly, so familiar, so right. Then he leaned away and met her eyes again.

Annalise opened her mouth, not sure what to say. She started to smile . . .

And then he really kissed her.

A kiss that was nothing like she'd ever experienced in his arms. He wrapped his hand around her neck and met her mouth with a sort of sweet desperation in his touch. Full and thorough, knowing her and drinking her in as if, indeed, he'd meant his words.

I would die for you.

Something broke free inside her, a flush of heat and life that she'd tamped away for years, afraid of the depths of her feelings, of her dependence on this man she didn't deserve.

Didn't deserve but had been given. Because of the great love of God, who'd loved her through Nathan, in sickness and health, for richer and poorer, for better or worse.

Especially better.

"I know you, and I love you."

She slid into Nathan's arms, kissing him back. He tasted like the outdoors, piney and a little wild, and she wove her fingers into his hair as he pulled her tight to his chest.

She'd forgotten what a strong man he was.

Now, his strength sparked a fire deep inside.

Nathan—amazing, kind, sweet Nathan—lowered her to the floor, his arms around her. Her heart left her as she clung to him, surrendered to his embrace, drinking in his touch, running her fingers along his beautiful face. Loving his gentleness, his strength, the gift of his love.

This was where she belonged, whatever her name might be.

When he pulled away, she felt his smile on her even before she opened her eyes. His gaze drank her in, a depth to his expression that resonated in his words. "I love you, Annalise. And Deidre. And whoever you might be in the future. As I heard Jason say yesterday, isn't a rose by any other name still a rose?"

"And now you're Romeo?"

When he grinned, there was the boy she'd fallen in love with, the man he'd been on their wedding night, the hero he'd become every day of their lives.

How had she ever thought him ho-hum?

He traced his hand down to her knee, to the scar there.

"It was a sparrow," she said, cupping her hand over his. "I remembered hearing in church how God watched even the sparrows, and I liked it. Held on to it, even when I was running from Him. It was better than a flower or a dove or a four-leaf clover."

"A sparrow." He ran his thumb over it before he kissed her again.

This time in his touch she tasted the freshness, the newness of the days before them.

"Ready to go home?" he whispered.

Annalise slipped her hand inside his jacket, to where his T-shirt met his neck. Ran her thumb over the hollow of his throat. Smiled. "Not quite yet."

&

"Now Helen's not answering. None of them are." Frank tossed his phone onto the dashboard of his rental. "I called the sheriff's office and they sent a cruiser by the house, but there's no one there."

"Calm down, Frank. We can't help anyone if we skid off the road." Boyd sat in the passenger seat with his hand braced on the dashboard. "And watch out for deer." Outside, the sun had begun to lie low upon the horizon, a sizzling burn of light.

He should have listened to his gut and brought Annalise with him, regardless of what Nathan said. "Welcome to northern Minnesota. Garcia could already be in Deep Haven; Annalise and her entire family might be dead—"

"Sorry."

No more than Frank was. He'd wanted to hit something when he walked into the coroner's office and took a look at the victim, the so-called Luis Garcia.

Only, not Garcia. He heard his own words echo back to him. "This is Ramos Steele, Garcia's right-hand man," he'd said quietly. "Garcia must have picked him up in California. We've never been able to capture him." Until now.

Until Ramos had somehow helped Garcia give the Canadian police and Frank's own team the slip.

"I'll try Nathan again," Boyd said, picking up the phone.

"I told him to find his wife, to hide her someplace safe. I didn't really think he'd listen to me." Frank touched the brakes as he rounded a curve. So maybe they didn't have to die en route to Deep Haven. But a lot could happen in two hours. Or four.

He couldn't erase the image of Helen walking into a trap in her living room. Garcia waiting for her in the darkness.

Never mind the thought of what he'd do to Annalise. To Colleen. How Nathan might die trying to protect his family. How his sons would perish with him.

Frank gritted his jaw as he came up too fast on a car, surged around it. "I should have moved them all that first day. Why didn't I listen to my gut?"

"We weren't even sure if they were in danger—"

"I knew it!" Frank slammed his hand on the steering wheel. "I knew it." He glanced at Boyd. "I've been doing this a long time. If they die, it's on me."

Oh, God. If he ever felt like praying, it was now. But he didn't even know where to start. How long had it been since he had a one-on-one with the Almighty? Maybe at his wife's grave. Yes, they'd had words then. Mostly Frank apologizing, but a few accusations thrown too. And some private resolutions made. The kind he'd broken over and over and over this week as he let Annalise and her family pull him farther into their lives.

Uncle Frank.

He should have stopped those words before they ever left his mouth. And as for meeting Helen . . .

He rubbed his chest. It tightened under his hand.

He shouldn't have betrayed her. No wonder she'd hung up on him—he'd turned into her husband. And by now, she knew that he'd lied to her.

Just what did he think would happen?

He could admit that he'd hoped she'd forgive him. That he'd be able to tell her on his own terms. That . . . that she'd let him stick around and be the guy she needed. He'd already been trying to figure out how to take a leave of absence, maybe even—

"Pull over, Frank. I'm driving."

He glanced at Boyd.

"Seriously. Pull over. You're upset and driving like a maniac, and getting us killed isn't going to help anyone."

Frank ground his molars together but pulled off at the scenic overlook.

Boyd got out, marched in front of the car, and yanked open the door. "Now."

How he wanted to throw a punch at him. But the kid had some sense. Frank climbed out, retreated to the passenger side, and buckled in. "Try to stay on the road."

"You try to get ahold of someone." Boyd pulled out onto the highway.

Okay, Frank did feel a little better with Boyd driving. At least then he could dial the phone without swerving.

Helen's phone went again to voice mail. "Helen, please call me. I'm so sorry—but this is an emergency. Annalise is in trouble—you're all in trouble."

He held the phone to his forehead, adding a prayer to his message. Maybe desperation made it a bit easier to pray. No matter what his history with God, for this moment he could pretend the Almighty was on his side.

"I know about Gina Sullivan."

Frank shot his partner a look.

Boyd kept his face forward. "I was talking with some of the other agents and they told me what happened."

"That was a long time ago."

"You placed Annalise right about the time you placed Gina. I think it's haunting you."

"*You're* haunting me. Drive faster."

"You're a legend in the agency, boss. No one hides people like you do. But you can't protect everyone. I know you wanted to save that girl . . . and that your wife dying nearly killed you, but you aren't in charge of everyone and you can't bear that burden."

"I promised them they'd be safe."

"That's not your promise to make."

Frank looked away. "I can try."

"And when you fail, it destroys you."

"I'm fine."

"Frank, you care about the people we place more than anyone. I know this isn't the first time you've been to Deep Haven since you placed Annalise."

"They have some great fishing in northern Minnesota."

"It doesn't work to act like you don't care, like it won't affect you, because it does."

Frank stared out the window, to the sun falling behind the trees, the darkening sky. "It's just a job."

"No, it's not. I know your story, Frank. I know your wife died. I've been your partner long enough to know that you're lonely."

"That's not true. I don't need anyone."

"Really, Uncle Frank?"

He glanced at Boyd. "Watch yourself."

"You know what? I think you didn't move Annalise because you became part of the family. You kept telling yourself that it was pretend, but in your heart it felt real. Very real."

He'd request a new partner after this was over. "I'm not stupid. I know it's not real."

"But why can't it be? Make it real."

Frank frowned. "What are you talking about?"

"You're tired, Frank. You're tired of this business. Tired of sleeping in different towns, of dismantling people's lives and reinventing them all over. You've let it get inside you, turn you angry."

He wasn't angry, was he?

Maybe he was. Maybe he was angry at the injustice and the horrors and the pain, furious that he had to be the one who made it worse.

He was angry that too many people had to pay for the crimes

of others. That too many mothers wondered where their children were. Like Annalise's mother, Claire O'Reilly.

He might never get her face out of his head.

"Frank, I have news for you. We're the good guys. And it's time for you to do what you do best."

"What's that?"

"Reinvent yourself. Give yourself a new identity. Be Uncle Frank—not the guy with the devastating news but the one who takes the grandkids fishing."

"I can't be Uncle Frank—"

"You already are, boss."

Frank saw himself playing Monopoly with Henry. And cheering at Colleen's games.

And helping Helen make popcorn.

You already are.

"But it's not real. Helen will never forgive me. Even if I tell her I want to stick around, you don't understand—her ex-husband lied to her. He betrayed her. And now so did I."

"So maybe you have to work at it. Prove to her that you're not him. Make her see that you're in this. That is, if you want to be."

Oh, he wanted to be. He wanted to be the one who shoveled her porch and watched her make pie and took her dancing. And held her hand through whatever future lay ahead.

Helen had made him feel again—or want to.

She'd made him into Uncle Frank.

If she forgave him, maybe he would figure out how to stick around, all the way to the end.

"Faster, Boyd. Drive faster," Frank said as he picked up the phone again.

❧

Frank's message boiled in Helen's chest all day: *You probably know about Annalise and why we did what we did. . . . It was for her safety . . .*

It had her thinking like some sort of spy movie—Annalise tangled up in trouble. Her daughter-in-law came home with Nathan shortly before Henry got off the late bus, and Helen couldn't help but march over there.

Just in case Annalise felt like explaining herself.

You probably know about Annalise.

Annalise was in the kitchen, peeling potatoes for dinner. "I have a meat loaf in the oven."

That's all she had to say? Who had her son married? And what secrets did the woman harbor that justified a sentence like *It was for her safety . . . ?*

In the next room, Nathan was dismantling his shotgun. Not a word to her about where Frank might be.

She refused to ask.

"Keep an eye on the potatoes, will you, Helen?" Annalise said, flashing her a smile, then disappearing to straighten the entryway.

Oh, the whole thing could drive her to her last nerve. Fine, if they wanted to pretend like today never happened . . .

The sun remained only a simmer of fire on the far horizon, nearly snuffed out from the day. It got dark so early in Deep Haven this time of year.

Helen checked the meat loaf in the oven, then took the potatoes off the stove and dumped them into the colander in the sink. Steam rose, slurring the windowpanes. After returning the potatoes to the pot, she opened the fridge and found the milk, the butter. Fished out the masher from the crock.

Annalise came from the entryway and slid into a chair. "Helen, we need to talk."

Helen poured in the milk and out of the corner of her eye saw Nathan appear. Nod. What, was he keeping secrets from her too?

She cut in butter and picked up the masher.

"Please, Mom. Sit down," Nathan said.

"I'm fine here." Helen leaned over the pot and began to mash the potatoes.

"Mom!"

Nathan's tone made her drop the masher.

"We have to talk about the cancer."

Oh. The cancer. So that's what this was about. Now she felt foolish. She glanced at Nathan with a thin smile. "I don't have cancer. They ran tests and think it might be something else, something treatable. I'm so sorry for the trouble I caused."

Nathan folded his arms over his chest as if he were talking to a child. "Mom, really? You're not just saying that to protect us?"

Helen swallowed the rock in her throat and tried to sound normal. "No. I'm sorry I didn't tell you, but I promise, I wouldn't *lie* about something like cancer." She picked up the masher and worked the potatoes into a fine puree and refused to listen to the accusing voices inside. She would have *eventually* told them.

"Helen . . . there's more."

It was the way Annalise said it, softly, with a tremor in her voice, that made Helen pause. Turn away from the potatoes.

Annalise twisted her hands together. "I don't know how else to tell you this than to just say it. I'm not who I said I was."

You probably know about Annalise . . . Helen took a breath, felt it burn through her. "Go on."

Annalise glanced at Nathan as if asking for permission.

The glance was a knife to Helen's chest. Her son had lied to her too.

"My name is really Deidre O'Reilly. I moved to Deep Haven twenty years ago under the Witness Security Program."

Helen stared at her, hearing the words but unable to unscramble them in her head.

"And Frank Harrison is my handler. Not my uncle."

Not my uncle.

"Helen?"

Not her uncle. Helen wrapped her arms around her waist, feeling hollow. "So. That's what the message today was about."

Annalise frowned. "What message?"

"Frank left a message to apologize. Said he was only trying to protect you." She studied Annalise, really looking at her. For a second, she saw the woman she'd met twenty years ago when Nathan brought her home for dinner. Blonde hair, a wan, almost-shaken look about her.

Helen reached for the chair and sat down. "Are you still in trouble? Is that why Frank was here? Why my son was sitting in the family room with his *shotgun*?"

She didn't mean for the words to slide out with quite so much edge. Especially once Annalise put her hand to her mouth as if shaking away tears. But what kind of woman put her family in danger?

"No, Mom," Nathan said quietly. "Not anymore. They put her here because she testified against a drug lord. He got out and tried to find her—which was why Frank was here. But they caught the guy."

Helen met Annalise's gaze, held it. "You came here because you were hiding?"

Annalise nodded.

"And . . . your family? Are they really dead?"

Annalise let out a shaky breath. "My parents are alive and living in St. Louis. I have a brother, Ben, and a sister, Kylie."

"And do they know you're alive?"

"My parents do."

"Oh. Your poor mother." Helen hadn't meant for that to escape, but she couldn't imagine letting go of Nathan, not knowing where he was.

She imagined it might be like living with the grief of a kidnapped child or an MIA soldier. Almost despising the hope that you couldn't surrender.

She wanted to take Annalise's hand. Instead she clasped her own in her lap.

"Frank left because his job here was finished," Nathan said.

Annalise nodded. "I don't think we'll see him again, Helen."

Just like that. Well. Okay.

Helen forced a smile. "It was nice meeting him."

"Mom—"

She held up a hand to Nathan. "I don't want to speak of him. It's enough to know that you're both okay." She looked at Annalise. "Does this mean you'll go back to your other life?"

Annalise frowned at her. "This is my life. You and Nathan and the kids."

"But you lied. You created a fake life."

"What part about this life isn't real? You? My children? I had no choice, Helen. I had to become Annalise Decker. This is me."

"And what about your family? Are you just going to let them think you're dead?"

Annalise looked as if she'd been slapped. "I . . ."

"We need to go to the game, honey," Nathan said softly. "It starts in thirty minutes."

"Oh. I . . . didn't realize it was so late." Annalise jumped up from her chair and went to the basement door, calling, "Henry, get your shoes on."

So this was how Annalise would be—unaccountable for her actions. For the pain she inflicted on her family. Helen shook her head in disgust.

Henry came up the stairs. "I'm hungry. What about supper?"

Helen got up, fury roaring in her ears, and headed toward the door. But she stopped there and turned. "We don't erase our past, Annalise. We learn from it."

She didn't look back as she pushed her way outside.

"Mom!" Nathan followed her onto the stoop, his hands in his pockets. He closed the door behind him. "Annalise didn't have a choice. She didn't want to lie to any of us."

"We're not the only ones she lied to—"

"We're going to tell the children later."

"I'm talking about the town of Deep Haven, Mr. Mayoral Candidate. Think they'll forgive us for this?"

His face whitened.

"You didn't think about that, did you?"

"I just found out this afternoon."

And yet here he was, forgiving Annalise? Acting as if everything was normal?

The woman had destroyed all his hope of being mayor. Made them into fools.

"I love her, Mom. She's my wife. And I'm not going to give up on us. I know she lied, but I promised to stay the course, all the way to the end, and I'm trusting in God's grace, every day, to get there."

He stood there, so much resolution in his eyes, and it hit her. "You're so much like your father, you know."

Nathan stiffened, his mouth opening.

Helen came back to him, stood with him under the porch light. "No, you don't understand. Your daddy loved you. He wanted more than anything to come back to us. I . . . just couldn't forgive him." She couldn't look at Nathan then, her eyes wet in the cold. "I turned him away that night he was killed. I told him he'd never see you again . . ." She wrapped her arms around herself as the wind chapped her wet cheeks. "He never gave up on you, even when I turned him away. You should know that."

She heard Nathan breathing and for a moment expected some kind of horrible accusation. Even heard it in her head. *You stole my father from me.*

Instead, she felt his arms circle her, pulling her close. "I love you, Mom. And I forgive you."

Oh, Nathan. She didn't know how she'd managed to raise such an amazing man, but she put her arms around him, holding on, burying her face in his jacket.

I'm sorry, Dylan.

She finally untangled herself from his embrace. He ran a thumb across her cheek, his green eyes kind.

Helen wiped the wetness away. "Listen, you and Annalise go to the game. I'll feed Henry and be there in a bit." She patted her son on his cheek. "Besides, I need to make popcorn."

"We don't need popcorn, Mom."

"Of course we do."

Back inside, Henry was pulling on his jacket, Annalise scooping the potatoes into a container.

"I'll feed him, Annalise," Helen said, glancing at her.

"I—"

"C'mon, Annalise. Mom will be there in a bit." Nathan held out his hand.

Henry shrugged out of his jacket. "Thanks, Grandma."

"What are grandmas for?" she said, kissing the top of his head.

"Thank you, Helen," Annalise said. Helen couldn't look at her. Nathan might be ready to forgive, but she wasn't sure how she might get there. Not yet.

As she watched them drive away in Nathan's sedan, their taillights vanishing in the night, she flicked on the radio. Neil and Vern spilled out the pregame radio chatter, and she could hear the crowd in the background. Still, they couldn't drown out Frank's words running in her head as she put the rolls in a basket.

It was for her safety, and I promise I didn't want to deceive you.

But they had deceived her, hadn't they?

She pulled out the meat loaf and set it on the stove. The ketchup had soaked into it, turning the meat savory, tangy. It was Annalise's recipe. Delicious, mouthwatering. Perfect.

Helen stared at it, the aroma filling the kitchen. Then picked up a towel, pressed it to her eyes.

How had she become so unforgiving? Why couldn't she be more like Nathan?

We don't erase our past . . . We learn from it.

Apparently she hadn't. She hadn't learned anything from the years watching Nathan grieve his father, just because she couldn't forgive. Did she want that again for him? For her grandchildren?

She could grow cold and lonely in that house across the street. Or . . .

Or she could forgive. She could love, despite her daughter-in-law's betrayals.

Helen shuddered to think how she might have treated the girl had she known her circumstances. She'd never been a woman tolerant of the worst. She only wanted the best. And if Annalise had shown up with her baggage . . .

Perhaps, in hiding Annalise's past, God had given Helen the daughter-in-law she had always hoped for.

I'm sorry. The words pulsed inside her. *I'm sorry, Annalise. I'm sorry, Nathan.*

Because life didn't just come with better . . . it came with worse, too. A worse that God could have fixed, perhaps, if she'd let Him, so long ago. She hadn't wanted to take the risk of a broken heart. Of getting hurt over and over again.

But wasn't that the nature of love? Risking betrayal? Forgiving? Wiping the slate clean and starting over?

Wasn't that the nature of God?

This was what Dylan needed that day so many years ago. A second chance. Unconditional forgiveness. Maybe Dylan would have kept betraying her. But if she'd forgiven him, she might have built a different legacy for her son. Instead Helen had reacted out of her pain and spent thirty years reaping the consequences.

"Lord, I'm sorry for not keeping my vows. For not trusting You to get me through the worse. For not loving."

"Grandma, are you okay?"

Henry stood in the kitchen, staring at her with wide eyes.

She smiled at him. "Yes. I think I am."

"Are we going to eat soon?"

She dished up some mashed potatoes, a slab of meat loaf, added a roll, and set Henry's plate on the table. "I have to make a call."

She dug out her cell phone—six missed calls from an unknown number.

Frank.

On the radio, she heard the singing of the national anthem. She turned the volume down and hit Redial, tousling Henry's hair as the call connected, rang.

Please, be there.

"You called me. Oh, thank God, Helen; you called me."

She hadn't expected quite so much exuberance. "Frank?"

"Listen, I'm on my way back to Deep Haven—I should be there in thirty minutes or—maybe longer."

He was coming back. She turned away from Henry, not wanting him to see her smile. Frank was coming back.

"I'm sorry, Frank, that I didn't tell—"

"Is Annalise with you?"

Oh. She tried not to be hurt. "No. She's at the game."

"The game! Of course. Okay . . . um . . ."

Something in his voice made her walk away from the table out of Henry's earshot. "What's the matter?"

A sigh trembled through the line.

"I know about Annalise. Is she in more trouble?" Helen glanced at Henry. He didn't seem to hear her. "What's going on, Frank?"

"Just stay put. I'm calling the sheriff. Annalise is still in danger. You all are, I think. Lock your doors; I'll be there as soon as I can."

"Frank—don't worry about me. You protect my daughter. I'll take care of Henry and me."

"I know you will." Silence, and then his voice softened. "When this is all over, we have to talk. I'm sorry I betrayed you to your family. But . . . if you'll let me, I'd like to stick around and . . . Well, I know I'm not the man you thought I was, but I'd like to be."

Oh, Frank. She cupped her hand over the speaker. "You're

exactly the man I thought you were. We just need a fresh start. And by the way . . . I don't have cancer."

Another beat of silence. "You don't?"

"I guess I'll be hanging around Deep Haven for a while."

On the other end of the line, she thought she heard a soft laugh. "Me too. Please, lock your doors. I'll be there as soon as I can."

"I'll be here, waiting."

18

"I WISH COLLEEN HAD STOPPED BY the house before the game. I would have liked to talk to her, to tell her I'm sorry." Annalise blew on her hands as they drove to the school. While they were at the Millers' hideaway, it had begun to sleet, turning the roads slick.

Her stomach churned with Helen's anger. In twenty years, her mother-in-law hadn't once yelled at her. It stung, but the questions lodged inside her. *What about your family? Are you just going to let them think you're dead?*

Yes, maybe it would be better if she stayed dead. So many questions, so many wounds to open.

Nathan turned in at the school lot. "I think Colleen owes you an apology."

"It's my fault, too. I was so afraid of losing her that I made her feel like a criminal."

"She had a boy in her room—"

"Who apparently came over to ask if he could go to church with her."

Nathan smirked. "Right, okay."

"What if she is telling the truth? Seriously, Nathan. I feared she was going to become me, and I didn't even listen to her. I didn't trust her."

"First of all, what's so bad about being you?"

"Not me, Annalise. Me, *Deidre*."

"Again. I didn't know Deidre, but I can't imagine she didn't have some qualities that made you who you are today." He pulled into a parking space. "But you don't owe Colleen a rundown of your past. You are her mother. And your job is to guide her toward her future. You've been doing that in word and deed her entire life. And in every moment, you've given her the best of yourself, the best parenting you can. Every piece of guidance, every ounce of pushing her to her future, is valid. It's not negated by your mistakes. So no, I don't think you owe Colleen an explanation or an apology."

He put the car in park. "Babe, I don't know who you were, but I know who you are. And that's the woman Colleen needs right now." He leaned over, took her face, and kissed her. "Get your pom-poms."

She caught his hand. "What are you going to do when the town finds out? It might destroy your mayoral race."

"Who wants to be mayor anyway?"

But she knew him too well to believe him, to not see the flash of sorrow in his eyes. If only she could figure out a way to fix this . . .

No. God would fix this. She'd have to let Him. Wasn't that

what trusting in His grace—His love—every moment was all about? Following Him even in the dark places to lead them to the light?

She got out and grabbed the gear. Inside the school, the gym was already alive, the pep band warming up, the teams in their circles, hitting the ball to each other. She searched for Colleen and found her practicing her serve, her hair pulled back in a ponytail, her skin flushed.

Annalise raised her hand. "Colleen!"

Her daughter turned, searching for her voice. Annalise smiled, waved.

Colleen's eyes widened as if she were surprised to see her. What, did she think one little fight would keep Annalise from attending the most important game of her daughter's career? She gave a thumbs-up even as Colleen shook her head.

"You can do it! Stay focused!"

"You used to play volleyball, didn't you?" Nathan said quietly next to her.

What a relief to finally nod, to slip her hand into Nathan's, to smile as they made their way to the stands. "I loved it and probably would have been pretty good until I fell in love with the wrong boy."

"Someday I'll be ready to hear about that," Nathan said, squeezing her hand.

Her gaze scanned the stands, searching for Colleen's wrong boy. Tucker had behaved himself like a gentleman last night at dinner— had it only been last night? It felt like a lifetime ago. She'd barely looked at him, consumed with her confession to Nathan. Now she wanted to talk to him, maybe let him apologize. To listen to him.

They'd establish a few ground rules. Like dating out in the open, under supervision. But she would try to give him the benefit of grace.

A fresh start.

Deep Haven fans packed the stands. She waved to a number of parents, spied Jason sitting with cute Harper Jacobsen, then followed her husband to the middle section.

Vern and Neil announced the team, and they stood for the national anthem.

Colleen kept staring at her, so much tension in her expression that Annalise wanted to cry. Clearly the last couple days—especially today's crisis—had drained her emotional edge for this game. *Oh, Lord, please help her.*

She gave her daughter another thumbs-up as the team huddled, then went to the bench.

They started Colleen at wing spiker.

"What position were you?"

"Same as Colleen—an outside hitter."

Nathan leaned close to her ear. "I feel like I'm just getting to know you."

She glanced at him. "No, you've always known me. Now you find out why. . . . C'mon, Colleen! She completely missed that set!"

"She'll get into her groove."

The crowd roared when the Huskies took the serve back. Annalise missed the popcorn, the camaraderie of Helen.

In fact, she couldn't remember a game she'd attended without Helen.

I had to become Annalise Decker. This is me.

And what about Deidre?

She barely heard Vern announce the score, the Huskies up by three.

Why would she want to be Deidre again? Deidre had been headed toward death.

Annalise was life and hope and a future. Annalise was the name of grace.

The only thing Deidre did was remind her how redemption felt.

She'd forgotten that. But surrounded by Deep Haven, cheering as her daughter finally landed an attack, as the Huskies topped the Wolves by ten, maybe it didn't hurt to remember. Maybe by wiping the past clean, by not ever revisiting it, she had stolen the depth and power of amazing grace.

Maybe that, too, was the message her mother offered her last night on the phone: grace.

Grace meant God knew her past and still offered her a beautiful future. An unbreakable happy ending.

Colleen rotated into the server position and aced her first shot.

"That's my girl," Nathan said beside her.

Their daughter took the ball, twirled it in her hands. Two points to the game.

They handed back the second service, but the Huskies set it up in a beautiful bump, set, attack.

The Wolves dug it out but drove the ball into the net.

One point to the first game. The Huskies could win this championship.

Colleen slammed the ball over the net. The opposite team dove for it with a one-handed dig. It flew into the rafters and the Husky team erupted in victory.

"They're going to sweep these," Nathan said.

Annalise's phone vibrated in her pocket. She pulled it out. How had she missed six calls? She checked the number and didn't recognize it.

Oh, sure. Poor Frank—he probably wanted to say good-bye. After all he'd done for her, she owed him that much.

"Hello? Frank, is that you?" Annalise pressed her hand to her ear, unable to hear. "I'm going out into the hall—just a moment."

She muted the phone, turned to Nathan. "It's Frank. I'm going out to the hallway."

He lifted his hand for a high five as she descended the bleachers and headed into the hallway while the girls lined up for a new game.

"Frank, are you still there?"

Shoot, the line had gone dead. Maybe she hit the wrong button. Or if he was still traveling, he might have gone through a dead zone.

She walked toward a quiet alcove by the fitness center, near the girls' bathroom, scrolling down for the number to call him back.

"Hang up."

The voice came from behind her. She jerked around as recognition slid through her—a smell, a snarl, a breath she'd never forgotten.

He held up his phone. "Thank you for taking my call."

Garcia had changed. Jail had made him leaner, scraped out the hollows of his face, turned his eyes darker. He was bald, too, under that hoodie, and the cobra around his neck seemed faded.

Funny how it looked more vivid in her nightmares.

"Deidre O'Reilly. Miss me?"

She should scream. But with the ruckus in the gym, who would hear her? And—too late. He pressed a gun against her jacket.

"Let's go for a drive."

She wouldn't move. "No. You'll have to kill me here."

"How about if I start with you and then go over to your house and wait for your husband and daughter? She's so pretty. We had a nice chat today."

His words slid through her like ice. He'd talked to Colleen?

"You . . . stay away from my daughter."

"She looks just like you, you know. And quite the volleyball star."

She raised her hand to slap him, but he caught her wrist, squeezed it. "C'mon, Deidre. Don't put up a fuss. You knew this was going to happen." He took her hand. "Don't make a scene now. If I have to go down, I'll take as many of your friends with me as I can."

She slipped her phone into her pocket, pressing the speed dial as he ushered her out of the school.

Sleet hit her jacket, ran down her back.

"We'll take your car."

"I don't have keys."

"I do."

If she'd had a doubt that Garcia had terrorized her daughter today, it vanished when he pulled out Colleen's keys. "I heard she just got her license."

She didn't know why Garcia had let Colleen go, but perhaps that was God, giving her this last measure of grace.

And maybe, if Annalise played things right, she could end this tonight.

Garcia opened the passenger door, then pushed her over to the driver's seat of the sedan. Handed her the keys. She looked around the parking lot for anyone she could signal to, maybe give enough of a smile for them to tell Nathan they'd seen her.

Everyone was at the game.

She prayed her call had connected.

"I changed my mind. Let's go home and wait for the family, shall we?"

Her hand shook as she inserted the key into the ignition. *Think.*

"How did you find me?"

"You're all I've thought of for twenty years, *chica*. And it's hard to hide your face when your husband is running for mayor, don't you think? Such a lovely family . . ."

She pulled out of the lot. *Think.* "They know where you are. They know you're here. . . . They'll look for you at the house."

He nudged the chilly end of his gun into her neck. "Maybe you're right. I'm a lonely man. Maybe we should run away together." He leaned close, let his sour breath wash over her. "I always told Blake that I'd take you in trade."

She refused to flinch.

Think.

Annalise drove up the hill, her mind whirring. She had to get him out of town—and fast. Maybe buy enough time for Nathan to figure out she'd vanished and come save her.

No, let God save her.

Please, God. You've brought me this far . . .

She tapped her brakes at the stoplight, and the car fishtailed on the sleet, nearly hitting a Jeep coming into the intersection. It swerved, slid into a display of pumpkins.

How many people had died at this light, slamming into oncoming traffic, and today, she had to get a good driver.

She righted the car and turned onto the highway headed out of town, reaching for her seat belt. "So where to?"

Think.

"Just keep driving."

She stepped on the gas, hiding a smile in the darkness. She hadn't lived in Deep Haven for two decades without learning its secrets, its legends, the stories that could save her.

"Maybe while you're in Deep Haven, you should visit a few of the sites? Like Cutaway Creek. Glorious this time of year."

"Shut up." He screwed the gun into her neck. "Do you know what I'm going to do to you? I'm going to take my time. I'm going to let you relive what it feels like to have your life stolen from you. Slowly. I'm going to watch you suffer, and you'll die knowing that when I'm done with you, I'm going back for your daughter."

She stared at the road ahead, the corner at the bottom of the hill. How many times had they driven by it, Nathan barely able to look at the craggy edge? But she had. Had once even pulled up and stared over the side. The bridge spanned an opening to the river that spilled out into the lake. One side, so lethal, with the twenty-foot drop into the frothy waves of Lake Superior, where the river flowed into it.

The other side into the rocky embankment of the river.

She'd only wound him. Just hit the side rail hard enough to stop them, shove him into the windshield. Maybe even knock him out.

Then she'd run.

"I'm not scared of you." The words emerged on their own, but even as she said them, she felt suddenly as if two hands settled over her. The fear seeped out of her.

She came around the curve . . . and gunned it.

"You're as stupid now as you were then—"

The car spun on the ice. A scream gathered in her throat, but she held it back as the sedan slammed into the guardrail. Her head jerked. The car ricocheted off with such force that Garcia slammed into her.

The car bulleted to the other side. With a crunch it broke through the railing and sailed over.

Annalise let the scream go then as her headlights shone on the river.

Then they hit—hard and fast, the light snuffing out.

She woke seconds later—or maybe she'd only been shocked, but she couldn't breathe. She lay sideways, the car crushed on the passenger side, her seat belt cutting into her carotid artery.

The sound of water rushed at her as the river filled the car through the passenger side window. The cold had teeth, snaring her breath as it crawled up her. She yanked at the belt and fought for the latch. "Please!"

Beneath her, Garcia slouched in the darkness, nearly submerged.

Annalise gulped for air as she thrashed. Her foot was caught down below, but she could barely feel it over the needles in her skin.

She found the latch. The seat belt snapped open and she arched upward, yanking her foot to free it.

The water worked up her body, over her shoulder, biting through her clothes. She'd already begun to shake.

Garcia lay unmoving in the liquid darkness.

She angled her neck toward the pocket of air at the visor. *Breathe, just breathe.*

Her foot wouldn't give.

The water seemed to stabilize around her ears. She had her face pressed to the velvety fabric of the roof, breathing in what little air remained in the pocket as she began to bang on her still-closed window.

Please, God. Oh, please.

She closed her eyes, willing herself to stay calm.

She didn't have to panic. She could choose to hope.

Choose to believe.

Choose to hold on to grace.

❧

Tuck just couldn't escape the Decker family. He'd be happy if he never saw another member again, and then Mrs. Decker nearly T-boned him, her face illuminated in the bright lights of the town's most notorious intersection. He'd swerved, plowed his Jeep into the curb, taking out the display of pumpkins piled up in front of the gas station.

Awesome.

What was her problem? And she didn't even slow down—just kept going, like she didn't see him. He watched her taillights as she punched the gas.

He turned down the volume of the game on the radio and let a descriptive word enter his brain as he got out of the Jeep, ducking his head against the sleet.

She'd made him bust out a headlight.

Oh, man.

He might have been at the game, might have been cheering on Colleen, but Mrs. Decker had taken care of that by ratting him out. He thought of her smug smile last night, pretending her way through dinner. How long did she wait before she pulled the family aside, told them a wild story about him?

He could only imagine.

And he wasn't about to forgive Colleen either after the way she just stood there in school today as if she wanted her brother to take him down.

He didn't even *want* to listen to the game. Wasn't sure why he'd spent the last hour driving past the school, then down to get a sandwich, then back toward the game. He didn't want to see her or anything.

He should just forget about the self-righteous Decker clan.

Tuck got in the car. Let the anger dig in him for a bit. Then he gunned it down the road after Mrs. Decker, just until she got to wherever she was going. He'd show her the damage and demand she pay for it. He wasn't cutting into his snowboard fund because of her.

Even from this far behind he could see her swerving. *Slow down, sheesh.* She passed the library, the coffee shop, heading up the hill . . . out of town.

What if she'd been drinking? He let the thought sit there, then dismissed it.

But why wasn't she at the game? That bugged him a little. As far as he knew, Mrs. Decker hadn't missed a game in the history of Colleen's life.

She turned into a lead foot as she sped down the hill. *Just try to outrun me, baby.* He gripped the wheel, glancing at the speedometer. He had snow tires on his Jeep. Her little sedan—he recognized it now as Colleen's dad's car—could be a snowboard for the amount of traction it had on this road.

Especially around the upcoming curve. He'd heard that someone had died thirty years ago around this curve. And Tuck himself had nearly hit the guardrail a couple times when he was just learning to drive.

He tapped his brakes. His car shimmied, slid.

What was he doing? He slowed, let his Jeep go to the shoulder, his heart thundering. He'd turned into a road rager.

Still, it bugged him. All her self-righteous preaching. The fact that she hadn't stopped at the intersection. Her crazy driving.

Why wasn't she at the game?

He sat there in the darkness, watching as her taillights shrank in the night. Then they disappeared, fast, a slash of red light into the trees.

Weird.

Now, as he sat on the side of the road, it all nagged him enough to pull his phone out of his pocket. Colleen wouldn't take her phone on the court, so he was probably safe.

"Yeah, hey, Colleen. It's me. I . . . This is going to sound weird, but I just saw your mom peeling out of town. She's acting weird. And she nearly hit me. Tell her she owes me a hundred bucks." Okay, that didn't end quite like he wanted, but hey, he could taste the lingering ire in the back of his throat. He sighed. "I guess I'll see you around. Hope you win your game."

He hung up. Upped the volume on the radio.

They were well into the second game. Oh, Colleen missed a spike.

Maybe Mrs. Decker didn't want to see them lose.

He put his car into drive, intending to turn around.

Do what you know is right. He hadn't been able to get Amelia's dad's words out of his head all day. Like he was haunted or something.

Still, maybe he'd just drive down the road, around the corner.

Then he'd go home and never see the Deckers again.

Hopefully.

Tuck slowed as he entered the curve, his headlight scraping the guardrail. Something had recently hit it. He drove across the bridge. Slowed. No lights in the long stretch of road ahead.

He pulled into the lot beyond the bridge, next to the overlook, and turned around.

His headlight revealed the gaping maw in the opposite rail.

No.

Oh *no*. He slammed his Jeep into park and barreled out.

"Mrs. Decker!" He scrambled across the road, fell, then flung himself at the rail, looking over.

The tin-can car lay on its side in the river below, the driver's side propped up on a boulder.

No! He pulled out his phone to dial 911.

Nothing. Of course—the walls of the gorge obscured the signal. "Mrs. Decker!" She could be dead in there . . .

And if she wasn't, she would be soon in that icy water.

Tuck searched for the path, the trail of dirt that led off-road tourists down to the edge, but couldn't find it. It didn't matter. His headlight shone over the river, and he scrambled to the edge of the bridge, began to climb down.

When his foot slipped on the icy rock, he fell, bumping and slamming into the stones, hitting the water.

The force, the ice-cold temperature, knocked his breath out of him. He gasped and fought the pain as he plowed through the water, the foam cresting up around his ears, down his jacket.

"Mrs. Decker!" *Please, let her not be underwater.*

He scrambled to the driver's door. Down here, away from the lights of his Jeep, he could barely make out the handle. He tried to open it, but it wouldn't budge. The river glistened in the darkness, flooding over him to his shoulders.

"Help!" The voice came from inside the window.

She was alive. "Mrs. Decker! It's Tucker Newman!"

"Tucker! Help—my foot's stuck! I can't get out!"

At least she had air. He climbed over the boulder, back to the cliff, rooted around until he found a rock, his hand nearly numb with cold.

"Get back!" He slammed the rock into her window and it broke, a spiderweb of glass. He kicked it away and leaned in.

The water filled the car nearly to the roof. Only her chin and head emerged from the water.

"It's going to be okay."

Except if he didn't get her out of there fast, it wouldn't be.

Whoa. There was a hand—an arm!—floating by her face. He scrambled away. "What the—?"

She shrieked, slapped at it. "Get me out of here!"

"Is there someone else in there with you?"

"I think he's dead. Here—pull me out!"

Tuck crouched on the boulder and reached in, caught her hand. It was ice. He grabbed her other hand and began to pull. Her head and shoulders were through the window when she cried out.

"I'm sorry!"

"No, it's not your fault, Tucker. My foot is pinned. You gotta get help. Please—go, get help."

"I can't leave you here."

"You can! Please!"

"Okay, okay—I'm just going to go far enough to get a cell signal. Then I'll be back. I'll be right back—I promise."

Tuck was turning when he heard the car shift, heard it skidding against the rocks.

The current was taking it under.

"No!" He slid back toward her, grabbed her hand. Slipped just as the car settled.

It pinned his leg against the rock, and pain shot through his body.

Mrs. Decker clung to him, clawing at his hand. "Wait—don't let go, Tucker. You're the only thing holding my head above water."

He wasn't going anywhere, not with his leg pinned. But he kept that to himself. She didn't need to know that they were both probably going to die.

&

Who wants to be mayor anyway?

Nathan's own words sat in the back of his head like mud as his gaze moved between the door, the court, and the crowd of Deep Haven friends.

It bothered him that he needed it so much. That he thought without the title, he was no one. So he'd never scored touchdowns or made millions or even redeemed the Decker name. A man wasn't tied to his name. A man was the guy he was at home or at work. Like Seb had said, every day proving himself to be a man of honor.

A man was the guy he became when his wife smiled at him.

That's what he needed.

Who wants to be mayor anyway?

Except he thought he'd do a good job. Help this town to a better place, economically, maybe even civically.

I'm talking about the town of Deep Haven, Mr. Mayoral Candidate. Think they'll forgive us for this?

Wow, he hadn't realized the depths of his mother's hurt over the years. But she was right . . . Deep Haven knew how to bear a grudge. So much for his mayoral bid. Or his real estate business.

Maybe they should move anyway.

But the truth about Annalise didn't have to come out. So Annalise had traded in her old name for a new one. So she'd made up her past. So she'd lied about everything that they knew about her. It was private family business. No one really needed to know.

Maybe he could still win his campaign.

"De-fense, de-fense!" He joined the crowd in cheering the Huskies. The cheer reverberated through the gym, turning the place deafening. No wonder Annalise escaped to a quiet place for her phone call. They'd fallen to a 21–15 deficit in the second game, and even Colleen seemed to be losing her focus. She kept glancing toward him in the stands as if looking for her mother, needing her for moral support.

He checked his watch. Annalise had been gone for nearly forty minutes, the entire second game. Whoever she was talking to must be important.

Frank? Had she said his name? Nathan couldn't remember.

He took out his phone. He could call, hope she'd answer, remind her . . . Funny, he had a voice mail. He hadn't heard it come in. He'd pick it up after the game.

The Wolves landed another point. Three more and they'd have to go to three games, a fifteen-point match.

The coach called a time-out, and Colleen took the bench, wiping a towel over her face.

She didn't move when the coach sent the team back in. Yeah, well, the pressure had gone to her head. She'd missed sets, spiked out of bounds, fumbled digs. She played like she belonged on JV. And it seemed as if she didn't care.

Nathan frowned as he watched her dig around her jacket and pull out—her phone?

Oh, c'mon, Colleen. She had better not be texting Tucker.

That thought felt a little hypocritical, seeing as Nathan had finally figured out the look on Jason's face that day by the theater. He'd seen it in the mirror a couple times when he was that age.

Whatever Jason and Harper were up to, it had Jason on the defensive.

Which meant it couldn't be anything good.

Nathan watched as Colleen held the phone to her ear, pulled away, and stared at it. She pressed a button, listened again.

Nathan could almost see her face transform, see it whiten, and his own chest tightened as her mouth opened.

Then she screamed.

She stood, dropped the phone, and screamed.

The ball landed in the middle of the Huskies' court as every player turned, watching Colleen run out into the middle of the game. Across the gym, toward—

"Daddy! Daddy—I think he took her! That man took Mom!"

Nathan was on his feet—he knew that much—but beyond that, nothing made sense. He made it down the bleachers to the floor and caught Colleen by her arms. "What are you talking about?"

Tears flushed her reddened face. "Tucker called. He just saw Mom driving out of town, and . . . The man—he had . . . he had a . . . a snake—" She lifted her trembling hand to her neck, her voice hiccuping out, unraveling. "And he took me today from the school parking lot . . ."

"Someone *took* you. Today?"

Nathan vaguely sensed the crowd hushing around him, barely sensed his hands tightening on Colleen's arms. "Did he hurt you?"

Only then did he see the bruise on her cheek, the swelling around her eyes.

Oh. He couldn't breathe. "What happened?"

"He told me that if I didn't go to the game or if I told Mom or you, he'd go to our house and kill everybody."

He cupped her face, kept his voice low, unsure how he was going to ask this—or if he could bear the answer. "Did he . . . ?" He swallowed. "Did he . . . ?"

"No, Daddy." She shook her head, and he wanted to weep with relief. He crushed his daughter to himself. *Thank You, God. Oh, thank You.*

"He just hit me because . . . because he said terrible things about Mom, and I called him a liar. He was waiting for her to come to the volleyball game and told me that if I told anyone, he'd kill us all."

Nathan closed his eyes.

"Nathan, are you okay?"

He turned to find Seb Brewster behind him, concern in his eyes.

Nathan's mouth had dried, his heart in his throat. No, he wasn't okay. Might never be okay. "I think someone has kidnapped my wife."

His voice might have echoed into Canada. The stands went still.

Seb stared at him. "What?"

Nathan looked at the crowd. Eli Hueston, Deep Haven's former sheriff, was on his feet, heading down the bleachers. With Pastor Dan and his wife, Ellie, behind him.

Jason had stood up in the top row.

Here it was, their family and all their secrets, about to be laid open in front of all of Deep Haven. He could hear the murmur growing.

But his wife was out there, maybe already dead. "My family is in trouble."

The murmur died.

"My wife is not who you believe her to be." He reached down, took Colleen's hand, and held it tight. "Annalise has been living here under an assumed name, in the protection of the Witness Security Program, for twenty years. She did it because she testified against a man who still wants to kill her. A man who I think has tracked her down." Nathan's chest webbed, stealing his words. "Who has taken her. I pray he hasn't . . ." He looked away, swallowed, his voice turning puny. "I have to find her."

Silence.

He heard the quiet and knew the faces of Deep Haven even without looking at them. He knew almost all of them, knew their fathers, their children, where they lived. He'd gone to school with half of them, helped most of them buy their homes. And they knew him, too.

Knew him as the son of a reckless, murdering drunk.

And now as the husband of a woman who'd betrayed them.

And suddenly he didn't care in the least.

"Annalise might not be the person you thought she was. But she's my wife and I love her."

Colleen held up her cell phone. "Tucker's not answering, and I don't know where he saw her. I'll keep trying, but maybe we can track his GPS."

Oh, the brilliant children of this generation. "Good idea."

"Kyle!" Eli signaled to his son, off duty and sitting with his girlfriend, Emma, in the stands. "Get on the horn to your office. Tell them to meet us at the school."

"Nathan!"

The voice made him turn.

Frank.

And to his shock, Colleen launched herself at the man, wrapping her arms around him. "Uncle Frank! Something's happened to Mom!"

Frank appeared as if he'd aged ten years since Nathan saw him eight hours ago. He seemed unsure what to do about Colleen's affection, slowly lifting his arms to hold her.

Personally Nathan wanted to grab him by the throat. "What happened? I thought you had him!"

Frank unlatched Colleen's arms from around his neck. Smiled

at her a moment, something of sadness in his expression before he turned to Nathan. "I did too. The body wasn't Garcia."

Colleen backed away from him. "You're not my uncle, are you?"

He pursed his lips as if not wanting to admit it before shaking his head. "But that doesn't mean I don't love your mom like my own daughter. I'll find her, Colleen. I promise." He pulled out his cell phone. "Did you say that Tucker called you? What is his number?"

Around him, Nathan heard the buzz of the crowd. Men had begun to flood off the bleachers.

Pastor Dan came up to him first. "We'll find her. He couldn't have taken her far." He clamped Nathan on the shoulder. "I'm headed to the station to call the volunteers."

Nathan stared after him. Really? But it seemed . . . yes. Seb had a circle of men around him, already mapping out the town. Eli had joined in a huddle with Kyle over by the radio booth.

"Wait—I don't want anyone to get hurt!" Nathan said.

Seb was pulling on his jacket as he moved past him. "It's not up to you anymore. You live in community, Nathan. When one is in trouble, we're all in trouble."

Frank had turned, following a group of men out the door. Nathan ran to catch up.

"Dad!"

He turned, and Jason had Colleen by the hand.

"Go back to the house!" Or . . . "Wait!" Nathan pulled out his phone, dialed. He wanted to weep when his mother answered. "Are you okay?"

"I'm fine. There's a deputy sitting at the table right now. But . . . are you? Frank called here almost an hour ago looking for Annalise. Is she with you? Is she okay?"

He looked at Jason. Colleen. They were watching him. And he was sick of lying. Sick of secrets.

"I don't know. Is Henry with you?"

"Yes, he's here and fine. Scared. We all are."

Him too. "Pray, Mom," he said. "Just pray." He hung up and turned to Jason. "Go home. I'm going to call John and see if he'll come down—"

"Dad, I'm eighteen. I'm not a child—"

"Really? Because I'm not so sure about that. I'm not an idiot, Jason. I finally figured out why you couldn't look me in the eye last night after I caught you with Harper. And I did catch you, didn't I? Maybe Tucker's a better guy than we thought—maybe it's my own son who needs to figure out how to grow up and be a gentleman."

Jason's face reddened.

"Go home, and wait for me. And pray that we find your mother."

Nathan gave Colleen a hard kiss on the forehead. Then he ran to the front door. The cruisers had already lined up, their lights flashing.

Frank huddled in an alcove near the building, a hand pressed to his free ear, barking into the phone.

Nathan jogged over to him. Frank held up his hand. "Yep. Got it." He hung up. "I got a GPS location of Tucker's call. He was down on the highway, just out of town. That gives us a place to start."

He signaled to Eli, who came over. Frank gave him the information.

"There's a lot of country outside of town," Eli said.

Nathan was still holding his phone and looked at it now. "Annalise called me."

Nathan punched the speed dial for his voice mail. He listened to the message, pressing his other hand to his frozen ear. Muffled voices . . . Wait . . .

Yes, she'd called him. Annalise had called him when Garcia took her.

He wanted to cry when he made out her voice. "Maybe while you're in Deep Haven, you should visit . . ."

No.

He closed his eyes. His heart stopped on her scream.

Oh, God, please . . . "I know where she is."

Frank and Eli turned to him. Nathan tasted a bullet, tinny and thick, in his throat. "I think she drove into Cutaway Creek."

"Let's go," Frank said. He jogged to another man, a dark-haired cop type standing by his rental, probably his partner.

Nathan stayed on his heels, grabbed for the back door.

"There's no use in my saying you should stay here, is there?" Frank said, yanking his door open. His partner got in on the driver's side.

Nathan shook his head.

"Get in."

Nathan never realized how far the creek was from town, how many heartbeats it took to get there.

Please, God. He didn't want to lose his wife in the icy waters of Cutaway Creek.

They rounded the curve, and he saw it first—the broken jaws of the guardrail where a car had broken through. Nathan had the door open before they stopped. A line of police cruisers and headlights piled up behind him, but he didn't stop for traffic, just ran out to the edge.

"Here! We're down here."

Flashlights swung toward the voice.

Tucker. Sitting on a boulder beside an overturned car, his foot braced on the frame, the water up to his shoulders.

He held Nathan's limp wife in his arms, her head in his lap. "Hurry!"

Nathan didn't wait for the EMTs, didn't care about the voices or the nightmares or the feel of the cresting water that could pull him under. He scrambled down the rocky wall and spilled into the water.

The frigid cold seared away his breath, but he didn't care as he launched himself toward Tucker.

"I'm sorry. I tried to keep her awake, tried to keep her talking—"

Tucker seemed nearly frantic but Nathan couldn't deal with him, not right now. Instead, he pulled Annalise into his lap.

No. This wasn't Annalise. This woman had the countenance of a specter—gray skin, eyes closed, stringy hair around her face.

This couldn't be his Annalise. Bright and beautiful, strong, full of life and hope. The grace of God.

No, this wasn't his wife. Because this woman was dead.

19

It was a beautiful day to die.

Deep Haven stilled under its last snowfall, and grace in the form of a million different flakes covered the rocks, the trees, the craggy ledges. Lacy blankets of frost climbed up the windows, and locals captured their words in the air. Winter in Deep Haven had slowed to a crawl, settled everyone in slumber, in a pocket of quiet.

A pocket of safety.

A place where Frank had sent her to die. Or . . . perhaps to be reborn.

She'd stood on the shoreline, hands in her pockets, breathing in the scent of spring. He'd told her that rebirth would be hard, like the coming of spring, with the runoffs from the hills swelling the rivers, the icy roads breaking through to mud, the black ice freezing in the morning. He told her to take her time waking, to tend her wounds from winter.

But he'd promised that, like summer, she would someday be whole again.

And she wanted to believe it. Wanted to wake from the nightmare. But it felt like punching through ice, this waking. She could hear voices, but she so easily settled back into the cold. More voices, calling her forth again to smells and sounds.

Yet the pocket of silence, the winter, called.

And pain waited in the light. There wasn't enough grace there for her to start over. To begin again. Dying felt so much easier.

"Annalise?"

She took a breath, felt it stiff and cold in her lungs.

"Honey, please wake up."

She felt the hand now, tight in hers. Annalise? But her name was Deidre.

Except she understood Annalise, too. Like a melody, deep in her heart.

"Mom."

This name she knew. Her eyes opened. And this face, so familiar. Blue eyes. Freckles on the cute, pert nose. Blonde hair long around her face. "Colleen."

Annalise spoke, but she could barely hear herself. She wore a mask over her nose, the air cold and bright, forced into her. She lifted her hand to move it and it pinched.

"Sweetie, you were in an accident."

Nathan. She knew him, too—his name a song, something she'd always sung. He looked like he hadn't slept for days, his white T-shirt rumpled, his hair a broom on one side.

Jason stood at the foot of the bed, looking younger somehow, a little beaten.

And then it rushed back to her.

She inhaled a quick breath. Moved the oxygen mask to one side. "Garcia—"

"Luis Garcia is dead," Nathan said. "He drowned. And you broke your foot. Do you remember what happened?"

A hospital. She recognized it now—the pink hanging curtain, the square television, flowers on the table, and . . . and get-well cards. They plastered the walls around her bed and hung pinned to the curtain. Pictures drawn by the hands of children papered the window, overflowed in a basket on the windowsill. So many cards.

"I was in an accident."

"A car accident, that's right. You went off the bridge."

No—no, that wasn't right. "I drove off the bridge," she said, her voice raspy.

Nathan gasped. "You *drove* off the bridge?"

"I didn't mean to. I just wanted to stun him, to get away. We went over. I thought I was going to die."

"You did die. Your heart stopped twice. You've been in a medically induced coma for three days while they rewarmed you." Nathan's mouth tightened to a grim line. "We could have lost you."

"How did you find me?" She accepted the straw of water from Nathan, let it soothe her parched throat.

"You called me," Nathan said. He smiled, something soft and sweet in his expression.

She smiled back. "That's right, I did."

"Mom! You're awake!" Henry bounded into the room and kissed her nose. "Oops, it's still cold."

"She'll warm up, Son," Nathan said. But she didn't miss the way he whisked his hand across his cheek.

Helen came in behind Henry, wearing a hat, a leather coat, her cheeks rosy. Her eyes warmed when she looked at Annalise. "Don't you scare us like that again. Ever." She squeezed Annalise's hand and gave her a smile, forgiveness in it.

Then, right behind her . . . "Frank?"

He looked younger, less angry, dressed in a flannel shirt, a pair of jeans. His eyes were soft. "Hey, kiddo," he said. "I was pretty worried."

He was? "You didn't have to stay."

Was that a blush? He glanced at Helen, who smiled at him. "I was thinking of maybe sticking around if that's okay."

"Uncle Frank is in love with Grandma!" Henry said.

Frank lifted a shoulder. "I like it here. I found this great house outside of town with fixer-upper potential." He glanced at Nathan. "For a guy with a fresh vision."

Really? Frank was staying?

Helen slipped her hand into his. "A house big enough for guests and family."

Frank looked at her and smiled, so much affection in it that Annalise almost didn't recognize him. "Yes. For family."

Maybe she *had* died, gone to a different, happier place.

No, this was the right place. The place she'd always known. A place she wanted to stay.

"How's Tucker?" She remembered him, too. How he'd apologized and kept her talking to try to keep her awake as the cold turned her body stiff, slowed her heartbeat. He told her about his dreams of being a snowboarder, his family, the loss of his brother.

How he cared for Colleen and just wanted to fit into her world.

Annalise looked at her daughter. "Please tell me he's okay."

Colleen's eyes glistened. "Yeah. He's okay. He has a broken leg, though. He probably won't be able to snowboard this season."

"Then he'll need some company. Maybe we can teach him how the Deckers play Monopoly."

Her daughter's mouth opened, a smile in her eyes. "Really?"

"I'm sorry I was so 'judgy.' You're right. I had to get to know him. I . . . I just didn't want to lose you, Colleen. Not yet."

"You're not going to lose me, Mom," Colleen said softly. She took her hand, squeezed. "Ever."

"And you're not going to lose me." Annalise looked at her family. "I'm sorry for not telling you who I really was."

"Oh, Mom," Jason said. "We've always known exactly who you are."

Really—how—?

"You're our mom!" Henry said and bounced on the bed.

"Henry, dude, take a chill there," Jason said, pulling Henry off the bed.

Nathan leaned closer. "And for better or worse, Deidre or Annalise, or whatever you want to call yourself, you're my wife." He kissed her on the forehead. "I'm not real partial to the name Esmeralda, however. Or Penelope. But I could learn to live with it."

She cupped her hand against his face, brushing the whiskers there. "Annalise Decker will do."

He sat on the bed, caught her hand, and pulled it to his chest, meeting her eyes. Just like he had that first time when she'd arrived, springtime in the wind, reborn and new, and walked into his life.

"My whole class made you cards," Henry said, pointing to a row of pictures.

"Beth Iverson sent cookies from the soccer team, but we ate them," Jason said. "Sorry."

"The PTA sent flowers, and the volleyball team sent cards, and the church sent a wreath, and the rest are from your Deep Haven fans. Apparently you could run for mayor in this town," Nathan said.

She held his gaze. "And you?"

He shook his head. "I think I have my hands full keeping you out of trouble." He smiled, nothing of guile in it. "Seb Brewster will make a wonderful mayor. Besides, I don't have anything to prove to anyone but you."

"I'm sorry, Nathan."

"Sweetheart, we've had enough excitement for the rest of our lives. Please, give me boring."

Oh, boring would be the last thing she'd have with this man. "No more secrets, I promise. I never meant to bring so much trouble here. I just wanted a place to hide."

"Lise, you might have thought you were hiding out in Deep Haven," Nathan said as he leaned down, his lips close to her ear, "but really . . . you were just coming home."

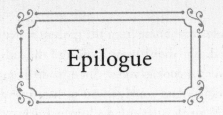

Epilogue

CLAIRE ALWAYS HUNG THE SPARROW on the tree last.

She'd bought it that first year after Deidre left. It helped erase from her memory the words, the fight over the tattoo. It didn't matter anymore—none of it did. Now the sparrow simply told her that, yes, God would watch.

Had to be watching.

After all, Claire begged Him each day for enough grace to believe, to pray, to hold on to hope. Even when she couldn't form the words.

Surely He knew the cry of her heart.

Outside, the St. Louis sky was washed slate gray, full of mourning despite the festive lights on the house, the sparkle from the tree. Claire had smelled snow in the air this morning when she fetched the paper for her husband. She'd asked Henry to pick up some salt on his way home from the grocery store, just in case it sleeted instead. She didn't want Kylie and the kids to fall when they came over for cookies today. She'd made them a fresh batch of snickerdoodles. And couldn't wait to hear granddaughter Joy recite her lines for the upcoming Christmas play or to hold baby Deidre Grace.

Ben might be by later too, after shooting hoops down at the gym before Lamaze class with Molly. Claire couldn't wait for the next grandbaby.

She couldn't have enough grandbabies.

For a moment, she watched the sparrow dangle on the tree, the light glinting off it, shiny, bright. She still hung the other ornaments, too. The plaster handprint two-year-old Deidre had made in Sunday school. The Popsicle-stick manger scene. The school picture glued to a star's center, cardboard covered with tinfoil.

In the picture, Deidre had such an overbite as she grinned, ten years old, her eyes shiny with Christmas hope.

The grief had lessened over the years. Just a bit. Or maybe Claire had simply accepted it a little more each year.

If one could ever accept saying good-bye.

Claire cupped the sparrow, fitting it in her hands, then drew in a breath and let it go.

Always letting go.

She put the empty ornament boxes into a plastic container and slipped on her shoes for the trek out to the detached garage.

Yes, the smell of snow seasoned the air. If they were lucky, they'd get a dusting before Christmas. Something about the snow always lightened her spirit.

She hoped Deidre lived where it snowed.

Claire shoved the container onto the shelf and was closing the door when she saw the Suburban drive up. She pulled her cardigan around her and waited in the cold while the driver got out.

She'd call him handsome, in a wool coat, dark-brown hair clipped short, green eyes that looked at her with such warmth, it unnerved her.

"Are you Claire O'Reilly?"

She didn't know why, but the question sent a sliver of ice through her. She should have been over the fear by now, should be made of steel.

But she'd always dreaded this moment, the one when they'd send an official to break the news.

After all this time, she still wasn't prepared.

Her throat tightened, her eyes burning. *Please . . .*

The passenger on the other side got out also. Claire heard the door slam and glanced over.

Her breath left her.

Oh . . .

She pressed a hand to her mouth, reached out for something. The man caught her hand.

"Mom?"

Claire still couldn't breathe, couldn't speak as she took in the woman. Tall and beautiful with blonde hair, those blue eyes. She knew this face, this smile, this woman. *"Deidre."* She let the name out, almost a whisper. And held her breath just in case—

"It's me, Mom. It's me."

And then Claire made a noise she didn't recognize, one she'd been holding in for over two decades, one that she'd allowed only God to hear.

"Oh, Deidre." Claire launched herself forward, but the woman had already caught her up, pulling her tight.

Claire closed her eyes and clutched her daughter—her grown, beautiful daughter—to herself. Breathing her in, the smell of her skin, the softness of her hair, the presence of her. Alive.

Alive.

Thank You. Thank You. "Please, tell me it's over."

"It's over, Mom."

She didn't want to, but Claire couldn't stop herself from pulling away, examining Deidre like she might a child. She cupped her hands on either side of her daughter's face. "You are so beautiful."

Then she laughed. Oh, Claire laughed, a full-out release of everything she'd clamped down for so long. Laughed and drew her daughter into another fierce hug.

Behind her, Claire heard voices. She stepped back.

Out of the car trundled a young man, tall, nearly an adult. For a moment, Claire flashed back and saw Ben in his teenage years. Behind him appeared another boy. Again, Ben, only this time with her daughter's adolescent smile.

And then a girl.

An amazing replica of Deidre, with long blonde hair, blue eyes, a tentative grin.

The daughter she'd lost, reincarnated right here in her driveway.

"This is my family, Mom. My husband, Nathan, and our sons, Jason and Henry. And this is Colleen. Your granddaughter."

Claire took Colleen's hands even as the girl glanced at her mom. "You're as lovely as your mother."

Colleen smiled.

"Are you really my grandma?"

Claire looked at the boy. *Henry.* Her husband would be thrilled to meet his namesake. Young Henry had something of mischief in his smile and stared up at her now as if the world hinged on her answer. She glanced at Deidre, who smiled at her.

Yes. Oh *yes*. "I am. In fact, I have a fresh batch of snickerdoodle cookies on the counter just for grandchildren. Want one?"

Henry nodded. "I love snickerdoodles! My mom makes the best."

Really. Claire pressed a hand to her chest, not sure if her heart still beat.

As he ran inside, Deidre came up to her mother, took her hands. Claire threaded the fingers with her own.

They stood under the glow of the house Christmas lights as snow trickled from the sky, falling to the ground in the gentle silence of amazing grace.

A Note from the Author

THIS NOVEL BEGAN on a flight to Portland. I sat next to a woman who was fidgeting in her seat, clearly distraught at some turmoil in her heart. After a few nudges from the Lord, I leaned over to ask her how she was and why she was going to Portland.

"To say good-bye to my daughter, who is going into the Witness Security Program." She looked at me wearing a haunted expression. "She witnessed a murder and now the family of the convicted killer is threatening her. She isn't safe."

I stared at her. "For how long will she be hiding?"

"Forever," she said.

I swallowed. After a moment: "How old is your daughter?"

"Twenty-one."

"Why don't you go with her?" I asked, not quite able to comprehend the magnitude of her loss. Not knowing if your daughter was alive, not seeing her get married, not knowing your grandchildren . . . so many unbearable sacrifices.

"I can't. I have a husband who is handicapped and two small children. They can't move."

I didn't pry any further, but my heart wrenched as I prayed

for her, and right then *You Don't Know Me* was birthed. At first I thought it might be the mother's story. But as I worked on it, I realized it was also the daughter's story. A story of secrets, of living another life. A story of second chances but also of regret. A story of grace and walking in it every day, hoping for a happy ending.

As I wrote, I discovered that *You Don't Know Me* was also a story of how secrets can burrow in and destroy our lives even when we believe we are protecting the ones we love. Big secrets and small ones. Like the kind a mother and daughter might keep or the kind a son might keep from his father. While we think that secrets protect our loved ones, secrets are a cancer, and instead of bringing peace, they eat away at our security. Instead of being able to forget the secrets, the longer we keep them, the more they invade our everyday thinking. We wake up with our secrets haunting us, and just when we think we've put them behind us, they creep up and remind us of our deceit. They keep us from believing that we deserve a happy ending. They keep us from accepting the grace that God longs to give us.

I owe credit to my pastor, Dale McIntire, for the church scene in chapter 9. He read that psalm; he spoke those words (or close to them). And as God would have it, he spoke not only to Annalise but to me. See, God wants to break through the identities we've constructed for ourselves, the fears we have of discovery, to say, "I see you. I know you. I know everything about you, and yet I love you. Period. You don't have to fear the truth with Me because I already know it. I know exactly who you are, and I still died to save you."

In that moment, I heard the words of "Amazing Grace"—"How precious did that Grace appear the hour I first believed" (or realized just how wretched I was and how much I needed the

Savior). This is the gift God gives us when we face those secrets that hold us captive. His grace. Salvation.

A fresh start.

We all keep secrets, and frankly many of us are living dual identities—the one the world knows and the one created by the secrets in our heart. God sees them both and He still loves you. More, He longs to set you free. He can free you. Heal you. Fix your marriage, your family, your situation. I know because I've seen Him do this in my life.

I pray that the truth sets you free to be the person God died for you to become. Thank you for reading *You Don't Know Me*.

Live in truth, my friends.

Susan May Warren

About the Author

Susan May Warren is the RITA Award–winning author of more than thirty novels whose compelling plots and unforgettable characters have won acclaim with readers and reviewers alike. She served with her husband and four children as a missionary in Russia for eight years before she and her family returned home to the States. She now writes full-time as her husband runs a lodge on Lake Superior in northern Minnesota, where many of her books are set. She and her family enjoy hiking, canoeing, and being involved in their local church.

Susan holds a BA in mass communications from the University of Minnesota. Several of her critically acclaimed novels have been chosen as Top Picks by *Romantic Times* and won the RWA's Inspirational Reader's Choice contest and the American Christian Fiction Writers Book of the Year award. Five of her books have been Christy Award finalists. In addition to her writing, Susan loves to teach and speak at women's events about God's amazing grace in our lives.

For exciting updates on her new releases, previous books, and more, visit her website at www.susanmaywarren.com.

Discussion Questions

1. *You Don't Know Me* opens with Claire O'Reilly traveling to Portland to say good-bye to her daughter. What questions and fears does she wrestle with? If you were Claire, what would you say to Deidre in that last meeting?

2. Annalise Decker appears to have the perfect life, but she keeps a number of secrets—big and small—from her husband, Nathan. At the same time, Nathan keeps the secret of his spending from Annalise. Do you agree with their belief that secrets are normal in a relationship? What do you think of Annalise's idea that secrets protect them? When have you kept secrets from someone you love? What was the result?

3. While Annalise and Nathan have a marriage that many people envy, Annalise has mixed feelings about the lack of "spark" in their relationship. Do you believe this type of chemistry is important in a marriage? How do things change for Nathan and Annalise throughout the story?

4. In what ways do we see Nathan haunted by his father's death? How does he try to prove himself to the people of Deep Haven? Have you ever felt pressure to escape a family legacy?

5. Witness Security agent Frank Harrison gives Annalise an impossible choice: to uproot her family and force them to assume new identities or to leave them behind. If you were in Annalise's place, which option would you choose? Why?

6. Colleen Decker not only resembles her mother physically, but Annalise also observes that Colleen shares personality traits with her younger self. What fears do these similarities raise in Annalise? Do you agree with how she responds to them? How do you feel about traits that you share with your own parents or children?

7. Why do you think Tucker Newman is so desperate for Colleen's family to like him? Have you ever felt a similar longing for approval?

8. Nathan comes home one afternoon to find Annalise painting the basement—the latest in a long series of home improvements. Why do you think Annalise has this urge to constantly redecorate, never satisfied with the house? Do you have areas of your life that you are constantly "remodeling"?

9. In chapter 9, Pastor Dan counsels his congregation, "Do not let your circumstances define God's love for you. He loves you. Period." How do you see characters in this story interpreting God's love according to their circumstances? Have you ever done the same?

10. Helen's sister Miriam challenges her on the lack of forgiveness that led to her divorce. What does Helen come to realize about how she treated her ex-husband, Dylan? How does it affect her reaction to Annalise's deception? In what circumstances have you found it difficult to forgive?

11. When he finally learned of his wife's cancer, Frank distanced himself to avoid witnessing her pain. How is that response challenged in his growing relationship with Helen? Have you ever felt tempted to avoid growing close to someone in order to avoid being hurt?

12. Thinking she'll have to leave Deep Haven, Annalise decides to pack a small bag of her belongings. What items does she choose to take with her, and what significance do they hold? If you could take only a few items from your home, what would you choose?

13. In the midst of her health scare, Helen resolves to begin "living large." What's on her list of things to see or do? What things would be on your list? Do you feel that you're living life to the fullest right now? Why or why not?

14. When he learns about the potential threat to his family, Nathan takes action to protect them—with nearly tragic results. Do you agree with his method? What would you have done in his place?

15. On the outside, Tucker looks like trouble, the quintessential bad boy. By contrast, Jason Decker looks like an honorable young man, the perfect student and son. How are both boys revealed to be different from their appearance? Have

you made similar assumptions based on a person's outward appearance? How do you respond if you find that your first impression was wrong?

16. Annalise fears how Nathan will react if she confesses her past and lets him see the person she once was. How does she come to feel about being fully known by him—both in her past and her present? Have you ever feared being fully known, by another person or by God?

17. Several characters in *You Don't Know Me* consider the idea of a second chance, of becoming someone new. Have you ever wished you could start over or create a new identity for yourself? In what circumstances? Are there ways that reinventing yourself can be a good thing?

18. How does Annalise finally come to view her past? Looking back on your own life, where can you see evidence of God's grace, even in times of difficulty or pain?

THE TEAM HOPE SERIES

Meet Team Hope—members of an elite search-and-rescue team who run to the edge of danger to bring others back. Unfortunately, they can't seem to stay out of trouble. . . .

A CHRISTMAS NOVELLA

A heartwarming story about family, traditions, and rediscovering the *real* magic of Christmas